CREEKTOWN DISCOVERIES

VOL *The* TWO

Sugarcreek
SURPRISE

CREEKTOWN DISCOVERIES

VOL *The* TWO

Sugarcreek
SURPRISE

WANDA E. BRUNSTETTER

BARBOUR
PUBLISHING

© 2022 by Wanda E. Brunstetter

ISBN 978-1-64352-922-6

33614082805440

eBook Edition:
Adobe Digital Edition (.epub) 978-1-64352-924-0

All scripture quotations are taken from the King James Version of the Bible.

All German-Dutch words are taken from the *Revised Pennsylvania German Dictionary* found in Lancaster County, Pennsylvania.

This book is a work of fiction. Names, characters, places, and incidents are either products of the author's imagination or used fictitiously. Any similarity to actual people, organizations, and/or events is purely coincidental.

For more information about Wanda E. Brunstetter, please access the author's website at the following internet address: www.wandabrunstetter.com

Image Credit: Richard Brunstetter III
Cover Design: Buffy Cooper

Published by Barbour Publishing, Inc., 1810 Barbour Drive, Uhrichsville, OH 44683, www.barbourbooks.com

Our mission is to inspire the world with the life-changing message of the Bible.

Member of the
Evangelical Christian
Publishers Association

Printed in the United States of America.

Dedication

To my Amish friend LeAnne,
a dedicated schoolteacher.

~

For God hath not given us the spirit of fear;
but of power, and of love, and of a sound mind.
2 TIMOTHY 1:7

Prologue

Lois Troyer took a seat at the kitchen table to read the letters she had received this morning from her newspaper column, Dear Caroline. The antique store she and her husband, Orley, owned was closed for the day, and Orley had gone fishing with his friend Lester. The house was quiet, and this was the perfect time for her to get some of the letters answered and sent back to the newspaper for publication.

Lois took a sip of peppermint tea, then slit open the envelope on top of the pile. "Dear Caroline," she read out loud. "My granddaughter is twenty-five years old and has never had a serious boyfriend. Whenever a young man takes an interest in her, she pulls away. I am concerned about her, because she works all the time and has a limited social life. I have tried to coax her into doing more social things, but to no avail. Is there anything I can do to help her? —Worried Grandma."

Lois pursed her lips. "Now, how should I respond to this letter?"

Chapter 1

Sugarcreek, Ohio

Lisa Miller rubbed her chilly arms against September's nippy breeze as she stood on the front porch of the Amish schoolhouse, ready to greet her young students, ages six to ten. The view from where she stood looked beautiful this time of the year, encompassing the resting farmlands surrounding the one-room schoolhouse. In the distance, trees had started turning gold, and the intense morning light made them appear to have a gilded glow. While Lisa breathed in the crisp air, she glanced at the neatened lawn in the schoolyard that was still being mowed weekly. It wouldn't be too many more weeks before winter would be upon them, and then the task of mowing would be finished for the year.

When Yvonne Yoder, the teacher who taught the higher grades, rang the bell, all the children from grades one to eight filed into the building.

Lisa smiled as each one came past. "Good morning," she said cheerfully.

"*Guder mariye*, Teacher." Six-year-old Nancy Burkholder looked up at Lisa and grinned.

"*Mir hen unser middaagesse mitgnumme*," said her twin brother, Nathan, as he held up his lunch pail.

Lisa nodded and spoke to the siblings in English, because it was important for all Amish children to learn a second language in their early years of school. "Yes, I see that you carried your dinner,

Nathan. Now both of you should put your lunch pails away, take off your wraps, and be seated at your desk."

The twins nodded and went obediently inside.

Keeping her smile in place, Lisa greeted the rest of the students, then stepped inside behind the last one and shut the door. What a privilege it was to be teaching at this school. Each of the pupils she taught filled her life with such joy. She couldn't imagine doing anything else. Since Lisa had no plans of getting married, she hoped she'd be able to teach right here at this school for a good many years. Although she'd had no formal training, Lisa, like all young Amish women chosen to teach at a one-room Amish schoolhouse, had been an excellent scholar back when she'd attended this school. How fortunate she felt to have been chosen by the school board to teach here seven years ago. The time had gone quickly, and she'd enjoyed every year.

After Lisa stepped into the main part of the schoolhouse, she was pleased to see that each of the children now sat at their desk with hands folded. Yvonne took her place at the front of the room and read a portion of scripture from the Bible. Following that, everyone stood to recite the Lord's Prayer. Afterward, Lisa led the students in singing a few songs. She enjoyed this part of the day so much—not just in the pleasure of singing herself but in listening to the children's blended voices as they sang with enthusiasm. Although school had only been in session a little over a month so far, the entire classroom seemed quite cooperative.

When the singing ended, Lisa worked with the fifteen younger ones on their reading, using the Dick and Jane series that was popular in the middle years of the 1900s. Lisa's scholars opened their reading material to the page where they'd left off from yesterday's lesson.

Meanwhile, Yvonne taught the twenty older children, ranging in ages from eleven to fifteen. Considering the size of the class, the children were well behaved and attentive. Not like last year when Lisa had dealt with two unruly eight-year-olds who talked out of turn and interrupted with questions that had nothing to do with the lesson. Those actions had been quite unnerving at times.

Things went well with the reading lesson until Lisa saw something furry out of the corner of her eye. Apparently the children must have seen it too, for several giggles, whispers, and snickers ensued.

The fluffy orange cat let out a loud meow. Then it darted close to where eight-year-old Gina Schlabach sat. The blond-haired girl bent down to pet the cat and squealed when it jumped up and onto her lap. But the skittish animal didn't stay there long and was soon on the floor again.

Lisa groaned. *A little unexpected excitement is not what we need this morning. Well, at least it's not a mouse. That would have really caused a stir—especially for me, since I have no love whatsoever for rodents.* Lisa had always been glad that her grandparents had several outdoor cats to keep the mice down.

She reached for the cat, but before her hands could touch the animal's furry coat, it zipped between her legs and made a dash toward the front entrance. The kids were all shouting, "Get it! Get it!" while Yvonne hurried to open the door. Instead of going out, as Lisa had hoped, the determined cat whipped around and raced to the front of the room.

David Stutzman, who'd recently turned fourteen, got up from his seat and took off after the cat. "I'll get him!" the boy hollered. The chase began, and soon two more of the older boys joined in.

There was no way Lisa or Yvonne could resume their lessons right now, so they stood on either side of the room and waited. A short time later, Johnathan Graber, the oldest boy in the class, got a hold of the cat, and everyone cheered. Lisa felt relief when the furry animal had been taken outside and everyone was back in their seats. *So much for a quiet start to the day.*

Things went smoothly the rest of the morning, and at eleven thirty, it was time for lunch. The students washed their hands before getting out their lunch pails. Then everyone took a seat at their desk. Following a silent prayer, the children and teachers began to eat.

From her teacher's desk, Lisa listened to the children visit with one another as they ate the food their mothers had packed for them. Most included sandwiches, but some children had a thermos filled with warm soup, as well as crackers and sometimes cheese. Most often an apple, orange, or cupcake was included for dessert.

Lisa's lunch today consisted of a swiss cheese and turkey sandwich, which her grandmother had insisted on making for her. The kindly woman had also included a thermos full of Lisa's favorite cinnamon herbal tea, as well as a lemon-flavored fry pie for dessert. Lisa appreciated her grandmother's thoughtfulness in choosing some of her favorite things. Grandma and Grandpa Schrock had been good to Lisa ever since she first came to live with them when she was seven years old, after her parents and paternal grandparents had been killed in a tragic accident. Lisa couldn't remember much about the part of her childhood that had taken place before the accident eighteen years ago. She did remember the horrible sense of loss she'd felt, waking up in the hospital with Grandpa and Grandma Schrock at her side and being told that she was the only one who'd survived when the van she'd been riding in with her parents and other grandparents had been hit by another vehicle. Even their English driver had died in the crash. Lisa's maternal grandparents had told her often that it was a miracle she hadn't been killed, and they'd said they felt blessed being able to raise Lisa.

A lump formed in Lisa's throat, and she tried to push it down with a drink of water. Even all these years later, it still hurt to think about her loss. She had no siblings, and when her parents died, she'd become an orphan. How grateful Lisa was that Grandma and Grandpa Schrock had gone to Indiana and brought her to their home in Ohio. She'd been shy around them at first and tried hard not to become attached, for fear of losing them too. But it had been impossible to live in the same house and not form an attachment with such a sweet, caring couple. Even so, Grandma and Grandpa had been the only people Lisa had allowed herself to get close to. Even Lisa's friendship with Yvonne was superficial, although the other schoolteacher had often said she considered Lisa to be her good friend.

Sometimes Lisa found herself envying others who were involved in their friendships, as they spent time together doing fun things and talking about their plans and dreams for the future. The emptiness inside could be disheartening at moments, but Lisa would always manage to push those feelings of envy aside, trying to refocus on anything else to take her mind off the sadness she felt.

I should be thankful for what the Lord has provided for me. And why am I so unsure about my future? Why can't I be like other people my age? Lisa took a few sips of her soothing, warm cinnamon tea. *What will I do someday when my grandparents are gone and I'm all alone? Will I be able to manage on my own without them?*

Lisa's attention refocused when Yvonne announced that it was time for the scholars to clear off their desks and go outside for the remainder of their lunch break.

Lisa looked at her half-eaten sandwich. Where had the time gone? *Guess that's what I get for doing too much thinking when I should have been eating,* she told herself.

"I see you're not finished with your lunch yet," Yvonne said when she approached Lisa's desk. "Why don't you go ahead and finish eating while I take the children outside?"

Lisa nodded. "Yes, thank you so much. As soon as I finish I'll be outside to join you."

"Take your time." Yvonne gave Lisa's shoulder a pat and followed the students out the front door.

Lisa felt guilty seeing her co-teacher go out alone with the children, so she hurried to finish her lunch and then slipped into her sweater and rushed out the front door.

Several of the older children had started a game of baseball, while some of the younger ones used the playground equipment. Lisa stood nearby, watching and remembering her days of playing in this same schoolyard. She'd been a shy child back then and was still shy when around adults—especially those she didn't know very well.

Soon recess was over, and it was story time, which Lisa had enjoyed as a young girl and still did as the teacher. She was reading the second book of a five-book series about a set of boy-and-girl twins who lived in Ohio. The children enjoyed the stories about the high-spirited twins, who seemed to find some sort of adventure at every corner.

Lisa wished she had a sibling—someone with whom she could share her innermost feelings and deepest desires. But then, if she had a brother or sister, they too may have died as a result of the accident that had taken four people from Lisa's family. One thing Lisa had never understood was why her life had been spared and not the others who'd been riding in the van that fateful day. It didn't make sense that she was alive but her parents and grandparents weren't. Grandma Schrock had told Lisa on more than one occasion that God must have a special purpose for Lisa's life. What it was, she couldn't imagine, but like her grandpa had said not long ago during their family devotions, no one should question why God allows what He does. Lisa hadn't fully accepted that idea though. Over the years, she'd questioned on more than one occasion the reason why God would allow certain things to happen.

"Teacher, when are ya gonna start readin' to us?"

Caught off guard by Nathan Burkholder's question, Lisa realized that although she held the children's book in her hands, she still had not opened it or begun to read.

She quickly opened the book to the page she'd marked with a ribbon the last time she'd read to the students and cleared her throat. The children seemed spellbound as she read to them about another adventure the fictional twins experienced. Truthfully, Lisa found herself enjoying the story right along with her young pupils.

After story time ended, Lisa taught an English lesson to her students and helped them work on their spelling.

The school day ended at three thirty, and Lisa and Yvonne said goodbye to their students.

"Feel free to go home whenever you're ready," Lisa told Yvonne. "I will do a few things to prepare for tomorrow's lessons, and then I'll close and lock the schoolhouse before going home."

Yvonne looked a bit hesitant at first but finally nodded. "*Danki.* I'll see you tomorrow morning, Lisa."

Half an hour later, as Lisa was about to pick up her things and leave the schoolhouse, a knock sounded on the front door.

I wonder who that can be. I bet one of the scholars forgot to take their lunch box or something else home with them.

Lisa went to the door. When she opened it, she was surprised to see a young, beardless Amish man with a crop of thick brown hair on the porch. She didn't recognize him and wondered if he was new to the area or visiting someone here in Sugarcreek.

"Hello." He offered her a friendly smile and reached out his hand. "My name's Paul, and I'm here to see about the work that needs to be done on the schoolhouse."

Lisa's brows furrowed. She had no idea what this man was talking about. "I—I am not aware of any work that needs to be done here at this time. Some repairs were done at the schoolhouse this summer, while school was not in session, so—"

"Oh, no," he interrupted. "This has to do with the window that got broken during a baseball game last week."

Lisa's forehead wrinkled. She felt more confused than ever. "We have no broken windows here. I'm one of the teachers, and if a baseball had hit one of our windows I would most certainly have known about it."

He reached under his straw hat and scratched the side of his head. "To ease my curiosity, and to make sure there's absolutely no broken window at this schoolhouse, would ya mind if I walk around the outside of building and take a look? Maybe the window got broke when you weren't here."

She was on the verge of arguing further with him, but his determined expression made Lisa believe that the best approach was to let him look. But she needed to see for herself as well. "I'll go with you."

"Sure, no problem." He stepped off the porch, and Lisa followed. They walked around the entire building, and sure enough, just as Lisa had said, none of the windows were broken.

Paul rubbed his chin. "Hmm. . .that's sure strange. I wonder why my uncle would ask me to come here if there were no broken windows." His cheeks colored as he eyed Lisa with a look of confusion. "Sorry to have bothered you, Teacher. . . . Uh, what is your name?"

"I'm Lisa. I teach the younger grades here."

"Nice to meet you. I'm new to the area, so maybe I misunderstood what my uncle said and came to the wrong schoolhouse."

She gave a slow nod. "*Jah*, that must be what happened all right." Lisa's skin prickled as Paul tipped his head and stared at her in a peculiar sort of way. She wished he would leave the schoolyard so she could get her bike and be on her way home.

"Well," he said after a few more seconds passed, "guess I'd better head back to my uncle Abe's shop and find out where I went wrong." Paul moved toward his horse and buggy, secured at the hitching rail. "It was nice meeting you," he said once more, only this time he called it out over his shoulder.

She gave a quick nod. "I hope you find the schoolhouse you're looking for."

"Danki."

Lisa watched as he climbed into his buggy and guided his horse out of the schoolyard. It was nerve racking enough that she'd been forced to talk to a complete stranger, but the fact that he was such a nice-looking man made her feel even more rattled.

Chapter 2

When Lisa rode her bicycle into her grandparents' yard that afternoon, she spotted Grandma pulling weeds in the garden. A good-sized pile of debris sat off to one side near the patch of flowers planted in a nice, tidy row. Lisa pedaled a little farther toward her grandparents' large white home with a wraparound porch. *It looks like Grandma's already gotten a good amount of the task completed. I shouldn't be surprised. I hope she still needs my help after I took so long to get home.*

Lisa's grandmother was a hard worker and liked to spend time in her garden. Sometimes it seemed Grandma could be a little obsessed with it. Like last year when she'd talked about getting a certain type of strawberry plant. A week later, she'd hired a driver and hunted at some different places around town until finally finding the ones she wanted.

Lisa parked the bike by the barn and hurried over to the garden. "Sorry I'm late, Grandma. I'd hoped to be here earlier, but I got waylaid at the schoolhouse."

Grandma's blue eyes appeared as sincere as ever when she looked up at Lisa and slowly shook her head. "Not a problem. I'm almost finished here, so why don't you go inside and rest a bit? I'm sure you're tired from teaching all day, not to mention the ride home on your bike."

Before Lisa could form a response, her grandmother quickly

added, "When we start supper you can tell me all about your day."

Lisa hesitated but finally nodded. "I'll go get changed and meet you in the kitchen."

"Take your time. I still have one more row to weed, and then I'll be in."

"Are you sure I can't help? I can hurry and get changed and be right back." Lisa paused to wipe her damp forehead.

Grandma shook her head a second time. "There's no need for that. You look hot and tired. I think a cold drink and a little time to rest would be good for you right now."

Lisa couldn't deny it. She'd pedaled hard coming home and had worked up a sweat.

"Danki," she said. "You always seem to know what I need—often before I realize it myself."

Grandma's brows furrowed as she cast a knowing look in Lisa's direction. "Now if I could just convince you to socialize more with young people your age..."

Here we go again. Grandma's always nudging me to get out there and spend more time with my peers. Lisa lowered her head and kicked at a small stone with the toe of her shoe. She knew exactly what her grandmother was leading up to. "I keep busy enough with my teaching job, and I don't need a boyfriend." *I honestly don't want to discuss this subject.*

She stepped onto the porch and hurried into the house before her well-meaning grandmother could say anything more. They'd had this conversation too many times, and Lisa didn't want to discuss it again. Although she felt sure that Grandma meant well, Lisa did not like to be pushed in a direction she didn't want to go—especially if it involved falling in love and getting married. Although a few young men, like Aaron Wengerd, had been interested in her, Lisa never allowed herself to get close to any of them. At her grandmother's insistence, she had attended a few young people's singings and other events but had always declined when any young man asked if he could take her home in his carriage. Since Lisa had no plans of getting married, it wouldn't make sense to lead on any would-be suitor.

She went to the kitchen and grabbed a bottle of water from the refrigerator. After touching her face with the cold bottle, Lisa twisted off the cap and took a long drink. *That sure hits the spot. Grandma was right when she said a cold drink is what I needed.* She closed the refrigerator door and headed out of the room to the hallway with the unfinished water in her hand.

Feeling more tired than she had realized, Lisa slowly climbed the stairs to her room. After shutting the door, she set her book bag on the floor by the desk.

Lisa liked the bedroom she had fixed up with a beach theme. It faced the sunny west side of the house and felt warm and comfy in the afternoon. But some days her room became too warm, like today. So she opened the window to allow air to flow in. It felt nice to soak up the quiet of her personal space as she stood looking out at the view of the countryside beyond her grandparents' property.

Lisa took another refreshing drink of water before moving away from the window and setting the bottle on her nightstand. *I can take my time since Grandma said she'd be a while yet.*

She slipped off her shoes and padded across the room to the closet to find one of her work frocks. Lisa picked one out, laid it on the bed, and plopped down beside it. She thought back to Grandma's comment before coming inside from the garden. *Grandma likes to encourage me to go and do things with people my age. I wish she'd realize that I'm not interested in doing that. Surely by now she must know that I'm not outgoing.*

Lisa stared at the tote she'd brought in with her. In addition to a few books, it held papers she needed to grade this evening. *My students are my focus. That's the way things have been for the last seven years. Even though my life isn't complicated and full of social obligations, that's fine with me. But I have to admit that sometimes it can be a little boring to spend so much time by myself.*

Every now and then, Yvonne would talk to Lisa about her plans and she'd try to include Lisa in them. But Lisa would always have some excuse as to why she couldn't join her fellow teacher. For now at least, all she needed to think about was resting a few minutes, getting changed, and going down to the kitchen to begin supper preparations.

———

"So now tell me about your day," Grandma said as she cut up some beets she'd brought in from the garden earlier and precooked.

Lisa turned from her place at the stove, where she'd been tending a skillet of fried chicken. "Things went along well until a *wusslich katz* got into the schoolhouse and created quite a stir when it didn't want to be caught."

Grandma chuckled. "A frisky cat would be enough to cause some excitement, all right." She took out a kettle and put the beets inside, then added some water and placed the pot on the back burner of the propane stove. "Were you able to get it out of the building without too much trouble?"

"Jah. One of the boys finally caught the critter."

Grandma got a faraway look in her eyes before going to the refrigerator to take out some carrots and celery. "Even though I'm sure I've told you this story in the past, I can't help retelling it. One day back when I taught school, my *hund*, Nipper, followed me to the schoolhouse and slipped in through the open door before I could stop her. The *kinner* thought it was great to have a dog attend school, and they made it clear they didn't want me to take her out." Grandma washed the veggies and began cutting them up. "Of course, if I'd let Nipper stay, she would have been a distraction, so I took her outside and told her to go home."

"Did she?" Lisa asked.

"No. That determined animal curled up on the front porch and waited for me till school was out for the day. I even caught some of the students giving her pieces of their sandwiches during lunch."

I remember this story. Lisa snickered. She liked how animated Grandma's voice had become and could almost picture the look of surprise Grandma must have had on her face. No doubt she felt a bit irritated, but most likely Grandma had thought it was kind of funny. That was how it usually went around here whenever one of their farm animals did something humorous or out of character.

"Did anything else unusual happen today?" Grandma asked.

Lisa poked a fork into the chicken to check for tenderness before responding. "The only other thing that caught me off guard was when a young Amish man came to the schoolhouse as I was getting ready to leave. I didn't recognize him and assumed he must be new to the area."

"Did he give his name or say why he was there?"

"He said he was Paul but didn't state his last name. He also informed me that he'd come to the schoolhouse to see about fixing a broken window."

Grandma's brows lifted. "What happened? Did someone throw a ball through one of the building's windows?"

Lisa shook her head. "There are no broken windows, and I told him so. But then he insisted on walking around the schoolhouse to check, just in case." She frowned. "So I went with him."

"How did that go?"

"Just like I expected. There were no broken windows."

"What happened after that?"

"He looked kind of embarrassed and said he must be at the wrong schoolhouse."

"I assume he left then?"

"Jah, but before he got into his buggy, he gave me a really strange look." Lisa scrunched up her nose. "It made me feel *naerfich*." She didn't mention that Paul had asked her name.

Grandma paused from her job. "Did he say anything specific that made you nervous, or was it just his *ausdruck*?"

"It was only his expression." Lisa lifted her shoulders in a brief shrug. "But maybe I was being too sensitive. Sometimes when people look at me a certain way, I imagine that they are thinking something about me, which may not be true."

Grandma pursed her lips. "Granddaughter, you worry too much about what others think."

Lisa gave no reply as she turned back to face the stove. She was fully aware of what her grandmother thought, so there was no point in talking about it.

———

Walnut Creek

"Are those some of the old milk bottles you got at the flea market the other day?" Lois peered over her husband's shoulder as he placed two of the more unusual ones on a shelf that had been built on one side of their antique store. She stepped back and grabbed out a tissue from her apron band to catch a sneeze.

"Bless you, *fraa*. Are you coming down with a *kalt*?"

"Danki for the blessing, and no, it's not a cold. My allergies act up sometimes when I've been dusting."

"That makes sense." Orley turned his head in her direction and pointed at the milk bottles. "Do you like them?"

She bobbed her head and stuffed her hankie back under the apron band. "From what I can tell, they look very nice."

"I think so too."

The bell on the front door jingled, interrupting their conversation. Lois turned to see who had come into the store and smiled as their friend Jeff Davis walked in. "Hello, Jeff."

"Hey, it's good to see you." Orley had a big grin on his face too as he stepped away from the milk bottle display and went to greet Jeff. "How have you, Rhonda, and that sweet baby girl of yours been?" He extended his hand.

"We're all doing well, and our precious Emily keeps us smiling every day. I have to admit, she has Rhonda and me in the palm of her little hand." Jeff gave Orley a hearty handshake then came over and encompassed Lois in a friendly hug. "How are you folks getting along these days?"

Orley bobbed his head. "Fine and dandy. We're still keeping busy buying and selling antiques."

Lois couldn't miss the twinkle in her husband's eyes. He loved the kind of work they were in and probably wouldn't know what to do if they ever had to give up their store. Lois enjoyed it too, but not nearly as much as Orley did. He often commented that just the smell of old things here in the shop gave him a sense of satisfaction. "Makes me feel in touch with the past," he'd said on more than one occasion.

"How are things going at the inn, Jeff?" Lois asked. "Is your new business doing well?"

He nodded. "It certainly is. We have reservations booked clear through the end of this year and into the next as well."

"That's good to hear." Orley gave Jeff's back a few pats. "We're glad things are working out well for you and Rhonda." He looked at Lois. "Isn't that right, fraa?"

"Absolutely."

"So now, what brings you into our store this afternoon?" Orley asked Jeff.

"I was in town picking up a few things for Rhonda and thought I'd drop by to see how you folks are doing."

"We're gettin' along well and keeping plenty busy." Orley gestured to the milk bottles he'd placed on the shelf. "I got those in recently, in case you're interested."

"I'm always interested in looking," Jeff said, "but I'd better not buy anything right now."

"No problem," Orley responded. "Feel free to come by anytime just to look around."

"Maybe one of these days you two can come over to our place again for another visit."

"That would be nice."

Lois stepped closer to her husband. "And perhaps you, your wife, and that little one of yours could come by one evening soon for supper. We would love to have you over, Jeff."

"I'll talk to Rhonda about doing that." He offered Lois a wide grin.

Orley ran a thumb and finger along his left suspender. "It would be real nice to take the time and do some catching up."

"I agree." Jeff paused and looked toward the door. "I'd like to look around to see what you've added here, but I'd better save it for another time. I have more errands to run right now."

"I'll give you a call to let you know what evening might work best for us and see what your schedule looks like."

"Thanks. I'd better get going." Jeff gave Lois another hug and shook Orley's hand again.

"Tell your wife we said hello, and give that precious baby girl a kiss from us," Lois said.

"I'll be sure and do that, and feel free to drop by the inn anytime to say hello when you're not working here and are in our area. I'm sure Rhonda would like to see you."

"We will." Lois watched as Jeff headed out the door; then she turned to face Orley. "What a nice surprise to see Jeff today. It's always good when someone we know and have mentored comes in to say hello."

Orley nodded.

"I'm glad we were given the opportunity to befriend them and see how the Lord worked things out for their marriage. We as humans can only do so much, but Jesus can work out any problem no matter how big it is."

"Jah." Orley pressed a palm against his chest. "I'm kind of disappointed, though, that no one since Jeff and Rhonda has come into the shop with a problem we can try to help them with."

"Husband, that's one of your special qualities that I've admired for a good many years. You have a wonderful gift for helping those in need, and it's made me grow in my walk with the Lord too." Lois touched his arm and gave it a few pats. "If it's meant to be, someone who is dealing with a problem and needs a touch from God will come into Memory Keepers." She pointed upward. "We just need to pray and be ready to share the Good News."

"Agreed."

"And while we are waiting for that person, or maybe more than one person, I will continue to try to help people who write letters to the Dear Caroline column. I so enjoy writing answers for their problems."

Orley leaned close to Lois and brushed a kiss across her cheek—something he would never do if a customer had been in the store. "I appreciate the fact that on occasion you have read me some of those letters and allowed me to offer a few suggestions."

"That's right," Lois said. "Together we make a good team, always trying to stay true to what the Lord has taught us in His Word."

"And relying on Him to help us respond out of love and kindness to those people who are hurting because of life's problems," Orley added. "So we'll wait patiently and be ready for the day when God sends someone into the store who may need our help."

Chapter 3

Sugarcreek

"We'd better hurry, or we're going to be late for church," Grandma announced as she and Lisa entered the kitchen Sunday morning. "I can't believe all three of us overslept. Guess that's what we get for staying up late last night to finish that thousand-piece puzzle."

"I think we were all determined to see the puzzle finished." Lisa reached for the multivitamin container and removed the lid. "It was a nice evening though." She took out a chewable tablet and replaced the lid. "I especially enjoyed snacking on popcorn and some of those yummy, lemon-filled *kichlin* you made yesterday morning."

"Those cookies did turn out well." Grandma laughed. "If I hadn't moved the plate away from your *grossdaadi*, I believe he would have eaten every last one." She opened the refrigerator and took out a bottle of milk. "I think since we're running late that we should all have a bowl of cold cereal this morning. We can eat as soon as your grandpa comes in from getting the horse and buggy ready to go."

"I'll get out the cereal and set the table," Lisa offered.

"I'm going to use up the blueberries that are left in the refrigerator. Those should go well with our food this morning." Grandma smiled. "While you're doing that, I'll also make some *kaffi*. We'll need some good, strong brew to help us stay awake this morning. Sure wouldn't want to fall asleep in the middle of one of our ministers' sermons. Not only would we miss a good message, but it would be most embarrassing if anyone saw us dozing off."

Lisa nodded, but her thoughts turned to other things. Grandma had gotten out the berries, rinsed them, and then placed them into a bowl. As Lisa went about getting the dishes and cereal on the table, she reflected on how things had gone during the three-hour church service she and her grandparents had attended two weeks ago. It had been held in their neighbor's barn, which was nice because they could walk over and didn't have to travel by horse and buggy. This morning, however, the service would be at the home of Yvonne's parents, two miles away.

Lisa had never voiced her thoughts, but attending church was one of the few Amish gatherings in her community that she didn't dread attending. The men and women sat on opposite sides of the building and ate at separate tables during the noon meal when the service concluded. She didn't have to worry about someone like Aaron Wengerd striking up a conversation with her or, worse yet, asking if he could take her out someplace, like he'd done at the last young people's singing. Lisa hadn't wanted to attend the event, but after Grandma kept insisting that she go, Lisa had finally given in. Unfortunately, other than singing, she hadn't enjoyed much else—especially the socializing that had occurred before and then after everyone was done singing. Since Lisa had come to the event with Yvonne, she'd had to wait until her co-teacher had finished mingling before she could go home. She'd promised herself that evening that she would not attend any more young people's social gatherings, even if Grandma pestered her about going.

Today, during church at least, as long as Lisa didn't make the mistake of looking directly at anyone on the men's side of the room, she would not have to worry about any of the young men making eye contact with her. And of course Lisa would do her best to keep her eyes on the songbook while they were singing and on the ministers when they spoke.

The aroma of fresh-brewed coffee caused Lisa's contemplations to dissolve like a puff of smoke. A few seconds later, Grandpa entered the kitchen via the back door. "The horse and buggy are all set to go, so as soon as we've eaten we can leave for church." He looked at Grandma. "Is breakfast about ready?"

She pointed to the table. "It's all set out, and we kept things simple so we could eat quickly. I rinsed off the last of the blueberries, so we can have them with our cereal."

"Good to hear." Grandpa went over to the sink and washed his hands. After he'd dried them on a kitchen towel, they all took their seats at the table and bowed their heads.

Dear Lord, Lisa prayed silently, *thank You for our food and for my grandparents. Without them, I'd be all alone in the world.* She swallowed against the constriction that had formed in her throat. *Please keep Grandma and Grandpa healthy and safe from all harm.*

Paul sat on one end of a backless wooden bench next to his seventeen-year-old cousin, Kevin, making an effort to keep his focus on the sermon being preached. Although the topic on the importance of humility was a good one, he found it difficult not to keep glancing at the women's side of the room, where a pretty blond schoolteacher sat. Although Paul knew nothing about the young woman other than that she taught at the schoolhouse where he'd mistakenly shown up, for some strange reason he felt drawn to her. He glanced toward the preacher then back at Lisa again. *Since she's not sitting by anyone her age, I wonder if she's kind of shy. I hope I'll be given a chance to talk to Lisa again. I'd like to find out more about her.*

He picked up his comb that had slipped from his black trouser pocket and put it away. At the same time, a baby across the room began to cry, and the mother tried to console it, but she soon got up to go take care of the little one.

Paul's attention was pulled back to the sermon when the minister, whose name he did not know, practically shouted, "There is no place for haughtiness in a Christian's life. The Bible tells us in Philippians 2:3–4, 'Let nothing be done through strife or vainglory;

but in lowliness of mind let each esteem other better than themselves. Look not every man on his own things, but every man also on the things of others.'"

Paul understood the importance of thinking more about others than oneself. He'd always tried to do that, even as a child when it came to sharing his toys. Unfortunately, some people, like his so-called used-to-be friend Ervin Yoder, didn't care whose feelings he trampled on. If Ervin had cared about the friendship they'd had since childhood, he wouldn't have stolen Paul's girlfriend. Paul had gone steady with Susan Lambright nearly two years, and he'd hoped to marry her. Then the night before he had planned to propose, he'd caught Susan in the arms of Ervin. Paul would never forget the feeling of betrayal that had smacked him in the gut like an angry wave when Ervin announced that he and Susan had been secretly seeing each other for the past three months. Paul had learned right then that things didn't always go the way a person had planned. He'd learn to be wary and keep up his guard.

Paul's lips pressed tightly together as he envisioned Susan holding Ervin's hand when she'd told Paul that although she had agreed to let him court her, she'd never really thought of him as anything more than a good friend.

Good friend? Are you kidding me? Good friends don't hold hands, kiss each other, and talk about their future together. Paul pulled his fingers into the palms of his hands. *I need to accept the bitter with the sweet and move on, no matter what disappointments life throws at me. That is the main reason I left Indiana and came here to Ohio. I just need to trust God and follow His direction. I'm sure He has a plan for my life that doesn't include getting married.*

During the noon meal that followed the church service, Paul's cousin Kevin introduced him to all the young men in attendance. Most of them, except for one fellow by the name of Aaron Wengerd, had welcomed him warmly. But when Aaron simply mumbled,

"Hello," before leaving, Paul figured there must be something about him that Aaron didn't like, or maybe the fellow was on the shy side.

Once they'd set up tables inside the building for the noon meal, the women brought out the different choices of bread, cheese, peanut butter, pickles, and beverages. Paul couldn't wait to grab a cup of coffee to recharge his battery. The men and children began to take their seats at the tables, and it wasn't long before the ladies did the same. Soon one of the ministers said it was time to pray, and the room quieted for silent prayer.

Afterward, the people rose, and lines began to form at the different tables; some were getting their drinks first, while others went for the food that had been set out.

Paul felt somewhat awkward, not knowing anyone besides his uncle, aunt, and two cousins at this nice-sized gathering. The church district Paul had been part of back in Indiana wasn't as large as this one. Paul would have to get used to its size since he'd chosen to live here. But he hoped after being here today he'd get to meet a good share of people. Paul had picked out his food and found a place to sit with the men. He saw the pretty young schoolteacher again, sitting beside an older woman with mostly gray hair. Paul's attentions were quickly diverted, however, when a young man sitting across from him said, "Hi, my name's Steven." He gestured to the teenage boy who sat next to him. "And this is my brother, Samuel."

Paul shook both of their hands. "It's nice to meet you. My name's Paul Herschberger, and I moved to Ohio to work as a carpenter for my uncle Abe."

Steven nodded. "We heard Abe's nephew was coming here. When Abe told our *daed*, he seemed excited about it."

Paul smiled. It felt good to know his dad's brother wanted him to be here. "So what do you fellows do for a living?" he questioned.

Steven opened his mouth, but Samuel spoke first. "Our parents live near your uncle's place, and the two of us work with our daed as horse trainers."

"Sounds like an interesting occupation."

"That's for sure," Steven put in. "There's never a dull moment when you're workin' with horses."

The conversation went well as they covered several topics. Paul felt as if he was getting to know them a little and felt pleased when Steven invited him to come by and visit sometime.

The awkwardness Paul had felt earlier began to subside. He finished what was on his plate before excusing himself to get a refill of coffee. A while after he returned to his place with Steven and Samuel, Paul's uncle came and got him, saying he wanted to introduce Paul to some of the older men. When they approached a short, stocky man with mostly gray hair, Uncle Abe made the introductions, "This is my nephew Paul Herschberger. He recently moved here from Indiana."

The older man grinned as he gave Paul a hearty handshake. "I'm Jerold Schrock, but most everyone calls me Jerry."

"It's good to meet you, Jerry."

"Likewise."

"My nephew's a carpenter, and he'll be working for me, unless he finds something else he'd rather be doing." Uncle Abe put his hand on Paul's shoulder.

"I doubt that I'd want to work for anyone else or do anything other than carpentry work," Paul said with a shake of his head.

"Your uncle does good work, and he treats his customers well," Jerry interjected.

Paul nodded. "I feel fortunate that in addition to providing me with a job, my aunt and uncle have invited me to stay with them and their family."

Uncle Abe leaned closer to Paul and spoke quietly. "Just a reminder, nephew, that since this is Sunday, our day of rest, we shouldn't be talking about work."

Paul struggled with the urge to remind his uncle that he'd brought up the subject, but he held his tongue and gave an agreeable nod instead.

Jerry looked over at Paul. "What made you decide to leave

Indiana and move to Ohio?"

Paul shifted his stance as he cleared his throat. "Well, I—uh—needed a change of pace. Thought it'd be nice to make a new start." He paused and looked over at his uncle. "So when Uncle Abe suggested that I move here, I jumped at the chance."

"Sometimes it's good to start over in a new place," Jerry said. "I did that after I met my fraa at a mutual friend's wedding." He glanced over at a group of older women sitting together across the yard. Paul assumed one of them must be Jerry's wife, but since the older man didn't point her out, Paul thought it would be impolite to ask.

"Where'd you live before moving to Sugarcreek?" Paul asked instead.

"I grew up in a town on the western side of Pennsylvania, not far from Pittsburgh." Jerry looked over at the older women again. "My wife, Marlene, lived in Sugarcreek, and I decided it would be a nice place to live too. So I found a job and moved here even before I asked her to marry me."

Uncle Abe chuckled. "You'd have been in for a big surprise if she'd said no."

Jerry gave a vigorous shake of his head. "I knew Marlene was the woman for me, so I wouldn't have taken no for an answer."

Paul couldn't help noticing the older man's determined expression. It made him wonder if he should have tried harder to woo Susan back instead of giving up and taking off for what he hoped would be greener pastures. Well, he was here now, and one way or another, Paul planned to make a new life for himself. Of course, he would probably remain a bachelor, because if there was one thing Paul knew, he could not allow himself to fall in love with any woman and set himself up for the possibility of getting hurt again.

While Lisa walked leisurely behind her grandparents as the three of them headed for their buggy, she heard Grandma ask Grandpa a question that made her ears perk up: "Who was that young man you were talking to after the meal?"

"His name is Paul, and he's new to the area. Fact is, the young man's Abe Herschberger's nephew."

"I see," Grandma responded as they picked up their pace a bit.

"Paul's a carpenter, and he'll be working for Abe."

"He's the same man I told you about that stopped at the school-house a few days ago when I was getting ready to leave," Lisa spoke up. "I—I was surprised to see him in church."

Grandma stopped walking and turned to face Lisa. "Did you have a chance to talk to him today?"

"No, but he looked my way several times, and it made me feel naerfich."

"He probably recognized you from when he stopped by the schoolhouse." Grandpa, who'd also turned to face Lisa, gave her a quick wink. "Paul seems like a nice man, so there was nothin' for you to feel nervous about."

Lisa offered no response. There was no point in trying to explain how she felt. Grandma always pressured her to be more social, and Grandpa sometimes made comments about her shyness, often saying that Lisa needed to quit acting like a turtle and come out of her shell. His words stung like the prick from a rosebush. So whenever possible, Lisa tried to avoid the topic of her not wanting to socialize. No one, not even her grandparents, understood how Lisa felt deep inside, and since she didn't want to talk about her inner feelings, Lisa would make sure it stayed that way.

Chapter 4

Lisa stood in front of the classroom, looking at the bulletin board her co-teacher had planned for some of the older students to decorate. Yvonne had developed a nagging toothache yesterday and had no choice but to go to the dentist this morning, leaving Lisa to teach all eight grades on her own. Lisa figured Yvonne would be back sometime this afternoon, and it would be good to save the harder subjects until then and do something creative during the morning session. So while the upper classes did their reading assignment, Lisa had her younger students color some leaves that the older students had drawn previously. Once the coloring was done, the third- and fourth-grade children cut the leaves out. When those had been finished, the fifth-grade girls put the leaves on the bulletin board while Lisa read her lower-grade students a story about a boy who liked to rake the leaves in his backyard and then jump into the pile. She'd taken the book about the twins home with her over the weekend and had forgotten to bring it back this morning, so she hoped the children would enjoy this book instead.

"Of course," Lisa said as she neared the end of the story, "when the boy jumped, the leaves scattered, so he had to rake them all up again."

A few hands went up, and Lisa allowed the pupils to ask questions.

"What would you like to know, Johnny?" Lisa pointed to the

dark-haired boy from the second grade.

"Have you ever jumped in a pile of leaves?"

Lisa smiled. "Yes, when I was a girl I did that many times."

"Do you still jump in the leaves?" the same boy questioned.

She shook her head. "But I do enjoy walking through leaves that have fallen from the trees this time of the year. I like to hear the crunch, crunch, crunch beneath my feet."

Another hand shot up. Lisa gestured to the first-grade girl. "What is your question, Linda?"

"Can we walk through the crunchy leaves after lunch during our outside recess time?"

"Yes, you certainly can, and I'd be happy to walk along with you."

"Can we rake the leaves and jump in the big pile?" This question came from eight-year-old Abner.

"If there's a rake in the toolshed out back, you can take turns raking the leaves," Lisa replied. "But you'll have to rake them in a pile again after you've taken turns jumping in."

All heads in the lower grades bobbed eagerly as the children looked at their teacher with happy smiles.

Just thinking about walking through the fallen leaves and watching the children rake and jump into the pile made Lisa feel like a kid again. She looked forward to the noon recess and walking briskly through the leaves with some of her scholars. The cool, refreshing autumn air would be an added bonus.

At lunchtime, since Yvonne had not shown up yet, Lisa told the children, according to their ages, to go wash up and get their lunches then bring them back to their desks.

While they ate, Lisa sat at her own desk, eating the first half of the ham and cheese sandwich her grandmother had prepared for her this morning.

Grandma's so good to me, she thought, savoring each bite. *Ever since I came to live with her and Grandpa, she's always been attentive to my needs. Grandpa's thoughtful too. I bet they treated my mother well when she lived with them. Maybe they're raising me the same way they did her.*

A lump formed in Lisa's throat, and when she took another bite of her sandwich, she could barely get it down. Although she remembered very little about the accident that had taken her parents' and paternal grandparents' lives, the pain of what had happened often crept to the surface of her thoughts. Lisa wouldn't know what to do if her mother's parents were taken from her too. She loved them both so dearly and knew without a doubt that they missed their only daughter. Despite the horrible pain they must have felt, Grandma and Grandpa Schrock had remained strong for Lisa and always tried to be cheerful and encouraging. She didn't understand where their strength came from.

Lisa reached for her bottle of water and was about to take a drink when little Anna Troyer, who sat in the front row, shrieked so loud Lisa nearly jumped out of her chair.

"What's wrong, Anna?" Lisa asked, approaching the child's desk.

"Look, Teacher—*iemense!*" Anna's chin quivered as she pointed at several ants crawling around on the surface of her desk.

"I'll take a look and see what I can do." Leaning over Anna's desk, Lisa peered into the child's lunch box and discovered that there were also ants in there. She tried not to let on, but the sight of them made her skin crawl.

Anna continued to howl, and Lisa quickly picked up the lunch box and took it outside after instructing one of the older boys to take care of the ants on Anna's desk and any that might have made their way to the floor.

After removing the sandwich, cookies, and apple from Anna's lunch box, Lisa placed them on the wide porch railing. At least it appeared that all of Anna's lunch, held in plastic bags, had been protected from the ants.

Being careful not to touch any, Lisa dumped the little insects out of the lunch box and onto the ground. Anna came outside with tears on her face and stood beside her. She pointed and watched the little black insects on the ground crawling away. "Look at them, Teacher. Did any get inside the wrappers and eat my food?"

Lisa gave Anna what she hoped was a soothing smile. "Nope, your lunch items seem sealed and you should be able to eat your food."

Upon closer look, Lisa saw that a few of the more determined bugs remained and appeared to be stuck to the sides of the lunch box. Upon closer inspection, she saw that the pesky insects were trapped in a drizzle of amber-colored honey.

"Did your mama make you a peanut butter and honey sandwich this morning?" Lisa asked Anna, who remained close to her.

Sniffling, the little girl nodded.

When Lisa sat on the porch step and looked up from her angle at the wrapping of the peanut butter and honey sandwich again, she noticed a small hole in the bag housing the bread. Apparently the honey had leaked out through the hole, and the ants saw it as an invitation to take up residence in the lunch box and enjoy a free meal.

"I don't want my sandwich now," Anna said with a whimper. "It might be full of iemense." She wrinkled her freckled nose. "Sure wouldn't wanna eat some icky bugs."

"I don't think any of the ants got into the bag, but if you don't want to eat your bread, I'd be happy to give you half of my ham and cheese sandwich. Does that sound good to you?"

"Jah." Anna took a seat on the porch step beside Lisa and leaned her head against Lisa's shoulder. "I like you, Teacher. You're real nice."

"Thank you." Lisa smiled. "I like you too."

At a tender moment like this, Lisa felt a strong desire to become a mother. But it would mean getting married, and that was something she would never do, no matter how much she loved being with children. So Lisa's only recourse was to keep teaching school for as long as possible and enjoy spending time with other people's children.

A few moments later, the same older boy Lisa had asked for help inside the classroom came out to let her know that the ants had been taken care of.

"Thank you for helping out."

"No problem. Besides, I've gotten rid of many spiders at home for my *mamm*. I catch 'em and then put the creepy crawlers outside for her."

"I'm sure she appreciates you doing that." Lisa reached up and put the rest of Anna's food in her lunch box.

He nodded then turned and headed back inside of the schoolhouse.

Lisa took Anna by the hand. "Let's go back to our desks now and finish eating."

———

As soon as everyone had cleared away their lunch boxes and cleaned off their desks, they all went outside to play. The older boys, and a few of the girls, showed no interest in frolicking in the leaves, so they got a game of baseball going. While they hooted, hollered, and cheered each other on, Lisa watched the younger ones have fun playing in the piles of leaves two of the third-grade boys had raked up. Although Lisa was tempted to jump in too, she held herself in check and stuck to walking back and forth in the crackling leaves. Several of the young girls trotted along with her, laughing and singing a silly song one of the children had made up as they walked along.

When recess was about to conclude, Yvonne showed up. "Looks like everyone's having a good time," she said.

"For sure." Lisa noticed a bit of swelling in her friend's jaw. "How'd it go at the dentist's? Did he figure out what was wrong with your tooth?"

Yvonne grimaced. "It's infected and I was given antibiotics."

"Oh, sorry to hear."

"The worst part is that I'll need to have a root canal done next Wednesday. So do you think you'll be able to handle all of the classes, or should I see about getting you a helper?"

"I managed fine this morning, so I'm sure it won't be a problem for me to teach all eight grades that day."

"Thank you." Yvonne released a deep sigh. "As much as I dislike the idea of going back to see the dentist, I'll sure be glad when the appointment is over with and my throbbing gum feels better."

Lisa nodded. Although she'd never had an abscessed tooth or a root canal, she'd heard from others that it wasn't the most pleasant thing.

Lisa continued to watch the children play with the leaves. One of the boys picked up an armful and tossed them into the air. The brilliant colors floated back down. Some landed on a boy's head, and the rest fell to the ground. He laughed and tossed some more. His act encouraged one of the other children to do the same thing. Lisa enjoyed hearing them laughing at one another, each wearing a few leaves on some area of their clothing. But soon the merriment ended as they'd brushed themselves off and walked together, visiting before going in for more lessons.

Lisa glanced at her co-teacher, who was also watching the children. *I'll be praying that things will continue to get better for Yvonne. We all can use prayer in our lives, and it's good to pray for those in need.*

She gave Yvonne's arm a few pats. "Recess is about over now. I guess we'd better let the children know it's time to go inside."

Since Paul's uncle was out of town and had given him the day off, Paul had decided to take advantage of this beautiful fall day and check out a few yard sales in the area. Because he was new to Sugarcreek, Paul would keep local for now, giving him a chance to get used to his surroundings.

So far he'd been adjusting well to living at his uncle and aunt's house. They had made the transition from his parents' home to their place pretty easy. Paul had told them right away that he would help out with the animals and anything else he could do to repay their generosity. He also let it be known that he was thankful for the job Uncle Abe had offered him. The pay wasn't bad either. In fact, Paul would be earning more than what he'd previously made working for his dad.

As Paul guided his aunt's horse and buggy down the road, he looked at the different houses, farms, and lay of the land along the way. Soon he saw a wooden sign that read Horse Training. *That must be where those two brothers live who I met after church last Sunday. One of these days I'll have to pop in to visit them and get a close look at how they train horses for pulling buggies, pony carts, and wagons.* Paul looked over in that direction again and saw someone working with a horse. Then he looked back at the road as a couple of cars were coming, reminding him that he needed to stay focused.

Paul saw a Yard Sale sign at the end of the next driveway, so he guided Aunt Emma's horse and buggy onto the property. It was probably wishful thinking, but Paul thought it would be great if he could find a specific old milk bottle that he'd been searching for. Although the chances were slim, it was worth looking.

Paul secured his aunt's horse to a fence post and entered. It didn't take long before he spotted an Amish man, who looked to be in his late fifties, walking up and down between the row of tables. He'd never seen this man before and figured he must not be from his uncle's church district because he hadn't seen him at church last Sunday. When the bearded man glanced his way, Paul gave a nod and moved in the direction of the first table. There were some fancy glasses and cups but nothing vintage, so Paul moved on to the next table.

"Looking for anything specific?" the Amish man questioned as he approached Paul.

"Yeah, but I probably won't find it here." He brushed a hand across his damp forehead. "Uh. . .is this your place? Are you the one hosting this yard sale?"

"Nope, I'm just here looking." He moved closer to Paul. "Mind if I ask what it is that you are seeking?"

"An old milk bottle like my grandmother used to have. It was an unusual one and she really liked it, but thanks to my clumsiness, the bottle got broken. I'd like to replace it for her, but it's doubtful that I'll ever find another one like it."

The man pulled a business card from his pocket and handed it to Paul. "My wife and I own an antique store, Memory Keepers, in Walnut Creek. Why don't you drop by sometime when you're in the area? We often have quite a few old milk bottles for sale, and some are available right now."

Paul's interest was piqued. "I just might do that." Even though anything he might buy in an antique store would no doubt be higher priced than a yard sale item, Paul didn't mind. He'd be willing to pay more if he could surprise his grandmother with a milk bottle identical to—or even almost like—the one he'd broken.

⁓

Marlene Schrock pulled out a chair and took a seat at the kitchen table. The house seemed quiet, since she'd finished using the washer for the day and the clothes were outside drying on the line. Lisa was teaching at the school, and Marlene's husband, Jerry, was away today, seeing a friend who'd had foot surgery, and no doubt he'd be a while visiting the man.

Marlene glanced at the three loaves of fresh bread sitting on the counter. Between doing laundry and baking bread, she had spent a good portion of the morning working. Now it was time to take a much-needed break with a cup of coffee and the chance to read this morning's newspaper.

I wouldn't mind a softer chair to sit on, though. She rose and pushed in the wooden seat. *I think I'll move out to the living room and relax in the recliner.* Marlene grabbed her things and got comfortable in the cozy living-room chair.

She did a quick read-through of some news articles and scanned a few ads, then turned to the page that featured the Dear Caroline column. Marlene was pleased to see her letter had been printed and Caroline had responded. After a few sips of coffee, she set the mug on the end table and eagerly read the message from Caroline out loud.

"Dear Worried Grandma: If your granddaughter isn't responding to any of the men who have shown an interest in her, she may not have met the right one. If you know a man you believe could be right for her, you might consider trying to get them together. Sometimes all it takes is a little nudge from a well-meaning matchmaker."

Marlene smiled and picked up her coffee mug for another drink. *Playing matchmaker is a good idea. Don't know why I didn't think of it myself. Now all I need to do is find the right man for Lisa.*

Chapter 5

"I'm going into town to run a few errands this morning. Would you like to go with me?" Lisa's grandfather asked her after they'd finished eating breakfast the first Saturday of October.

She looked across the table at her grandmother, but before Lisa could voice the question that had come to mind, Grandma smiled and said: "Now don't you worry about the *gschaar*. I am perfectly capable of washing and drying the dishes myself. You and your grossdaadi don't get much one-on-one time, and I think you should go along with him." She bobbed her head a couple of times for emphasis. "It'll be a nice outing for both of you." Grandma stood and picked up the juice container to put away in the refrigerator.

Lisa's mind raced as she thought of a few more excuses, but knowing her grandmother, nothing would be convincing enough. Even when debating about something with Grandpa, Grandma could be very persuasive and quite often won out. While Lisa had no desire to go to town today, where she would likely have to make conversation if she and Grandpa ran into someone they knew, Lisa figured she might as well give in.

Her grandmother moved to the sink and began to rinse out the bowl used to prepare their scrambled eggs.

With a slow nod, Lisa looked over at Grandpa and gave a forced smile. "I'll be ready to go with you as soon as I help Grandma clear the breakfast dishes. It's the least I can do to help out so she doesn't have to do everything herself."

"No problem," he said. "I'll get the horse and buggy ready and be waiting for you outside."

⁓

When Lisa entered the barn a short time later, the odor of sweet-smelling hay assaulted her senses. She paused by the door, listening to the crackle of dry straw being spread in a stall. Apparently Grandpa wasn't ready to go yet.

Lisa headed in the direction of the sound and found him raking fresh straw across the floor in her horse's stall. The gentle mare she had named Pet stood in the corner of the cubicle, munching on what was left of the oats Lisa had fed her earlier this morning.

Grandpa looked away from his chore and smiled at Lisa. "I'll get my horse out as soon as I'm done here. You can wait for me in the buggy if you want to."

She shook her head. "I'd rather do something more meaningful than stand around wasting time. How about if I take Benny out of his stall and get him hitched to the buggy?"

He grinned at her. "Danki, Lisa. I appreciate your willingness to help."

"I'm happy to do it." Lisa lingered as he resumed his work. *Maybe we could do something fun together while we're out today.* "Grandpa, while we are in town maybe we could look for another puzzle to work on."

He chuckled. "Sure, we can check out a couple of places I know of that usually have a variety of them." He stepped out of the stall to bring in more bedding.

"I've got a little spending money on me. I was also thinking maybe we could stop and get some ice cream."

"I might be up for a treat while we're out shopping. You know me. . . . I never turn down a dish of ice cream," he teased.

"Okay, I better get busy hooking Benny to the buggy." Lisa hurried to the next stall, where Grandpa's horse waited. Given all that her grandparents had done for her, offering to help whenever needed was the least she could do.

⁓

Walnut Creek

Paul secured his uncle's horse, Cinnamon, at the hitching post outside the antique store and stepped down from the open buggy he'd also borrowed from his uncle. When Paul left Indiana, his own horse and buggy had remained behind under the care of his folks. Paul's intent was to have them brought out here once he felt certain that he liked living in Ohio and wanted to stay. Paul hadn't even been here a month yet, so he couldn't be sure; but he liked the lay of the land, and working for his uncle had been going well. Unless something came up to change his mind, he would most likely be staying. Before winter set in, he hoped to have his own horse and buggy with him. When Paul felt ready, he would either buy or rent a place of his own. He wouldn't feel right about staying with his aunt and uncle indefinitely—especially since they still had two children living at home.

Paul let his thoughts drift away and focused on the antique store he was about to enter. He'd been eager to come here ever since he'd met the Amish man who owned the business. The building sat in a good location, and the fact that it was on a main street made it quite visible. Paul couldn't help but notice the vintage-looking WELCOME sign on the front door. When he opened the door, a bell near the top jangled.

Paul's senses awakened as he entered the building and breathed in the distinct odors of leather, wood, and something else, mixed with a musty aroma. His eyes scanned many kinds of old items. *I'm guessing this shop is pretty good sized. There must be plenty of interesting things in this store.*

Paul glanced around at the narrow aisle for walking between the table displays on both sides. A glimmer of sunlight shining through one of the windows made the silver and crystal vases look more appealing. Antique wooden cabinets had been filled with collectible plates, china cups, and thimbles in various sizes and colors. Rusty and paint-distressed signs advertising various businesses hung on one wall. Old clocks and musical instruments decorated another wall, and another area of the shop was full of old farm tools. Rustic-looking furniture had been scattered about the room, along with cedar chests, trunks, vintage kitchen items, and stacks of old books. There were so many things Paul hardly knew where to look first. But one thing was certain: he wouldn't leave here before seeing what their old milk bottles looked like. Paul hoped that among the bottles they had in the store there'd be the one he'd been searching for.

"Well, hello there." Orley Troyer stepped out from behind the front counter and shook Paul's hand. "You're the young man I met at a yard sale a few weeks ago, aren't you?"

Paul nodded. "I was the person looking for a particular old milk bottle, and you invited me to stop by your shop and see what kinds of bottles you have for sale."

"Yes indeed. The old milk bottles I have are right over there." Orley pointed to a shelf on one wall. "There are some nice ones too, so maybe one of 'em will catch your eye."

"Thanks. I'll go take a look." Paul headed in that direction. When he reached the shelf, he looked each of the bottles over carefully. He had to admit there were some nice ones for sale but nothing quite like the one his grandma used to own.

He turned to face Orley. "Sorry, but I don't see the one I've been looking for here. Are these the only milk bottles you have?"

The older man nodded. "I'm always on the lookout for more, however. So if you'd like to provide me with a phone number where you can be reached, I'd be happy to give you a call if I get more in."

"Thanks, I'd appreciate that." Paul reached into his jacket pocket for the notebook and pen he usually carried but found nothing except a hankie. "Would you have something I can write my phone number on?"

"Of course. There's a stack of writing pads on the counter up front."

Paul followed Orley, and when they reached the checkout counter, an Amish woman joined them.

"I'd like you to meet my wife, Lois." Orley gestured to the auburn-haired lady.

Paul shook the smiling woman's hand. "It's nice to meet you. I'm Paul Herschberger."

"This young man and I met at a yard sale a few weeks ago," Orley explained. "He came in to check out the antique milk bottles here in our store, but none of the ones we have resemble the bottle he's been looking for."

"That's too bad. We can let you know if we get any more in," she said in a kindly tone.

"I told him the same thing." Orley handed Paul one of the tablets and a pen.

After he wrote down his uncle's phone number, he handed the tablet back.

Orley tore off the piece of paper with the phone number and gave the remainder of the notebook to Paul. "You're welcome to keep this. Oh, here's a pen too. We recently had them made with our business name—Memory Keepers—to give out to our customers."

With a "thank you," Paul accepted the tablet, noting that in addition to the name of the store, it included a phone number and address. "I'd best get going. I have a few other stops I need to make today. Again, it was nice to meet you, Lois, and good to see you again, Orley."

Lois nodded, and Orley grinned. "It was nice seeing you as well," they said almost at the same time.

Although a bit disappointed about not finding the right milk bottle, Paul was glad he'd stopped by Memory Keepers. The Troyers were a friendly couple, and he'd enjoyed seeing their store. Something about being among so many vintage items gave Paul a sense of peace and satisfaction.

"Fall is sure a pleasant time of the year," Lisa's grandfather commented as they drew closer to town.

"Jah, I enjoy seeing all the pretty-colored leaves." As they approached an Amish farm, Lisa looked to her left, noticing that the grain silo had recently been filled. A herd of cows grazed inside a fenced pasture, and several chickens ran about in the yard. She fought the urge to wave at the homemade scarecrow wearing a black hat, standing tall in the field of corn that had already been harvested. No doubt that scraggly scarecrow would be torn down before the harsh winds of winter blew in.

In some ways Lisa dreaded the cold winter months. But there were good things to look forward to, such as sledding when the ground was covered with snow, ice-skating on frozen ponds, and caroling a few days before Christmas. Lisa also looked forward to the annual Christmas program put on by the schoolchildren for their families.

"You've grown awfully quiet all of a sudden." Grandpa nudged Lisa's arm.

"Just thinking is all," she responded.

"About anything in particular?"

"It was nothing important. I was having a few thoughts about the upcoming winter months. It'll be here before we know it."

"That's for sure. When I was boy, time seemed to drag on, but the older I've gotten, the quicker the days seem to go flying by."

Lisa didn't think time moved much differently than when she was young, but then she hadn't thought that much about it either. Her schedule could be busy while teaching the children, but usually weekends were pretty laid back and she had time to do the things she wanted, like help out her grandparents, read one of her newest novels, or enjoy a stroll down the road, appreciating the sounds and views of nature.

As the horse clippity-clopped into town at a pretty good pace, Grandpa pulled back on the reins to slow the gelding.

When the hardware store came into view, Grandpa guided his horse to the closest hitching rail. Lisa climbed down and secured the animal. After Grandpa joined her, they went inside the store. "As soon as I find the paint I'll see what they've got for puzzles here." He smiled.

"Okay, I think I'll take a look around and see what else they have in the store. There could be something new since the last time I was here." Lisa headed in the opposite direction.

While Grandpa looked for paint and a new puzzle plus a few other supplies, Lisa wandered up and down the aisles, although not searching for anything in particular. She wished the Christian bookstore in town were closer. If it were, she'd go there to browse around while Grandpa did his shopping here.

I should have asked him to drop me off there before coming here, Lisa thought. *Oh well, I'm in this store now, so I may as well make the best of it. Maybe Grandpa would like my opinion on the paint he's getting for the kitchen.*

Lisa pivoted to head back to the paint section, but she came face-to-face with Aaron Wengerd.

"Hello, Lisa. How are you doin' today?" He offered her a wide smile.

Her cheeks heated as she dropped her gaze to the floor. "I– I'm fine." Remembering her manners, she quickly added, "How are you?"

"Doin' okay." Aaron cleared his throat loudly. "Say, I have a question to ask."

Lisa forced herself to look at him. "What?"

"There's a young people's singing planned for tomorrow evening. I was wondering if you're planning to go."

Lisa shook her head. "Probably not."

"How come?"

She merely shrugged in response.

"I'd be happy to come by your grandparents' place and get you."

She glanced around, hoping her grandpa would show up and come to her rescue. "I. . .uh. . .well, if I do go to the singing, I'll probably walk, since the people hosting the event don't live far from Grandma and Grandpa's house. But danki for asking."

"It's not safe for you to be walking alone, especially after the singing when it's dark."

"I'll be fine. I've walked by myself many times."

"But I don't think—"

"There you are, Lisa," Grandpa said, carrying the bucket of paint in one hand as he started down the aisle toward her. In his other hand he toted a basket with a puzzle he'd found along with a few other items. "I've got what I need, and I'm ready to go." He gave Aaron a nod. "Sorry to interrupt your conversation with my grand-daughter, but we have some other stops and need to get going."

Aaron opened his mouth as if he might say something, but in a hurry to get away from him, Lisa mumbled a quick goodbye. Then she took hold of her grandfather's arm and hurried away.

"I see you found a puzzle for us to start on." Lisa stayed in step with him.

"Jah, this one is a fall scene, and it caught my eye right away." He raised the basket toward her.

"That's a nice one. I'm sure it will be fun to put together."

Grandpa nodded and began speaking in Pennsylvania Dutch. "What'd Aaron want?" Grandpa asked as they approached the checkout counter, where someone else was being waited on with a shopping basket.

"He asked if he could pick me up for the singing tomorrow evening."

"What'd you tell him?"

"I said I probably wouldn't go, but if I did, I'd walk."

"Did he press the issue?"

"No, but only because you came along at just the right time."

Grandpa made a little grunting sound. "That fellow is persistent. I would be surprised if he doesn't show up at our house tomorrow evening and try to persuade you to go with him to the singing."

Lisa's jaw clenched. "He'd better not," she whispered. "Because if he does, I'll refuse to go."

Grandpa chuckled. "If anyone's going to take you, it'll be me. Aaron's right about one thing—you shouldn't be out walking alone."

Chapter 6

"Are you going to the young people's singing tonight?" Yvonne whispered to Lisa after they'd taken their seats on the women's side of the room before church started Sunday morning.

Lisa shrugged. "How about you?"

"Jah. I missed the last one, so I thought it'd be nice to attend this singing." Yvonne gave Lisa's shoulder a little bump. "I hope you can make it."

"Maybe so." Lisa glanced at the men's side of the room and noticed Aaron staring at her. She quickly dropped her gaze. *If it weren't for Aaron, it would be easier for me to attend that singing tonight. I really wish he'd stop pursuing me. Surely by now he must realize that I'm not interested in a relationship with him.*

Lisa had been around Aaron throughout most of their school years, and she'd never been a fan of his pushy demeanor. At least that's how she perceived him to be. Yvonne, on the other hand, had mentioned him in passing a while ago, saying she thought he was easy to get along with and quite good looking. Lisa wished Aaron would set his sights on her friend and forget about pursuing her, but she figured it wasn't her place to suggest it.

If by some chance Lisa were to ever fall in love, it would have to be with a very special person. She frowned. *I can't believe that by now Aaron hasn't figured out that I do not want to date him.* She twisted her fingers around the ties on her head covering. *Or anyone else for that matter.*

The room fell silent when the church district's three ministers entered the building and headed to the front of the congregation, where they took their seats. Lisa felt relief when the service started and she could focus on the first songs from their church hymnal, the Ausbund. She loved to sing, and she always felt encouraged by the words.

About halfway through the sermon, Lisa made the mistake of glancing across the room again. Her face heated when she saw that carpenter fellow, Paul, looking at her with a curious expression. At least she thought it was her he'd been focused on. Maybe it was just her imagination. But there was something about the fellow that sparked a little curiosity. She felt certain that he was nothing at all like Aaron. Although Lisa didn't know him that well, Paul seemed quieter and more polite than Aaron. But she figured it didn't really matter what Paul was like, since he was a stranger to their community and might not even be staying.

Pulling her attention back to the preacher's message, Lisa reflected on Proverbs 22:6, the scripture verse the minister had quoted: "Train up a child in the way he should go: and when he is old, he will not depart from it."

Although Preacher Sam spoke primarily to the parents, Lisa felt that the message was appropriate for her and Yvonne since they were teachers. Every child in their classroom needed guidance, not only to gain a sound education but also to shape their behavior. It was a privilege for Lisa to take part in training the young children who were in her care during school hours. It was a privilege to see her students gain knowledge and acquire good study habits. A solid education and good work ethic would be necessary when the children grew up, learned a trade, and got a job. Lisa thought about how most Amish young people, including herself, contributed to their family's income. This showed their sense of responsibility for those they lived with and cared for.

Being careful to keep her eyes on the minister who was still speaking, and not on any of the young men across the room, Lisa's focus returned to the elderly man's sermon.

⁓

When church ended and everyone filed out of the buggy maker's shop, Lisa heard her name being called. She glanced to her right and saw one of her students, Nancy Burkholder, heading her way.

"Teacher, guess what I got for my *gebottsdaag* yesterday?" the child asked with all the enthusiasm of a seven-year-old.

Lisa leaned down so that she was eye level with the young girl. "What did you get for your birthday?"

"I got a pony." Nancy glanced at her twin brother, Nathan, who stood near their ten-year-old brother, Simon. She looked at Lisa again and blinked a couple of times. "Uh. . .guess the little horse isn't really mine. It belongs to me and my *bruder*, since *Mamm* and Daed gave it to the both of us."

Her twin brother approached. "Our pony is real friendly, and she likes to be petted."

Lisa smiled. "A pony is a nice gift. I hope you and your sister will take good care of it."

Nathan grinned from ear to ear.

Nancy bobbed her head. "We're gonna brush and feed her whenever our daed says. And someday when we get older, Daed's gonna teach us how to train her to pull a cart with us in it."

"I can't wait to help train our pony." Her brother's voice grew louder.

"Me too." Nancy stepped closer to Lisa.

"Sounds like something for you to look forward to." Lisa gave the little girl's shoulder a gentle squeeze. "Did she have a name when you got her, or did you and Nathan get to choose a name?"

"Daed said we could choose." Nancy wrinkled her nose. "Nathan wanted to call her Slowpoke, on account of she don't move too fast. But I said we should name her Brownie, 'cause she's the color of chocolate."

Nathan looked at his sister. "I liked the name Slowpoke. You wanted to name our pony after food, and that's kinda *dumm*."

"That's okay. Other animals are named after food—like Abe Herschberger's horse named Cinnamon." Nancy pointed toward the fenced-in field where all the buggies and horses were held. "I thought Brownie was a cute name."

"Which name did you end up with for the pony?"

"Neither. When we couldn't decide, Mamm stepped in and said the pony should be called Daisy, which was the name of the pony she had when she was a *maedel*."

"Did your daed suggest a name for the pony?" Lisa questioned.

Nathan shook his head with a defeated expression. "Nope. Daed said the name Mamm wanted would stand."

Nancy's lower lip protruded. "So now we're stuck callin' the pony somethin' neither of us like. Mamm said if Nathan and I had agreed on a name, she wouldn't have stepped in."

"That was a good lesson to learn, jah?"

Nancy nodded. "I hope when I'm a *mudder* someday, I don't have *zwilling* babies." She wrinkled her nose for the second time.

"How come?" Lisa questioned.

"Cause if I had twins, then they'd hafta share their birthdays like me and Nathan do every year."

Nancy's twin didn't comment about the possibility of her having twins someday. He just shrugged his shoulders and headed back over to where his father sat, visiting with some of the other men.

Since I'm never getting married and having children, giving birth to twins is something I'll never have to worry about, Lisa told herself. She figured raising twin babies would be more difficult than having a single baby. And she could definitely see where twins having to share a birthday, and even their gift, would be hard.

Nancy bumped Lisa's hand and tipped her head to one side. "Think I hear my mamm callin' me, so I'd better go. See you at school tomorrow, Teacher."

Lisa gently squeezed the young girl's hand. "You can count on it."

Nancy grinned before turning away and skipping off to see what her mother wanted.

A moment later, Yvonne stepped up to Lisa and said, "Have you made up your mind yet about going to the singing tonight?"

Lisa drew in a breath of air and released it slowly. "Unless I change my mind between now and then, guess I will go, but only because I enjoy singing."

"I like it too," her friend said, "but I wouldn't mind if some nice-looking young man asked if he could take me home when the singing is over."

"Are you thinking of anyone in particular?"

Yvonne gave a slow shake of her head. "No, not really."

"Are you sure about that?"

A flush of pink swept across Yvonne's cheeks as she tucked her arms in close to her sides. "I'd rather not say.

"Okay." Lisa gestured to the barn, where the men had been busy turning the wooden benches they'd sat upon during church into tables. "Guess we'd better go inside and help the other women get the light meal set out on the tables."

"What time should I pick you up?" Grandpa asked when he dropped Lisa off that evening at the home where the singing was taking place.

"It should be over by nine," she replied.

"All right I'll come back to get you then. Unless," he added with a wink, "some handsome young fellow should ask if he can bring you home. If that happens, just call and leave me a message. I'll go out to the phone shack at a quarter to nine to see if you have called."

Lisa shook her head vigorously. "That won't happen, Grandpa, because I have no intention of riding home with anyone but you."

"All right then, have a good time." He reached across the buggy seat and gave her arm a tender squeeze.

Lisa stepped down from the buggy and hurried toward the oversized buggy shed where she saw Yvonne and some other young people heading. She had almost caught up to Yvonne when Aaron came alongside her.

"Hey, Lisa." He grinned at her, and in a most pleasant voice, he said, "I'm glad you could make it tonight."

She gave a brief nod and hurried on. By the time Lisa joined Yvonne, she had already gone into the building and was talking to David and Katie Hostetler, who had hosted the event.

Lisa held back, not wanting to interrupt. Feeling timid and out of her comfort zone, she stood off to one side near the beverage table. Hopefully Yvonne would see her once she had finished talking to the Hostetlers.

Fidgeting with the ties on her head covering, Lisa glanced around the spacious room where several tables and benches had been set out to accommodate those who had come for the pre-singing meal.

I hope no one says anything to me about why I haven't been to the last couple of singings, Lisa thought. *In fact, I'd be happy if nobody but Yvonne said anything to me this evening. I just want to eat, sing, and go back to the comfort and safety of my grandparents' home.*

"I'm glad you could make it," Yvonne said when she joined Lisa a few minutes later.

"Well, I do enjoy singing." Lisa spoke quietly.

"Jah, me too." Yvonne gestured to a group of young people across the room. "Looks like we have a good turnout tonight for our young people's gathering."

Before Lisa could comment, their hostess announced that it was time to eat. She then explained which side of the room the young men would sit on, which, of course, was across from where the women would sit to eat and also sing.

Once everyone had a paper plate and had made their way through the line, Lisa took a seat at the end of one table, next to Yvonne. After the young people were seated, all heads bowed for silent prayer, and then everyone began to eat. In addition to plenty of pizza, several fresh vegetables had been cut up to enjoy along with three flavored dips—ranch, onion, and garlic. The beverages consisted of individual bottles of water, several jugs of homemade root beer, and tall pitchers of lemonade.

Lisa had chosen two slices of Hawaiian pizza, which included ham and pineapple in addition to onions and cheddar cheese. This was one of Lisa's favorite kinds of pizza, and as she savored each bite, she came to the conclusion that coming here had been worth it, if only for the food.

Paul hadn't been to a singing in some time—ever since Susan broke up with him—and was enjoying this introduction to singings in Sugar-creek. He'd visited with a few of the young men before and during supper. Everyone seemed friendly and welcoming, for which he was glad. It helped to make the transition of moving from Indiana to Ohio a bit easier. He really wanted to fit in but knew it would take time before he established any close relationships in this Amish community.

Paul opened the songbook he'd been given and turned to the page that the song leader announced. The words to the song "Just a Little Talk with Jesus" blurred on the page as his thoughts led him in another direction. *I bet once the singing is over, a good many of the fellows here tonight will be offering to give certain young women a ride home in their buggy.* He shifted on his chair. *Well, I won't be one of them. Besides the fact that I'm new here and don't know any of the girls well enough to invite them to take a ride in my buggy, I would not want to lead any woman to believe that I might be interested in courting her. No, that would not be fair.*

After the singing ended and Lisa, with a strained voice from singing so many songs, had said goodbye to Yvonne, she went outside to wait for her grandfather. She hoped he would get here soon, because the wind had picked up and the chill in the air caused her to shiver.

"What are ya doin' out here in the cold?"

Lisa turned at the sound of Aaron's voice. "I'm waiting for my grossdaadi," she said. "He will be picking me up soon."

"There's no need for that. I'd be happy to give you a ride." He leaned closer to her ear—so close she could feel his warm breath.

Lisa shook her head determinedly. "I told you—Grandpa's coming for me."

"What time did he say he'd be here?"

"Nine o'clock."

"Well, it's only eight thirty, so there's no sense in your standin' out here for half an hour. If we go now, I can have you home before your grandpa even leaves his house."

"No thanks."

"Oh, come on, Lisa. Stop playing so hard to get. Most young women your age are married by now, and you're not even going steady with anyone."

Lisa's facial muscles tightened as she pressed her lips together in a grimace. "Please, Aaron, stop bothering me."

"Aw, don't be like that." He got right in her face. "You know you want to."

"Are you deaf? Didn't you hear what she said? Please stop badgering Lisa."

Aaron tuned to face Paul, the newcomer, who had stepped between them. "You're new here, aren't you?"

"Jah," Paul replied. "I came in September."

"So what gives you the right to stick your *naas* in where it's not wanted? Whatever I say to Lisa is none of your business."

Lisa held up a trembling hand and shook her head. "There's no need to argue about this." She turned to face Paul. "As I've already told Aaron, my grossdaadi is picking me up, and he should be here soon." She moved quickly away from the men and rushed out to one of the hitching posts to wait there. As much as Lisa had enjoyed the meal and time of singing after they'd eaten, she wished she hadn't let her grandparents or Yvonne talk her into coming here tonight. Unless something happened to change her mind, this would be the last singing she would ever attend.

Chapter 7

"How did the singing go last night?" Marlene asked, sitting next to Lisa during breakfast the following morning. "Since you went straight to bed when you got home, I didn't have the chance to ask." She couldn't help being curious about the event. Marlene hoped that Lisa had enjoyed her time there and that maybe one of the young men may have taken an interest in her.

Lisa's neck bent slightly forward, and her voice cracked when she spoke. "The food and singing were okay, but afterward. . ."

"What happened, Lisa? Did something occur that upset you?"

"Jah." Lisa took a sip of apple juice and set the glass down. "Aaron wanted to give me a ride home, and after I told him that Grandpa would be coming to get me, he kept insisting." She paused to take another drink. "Then that new fellow, Paul, came along and put Aaron in his place."

"Oh dear, that must have been quite embarrassing for you." Marlene spoke in a soothing tone as she gave her granddaughter's arm a gentle pat.

"Jah, it was. I appreciated the newcomer's concern for me, but it really was not his place to say anything to Aaron." Lisa straightened her shoulders. "I was doing fine by myself."

Hmm. . .it's interesting that the new fellow would do something like that—pretty bold, in fact. It may not be appreciated, but I'm just going to come right out and say what I'm thinking to Lisa. "I wonder if Paul might be interested in you."

Lisa gave a quick shake of her head, and her expression collapsed as if it were a pricked balloon. "Of course not, Grandma. We barely even know each other. I'm surprised you would even think such a thing."

Marlene glanced over at Jerry as he chewed on a piece of his buttered toast. She wasn't through with this topic and hoped he would say something to help.

Her husband winked at her and took a sip of coffee. "Paul seems like a nice person," he said from his place at the head of the table. "His uncle speaks highly of him."

Marlene couldn't help feeling pleased with her husband's effort at continuing this topic. She hoped they could bring about a spark in their granddaughter's way of thinking about Paul. If there was a possibility that he might be interested, maybe Lisa would give him a chance in the future.

"When did you last talk to Abe?" Marlene questioned.

He picked up the salt shaker and sprinkled some salt on his poached eggs. "When he came into my harness shop last Friday."

"Oh? What did he have to say?" Marlene's interest was piqued.

"He mentioned that Paul has a good work ethic, not to mention some mighty fine woodworking skills."

"Is Paul planning to remain in Sugarcreek permanently, or is he only here temporarily?"

"I'm not sure, but from the sound of things, I believe that Abe thinks his nephew plans to stay. But you can never tell with a young, single man. Paul might have an *aldi* back home, or he may find a girlfriend while he's living here."

"What do you mean by that?"

He tugged on his beard. "If whatever he's looking for here in Ohio happens, then I'm sure he'll want to stay. But if things don't go right, and Paul isn't as happy as he'd hoped to be, then he'll probably return to Indiana at some point."

"I suppose that makes sense." Marlene looked over at Lisa to see her reaction, but to her disappointment, her granddaughter said nothing, apparently absorbed in finishing her meal. As her granddaughter continued to eat and then poured herself more apple juice, Marlene wondered what exactly Lisa had on her mind.

Marlene rose from her chair. "I'd like another cup of coffee. Husband, would you like another one too?"

"Sure, that sounds good, since I'm not quite finished with my eggs."

She refilled their cups and brought them back, taking her seat again. A little more small talk transpired between her and Jerry, while their granddaughter continued to eat in silence.

Finally, when her scrambled eggs and toast had been eaten, Lisa bowed her head for a final silent prayer then cleared her dishes and put them in the sink. "It's later than I thought, and I need to get to the schoolhouse, Grandma. Would you mind doing the dishes without my help this morning?"

"Not at all," Marlene responded. "You go on ahead, and I hope you have a good day."

"Danki. I hope Grandpa's and your day goes well too."

As soon as Lisa went out the door, Marlene looked over at her husband and said, "What would you think about hiring Abe's nephew to build and install some new kitchen cabinets for us?"

His bushy brows furrowed. "You want new kitchen cabinets all of a sudden?"

"It's not sudden, Jerry." She gestured to the old cabinets across the room. "Those have been here since we first built this home, and they are getting a bit dilapidated, don't you think?"

He gave a quick shrug. "I suppose so, but. . ."

"It would sure be nice to do some updating in the kitchen. After all, I spend a good deal of my time in here, you know."

"Jah, that is true." He sent her a heart-melting smile. "I'll get a hold of Abe and see if one of his crew can come by to take a look at the old cabinets and then you can discuss what kind you'd like to have built that will replace the old ones."

Marlene shook her head. "I don't want just anyone who works for Abe. As I stated previously, I'd like it to be Paul."

The wrinkles around Jerry's blue eyes deepened as he pointed at her. "You wouldn't be trying to get our granddaughter and Abe's nephew together, now would you?"

A warm flush ran up the back of Marlene's neck and spread quickly to her cheeks. After all their years of marriage, Jerry knew her quite well. "It wouldn't hurt to try." Marlene fiddled with her napkin. "I mean. . .how's Lisa going to get to know this newcomer if she doesn't spend some time with him?"

Jerry lifted his gaze toward the ceiling and gave an undignified grunt. "Do I have to remind you that Lisa teaches school all day? You'll be the one who'll get to know him, *fraa*, not her."

Marlene tapped her knuckles lightly against the tabletop. "Guess I hadn't thought it all the way through."

"So it doesn't matter who comes to build and put in the new cabinets?"

Marlene pressed her lips together as she mulled things over. "No, I'd still like Paul to be the one. If I get acquainted with him, then I'll have a better idea if he could be right for Lisa."

Jerry shook his head slowly and muttered, "Okay, dear wife, I'll see what can be done."

She smiled. Already a plot had formed in her mind. *After all, Dear Caroline did suggest in her reply to my letter that I play matchmaker.*

———

As Lisa waited on the porch of the schoolhouse for the students to arrive, she thought about the curious expression she'd seen on her grandmother's face this morning when the topic of Paul came up. When Grandma stated that she wondered if Paul might be interested in Lisa, it was all she could do to keep from fleeing the room. *Why would my grandma even suggest such a thing? Is she that desperate to get me married off?*

Another thought hit Lisa that had never occurred to her before— perhaps one or both of her grandparents felt that it was time for her to move out. Maybe they believed they'd taken care of her long enough. Lisa was, after all, twenty-five years old.

Should I bring the subject up—see if they would like me to find someplace else to live? she asked herself. *Or would it be better to wait and see if either of them brings up the topic of Paul being interested in me again?*

Lisa's thoughts scattered when her first two students, Nathan and Nancy, arrived. A few feet behind them plodded a female, mid-sized dog with floppy ears and a thick coat of curly brown hair that looked like it needed a good brushing. The animal was obviously not a purebred, nor had it been well cared for. Lisa figured it might be a cocker/poodle mixture. One thing was certain: the floppy-eared critter did not belong here at school.

"Is this your dog?" Lisa asked the twins. "Because if it is, you'll need to tell her to go home."

They both shook their heads. "The hund was walkin' along the road and started followin' us when we went by," Nancy replied. "Our brother Simon told it to go home, but it kept walkin' behind us."

"Finally Simon picked up a stick, and the dog took off," Nathan put in. "But then after our bruder held back to wait for some of his friends, that hund showed up again and followed us the rest of the way here."

"Do you know who the dog belongs to?"

"Nope. I bet it's a stray." Nathan approached the dog and reached out as if to pet it.

"Be careful," Lisa cautioned. "The dog may not be friendly, and she could even bite."

"I don't think so, Teacher." Nathan shook his head. "See the way the mutt's tail is waggin'? My daed always says that when a hund wags its tail, it's a sign of friendliness." He grinned up at Lisa. "Ya know how come a dog has a lot of friends?"

"I have no idea."

"Cause it wags his tail 'stead of his tongue." Nathan slapped his knee and laughed, and his sister joined in. "Ain't that *schpassich*, Teacher?"

Lisa chuckled. "Yes, it's funny."

Nancy patted the dog's head and was rewarded with a slurp on her hand. "See, Teacher, the hund don't bite."

"You're right, but let's not encourage her. She might never go home."

"Can we bring her into the schoolhouse with us?" Nathan asked, stepping onto the porch.

Lisa shook her head, remembering the day when a cat got in. She had no doubt that allowing the dog inside would cause a stir among the children, which in turn would mean that lessons would not get done.

She clapped her hands and pointed toward the road. "Go home, doggy! Go back to where you belong!"

The dog released a whimper but didn't budge.

Lisa frowned. "That's just great. Now what am I supposed to do?"

"If the hund's a stray, she ain't got no home to go to." Nathan joined his sister in petting the dog.

"Oh, that's really not a good idea. I wish you—"

Lisa's comment was cut short when Yvonne showed up. "Sorry I'm late. My horse must have thrown a shoe sometime yesterday, so I had to walk this morning."

"It's okay," Lisa said. "Nathan and Nancy are the only students who have shown up so far. Them, and this mangy hund." She pointed to the dog.

"Is it the twins' dog?" Yvonne asked.

"No. Apparently it's a stray, or maybe she belongs to someone locally and wandered off their property, although I've never seen the mutt around before."

Yvonne leaned down and appeared to be scrutinizing the dog. "I don't remember seeing her either."

"Neither have we," the twins said simultaneously.

Lisa pointed at the dog. "I told her to leave, but as you can see, she doesn't listen too well."

"Maybe the dog's lost and can't find her way home." Yvonne gave the animal a few pats. "Is that how it is, girl? Are you confused about where you live?"

The dog tipped her head back and gave a *Woof! Woof!*

"We wanna bring her into the schoolhouse, but Teacher Lisa said no." Nancy's lower lip protruded.

"Your teacher is right," Yvonne said. "It's not a good idea to bring the hund inside, but if the dog's still out here when you go out for recess, you can pet her then."

Lisa resisted the urge to roll her eyes. If the children kept petting and making over the dog, she'd probably never leave.

———

"Before you head to town to pick up those supplies I asked you to get earlier, can I speak to you for a few minutes?"

"Sure, Uncle Abe." Paul turned at the sound of his uncle's voice and walked back to the woodworking shop. "Is there something else you need me to get?"

"No, just what's on the list I gave you. What I wanted to tell you about is a potential job." Uncle Abe stood in the entrance of his shop. "When I checked for phone messages a few minutes ago, there was one from the harness maker, Jerry Schrock."

There was a pause, and Paul waited silently for his uncle to continue.

"Jerry mentioned that his fraa would like some new cabinets in her kitchen, and he asked if you would come by and talk to her about the project."

"Why me?" Paul asked. "Since you're the boss, and you've known the harness maker awhile, I would think he'd want you to be the one to do the job."

Uncle Abe reached under his straw hat and rubbed a spot on his head just above his right ear. "I don't know the reason, but he made it clear that his wife specifically asked for you."

"Hmm..." Paul tipped his head to one side and blinked a couple of times. "But I've never even met Jerry Schrock's fraa."

Uncle Abe shrugged, holding both hands palms up. "I'm not the best at understanding women—not even my own wife. All I know is, it's a potential job, so I'll give you the Schrocks' address and you can drop by there on your way to or from town—whichever time you choose. Okay?"

Paul nodded. What else could he do? He didn't have much choice, since his uncle was also his boss.

———

"Go away! You can't come with me," Lisa shouted while glancing over her shoulder on the bicycle ride home that afternoon. The determined dog had hung around the schoolyard all day, barking excitedly during the pupils' recess and lapping up all the attention the children gave. Then for some unknown reason, the mutt had decided to follow Lisa home.

Why me? she wondered, pedaling harder to pick up speed. *I could understand if the hund had chosen to follow one of the children as they headed to their house after school. An animal like that needs kinner to play with, not an old maid schoolteacher who has better things to do than care for a pet.*

Yip! Yip! Yip! The strong-willed animal caught up with Lisa and ran alongside her bike.

"Go back! You can't come home with me," Lisa hollered, but the now-panting dog wouldn't let up.

Lisa kept going until her grandparents' house came into view. When she approached the driveway, she put on the brakes and looked down at the dog. "Please go away. I can't take care of you."

The mutt looked up at Lisa and cocked her furry head. Either she didn't understand or wasn't about to back down.

Heaving a hefty sigh, Lisa rode her bike up the driveway and into the yard, where she noticed a horse and market buggy parked at the hitching rail not far from the house. Grandma obviously had company, and Lisa didn't want to interrupt their visit, but she needed to get inside and away from the determined dog.

Lisa parked her bike near the barn and sprinted toward the house. But before she could put one foot on the porch, the pooch leaped up, knocking Lisa off balance and causing her to fall.

Groaning, she tried to get up, but it was an impossible task with the dog lying on top of her, slurping Lisa's face with her icky wet tongue.

"Need some help?" a deep voice called.

"Jah, I sure do." Although the dog was relentless with her slurpy kisses, Lisa managed to roll onto her side. Through half-closed eyelids she could see the man who had asked her the question. *Paul Herschberger? What's he doing here?* she asked herself. *Oh, I'm so embarrassed.*

Chapter 8

"From the way that hund of yours is gifting you with all those kisses I'd have to say that the pooch must really love you." Paul laughed.

Lisa frowned. "It's not funny, and she's not my dog."

"It's a little funny." He held out his hand toward her. "Looks like you might need some help getting up."

"I'm fine." Lisa pushed the dog aside and scrambled to her feet. "I just hope that silly critter doesn't have any fleas."

Another booming laugh escaped Paul's lips. "Now that was really funny. I mean what dog running around outside doesn't have a problem with fleas? If you're worried about it, maybe you should get her a flea collar."

Choosing not to comment, Lisa looked away from Paul and brushed at the dirt, blades of grass, and loose dog hair that had stuck to her dress. "The hund isn't mine," she said a few seconds later, while forcing herself to turn and look at him. "She followed two of my students to the schoolhouse this morning and hung around there all day. Nobody knows who the dog belongs to."

"So you brought her home with you?"

Lisa shook her head. "She followed me, running alongside my bike most of the way."

Grinning, Paul reached down and petted the dog's head. "Seems like a good-natured hund."

Lisa looked down at the mutt and frowned. "She's a *pescht*."

"Are you gonna keep her, even though she is a pest?"

"No way. I'll try to find out where she belongs."

"I bet she'd make a nice pet."

"If I can't find out where she lives, would you like her?"

Paul shook his head. "There are too many animals at my uncle's place now, and since I don't have a home of my own yet, I can't take on the responsibility of a dog."

"I don't want a dog either." Lisa cringed when the mutt licked her hand.

"Oh, but apparently she wants you." Paul winked.

Feeling less intimidated in his presence, Lisa voiced another question: "What brought you over here today? You obviously came out of the house and not my grossdaadi's harness shop."

"You're correct. I came to talk to your *grossmammi* about some new kitchen cabinets she wants built."

Lisa's eyes widened a bit. "Really? She hasn't said anything to me about remodeling the kitchen."

Paul shook his head. "Not redoing the whole room, just replacing the old cabinets."

"Oh, I see."

Woof! Woof! The floppy-eared dog sauntered up the porch stairs and flopped down with a grunt near the door.

I can't believe that silly mutt is making herself right at home on the porch. Next thing she'll be making me feeling obligated to feed and water her. Lisa was glad for the diversion, because observing the way Paul looked at her right now made her feel squeamish. It was as if he was studying her face.

Lisa was tempted to ask why he had begun staring at her with his lips slightly parted, but she decided it was best not to say anything. All Lisa really wanted to do right now was get into the house.

"Umm. . .it was nice seeing you again, but now, if you'll excuse me, I need to go inside and see about helping my grandma get supper started." She hurried past Paul and up the porch stairs.

"No problem. I'm sure we'll see more of each once I get started on your grandmother's cabinets. Oh, and good luck with your furry friend," he added with a chuckle.

Lisa grimaced as she skirted around the dog and went into the house. She'd had enough excitement for one day.

⸺

"I'm glad you're home," Marlene said when Lisa entered the kitchen. "I have some good news to share."

"If it's about getting new cabinets, I already know." Lisa removed her heavy sweater and hung it on the wall peg across the room. "I spoke to that newcomer, Paul, soon after I came into the yard."

"Oh, I'm glad you were able to visit with him."

"We didn't have much of a visit, Grandma. We only talked about the reason for his visit, and the pesky hund lying on our front porch."

Marlene's brows furrowed. "What dog on the porch? Is it our neighbor's collie that likes to come over here sometimes just to chase our poor *katze*?"

"No, it's an unkempt stray that wandered into the schoolyard today. She looks like a cocker/poodle mix, and I don't know if she likes to chase cats or not."

"Well, for goodness' sakes, why is the dog here if she's a stray?" Marlene headed out of the kitchen and opened the front door. "You're right, there that hund is, just lying on the porch," she called toward the kitchen. "The dog appears to really need a bath and a good brushing too."

"Maybe she'll leave in a while," Lisa hollered from the other room.

The dog looked up at Marlene and wagged its tail. Those big brown eyes of hers seemed to call out to Marlene, and it touched her heart. *The poor thing must be lost, and who knows for how long?* Closing the door, she headed back to where her granddaughter was.

"Let's have a seat at the table and I'll tell you the details about the hund," Lisa said.

"Good idea. I'll fix us some lemon-mint tea to drink while we visit."

"That sounds nice. It's kind of nippy out there this afternoon, and I need something to warm my insides." Lisa got out the teacups while Marlene heated the water. A short time later, they sat at the table with their beverages and a few sugar cookies.

"So you don't have any idea who the dog belongs to?" Marlene asked after Lisa had told her the whole story.

"No, I don't, but I intend to find out, because the pooch sure can't stay here."

"Why not? It sounds as though she's taken to you and would no doubt make a nice pet."

Lisa dunked a cookie into her tea and ate it quickly. "I don't need a pet, Grandma, especially one with a slurpy wet tongue. Besides, I'm sure she belongs somewhere, and there's no doubt some people living in the area who are most likely missing their dog. I'm going to make every effort to find the mutt's owner."

"How will you go about doing it?"

"I'll ask around, put up some posters in various places, and if necessary, take out an ad in our local paper."

Marlene took a sip of tea and dabbed at her lips with a napkin. "That's all well and good, but in the meantime, you can't let the poor pooch stay out on the porch whining." She tipped her head. "Can't you hear her, Lisa? No doubt she's hungry and probably lonely too."

Lisa blew out a noisy breath. "All right, as soon as we're done with our snack, I'll give the hund some cold meat loaf from Saturday night's meal. With your permission, that is."

Marlene reached over and patted her granddaughter's arm. "Of course it's all right. It would probably have gone to waste anyway, since your grossdaadi's not that thrilled about eating leftovers more than one day. And after he and I had meat loaf sandwiches last evening while you were at the singing, he made it clear that he wouldn't want more of the same any other night this week."

Lisa smiled. "That sounds like Grandpa, all right."

"In a few minutes I'll have another look in the refrigerator and see if I can find something else to feed that poor dog." Marlene nibbled on the last cookie she'd set out. *It's been some time since we've had a dog here on the property. It might be nice to have a watchdog, and it could very well be this one, unless Lisa finds its owners in the near future.*

With her elbows on the table, Marlene leaned forward and spoke in a bubbly tone. "I'm ever so excited about having new cabinets made for this old kitchen. I believe Abe's nephew will do a good job, because I'm sure his uncle would not have hired him as an employee unless the young man has talent." Marlene gazed up at her old cabinets with a wide smile. "Yes, even having new doors will give this room a much-needed update, and all new cabinets. . .well I'm sure they will be a huge improvements over these old ones."

"I'm happy for you, Grandma," Lisa said. "You work hard around here and deserve to have a nice kitchen."

"I may not be deserving of it, but some new cabinets will surely be nice." Marlene hoped Lisa would not catch on to the fact that she'd asked Paul to do the job in hopes that it might give him and Lisa a chance to get better acquainted. *And who knows,* she thought, smiling inwardly, *a romance might develop between them.*

When Lisa finished her snack, she tossed her napkin in the garbage can and put her cup and saucer in the sink. "Guess I'll take the meat loaf out to the mutt now."

"Don't forget to give her a bowl of water. She's probably as thirsty as she is *hungerich.*"

"Okay, Grandma."

Lisa took the meat loaf from the refrigerator and placed it in an unbreakable dish. Meanwhile, Grandma stood by in the kitchen watching her gather the items needed. "Your grandfather is going to think we want this dog," she commented.

"Not if we tell him we are only taking care of the animal until I find her owners." Lisa got a small bucket from the utility room, rinsed it thoroughly, and filled it with fresh water.

"That's true, unless. . ."

"You think Grandpa might like to have the dog around?"

"Maybe." Grandma shrugged her shoulders and motioned for Lisa to lead the way. "Hopefully that meat loaf will help to fill the dog's stomach, but she is fairly good sized and may need more than that small portion to meet her needs." Grandma opened the front door, and when Lisa stepped outside, she wasn't the least bit surprised to see the vagrant dog lying in the same spot she'd left her.

As soon as Lisa set the plate of food and the water bucket down, the predictable animal jumped up, gave it a couple of sniffs, and wolfed the food right down. After licking the plate clean, the pooch lapped up all the water and sat near the spotless dish, looking pathetically up at them.

"Did you see that?" Grandma asked as she stood by the open door.

Lisa nodded as she watched the process from a chair on the porch where she'd taken a seat. "The poor thing acts like she hasn't eaten or drunk water all day. I wonder how long it's been since she had her last meal."

"One thing's for certain, she hasn't been combed, brushed, or bathed anytime recently." Grandma gestured to the dog. "Just look at all those tangles and her matted hair. And I bet she would appreciate something more to eat. I'll go take another look in the refrigerator and see what else I can find," she commented before going inside and closing the front door.

The dog continued to sit near the clean dish, looking up at Lisa like she wanted more food.

Lisa picked up the empty bucket and stepped into the yard to refill it with cool, fresh water from the spigot. The four-legged animal, however, didn't budge from the porch. Lisa carried the bucket back up to the same spot and set it down. About then Grandma came out with something in a container.

"What did you find for our furry friend?" Lisa tilted her head.

"I found some leftover scrambled eggs from a few mornings ago." Grandma tapped the contents onto the plate and stepped back while Lisa watched.

"There she goes again, inhaling the food." Lisa couldn't keep from rolling her eyes.

"I have to say, this is a nice way to get rid of leftovers. One thing's for sure—the garbage can won't get as full as long as this critter stays here." Grandma took the chair beside Lisa.

Lisa hated to admit it, but she'd already begun to develop a soft spot toward the mutt, which was not a good thing. And it appeared that her grandmother might be feeling the same way about the dog. The only answer to the problem was to find out who owned the dog, and quickly.

On the trip back to his uncle's place, Paul thought about Lisa and how she reminded him of someone he'd once known, but he couldn't think of who she could be or where he might have met her. He wasn't even sure what there was about Lisa that seemed familiar, and it really bothered him.

"Makes no sense," Paul mumbled. "This is my first trip to Ohio since Uncle Abe and Aunt Emma moved here from Indiana, so I couldn't have met Lisa before."

He realized that this young lady had a way of amusing him. And she was nice looking with a pleasing smile, although he hadn't seen her smile that often. Paul had also noticed that Lisa seemed to have some sort of a hard shell around her. She'd acted distant and unfriendly at times, and he wondered why. *I hope I haven't done or said anything to upset her. I'd like to get better acquainted with Lisa, as well as her family.* Paul thumped his forehead. "I need to quit thinking about this, because in the long run it's really not that important. My focus should be on doing a good job as a carpenter and keeping so busy that I'll forget about the pain of my past."

Paul relaxed his grip on the reins and gave Cinnamon the freedom to trot. While the mare hurried toward home, Paul tried to change his train of thought to the mixed-breed dog Lisa had tried to pawn off on him.

Like I need a hund to complicate my life. He shook his head. *But if I were a betting man, I'd lay down a good bet that when I return to the Schrocks' home again, that overzealous animal will still be there. And I'd also bet that Lisa will have given the dog a name and be calling the pooch her own.*

Chapter 9

"That hund of yours sure misses you when you're at the schoolhouse all day." Grandma pointed at the dog sitting next to Lisa's chair at the breakfast table with her head on Lisa's knee.

"She does have you here during the day to keep her company."

"True, but I believe she still favors you, and I think she knows you're about to leave again," Grandpa put in.

Lisa's forehead wrinkled. "She'll like it even less when she's put in the pen you made so she won't be able to follow me to school."

"I'd keep her in the house with me all day," Grandma said, "but Paul will be coming over sometime later to take out the old cabinets, which means either the front or back door could be left open for a while. So if Maggie were to get out, she'd no doubt head straight for the schoolhouse, like she did the other day when I went out to get the mail and forgot to shut the door."

"Jah, the best place for her is in the pen when I'm not here, because she wants to follow me everywhere." Lisa couldn't believe it had been two weeks since Maggie showed up at the schoolhouse with Nancy and Nathan and then followed Lisa home when school let out. She'd tried unsuccessfully to find the dog's owner, even paying for an ad in their local newspaper, but with no response. Lisa hadn't meant to become attached to the pooch, but the determined dog had managed to worm her way into Lisa's heart. So when her grandparents gave their approval, she'd given the lovable pooch a name and decided to keep her.

Lisa glanced at the battery-operated clock on the far wall. "I'd better get going. Today we're having some special guests at the schoolhouse, and I need to make sure that everything's neat and tidy."

"Who are the special guests?" Grandpa questioned.

"I'll tell you both about it when I get home this afternoon."

Grandma smiled. "Jah, we'd like to hear all the details."

Lisa gave Maggie a nudge to remove the dog's silky head from her lap and pushed back her chair so she could leave the table. "Be a good girl while I'm gone, Maggie."

The dog wagged her tail and let out a shrill-sounding *Woof! Woof!*

Grandpa chuckled. "She's a *schmaert* hund, and I bet she understood exactly what you said."

"I agree Maggie is a smart dog." Lisa put her dishes in the sink. She didn't bother to ask if Grandma wanted her to help with the dishes before she left, because she already knew the answer. Whenever she asked that question on a school day, her grandmother always told Lisa to go ahead—that she would take care of the dishes.

"I'll put Maggie in her pen when I head out to my shop," Grandpa said.

"Danki." Lisa gave both her grandparents hugs, patted the top of Maggie's head, and went out the door, carrying her insulated lunch bag inside the tote she took with her to the schoolhouse every day.

⁓

The first part of the school day had seemed to drag by as Lisa waited for the English couple to show up. They were friends of someone Yvonne knew and often put on performances for children's birthday parties as well as some other special events. Yvonne's neighbor Gayle would be bringing the couple by about an hour before school ended for the day.

Lisa glanced up at the clock. *It shouldn't be too much longer now.*

I can't help but feel the children's excitement.

Five minutes later, a knock sounded on the schoolhouse door, and Yvonne went to answer it. When she returned, a middle-aged man and woman were with her. The woman carried a bright purple suitcase, and the man held a large multicolored canvas tote. The couple stood off to one side, while Yvonne walked up to the front of the room.

"Children, I'd like you to meet Mr. and Mrs. Brown. Mr. Brown is going to show us how he makes twisty animal balloons, and Mrs. Brown will demonstrate how she talks for her puppet without moving her lips."

All eyes were centered on the man and his wife as they joined Yvonne and Lisa up front. Mrs. Brown went first. She placed the suitcase on the floor, opened the lid, and lifted out an oversized, silly-looking puppet with bright red hair. The puppet had been dressed in a pair of faded blue jeans and a shirt nearly the same color as its hair.

Mrs. Brown took a seat in the chair Yvonne had provided and placed the puppet in her lap. "Boys and girls, this is my friend Charlie." She looked at the puppet and said, "Say hello to the boys and girls."

The puppet's mouth opened wide, and in a loud, high-pitched voice, it said, "Hello to the boys and girls."

Mrs. Brown shook her head. "No, Charlie, just say an easy hello."

"An easy hello."

Mrs. Brown gave her head another good shake. "No, no. . .just say hello, Charlie."

"Hello, Charlie."

Lisa, along with Yvonne and most of the students, laughed. Some of the children, however, sat staring at Charlie with eyes open wide, as though they couldn't believe what they were seeing or hearing. Although Lisa knew the puppet wasn't really talking, Mrs. Brown's lips didn't move, so it certainly appeared as if Charlie had spoken.

Lisa continued to watch with full attention as the talented

woman finished her routine. When she put Charlie back in his suitcase, Mr. Brown stepped forward.

"How many of you like balloons?" he asked.

All hands shot up.

"Well, that's good. Today I'm going to blow up a balloon and then create some bubbles and twists till it looks like a dog." He opened his tote and withdrew a skinny-looking brown balloon, stretched it several times, and put the opening of the balloon up to his mouth. As Mr. Brown blew, his cheeks puffed out and his whole face turned red. Lisa hoped the man wouldn't pass out. Something like that would no doubt scare the children—and Lisa too, for that matter.

Stop worrying, Lisa told herself. *Just try to relax and enjoy the program.*

Mr. Brown kept blowing until the balloon was inflated. Then his fingers moved swiftly as he made several bubbles, securing them in place. Finally, what looked like a wiener dog appeared. Using a black marking pen, he drew a face on the dog.

The students sat spellbound as Mr. Brown made several more twisty creations that included a poodle, a monkey, a lion, a hummingbird, and even a bouquet of flowers. He kept blowing and twisting until everyone in the class had been given a balloon, including the teachers.

"Would anyone like to try blowing up a balloon?" Mr. Brown asked.

Three of the older boys raised their hands, so Mr. Brown gave them each a balloon.

Lisa watched as the boys, one from her class and two from Yvonne's, stretched their balloons and then tried to blow them up. Their faces turned red as they tried unsuccessfully to inflate the balloons.

"This is too hard," one of the boys said with a frown. "I think these must be trick balloons."

"No, they're not." Mr. Brown shook his head. "It just takes

practice and lots of hot air."

Everyone laughed, including Lisa. It felt good to take some time out from teaching and allow the students to have a little unexpected fun.

"Can I try?" Abner, who was in the third grade, raised his hand.

Mr. Brown looked at Lisa, and when she nodded, he handed the boy a balloon.

It was hard for Lisa not to step in and tell her young student that he'd tried long enough as she watched him huff, puff, and turn red in the face.

"Pause for a breath and stretch the balloon a little more," Mr. Brown coached.

Abner did as the instructor said, but when he tried again, the balloon still did not inflate. With a determined expression, the boy continued to blow until he fell out of his chair and onto the floor.

"*Ach*, my. . .I think he's fainted." Lisa rushed forward and so did Yvonne, along with Mr. and Mrs. Brown. They all squatted beside Abner, but before they could say or do anything, his eyes popped open and he sat up. "I'm okay. *Ich is bletzlich umechdich warre.*"

Mrs. Brown looked at Lisa. "What'd he say?"

"Speaking in Pennsylvania Dutch, Abner said that suddenly he fainted," Lisa replied. She helped the boy to his feet. "You'd better sit back down and rest awhile."

"I'm okay," he insisted, holding tightly to the balloon.

"All right, but no more blowing today," Lisa said. "You can take the balloon home and practice if you want, but if you feel like you're going to pass out, you should stop and rest."

"Your teacher is right," Mr. Brown interjected. "You never want to keep blowing if you feel that you might faint."

"Well, boys and girls," Yvonne spoke up, "let's put our hands together and thank Mr. and Mrs. Brown for coming today and entertaining us with Charlie and so many balloons."

The students all clapped and said thank you.

Mrs. Brown took her puppet out of the suitcase again and said,

"Say goodbye to the boys and girls, Charlie."

The puppet's mouth opened, and it said loudly: "Goodbye to the boys and girls."

The children clapped again, and Lisa smiled. This had been a good day, and she was eager to go home and tell her grandparents about it.

Walnut Creek

Lois sat at the kitchen table with the letters she'd recently received for her Dear Caroline column, trying to concentrate on the question that had been asked of her in the first letter. It was hard to stay focused on her task when she was worried about Orley as she waited for him to get back from his doctor's appointment. Her dear husband hadn't been feeling up to snuff lately, and she'd prompted him to see their doctor. Orley's appointment had been for three o'clock this afternoon, and they'd closed the antique store early so he could go. Lois had assumed she would go with Orley, but during lunch, he'd informed her that he preferred to go alone. Lois had felt left out and a little bit hurt when he'd made the announcement, but she'd kept quiet. If he preferred that she not be with him when he saw the doctor, she would respect his wishes.

I hope there's nothing seriously wrong with my husband. Lois tapped her pen on the writing tablet before her. She remembered her mother saying when Lois was a young girl, *"Never expect the worst, but if it comes your way, ask God to help you deal with it."*

Tears sprang to Lois's eyes, and she blinked them away. It made her sad to think that her mother had passed away so unexpectedly, just a few weeks before Lois's eighth birthday. A young girl with no siblings and an overly strict father needed her mother.

If Orley and I could have had children, we probably would have made our share of mistakes while raising them, Lois thought. *But we would have done our best to teach them God's ways and raise them in a loving manner, without being harsh and demanding, the way my father was when I lived at home.*

Lois directed her thoughts back to the letter a reader of the Dear Caroline column had written. It was from a woman who had been reunited with her sister who'd run away from home when she was a teenager. The sisters were having a hard time reconnecting, since they hadn't seen each other for thirty years.

Lois rubbed her forehead. *If I had a sister or brother whom I hadn't seen in many years, I'd make every effort to reunite with them. What a joy it would be to get reacquainted.* She jotted down a few comments on her notebook to use when she felt ready to fully answer this letter.

Lois was about to move on to another letter when she heard a vehicle pull into the yard. Hurrying out of the kitchen and to the front door, she was pleased when she opened it and saw Orley getting out of his driver's car.

Lois stepped out and gave the man behind the wheel a wave. "How'd your appointment go?" she asked when Orley joined her on the porch.

"Let's go inside, and I'll tell you about it."

"Okay." Lois led the way to the living room and took a seat on the sofa. Orley had barely seated himself in his recliner when she said, "What did the doctor say when you told him you've been feeling poorly?"

"Well, let's see now. . . . First off, his nurse had me take off my shoes and step onto the scale to see how much I weighed. Then she took my temperature and checked my blood pressure." Orley shifted on his chair. "When the doctor came into the examining room and I told him my symptoms, he felt around on my neck, listened to my heart, and also looked in my mouth, ears, and even my eyes. After that, he asked me a whole bunch of questions."

"Did he give you a diagnosis?"

Orley shook his head. "He had his receptionist schedule me to have a few tests run that'll include blood work. I'll be getting that done tomorrow morning, and I have to go to the lab having fasted for twelve hours."

"You probably shouldn't eat anything after supper tonight, then."

He gave a nod, followed by a noisy yawn. "Right now, though, if you don't mind, I'm going to take a little nap."

"You go right ahead. If you're still sleeping by the time supper's ready, I'll wake you."

"Danki." Orley's eyelids closed, and a short time later, his heavy breathing let Lois know that he'd fallen asleep.

Lois said a silent prayer on behalf of her dear husband and then tiptoed quietly from the room to finish the letters she hadn't yet answered. Hopefully they would know something soon as to the reason Orley had been so tired and had begun to put on weight lately.

Sugarcreek

Paul was about halfway done removing the old cupboards in Marlene's kitchen when he heard Lisa's dog barking from her pen. He hadn't been the least bit surprised when he'd showed up today and seen the dog. When he'd mentioned it to Marlene, she had explained that when Lisa couldn't find the rightful owner, she'd decided to keep the dog and had named her Maggie.

Yep, I was right all along, Paul told himself as he hauled another load of wood from the old cupboards outside.

When Maggie continued to yap, Paul walked around to the side of the house where the pen had been built and nearly bumped into Lisa. "Oops. . .sorry. I didn't realize you were home." He took a step back from her. "But then I should have figured it out with the way your dog, Maggie, was carrying on."

Lisa's cheeks reddened as she stared up at him. "I—I guess my grandma must have told you that I kept the dog and named her."

"Jah." He looked at the pooch, whose barking had turned to a pathetic whine as she pawed from the inside of her pen at the gate holding her prisoner. "Looks like your hund wants out of there pretty bad." Paul looked back at Lisa while gesturing to the desperate dog.

Lisa gave no response to Paul's statement as she let Maggie out of her pen and headed for the house with the dog prancing right on her heels.

Chuckling to himself, Paul put the pieces of wood on the pile with the rest of the cabinets he'd torn out and then hurried back to the house.

When Paul entered the kitchen, he saw Lisa sitting at the table with her grandma. Maggie lay on the floor, close to Lisa's chair.

"Come join us for a glass of apple cider and some banana bread." Marlene motioned to the chair closest to where Lisa sat. "You've been working hard this afternoon and deserve a break."

There was still a little more that Paul needed to get done, but Marlene's offer was hard to turn down. "Sounds good. But I'd better wash up first. My hands are really dirty."

"No problem. Remember, the bathroom's down the hall and to the left." Marlene smiled. "Lisa was about to tell me about her day at school, but she can wait till you get back."

Paul nodded and headed down the hall. He'd noticed Lisa's pinched expression when her grandma had given him the invitation to join them for some refreshments. Was she annoyed by his intrusion? Maybe Lisa didn't feel comfortable talking about her day at the schoolhouse with Paul present. Whatever the case, she'd have to get over it, because he wasn't going to turn down the tasty snack that had been offered.

Paul stepped inside the bathroom and stood in front of the mirror, washing his hands. *I wonder what Lisa will have to say when she finds out her grandma invited me to stay for supper.*

Chapter 10

While Paul was down the hall washing his hands, Grandma informed Lisa that he would be staying for supper.

I was hoping to relax this evening with only Grandpa and Grandma. Lisa felt her frame stiffen. She felt awkward enough with this fellow on the premises but even more so with him staying for their meal. Lisa remembered how Paul had stared at her so strangely a while back. She still felt unsettled by him doing that, and she wondered why he had. She'd hoped Paul was done, or at least he'd be leaving soon after being there all day. *I guess Grandma had other ideas for this evening. After all, she's only being hospitable, and she likes to do the right thing for others.*

Lisa refocused her attention to the room. The kitchen was definitely in disorder without the old cabinets in place. The upper ones were absent of their dishes, glassware, spices, and dried food goods, along with the lower cabinets that had also been emptied of all of their contents. Grandma seemed all right about making do with this project that had disrupted her usually orderly kitchen, and apparently having a guest for supper in the midst of this disarray didn't bother her in the least.

Lisa hadn't given any thought to remodeling the kitchen, for to her, it looked fine the way it was. *It will no doubt look a lot nicer and more modern when it's done,* she thought. *It'll be interesting to see how things look when Paul has installed the new cupboards in the next day or two.*

Lisa looked at all the boxes stacked up on one side of the room that contained everything that had been in the cabinets. "But Grandma, our kitchen is torn apart right now," she said. "Do you really think this is a good time to be entertaining?"

Grandma flapped her hand. "Oh, Paul doesn't mind. He seemed more than willing to eat with us when I asked him to stay for supper." She gestured to the stack of boxes. "And of course we'll eat in the dining room so we don't have to look at all this clutter."

"What did you plan for the meal?" Lisa asked.

"I made a chicken-n-stuffing casserole and put it in the refrigerator this morning." Grandma snapped her fingers. "Which reminds me—I need to get that in the oven right now." She got up from her chair and moved quickly across the room. "I'm glad Paul's able to join us for the evening meal. It'll give us all a chance to get to know him better."

Lisa didn't voice her thoughts to Grandma, but she saw no reason to get to know the young man at all. He was here to do a job, plain and simple, not socialize with the family or stay to eat supper with them.

While her grandmother got out the casserole and placed it in the oven, Lisa cleaned out her lunch box and put it away. She'd just finished up when Paul reentered the room.

Lisa's grandma gestured to the table. "Let's have a seat now so we can enjoy our snack. I just put a casserole in the oven, and it'll be an hour or so before we can eat it, so the banana bread will get us by till then."

"Sounds good." Paul pulled out a chair at the table and took a seat.

"Should I go out to the harness shop and see if Grandpa would like to join us?" Lisa asked.

Grandma shook her head. "He went into town to pick up a few things, and he's not back yet."

"Oh." It was hard for Lisa to hide her disappointment. She felt uncomfortable around Paul, and if Grandpa could join them, he would surely engage Paul in conversation. Then Lisa could go to her room for a while to read one of the books she'd picked up at the library recently. She would come down in plenty of time to set the table and help Grandma with any last-minute supper preparations, of course. But as it was, Lisa felt obligated to sit and make small talk, or at the very least smile, nod, and pretend to be interested in whatever conversation Grandma got started with Paul.

Would it be too rude to excuse myself and pass up the banana bread and cider? Lisa wondered. *I could say that I've developed a headache.* Lisa's conscience pricked her, and she flinched. But then, that would be wrong because it'd be a lie.

"So now, tell us about the special visitors you had at school today," Grandma said after she'd taken a seat beside Lisa.

Lisa glanced at Paul then back at her grandmother. *I wish he wasn't a part of this conversation. He came here to work, not sit at Grandma's table, listening to what I have to say.*

Seeing Grandma's expectant expression, Lisa knew she couldn't sit here without sharing what had happened at the schoolhouse this afternoon. She took a quick drink of her apple cider and gave an overview of what had occurred with the woman who'd done ventriloquism and her puppet.

Grandma laughed. "I bet it was fun to watch someone speak without moving their lips and make her voice seem as if it were coming from the puppet's mouth."

"Some people call that 'throwing your voice,'" Paul interjected before Lisa could respond. "Of course, the ventriloquist isn't actually throwing his or her voice," he added. "Because they're talking without moving their lips and speaking in a different sounding voice while moving their puppet's mouth, it appears as if the puppet is talking."

"You seem to know a lot about ventriloquism," Grandma said, pouring more cider into Paul's glass.

He shrugged. "Not really. I just read an article about it in a magazine one day." Paul took an unbuttered slice of banana bread and quickly ate it.

Lisa picked up a piece and spread a thin layer of butter on it before taking a bite. "This is good *brot*."

"I agree this is good bread," Paul chimed in.

Grandma smiled. "I'm glad you both like it. We just need to be careful and not eat too much or it'll spoil our supper."

"No problem there. When I've been workin' hard all day, there's always plenty of room in my belly for food." Paul gave his stomach a few thumps.

Grandma pushed the plate of banana bread closer to Paul. "Then by all means, help yourself to some more."

"Thanks!" This time, Paul took two pieces and slathered them with twice as much butter as Lisa had used. She could hardly keep from lifting her gaze to the ceiling and rolling her eyes.

Doesn't this man have any willpower at all? I'm sure he must have eaten lunch today. Surely Paul can't be that hungry.

Lisa cleared her throat and looked at Grandma again. "Would you like to hear what talent the other guest who came to the schoolhouse shared?"

Grandma smiled. "Of course I would."

"He made animals and flowers out of the different-colored balloons he blew up and twisted in several places."

"Did he blow them by hand or with a pump?" Paul asked.

"By hand," she replied.

"You need a lot of air to do that."

Lisa gave a nod. "The man's face turned pretty red when he was blowing those balloons up. Some of the boys in the class wanted to try blowing up a balloon, and one of the younger ones insisted on trying and ended up passing out."

Grandma's eyes widened. "Oh, dear! I hope he was all right."

"He woke up quickly and was fine—just embarrassed is all."

"I would have been too." Paul finished his banana bread and pushed away from the table. "I'd better get the last of those cabinets taken outside now." He looked over at Grandma and said, "Danki for the snack you provided. Both the cider and banana bread sure hit the spot."

"You are most welcome." She offered him a broad smile. "Since you'll be putting in the cabinets tomorrow or the next day, you should join us for supper that evening too."

Lisa was shocked by Grandma's quick invite. *Why, Grandma? We haven't even had the first meal yet.* She wondered just how the young man would respond to her grandmother's invite. Lisa hoped he would decline the kind offer.

"That's very kind of you, but I wouldn't want to impose," Paul replied.

Grandma shook her head. "It will not be an imposition at all."

"Can I let you know tomorrow? My aunt may be planning something special, and I wouldn't want to disappoint her."

"Of course. You can give me your answer about supper when you get here tomorrow or the next day."

Paul nodded and moved across the room to gather the pieces of another cabinet he'd torn out.

"Lisa, would you please open the back door and hold it for him?" Grandma gave Lisa's arm a little nudge.

"Sure." Lisa got up from the table and did as her grandmother had asked. After Paul went out, she closed the door and returned to the kitchen to remove her glass and plate from the table.

"Paul seems like a nice young man, don't you think?" Grandma looked steadily at Lisa.

Lisa shrugged. "I really can't say. I don't know him well enough."

"Well, there's no better way to get acquainted with someone than while eating a meal." Grandma smiled. "Don't you agree?"

"I suppose." *But who says I want to get to know Paul?*

⁓

"This is one tasty casserole." Paul looked over at Jerry. "*Dei fraa is en gudi koch*, and I'm glad she invited me to join you and your family for supper this evening."

"I can't argue with that." Jerry looked over at Marlene and grinned. "My wife is a very good cook. Maybe the best in the whole state of Ohio."

She reached over and poked his arm. "Don't you go exaggerating, now."

"I'm not. In my opinion, you're the best." He helped himself to more casserole.

"I think you're just a little bit prejudiced."

Jerry shook his head. "No, I'm not—just stating facts as I see 'em is all." He let out a resonating chuckle. "Well, maybe I should've said, 'as I taste 'em.'"

Marlene smiled, and when she heard a grunt from across the room, she looked over and saw Maggie reposition herself as she lay sleeping. The dog was well behaved, and as long as there was food in her dish, she rarely begged for scraps from the table. Marlene was glad Lisa had decided to keep the dog. Not only was Maggie a good companion for Lisa when she was at home but she kept Marlene company during the days when Lisa taught school.

Looking away, Marlene glanced over at Lisa, who sat beside her. She seemed kind of sullen this evening and hadn't said more than a few words since they'd sat down at the dining-room table. Of course Jerry had monopolized a good deal of the conversation so far, as he'd asked Paul several questions about the new cabinets he would be installing in the kitchen. They'd also discussed their common interest in fishing and agreed that they might plan a fishing trip with each other sometime before winter set in or perhaps in early spring. Marlene had spoken up and asked if Lisa would like to go along, since she also enjoyed fishing. Lisa's only response had been a mumbled, "We'll see."

Paul seems like such a nice fellow, Marlene thought. *He's polite, friendly, and good looking. I sure hope he takes an interest in my granddaughter, and that once Lisa gets to know him better, the feeling will be mutual. Jerry and I won't be around forever, and Lisa's going to need someone after we're gone.*

Paul glanced over at Lisa and was about to ask her a question when her grandpa posed another one of his own.

"How long have you been doing carpentry work, Paul?" Jerry asked.

"I started working in my daed's furniture shop when I was sixteen. As a young boy I liked to mess around learning the names of the tools; Dad took the time to show me the different types of wood he'd use for jobs, and it seemed after that I always had some kind of project going," Paul replied. "When Dad saw that I had a knack for it, he invited me into his shop and taught me the proper way to use woodworking tools and gave me many good tips on how to build things." Paul laughed. "My mamm said that she always knew where to find me if I wasn't in the house or barn doing chores, because my favorite place to be was in the shop with Dad. Shortly before I moved here, Dad started making and selling rustic-looking pieces of furniture in the store for people who owned cabins in the woods or just wanted a woodsy feel in their homes. I enjoyed working with him in that area of the store too."

Jerry nodded. "That's how it was with me and my daed. I liked the smell of leather and hung out in his harness shop every chance I got. Eventually, we became business partners, and after Dad died, I took over the business."

"It's nice when a business can stay in the family—passed from one generation to the next," Marlene chimed in.

Jerry's forehead wrinkled. "Only I have no one to take over the harness shop when I've passed from this world into the next."

"No sons or sons-in-law to follow in your footsteps?" Paul asked.

Jerry gave a slow shake of his head. "Marlene and I were only blessed with two children: a daughter, Caroline, and a son, Andrew." His normally bright blue eyes had lost their sparkle, and his mouth turned down at the corners. "Both of them are deceased, and so is our son-in-law, Raymond."

"I'm sorry for your loss." Paul could almost feel the depth of the man's pain. Did he dare ask what had taken the lives of this elderly couple's children? Would it be too bold or cause them heartache to talk about it?

"Our son died when he was a boy and got hit by a car while he was riding the new bike we had given him for his ninth birthday," Marlene spoke up. Her voice quivered a bit as she spoke. "And our daughter—Lisa's mother—along with her husband and his parents, were killed when the vehicle they were riding in was hit head-on." Marlene looked at Lisa, who sat without speaking as she stared at her half-eaten meal. "Our granddaughter, their only child, was with them, but by some miracle, Lisa survived the crash with only minor injuries. Soon after her parents' and grandparents' funeral, we brought her here to live with us."

Paul sat in stunned silence for several seconds before extending his condolences. He knew now why Lisa reminded him of someone. She was the same girl he'd gone to school with in Goshen, Indiana. He just hadn't realized it until this minute.

Should I say anything? Paul asked himself. *How would Lisa react if I told her I was the boy who used to walk her home from school and had blurted out on more than one occasion that I planned to marry her someday?* He shifted on his unyielding chair. *Or would it better to keep quiet about this—at least for now?*

Chapter 11

"No! No! No!"

At the sound of her granddaughter's shrill screams, Marlene rushed from her room where she'd just gotten dressed. Holding on to the railing, she made her way swiftly up the stairs. When she entered the room Lisa occupied, she saw the young woman rolling from side to side as she continued to shout, "No! No! No!"

"Lisa, wake up." Marlene placed her hand on her granddaughter's arm and gave it a gentle shake. When Lisa's shouts turned to a deep moan, Marlene shook her arm again, a little more forcibly this time.

Lisa's eyes opened, and she blinked several times as she sat up in bed. Her face and nightgown were soaked with perspiration. "Wh–what's wrong, Grandma?"

"You were shouting in your sleep. I believe you must have been having a nightmare." Marlene took a seat on the edge of the bed. "Do you know what you were dreaming about?" She noticed the protruding tendons on Lisa's neck as her breaths burst in and out. Marlene sat close, waiting for her granddaughter to respond to the question.

"I—I was there, Grandma."

"Where?"

"At the cemetery, watching my mamm, daed, and other *grosseldere* being lowered into their *graewer*."

"You dreamed about your parents and grandparents being lowered into their graves?"

Lisa swept a shaky hand across her forehead before nodding. "I barely remember the event, but I saw it in my *draame* just like it was happening right then."

Marlene leaned closer and gave Lisa a hug. "Sometimes dreams bring us back to a time we barely remember, and other dreams are wild and make no sense at all."

"But why'd I have this draame now? I don't think I've ever dreamed about watching my family's burial before."

"It may have been due to the discussion that went on at the supper table last night, when we told Paul how you'd lost your parents and grandparents and the miracle of your survival." Marlene moved her head slowly up and down. "That might have triggered the memory in your mind, and then it was brought forth in a dream while you were sleeping."

Tears formed in Lisa's eyes, and when she blinked, several escaped and rolled down her cheeks. "I don't want to remember that day. It makes me *bedauerlich*."

"Of course it makes you sad." Marlene patted Lisa's back. "Everyone feels saddened when they lose a loved one. And you lost more than just one family member during the accident, which makes it doubly hard."

"I wish you hadn't talked to Paul about it. He didn't know my family, and it's none of his business." Lisa's lips pressed into a thin white slash as she folded her arms across her chest.

I didn't mean to be insensitive to her feelings. Marlene hesitated as she put her thoughts in order. *But I'd like to express my thoughts on the subject in an honest and caring way.*

"That's true, but his kind words, spoken in a soothing tone of voice, showed the sympathy he felt for you and us."

"I barely even know Paul, and I don't need his sympathy." Lisa pushed the covers aside and got out on the opposite side of the bed from Grandma. "I need to wash up, get dressed, and go downstairs to help you with breakfast." She glanced at the battery-operated clock by her bed and pushed the button on top of it to the Off position. "Since you woke me before the alarm went off, I should have plenty of time to take a shower and wash my sweaty body. Sure wouldn't want to put clean clothes on the way I am right now and then go off to teach school."

Marlene rose from the bed and moved toward the door. "I'll put the kaffi on and see you downstairs."

Lisa nodded slowly.

I think my granddaughter's put out with me and her grandpa for talking to Paul about the tragic loss of her parents and other grandparents. Lisa still misses them and obviously doesn't want to talk about it, but part of healing is being able to share our hurts with others and accept their sympathy. Marlene clung to the railing as she descended the stairs. *That certainly helped me when our son and daughter both died.*

As Lisa stood at the stove, scrambling eggs in a skillet, she thought about the terrifying dream she'd had. She couldn't remember ever having a nightmare like that before and hoped it would never happen again. Lisa didn't want to remember the details of her family's funeral or burial, and she had blanked out most of her earlier childhood when her parents and paternal grandparents were still alive. Even snippets from the past, which sometimes flitted through her mind, caused Lisa to feel fearful and despondent. She'd convinced herself that the only way she could be happy was to keep her focus on the present and refuse to give in to thoughts of the past. Staying busy so her mind couldn't wander also helped.

Teaching the children has given me a wonderful purpose, just like taking care of Maggie. Lisa smiled as she looked over at her dog lying by the kitchen's back door. *I'd say she's pretty content at this point in time. My life is good here, and I'm happy living with my loving grandparents, so I don't need anyone else.*

Although Lisa's biggest fear was losing her maternal grandparents, there was nothing she could do to prevent people she knew from dying. All she could do was try to keep herself from becoming too emotionally attached to anyone, even her grandparents, whom she loved and respected. That had not been easy, though, since she'd been living with them for so many years, and they had provided for her needs. There'd been a few times when she'd let her guard down and talked to Grandma or Grandpa about her feelings, but then she would pull back into her protective shell. The one thing Lisa could not allow herself to do was fall in love with a man and get married. If she did, it would put her in a vulnerable position of possibly losing her husband or children if some tragic event should occur. It was better to stay single than to risk being hurt again and left all alone.

"Is breakfast ready?" Grandpa's question drove Lisa's thoughts aside. She hadn't realized he'd come inside.

"Uh, almost." She looked down at the eggs she'd been scrambling and frowned. They hadn't even cooked at all. *What's going on with this stove?* That's when Lisa realized that she had not turned on the gas burner. *Boy, I need to get my head on straight. The bad dream from earlier is still bothering me, and it's beginning to affect my normal routine.*

She quickly turned the burner on and began stirring the eggs again.

"Where's your *grossmudder*?" Grandpa asked.

"Grandma's in the dining room setting the table."

"How come we're eating in there? We're not having company for breakfast." Grandpa moved closer to the stove and looked at her over the top of his reading glasses. "Are we?"

She shook her head. "With the kitchen missing its cabinets, Grandma said she didn't enjoy eating in here and looking at the vacant spaces."

He chuckled. "That sounds like my fraa, all right."

"What sounds like your wife?" Grandma asked, stepping into the kitchen, sandal footed.

He slipped his arm around her waist and pulled her close to

his side. "Nothin' important. I love everything about you, from your cute little turned-up nose, all the way down to your dainty toes. And you're a good cook too," he added.

Grandma poked his arm. "You're such a charming tease."

"I'm not teasing. You're everything a man could want."

They kissed, and Lisa looked the other way. She was glad that her grandparents loved each other, but she felt like an intruder when they displayed their affection in front of her. Although Lisa would never have admitted it, she envied them a bit, for she would never know a love like theirs.

"While you were out doing your chores, did you think to stop at the phone shed and check for messages, Jerry?" Grandma asked.

"Sure did. There was just one from Paul."

"Oh, what'd he have to say?"

Lisa's ears perked up at the sound of Paul's name. Although the eggs were done, she continued to stir them around in the skillet, waiting to hear what Grandpa said next.

"He wanted to let us know that he'll be over around ten o'clock to install the new cabinets, but he won't be able join us for supper tonight because his aunt invited some friends to come over to their house this evening, and she wants them to meet Paul. He said he thought it would be good to call now and let us know so you didn't plan a big meal that would include him."

"Oh, that's too bad. Paul's such a nice young man. I was really hoping he could join us again."

Lisa couldn't miss the tone of disappointment in Grandma's voice. She glanced over her shoulder and noticed her grandmother's furrowed brows. She was obviously disappointed, but Lisa felt relieved.

"If you're not too busy, do you have a few minutes to talk with me?" Marlene asked when she stepped into her husband's harness shop soon after Lisa left for the schoolhouse.

"I am never too busy to talk to you, my love." Jerry placed the piece of leather he'd been holding onto his workbench and suggested she pull up a chair.

Marlene sat on the metal folding chair customers sometimes used when they brought a harness or some other leather object in for repairs. More often than not, Jerry would sit and visit with his customers after they'd told him what they needed to have done, so he'd made sure to have a few extra chairs in the shop.

"How's it going out here?" Marlene asked.

"It's goin' fine. I just got some phone calls made to a couple of customers, and I was about to begin my leather work. Everything all right at the house?"

"Jah, things are fine, and it shouldn't be long before Paul shows up to begin his work."

Jerry looked up at the battery-operated clock on the wall. "Yep, he'll be here pretty soon. Did the dog follow you out this morning to the shop? I've got her treat, and you know how much she likes those doggy biscuits I bought."

"She came out the door with me, but then headed out back behind the house. I'm sure she'll come by for a biscuit when she's ready."

He nodded.

I feel like I'm such a worrywart coming out here and venting my feelings about our granddaughter. Marlene fiddled nonstop with the edge of her apron and remained quiet as she sat there.

Jerry smiled, and then his brows crinkled. "Okay, fraa, I'm sure that something is up by your nervous actions."

"I'm concerned about Lisa."

Jerry lifted his hands so his palms faced the ceiling. "You're always worried about our granddaughter. What has she done that concerns you now? Is it because she was quiet and seemed preoccupied during breakfast?"

"Jah, to a point. After what happened earlier this morning, I kind of expected she would be quiet while we ate. Lisa always pulls into her shell when something traumatic happens or if she's having a bad day and doesn't want to talk about it."

Jerry's eyes widened. "What happened this morning that involved Lisa?"

"After you went outside to do your chores, while I was getting dressed, I heard Lisa screaming, 'No! No! No!'" Marlene clasped her hands together. "So I hurried up to her room and found her moaning as she rolled back and forth on the bed."

"Was she feeling *grank*?"

"No, she wasn't sick. Her eyes were closed, so I knew she was asleep."

"Was she having a bad *draame*?"

"Jah. I woke her, and she told me that she'd been dreaming about the day her parents and other grandparents' bodies had been laid to rest." Marlene reached over and touched his arm. "The poor girl was drenched in sweat and quite shaken."

"Were you able to comfort her?"

"I believe so, but Lisa's such a sensitive young woman, and she rarely opens up and says what she's really feeling. I think she holds too much inside."

"You're probably right, but we can't force the girl to talk about her feelings if she doesn't want to." Jerry rubbed his temples. "I can still picture our granddaughter's face the day of the funeral and graveside service. She pressed her hands against her ears and kept shaking her head, as if in denial." He released a heavy sigh. "Then when the last shovels of dirt had filled in those four graves, the poor child collapsed on the ground with sobs louder than any I've ever heard."

Marlene's chin trembled as she slumped in her chair. "Jah, it was heart wrenching when you carried her screaming all the way to our carriage."

Jerry reached over and clasped Marlene's hand. "We both tried so hard to be supportive of our granddaughter that neither of us really had the chance to grieve properly that day."

"That is true," she agreed, "but I spent plenty of days, and nights too, grieving the loss of our daughter, son-in-law, and even Lisa's other grandparents who we barely knew. Of course, I had to do my grieving when Lisa wasn't in the same room. Many nights back then she had horrible nightmares, but it's been a long time since she had one, and it really shook her up." Marlene looked off across the room. *It's interesting how the strong negative memories can be put away and then, one day, released,* she thought. She reached behind the band of her apron, pulled out the tissue she'd tucked there this morning, and wiped her tears. "I can't help worrying about Lisa. We're not getting any younger, Jerry."

He nodded.

"I am determined to see the granddaughter God gave us to raise happily married so she will have a helpmate and someone to love and care for her when we are gone."

"I understand your reason for wanting Lisa to find a husband, but we cannot make it happen. We can only pray and ask the Lord to find our granddaughter someone, if it's meant to be. Also, if and when the right man comes along, it must be Lisa's decision whether to marry him or not."

"But that's not likely to happen if she continues to keep people at arm's length."

"We just need to remain supportive, and like I just said, remember to pray often for her."

And perhaps, Marlene thought, *if Lisa spends more time with Paul, she will see that he's the one.* Marlene had to admit that she didn't know the young man very well, but from the moment she first met Paul, she had a feeling that he was indeed the right man for their granddaughter. She just needed to figure out a way to get Paul and Lisa together so they could get to know each other well. Sometimes in matters of the heart, people needed a little nudge.

Chapter 12

Walnut Creek

"I'd like to go with you today," Lois said as she and Orley stood together in the kitchen on the morning of his doctor's appointment. "I want to be there when the *dokder* gives you the results of the blood test you had ten days ago."

Orley shook his head. "There's no need for that. I can tell you what the doctor said after I get home."

Lois couldn't help feeling discouraged by his response, but she wasn't too surprised, because he'd said things like this to her before when it came to his health. "But you might leave something important out," she argued. "And what if there are questions I would like to have answered by the doctor, and they're not questions you would think to ask him?"

"Are you saying that my memory is bad?" Orley squinted as he thumped the top of his partially bald head.

That's not what I'm trying to say at all. Why won't you just let me come along with you? Lois pursed her lips as she leaned against the counter and released a frustrated sigh. Orley's driver would be here soon, and if she couldn't get her husband to agree that she should go along to his appointment, then he'd be going there alone, and she'd spend the rest of the morning waiting for his return and trying not to worry about his health.

What if there is something seriously wrong with Orley? Lois asked herself. *Would he open up and give me all the details? Or would my dear husband keep quiet in order to shield me from the truth so I don't fret?*

Orley stepped forward and placed his hand on her arm. "All right, Lois, you can accompany me to the doctor's, but only on one condition."

She tipped her head back and looked directly into his eyes. "And what would that be?"

"You let me ask my questions first, and then if you have any of your own, you can chime right in." Orley lifted his glasses and rubbed the bridge of his nose.

Lois bobbed her head. "Jah, I can do that."

"Good, then you'd better get your jacket, outer bonnet, and purse, because I just heard a vehicle pull into the yard, and it's no doubt our driver."

Lois smiled. She was glad Orley had conceded and agreed to let her go with him today. Knowing her carefree husband, he would no doubt ask very few questions of the doctor. So it was good that she would be there to ask her own set of questions and find out everything they needed to know about Orley's health.

⁓

"That was some fine work you did on the Schrocks' cabinets." Paul's uncle gave him a pat on the back. "I had stopped by their place to give them the bill and let them know that if they had any questions not to hesitate to ask. They were happy with the work and even mentioned that they liked having you there during the whole process." His uncle's tone was laced with satisfaction. "Yes indeed, I did a good thing when I invited you to come here to work for me. Sure hope you stay put and don't move back to Indiana."

"No way!" Paul responded to his uncle's statement. "I have no intention of moving back to my hometown. There are too many unpleasant memories for me there, and so far I've been liking it here in Ohio. In fact, this could end up being the place where I decide to put down roots." Paul leaned against the desk in Uncle Abe's office.

"Are the unpleasant memories because of the girlfriend who

dropped you for your best friend?"

Paul's mouth nearly fell open. "How'd you know about that?" He had deliberately not said anything about his breakup with Susan because it was his personal life and he'd seen no reason his uncle, aunt, or anyone else in Sugarcreek should know about his friend's betrayal.

"Your daed told me." Uncle Abe took a seat behind his desk. "I'm guessing from your look of displeasure that he wasn't supposed to say anything."

Paul couldn't deny his uncle's words. He guessed that Dad telling Uncle Abe about his personal matter wasn't the end of the world. But with the surprise of the reveal still in the air, Paul stood there with no words to say to his uncle. It was an awkward silence as Paul barely managed to nod.

"Well you know how your daed is. He worries about his kinner, even if they aren't little children anymore." Uncle Abe drummed his fingers along the top of his desk. "My brother's a caring person and always has been. Even when we were kinner, he acted more like a daed than a big bruder to me and the rest of our siblings. If one of us got sick, he felt bad and always asked if there was anything he could do to help us feel better." Paul's uncle chuckled. "I kinda liked it, though, 'cause whenever I got in trouble with my mamm or daed, I could always count on my brother Daniel to offer me sympathy."

Paul smiled. "You're right, my dad is a caring person. I guess it's okay that he told you about me and Susan Lambright breaking up. The whole thing is hard for me to talk about, and I'm glad to be living here where I don't have to see her and Ervin Yoder together anymore."

"What you went through will just be a distant memory when you meet the right woman and fall in love." Uncle Abe's words were spoken in a soothing tone of voice. It kind of reminded Paul of the way his own father often spoke to him—full of sound advice but never pushy or controlling.

Paul thought about his mother and how she could sometimes be a bit overbearing when it came to trying to convince Paul or one of his brothers that she knew what was best for them. When he and his siblings were children, there wasn't much they could do about it, but as adults, sometimes Paul and his brothers had to stand up to their mother and remind her that they were grown men and had the right to make their own decisions. Mom would usually back off and say she was sorry, but there were times when she kept pushing. This was yet another reason Paul liked living here—no one was pressing him to do certain things he didn't want to do or to think the way they thought.

Paul wasn't sure that what Uncle Abe had said about him meeting the right woman and falling in love would ever happen, because he definitely was not looking for love. But if a woman should ever come his way who he believed was the right one, he'd make sure to pray about it and seek confirmation from God before proceeding with a permanent relationship.

For some reason, an image of Lisa's face overtook Paul's thoughts. *Now why am I thinking about her right now? Maybe it's because the last time I saw Lisa, I discovered that we knew each other when we were kinner. Of course,* he reminded himself, *Lisa obviously did not remember me, or she would have said something. I have to wonder if she blocked that part of her life out of her memory by choice; or could the trauma from the accident she and her family were involved in have resulted in partial amnesia?*

Paul felt a warm flush creep across his cheeks as another thought came to mind. *If Lisa's parents hadn't died and she'd continued to live in Goshen, I wonder if I would have ended up dating her. When I was a boy, I did believe I would marry Lisa someday.*

"What's wrong, Paul? Your face is red as a ripe apple, and the sweat on your forehead makes it appear that you might be overheated. Is it too warm for you here in the shop this morning?"

Uncle Abe's questions drew Paul out of his musings, and he moved away from the desk. "Jah, it is a little warm, but I'll be fine once your driver comes and we head out to do that job you had scheduled for today."

"That should be soon," Uncle Abe said. "So while I do some paperwork here in my office, would you please go out to the main part of the shop and make sure that all our supplies are ready?"

"Sure thing. I'll let you know when Herb gets here." Paul made a beeline for the door, eager to do something that would get his mind on something other than Lisa.

When school was over for the day and the children had all gone home, Lisa said goodbye to Yvonne before she stepped out the front door and nearly tripped on the curly-haired dog lying on the porch. "For goodness' sakes, Maggie, what are you doing here?"

The dog looked up at her, whined, and wagged her tail.

"What's going on? Who are you talking to?" Her coworker poked her head outside of the door.

"It looks like my dog missed me today and came to see me home."

"Oh, I heard you talking and thought maybe a student had come back for something they'd forgotten." Yvonne came out from the doorway and gave Maggie a few rubs on her flanks. "Your dog is sure sweet and friendly."

"Danki, and jah, I have to agree. Maggie has a way of warming hearts. It started with me and Grandma, which is why we ended up keeping the mutt." Lisa pointed at Maggie. "Guess I'd better go home with my furry companion now."

"All right, I'll see you tomorrow." Yvonne smiled and went back inside the schoolhouse, no doubt to finish cleaning the blackboard and gather up her things.

Lisa looked down at Maggie again and tapped her chin. *I wonder how you escaped the yard without Grandma knowing.* At this moment Lisa wished her dog could talk. She didn't know whether Maggie had been in her pen and somehow gotten out or if she'd been inside the house with Grandma and snuck outside when the door had been left open. Either way, Maggie should not have been out on the road by herself. She could have gotten hit by a car.

"Come on, girl." Lisa clapped her hands and started down the steps, glancing over her shoulder to see if the dog was coming. She needn't have worried, because Maggie was right on her heels.

When Lisa climbed onto her bicycle, she called to the dog and pointed as she commanded her to stay on the side of her bike farthest from traffic.

Maggie was obedient, and the only thing negative she did along the way toward home was bark at a few cars going in the opposite direction.

Lisa felt relief when they made it home safely without any problems. She shuddered to think of what could have happened when Maggie left her grandparents' yard this afternoon and headed for the schoolhouse with no supervision.

Was she really that desperate to see me? Lisa asked herself. *Maybe my hund has insecurities like I do and wants to be with someone who makes her feel safe.*

When she pedaled her bike up her grandparents' driveway, Lisa spotted her grandmother getting out of one of their driver's vehicles. Lisa parked her bike near the house and waited for Grandma to join her on the porch, where Maggie had already found a comfortable spot to lie down.

"How was your appointment?" Lisa asked, remembering that Grandma had mentioned this morning that she planned to see the chiropractor.

"It went well. My sore shoulder feels much better than it did yesterday." Grandma took a seat in one of the wicker chairs and motioned for Lisa to do the same. "When you came in on your bike, I saw that Maggie was with you and felt relieved. The little *schtinker* slipped out the front door when I went to get the mail shortly before my driver, Ida, picked me up. I called and called but she kept running, and then Ida showed up and I had to either go or be late for my appointment." Grandma looked down at Maggie, who lay with her eyes shut, apparently sleeping. "Did she end up at the schoolhouse?"

"Jah. I discovered her on the porch when I came out after the students had left for home." Lisa drew in some air and released it slowly. "She did well staying with me on the way home, but I shudder to think of what could have happened if she'd wandered out into the road on the way to the schoolhouse when she was by herself." She leaned down and stroked the dog's silky ears. "I've become attached to Maggie, and I want to keep her safe."

Grandma nodded. "Of course you do, and I'll do my best to make sure she doesn't get out again."

~

"I can't believe you've been diagnosed with hypothyroidism," Lois said after she and Orley left the doctor's office and stood waiting outside the building for their driver to pick them up. "No wonder you've been so tired and have gained some weight you've been unable to lose."

"I've also had some joint pain and noticed my fingernails have become really brittle, not to mention that I have experienced an intolerance to cold. I thought they were just signs of old age creeping in." Orley shrugged. "But at least what I have can be controlled by taking thyroid medicine. I will have to get my blood tested from time to time, though, in case the dosage needs to be adjusted."

"I'm so glad I talked you into seeing the doctor and that it was diagnosed quickly. And as the doctor explained, hypothyroidism develops slowly and may go unnoticed for a long time. I was surprised when he also stated that if left untreated you could develop other symptoms, such as high cholesterol; a slow heart rate; puffiness in the face, feet, or hands; a loss of balance; hoarseness; or eyebrows that have thinned or completely diminished."

"Too bad there isn't something natural I can do about my sluggish thyroid to make it work better." Orley frowned. "I hate taking pills."

"Tsk, tsk," Lois said. "Don't forget, the doctor also suggested taking iodine supplements because it's an essential mineral for good thyroid function." She touched his arm. "He also talked about making some dietary changes and reminded you of the importance of regular exercise."

Orley stroked his throat and grimaced. "Wish I was a kid again and could be healthy as a horse like I once was."

"Not all horses are healthy, you know."

Orley was about ready to comment when their driver pulled up. "Good," he muttered under his breath. *Now at least we won't have to talk about this anymore. Of course, the subject will probably be brought up again after we get home.*

Chapter 13

Sugarcreek

The first Saturday in November was Paul's day off, so he had decided to make a stop at the Christian bookstore in town to pick up a book his aunt had ordered a few weeks ago. Running errands for Aunt Emma when he was free to go was the least Paul could do, considering that she did his laundry and fed him most meals. When Paul first moved in with his aunt and uncle and started working for Uncle Abe, he'd insisted on paying something for his room and board. But he looked forward to the day when he could rent or buy his own home. He liked the idea of being completely independent.

On his way to the bookstore, he noticed a place for sale. It had a good-sized home on sprawling property and a few outbuildings as well. Paul could see that the place had electricity connected to it, and if he was really interested in buying the home, after he'd made the purchase the power would have to go. But for now he was only looking and getting a feel for the area. At this point he could easily look farther out from town and see what else was available.

He coaxed his horse to move more quickly by jiggling the reins. *Maybe out of curiosity, I should do some pricing on the homes around the area.*

It wasn't long before the businesses came into view, and Paul watched for the bookstore.

As usual on weekends, a good number of cars and people were

in town. He hoped to find a place available at one of the hitching rails to secure his horse and buggy and was pleased when he spotted one. No cars had been parked close, which was good. It wasn't often that a car would try to park near the horse and buggy areas, but there were those rare times.

Paul guided his horse, Chester, to the hitching rail and climbed out of his buggy. He felt at ease riding in his own rig again and had missed it. At least Paul could leave some of his personal things in the carriage and know that they would be at his disposal any time of the day or night. Both Chester and Paul's closed-in buggy had been transported to Sugarcreek a week ago, and he was glad to have them. Paul had missed the well-behaved gelding. Chester also had plenty of get-up-and-go when it was needed, which Paul appreciated. Neither his aunt's nor his uncle's horse, although dependable, had the energy Chester did.

Paul secured the horse and gave him a gentle pat. "You behave yourself while I'm gone now, ya hear?"

Chester's ears pricked up, and he nickered. Paul took that as a sign that his horse had been listening and understood his master's request, although some would say that the average horse would not understand Pennsylvania Dutch or English.

As Paul headed toward the bookstore, he thought about where else he'd like to go while in town. When Paul entered the place of business a few minutes later, he heard soft music playing in the background. Several shoppers mingled among the books and other items displayed around the store. The Mennonite woman up front by the register smiled as Paul approached. "Hello there. If you're looking for anything special just let me know."

Paul nodded and had just started down an aisle when he spotted Lisa's grandmother looking at some of the gift items.

"Hello, Marlene," Paul spoke in Dutch in a quiet tone as he stepped up beside her, not wanting to disturb the other patrons. "How are you today?"

"I'm doing just fine. Are things going well with you?"

Paul gave a nod. "Have you been enjoying your new kitchen cabinets?"

Wearing an enthusiastic smile, she bobbed her head. "Oh, jah, very much. You do good work, Paul, and I appreciate your efforts in making the cabinets just the way I had wanted."

"I'm glad you're happy with them."

"What brings you into the Christian bookstore this morning?" she questioned.

"Came to get a Bible study book that my aunt ordered."

"I came to buy a few books for my granddaughter, but as you can see, I've been looking at a few gift items as well." Marlene gestured to a variety of religious plaques on the display table. "During Lisa's free time she can often be found reading a book. She especially has a fascination with history and enjoys reading novels or nonfiction books that are set during historical times."

"I see." Paul was tempted to tell Marlene that he knew Lisa when she was a girl and mention how she had liked to read back then too. But he decided it was best not to say anything, at least at this time.

Paul glanced at the rows of books on the shelves. Although he wasn't much of a book reader, he didn't mind looking at magazines like the *Connection* or the woodworking publications.

"I wish Lisa had more of a social life. She's been reserved and has kept to herself a lot ever since she came to live with us after her parents died." Marlene heaved a heavy-sounding sigh. "She needs to spend time with other young people her age. Maybe then she would become more social instead of distancing herself so much."

Paul let what she'd said sink in. *I thought it was me or the things I've said that made her clam up.* "So it's not just me she acts quiet and kind of timid around?"

"Oh no. Lisa is that way with almost everyone. It took several years for her grandpa and me to get her to open up and talk more to us." Marlene shifted the sack she held over to her other hand. "But Jerry and I have kept trying, and some of the barriers have come down—at least between us and our granddaughter. And of course she was able to pursue a teaching career and has done well around the children."

"That's good to hear." Ever since he was a boy Paul had taken pleasure in fixing things, and at the moment, he wished there was something he could do to fix Lisa so that she would become the happy, carefree young girl he used to know. But was that same person still in there, or had Lisa closed the door on her past?

Maybe if I try to befriend her, I'll succeed, he thought. *I just need to figure out something we can talk about that she might be interested in. I'd like to be the one to help Lisa step out of her comfort zone and become more outgoing. Maybe I could ask her what she likes to do as a hobby, or I could talk to her about Maggie. Guess now isn't the time to be thinking about this, though. I need to get my errands run.*

Paul said goodbye to Marlene and headed for the counter to pick up his aunt's book. Right now his goal was to drop the book off to Aunt Emma after he left the store, and then he'd be heading to Walnut Creek to see if Orley Troyer had gotten any new milk bottles since the last time he'd visited Memory Keepers Antique Store.

Walnut Creek

Lois had gone to the post office to get the mail she'd received from her Dear Caroline column, and when she returned to the antique shop she found Orley sitting behind the front counter with a disgruntled expression.

"What's wrong?" she asked, approaching him.

"I've been going over the mail we received at home this morning and brought to the shop because we were running late and didn't have time to go through it there."

"Is there something in the mail that has you upset?"

"Jah." Orley shook his head as he held up a piece of paper. "It's a note from our bank, letting us know that a check one of our out-of-state customers gave us two weeks ago bounced." He released a puff of air. "Now we're stuck paying the fee."

Lois was about to comment, but Orley rushed on. "In addition to that, we're out the money we thought we'd made when that antique desk the man bought left our store."

"This kind of thing can happen sometimes," Lois said. "We'll need to be more careful and make sure that unless we know the customers personally we ask for proper identification, as well as a working phone number, whenever we take a check."

Orley nodded. "Jah, and since we aren't set up to take credit card payments and have always expected our customers to pay with cash or a check, we take a chance whenever someone pays by check and we know very little, if anything, about them."

"That's especially true if a customer is from out of town."

"It can be downright frustrating." Orley reached for two pieces of candy from the bowl they kept on the counter for customers to enjoy and popped one into his mouth.

Lois frowned. ""You eat too many *schleckerei*, husband, and the candy won't remove the frustration you're obviously feeling right now."

He shook his head. "I don't eat too many sweets."

Lois pointed to the candy dish. "I've noticed that this bowl of candy has gone down considerably since we first set it out, and I don't recall seeing many of our customers helping themselves to any of it."

Orley gave no response as he averted his gaze.

"I'm not trying to pick on you this morning, but too much sugar is bad for a person's health, and you're already dealing with one health issue due to your hypothyroidism." She paused for a few seconds then continued. "You're doing well so far on the medication the doctor prescribed, but you sure don't need another problem if your blood sugar gets out of control."

Orley put the other piece of candy in his mouth. "I'm fine, so don't worry. A little bit of sugar never hurt anyone." He looked at Lois pointedly. "I hope you don't start hiding candy and other sweets from me like that woman I read about in *The Budget* the other day."

"What woman? What did it say about her?" Lois questioned.

Orley rested his elbows on the countertop. "Apparently her husband was hooked on a certain kind of candy, and so she decided to hide it someplace where she thought he'd never find it."

Lois leaned forward, eager to hear more of this story. "Did she discover such a place?"

"Sure enough. That determined lady placed the candy in a plastic ziplock bag and hid it in the top part of the toilet tank." He scrunched up his nose. "Can you imagine such a thing?"

Lois chuckled. "No, I certainly can't. And don't you worry, because I would never go that far to hide candy from you." She shook her finger at him. "But if you don't behave yourself, I might quit buying it to set out here in the store."

He gave her a pouty little-boy look, with his lower lip protruding. "I won't eat too much candy. I promise."

Lois was about to comment when the bell on the front door jangled and a customer stepped in. This discussion, if it needed to go further, could wait for another time.

Orley smiled at the young man who had entered the shop, and he stepped out from behind the counter. "Guder mariye. It's nice to see you again, Paul."

"Good morning. It's my pleasure to see you too." Paul gave Orley a hearty handshake. "I came in to see if you may have gotten any more milk bottles since the last time I came here."

Orley gave a nod. "A few. I'd planned to call and let you know, but I misplaced your number. Would you like me to show them to you now?"

"Jah, please do."

Orley led the way to the section in the store where a large selection of old bottles and jars were displayed. He gestured to the five new milk bottles. "Are any of those close to what you've been lookin' for?"

"Unfortunately, none of them are like the old bottle that used to belong to my grandma." Paul shook his head. "Sure wish I hadn't accidentally broken hers."

Orley reached under his glasses and rubbed the bridge of his nose. "I sure feel bad about losin' the phone number where you could be reached. If you'll give it to me again, I'll put it in a safe place and give you a call when I get more vintage milk bottles in the store."

"I'd appreciate that." Paul told Orley the number, and Orley wrote it down on the small tablet he'd taken from his trousers pocket along with a pen.

"Have you been keeping busy with your carpentry work?" Orley asked, taking their conversation in another direction.

"Definitely. My uncle's business is growing, and we've been busier than ever lately. If things keep going like they are currently, he may have to hire another carpenter who is able to work full-time."

"How many people does he have working for him now?"

"Just me and my seventeen-year-old cousin Kevin. My uncle is still hands-on with his business, so when he's not out giving bids to prospective customers about work they want done, he's on the job working with me, Kevin, or Gary Yoder, who started working for my uncle a few months before he hired me. Gary has his own business raising goats, so unfortunately he can only work part-time for my uncle."

"It's great that Abe's business is doing so well. Not every business can say the same."

"I understand. I heard that many of the restaurants in the area are short on help so they've had to cut back on the hours they're open for business."

Orley rolled his shoulders, as if his shirt was causing discomfort. "It's a shame that so many young people these days either don't want to work anymore, or they're only looking for high-paid positions. Back when I was still single, I rarely was out of work. Course I wasn't picky and would have done most any job that had been offered to me." He looked right at Paul. "You strike me as bein' the same way. Am I right about that?"

Before Paul could respond, another customer entered the store. Since Lois had gone to the back room with their mail from both home and the store, Orley excused himself to go wait on the middle-aged English woman. As he approached the front of the store, he noticed that the bowl of candy was missing from the checkout counter. *That fraa of mine—she worries too much about my health, and apparently she doesn't trust me either.*

Although Paul hadn't found what he'd come for, he figured he might as well look around to see if anything else might catch his eye. So after Orley walked away, Paul meandered around the store, checking things out. Orley and his wife had acquired some pretty nice things to sell in their antique shop. One unusual piece in particular that he'd noticed in the old tool section caught Paul's eye. It was an antiquated-looking drill that hadn't been used in a good many years. Paul was tempted to buy it but changed his mind since it wasn't something he would use on the job and would end being just a novelty piece.

While browsing farther along the other side of the store, Paul noticed several old books that made him think of Lisa. He remembered once again how, when they were children, she had been a bookworm—always reading in her free time. After talking with Lisa's grandmother this morning, Paul believed he may have discovered a topic that he could discuss with Lisa. As soon as he got the chance, he would invite Lisa to come here to Memory Keepers with him and show her the old books they had for sale. He hoped she would be willing to accompany him.

And who knows, Paul thought, feeling a ray of hope, *the topic of books might give Lisa a spark of enthusiasm, and talking about books could even jog her memory.*

Chapter 14

Sugarcreek

A brisk breeze blew in through an open window in Deacon Herschberger's buggy shed where church was being held. Lisa shivered, wishing she had put on something heavier before rushing out the door. She'd noticed that the majority of the congregation had worn heavier clothing today. She felt silly only having her lightweight shawl for warmth. *What was I thinking? I should have gone back into the house before leaving for church and gotten my black jacket to wear under the shawl.*

Lisa rubbed her chilly hands together, hoping to warm them up and wishing someone would close the window on the women's side of the room. There was no doubt about it—the colder weather had arrived, and like it or not, soon winter would be upon them.

Of course, Lisa thought, *despite the frigid weather that will be coming within the next few months, there'll be good times to look forward to. The schoolchildren will enjoy frolicking in the snow during recess. We'll also have sledding, ice-skating, and caroling as we approach the Christmas holiday.* It was fun to take part in some of the outdoor activities—especially when Lisa could do it with her students. But when it came to doing things with other young people her age, Lisa usually turned down most invitations that involved outdoor winter activities. Since she loved to sing, Christmas caroling was the only exception.

When another waft of air blew in, Lisa wrapped her shawl

around her shoulders a little tighter, and her attention returned to the sermon being preached on the topic of friendship. The minister quoted from the book of Proverbs, chapter 18, verse 24: "A man that hath friends must shew himself friendly: and there is a friend that sticketh closer than a brother."

Lisa listened as the preacher went on to say that everyone needs good Christian friends for fellowship, for fun times, and to share one another's burdens.

"It's not good for people to close themselves off from others for fear of getting hurt. We are all imperfect and make mistakes, but mistakes can be forgiven." The minister's gaze traveled around the room. "Ecclesiastes 4:9 says: 'Two are better than one; because they have a good reward for their labour.'"

Lisa pressed her body firmly against the unyielding wooden bench she sat upon. It hadn't been as though no one had ever invited her to events in the community. Others might see her as the unfriendly type, but they didn't understand Lisa's need to protect herself from the possibility of having her heart being broken by allowing anyone besides her grandparents to get close to her. Other than Yvonne, Lisa had no friends near her age, and the truth was Lisa and Yvonne didn't see each other much outside of teaching school and attending church every other Sunday.

Am I going against God's Word by not establishing more friend-ships? Lisa wondered. *Should I attend more young people's gatherings and try to engage in conversation with those I don't know very well? Do I dare take a chance?*

The pounding of hooves in the yard outside the shop brought Lisa's thoughts to a halt. She craned her neck to look out the window. *Oh no! It looks like some of the horses broke free from the hitching line.*

⁓

When Paul heard the commotion outside, he knew instinctively what had happened. He also knew that if the horses weren't rounded up quickly, they could leave the yard and end up out on the road.

Without hesitation, he left his seat and followed three other young men out the door. Although it would mean missing part or all of the minister's sermon on friendship, Paul did what he felt was right. Someone had to get the horses secured again, and it would take more than one man to do it.

When Paul stepped into the yard, he quickly held up his arms as one of the five horses approached, tossing its head from side to side. "Whoa, now. Steady, boy." Paul reached out to grab the horse's halter, but a second horse passed by in a flash, followed by two more energetic horses.

Paul continued to wave his arms, as did the other three men who had come outside to help get the horses back where they belonged. Apparently none of the stubborn animals wanted to be caught, for they kept running around the yard, leading the men on a merry chase.

Just then, Aaron Wengerd came out of the shop and joined the pursuit, but the horses kept going at lightning speed. They circled the building where church was still taking place, thundered across the front lawn, and headed in the direction of the barn.

In some ways Paul felt relieved that his horse wasn't among those that had broken free. On the other hand, Chester would have been easy to catch, because all Paul would have had to do was just give a whistle and the gelding would've come right to him. Even Uncle Abe's horse, Cinnamon, would have been easy to catch. These crazy horses, however, weren't familiar with Paul, and he wasn't even sure who owned them.

As luck would have it, or by divine intervention, all the horses went straight into the barn.

"Let's put 'em in the stalls," one of the men hollered. "Then we can go out to the hitching line and make sure all the other horses are still there and secured."

Paul was the last man to enter the barn, and after quickly shutting the door, he joined the others in getting the horses put safely in stalls. Once that was done, they headed out to the area where the horses had been tethered.

Paul felt relief seeing that Chester had remained secure, along with all the others. Apparently only part of the line had broken, which should be easy to fix.

"Let's head back to church now. The horses can remain in the barn, and we can take care of the line after our service and noon meal is over," one of the other men directed. He had the beginning of a beard, which indicated that he was newly married.

Paul gave Chester a few pats, told him to be good, and started back toward the shop. Hopefully they hadn't been gone long enough to miss the rest of the minister's sermon. Paul had enjoyed listening to the scriptures that the preacher had quoted on the topic of friendship. He wondered if Lisa had appreciated them too.

Paul swiped a hand through his damp hair. *There I go thinking about her again. Why can't I get Lisa out of my thoughts?*

Before reentering the buggy shed for church, Paul tucked the ends of his rumpled, sweaty shirt back inside the front of his black trousers and made sure his vest looked okay. It was a miracle that he and the other fellows who'd chased after the horses and done all that waving looked even halfway presentable now.

After the noon meal was over, some people left for home, while others sat or stood around visiting for a while. Paul had helped repair the hitching line and scanned the remaining people to see if he could locate Lisa anywhere. He saw no sign of her talking to any of the women who remained and didn't see her grandparents either. Had they left without him noticing, or could they be in the house talking with the hosts of today's church service?

Paul glanced at the field where the buggies had been parked and saw Lisa walking toward one of the carriages, which he assumed belonged to her grandfather. He rubbed his hands briskly together to warm them from the cold. *This is my chance to talk to Lisa, so I'd better take it now, before she leaves.*

He hurried across the field and reached Lisa before she stepped into the buggy. "Hey, Lisa, can I talk to you for a moment?"

She turned, and a flush of red erupted on her cheeks. "Umm. . . sure."

Paul took a few more steps until he stood beside her. "I stopped by Memory Keepers Antique Store yesterday and noticed that they have quite a few old books." He transferred his weight from one foot to the other. "So I was wondering if you'd like to go there with me this coming Saturday."

"How did you know I like to read?" Lisa looked at him with a curious expression.

"Umm. . ." Paul hesitated, giving a little kick to a clump of weeds. He had wanted to talk to her days ago, in order to get to know her better, but hadn't had the opportunity until now. He felt funny at this point using the information from what Lisa's grandmother had told him about her and then utilizing it to try to convince this young woman into going to the antique store with him.

I'd best be honest with Lisa. "Your grandmother told me the other day that you liked to read historical books. And when I was at Memory Keepers I noticed they had a shelf with a nice amount of old literature there."

"And you thought of me?" Lisa spoke in a soft tone as she tilted her head from side to side, as though trying to decide. Finally, when Paul thought she was not going to answer, she said in a near whisper: "Jah, that would be nice."

Looking straight into her eyes, Paul smiled. "That's great. How about if I come by and pick you up around ten o'clock Saturday morning? Or would you rather leave later than that?"

"Ten is fine."

"Sounds good." Paul couldn't believe Lisa had agreed to go with him, and he hoped she would enjoy visiting the antique store and looking at the old books.

"Are ya ready to go, fraa?" Jerry asked, nudging Marlene's arm as they stood outside of the buggy shed.

She could see her granddaughter standing near their carriage with Paul. *I hope in time a spark of interest will grow between them.*

Marlene looked at Jerry and shook her head. "Not quite. Let's wait till Paul and Lisa are finished talking." She pointed toward their buggy. "And let us keep our voices down so no one hears us talking."

A good many people were still milling about getting ready to go, and some were in the process of leaving on foot or with their horse and buggy. Marlene didn't want her and Jerry's private conversation to be heard by anyone.

The wrinkles in Jerry's forehead deepened. "Why do we have to wait? It's chilly out here, and I'd like to get home. I'm sure Paul and Lisa won't mind if we show up at our buggy while they are talking. I mean, what could they have to say to one another that they wouldn't want us to hear?"

"I'm cold too, but they shouldn't be long." Marlene rolled her eyes. "And seriously, Jerry, can't you remember how it was when you were a young man speaking to a girl you might have an interest in?"

His brows lifted high on his forehead. "Has Paul given you some reason to believe he's taken an interest in our *grossdochder*?"

"He hasn't actually said so, but I've seen the way he looks at her."

"Oh? How's that?"

"Your voice is getting louder." Marlene placed one finger against her lips and made sure she spoke quietly. "You know very well what I'm talking about. Now can we stay here on the porch until Paul moves away from our carriage?"

Jerry gave a quick nod and stuffed his hands inside of his jacket. "I'll wait as long as you say, dear matchmaker. It would be nice if that young man took an interest in our granddaughter."

I agree. Marlene made no comment as they remained on the

porch. *I can't help being curious about what he's saying to Lisa.* When she saw Paul move away from their buggy and head toward the line of horses, she touched her husband's arm and said, "Okay, we can go now. Let's not keep our granddaughter waiting."

Now it was Jerry's turn to roll his eyes. "You're so predictable."

~

Lisa watched as Paul walked away. She couldn't believe she had agreed to go to the antique store in Walnut Creek with him. *What was I thinking?* she asked herself as she climbed into the back of her grandfather's buggy. Lisa looked off toward the road as another buggy pulled out to leave. *Guess I took today's sermon on friendship to heart. When the minister spoke on the subject, I couldn't help feeling as though he was speaking to me.*

Lisa's thoughts refocused as she saw Grandpa head over to the hitching line to get his horse. A few minutes later, Grandma showed up and climbed into the buggy. She turned to look at Lisa and smiled. "Was that Paul I saw you talking to a bit ago?"

"Jah. He mentioned that the antique store in Walnut Creek has some old books for sale, and he asked if I'd like to go with him this Saturday."

Grandma gave Lisa a wide smile. "It was nice of him to think of you. I'm sure you'll have a good time browsing around the antique store—especially if there are old books to look at."

Lisa nodded. She hoped her grandmother wouldn't make a big deal of this. She wasn't going on a date—it was just a friendly trip to look at some vintage books.

"Will Paul be picking you up, or are you supposed to meet him there?"

"He said he'd pick me up around ten o'clock Saturday morning."

"That'll be nice. It will give you two a chance to get to know each other a little better."

"I suppose." Lisa sucked in her lower lip while dropping her gaze to her lap. *Great. Looks like she is going to make something out of this.*

"Aren't you eager to get better acquainted with Paul? Or is there something you don't like about him?" Grandma questioned.

"I have nothing against him, and I don't know Paul well enough yet to decide whether there is something I don't like about him," Lisa answered honestly. "After the message we heard today on friendship, I thought it would be good if I tried to be a little friendlier, so I agreed to go to the antique store with him."

"That's *wunderbaar*, Lisa. You need more friends." There seemed to be a twinkle in Grandma's eyes as she smiled at Lisa.

Lisa wished now that she had never told her grandmother about Paul's invitation. But if she'd kept quiet about this, then when he came to pick her up, she would have to offer her grandparents some sort of explanation.

She felt relieved when Grandpa showed up and got his horse hitched to the buggy. Hopefully now Grandma would take her attention off Lisa and focus on something else, because usually she and Grandpa had plenty to talk about on the way home from anywhere. Most likely today it would be about the horses that broke free from the line and created a ruckus outside the shop where church had been held. In fact, Lisa hoped the topic was brought up as soon as Grandpa got into their carriage. She sure didn't need him to start asking questions about why Paul had been talking to her outside the buggy.

"Everyone set to go?" Grandpa asked, taking up the reins.

"I'm ready," Grandma replied.

"Me too, and I think I'll take a nap on the way home." Lisa leaned against the back of her seat and closed her eyes. At least this way she wouldn't have to answer any questions.

Chapter 15

Paul snapped the reins to get Chester moving faster. He thought about how he'd fussed earlier over which shirt to wear and ended up choosing his new pale purple one. But then he'd spilled some hot chocolate down the front of it before he left to pick up Lisa and had to change into one of his older light blue shirts.

Paul reflected on how his aunt had come into the room before he'd left and said she'd thought he had been wearing a new shirt earlier. Paul's ears had burned with the embarrassment he'd felt when admitting that he'd managed to drip hot chocolate on the shirt. Aunt Emma had put Paul's mind at ease, though, when she'd told him in her usual calm voice not to worry, that she would put something on his new shirt to keep it from staining and would soak it for a while too. She'd also assured Paul that the older shirt he'd changed into looked fine. Then, just before Paul walked out the door, Aunt Emma had said she hoped he would have a nice time visiting the antique store with Lisa.

Paul had sure been surprised when Lisa agreed to go with him to Memory Keepers. He hoped she would find some books she liked and wondered if Lisa would be more talkative today.

I'll have to make it my job to see that she is, he told himself as he urged his horse on.

Paul wondered if Lisa had spoken to her grandmother about him knowing she had a love for reading. He hadn't handled what he'd learned with much thought and didn't want to cause a problem between Lisa and her grandmother.

Paul's plan was to gain Lisa's trust, and if and when she began to open up more, he would tell her that they used to know each other when they were children. If he could get her to remember that, it might bring other things from the past into focus as well.

Paul felt good about the possibility of helping Lisa and wished he had thought to do it sooner—when he'd first realized who she was.

"Better late than never," he said aloud. "But I can't rush into it. I need to wait for the right time to tell her."

Chester's ears twitched, and he let out a whinny.

"That's okay, bud. I wasn't talkin' to you." Paul grinned. Chester had always been attentive to his words, even if the shiny brown horse didn't always understand what had been said.

When the Schrocks' place came into view, Paul slowed Chester and guided him up the driveway. He angled to the right, stopped at the hitching rail, and stepped out of the buggy. Paul had just secured his horse when Lisa came out of the house. She wore a black shawl over an aqua dress, which went well with her blond hair peeking out the front part of her stiff white head covering. Lisa walked with her head held high, but her gaze seemed to be on Chester rather than Paul.

"You have a nice-looking *gaul*," she said. "I like the white blaze on his head."

"Me too." Paul smiled and gave the horse a few pats. "His name is Chester, and he's usually quite friendly, even to strangers."

Lisa reached up and stroked the horse's neck. "Hello, Chester. I'm glad to meet you."

Chester flicked his ears and bobbed his head, as though he'd understood what she had said.

Paul chuckled. "I think he agrees with you."

Lisa looked at Paul, and when she gave a brief smile, he got a glimpse of the Lisa he'd known when she was a girl.

"Shall we head out?" he asked.

"Jah." Lisa climbed in and seated herself on the left side of the buggy, which was where the passenger up front always sat.

Paul released Chester from the rail, climbed in on the right side of the buggy, and took hold of the reins. Then he backed his horse up and headed down the driveway. "Even though it's a little chilly, at least the sun's shining today," Paul commented as he turned his horse and carriage onto the road.

"Jah."

He glanced over at Lisa and saw that her fingers were clutched tightly around her purse straps as she stared straight ahead. Paul wondered if he should try to strike up a conversation at this point or just ride quietly into Walnut Creek.

Guess I'll keep quiet unless she says something to me, he decided. *Maybe we both need to just relax and enjoy the scenery.*

Walnut Creek

When Lisa entered the antique store, where a vintage WELCOME sign and the chime of a bell above the door greeted them, her eyes widened. She had never been in this shop before, and she detected the scent of old wood, leather, dust, and a strange musty odor. From where she stood, Lisa's eyes began to study many of the old things that were on display around her. She was fascinated with the uneven texture of chipped paint on a distressed cabinet and the crisp white doilies draped over some of the end tables. Most of the aisles were narrow, with table displays on both sides and shelves and more antique furniture along three of the walls. Lisa was eager to check it all out.

"Let's go up to the checkout counter before we start looking at things," Paul said. "I'd like you to meet the owners of Memory Keepers."

Lisa hesitated, but when Paul gave her arm a tug, she followed him to the front of the store where a middle-aged Amish couple stood.

When they stepped out from behind the counter, Paul greeted them with a handshake, and then he gestured to Lisa. "Orley and Lois, I'd like you to meet my friend Lisa Miller." He turned to face Lisa before gesturing to the Troyers. "These nice folks are Orley and Lois."

Lisa's face warmed as she shook hands with the Amish couple. It had taken her by surprise when Paul referred to her as his friend, since they didn't know each other very well. *But then,* she reasoned, *it would have sounded odd if he'd called me his acquaintance.*

"It's nice to meet you, Lisa," Lois and Orley said at the same time.

Still feeling a bit shy, she gave a quick nod. "Nice to meet you too."

Orley looked at Paul with furrowed brows. "Sorry to say, but I haven't gotten in any new milk bottles since the last time you were here."

"That's okay," Paul responded. "We mostly came by so Lisa could look at your old books. She's a schoolteacher and likes to read."

"We have plenty of books here to look at." Orley pointed to one of the shelves across the room. "Maybe there will be something there to your liking."

"Okay, I'll take a look." Lisa began moving in that direction and paused to glance over her shoulder to see if Paul would join her. Instead of following her, he continued to visit with the Amish couple.

Making her way down one of the aisles, Lisa paused to slide her fingertips over the wood grain of a handmade cheese board. She was fascinated with several old trunks with leather handles, a pitted metal oil lantern, some cigar boxes with polished stone inlays, and an intricate thimble collection. She had never seen so many vintage items all in one place and hadn't even viewed everything.

As Lisa approached the bookshelf, the old wooden floorboards creaked beneath her feet. Even the ceilings and walls of the building had a vintage feel about them.

She reached up to pull one of the books off the shelf and noticed a cloth Amish doll with no face. A doll such as this was no longer played with by most Amish children the way it had been many years ago. Lisa had read once that the dolls were left faceless because everyone was alike in God's eyes and that lack of facial features agreed with the Bible's commandment against graven images. She'd also read that antique Amish dolls made for and used by Amish children from the past were highly collectible and could sell for as much as $1,000. However, the newly made faceless dolls found in many tourist shops in Amish country sold for much less.

Lisa had never owned a doll without a face like the one her grandmother had sitting on a straight-backed chair in her sewing room. When Lisa had first come to live with her grandparents, Grandma had let her play with the doll. Although she'd thought it was strange for the cloth doll to have no face, Lisa had found comfort in holding it. Even now, whenever she saw the faceless doll in Grandma's sewing room, Lisa was tempted to pick it up and give it a hug.

She turned her attention back to the book she held and opened it to the copyright page. It had been written in 1952 and was about two young orphaned sisters who had been sent to a boarding school that was owned by a mean woman who treated the children who lived there badly.

Lisa bit the inside of her cheek. *If it weren't for Grandpa and Grandma taking me in, I'd be an orphan too. I'm ever so thankful that they have always been kind and treated me well.*

She put the book back on the shelf and reached for another, but before she could open it to the first page, Lois stepped up to her.

"Have you found any books that interest you?" she asked.

Lisa shook her head. "Not yet, but then I've only looked at one."

"The book you're holding in your hand?"

"No, this is the second one I've pulled off the shelf, but I haven't really looked at it yet." Lisa held the musty-smelling book against her chest.

"I enjoy reading and writing too," Lois said.

"Are you an author?"

Lois's cheeks colored a bit. "Oh, no, nothing like that. I do enjoy writing letters though."

Lisa wasn't sure how to comment, so she merely offered the older woman what she hoped was a pleasant smile.

"Paul mentioned that he's from Sugarcreek. Is that where you live?" Lois questioned.

"Jah."

"Sugarcreek is a lovely town. Sometimes Orley and I go over there just to eat at the big Dutch Valley Restaurant. Oh, and we always enjoy looking at the giant-sized cuckoo clock in Sugarcreek." Lois grinned as she bobbed her head. "The huge timepiece was built in 1972, and every thirty minutes, Bavarian music is played as a three-foot doll-like couple on tracks dance the polka." Lois grinned. "But then, you probably knew all that."

Lisa nodded. *This woman is so outgoing and friendly,* she thought. *I suppose she has to be since being a business owner means greeting people on a regular basis.*

"Have you always lived in Sugarcreek?" Lois asked.

"No, I came there when I was a young girl, still in school. I lived in Indiana before that."

"That's a lovely state too. What prompted your parents to move to Ohio?"

"My parents died in an accident, so I went to live with my grandparents."

"I'm sorry for your loss." Lois placed her hand on Lisa's arm.

Lisa's fingers flexed around the book she held as her gaze bounced from place to place. She felt uncomfortable talking about this, especially with a person she hadn't met until today.

Lisa placed the book back on the shelf. "I've developed a *kopp-pweh,* so I'm going to tell Paul that I'd like to go."

"I'm sorry to hear you have a headache. Perhaps the musty aroma from the old books is the cause." Lois's words were spoken in a soothing tone.

"Jah, maybe so." Lisa hurried back to the place where Paul stood talking to Orley. "I think the smells in here have given me a headache," she said. "Take your time if you want to look around. I will wait for you in the buggy, and don't hurry on my account. I'll be fine."

Wincing as though he felt her pain, Paul said, "That's too bad, but you don't have to wait alone. I don't need to look at anything in the store today, so we can head out right now."

Lisa felt all her tension release. Although the musty-smelling books may have been part of the reason the headache had come on, most likely it came about from being put in a position where she had to mention her parents' deaths. Lisa was glad the conversation had ended before Lois could ask her more questions.

After Paul and Lisa left the store, Lois joined Orley up front to go over some paperwork they hadn't gotten done yet this morning.

"Paul's friend seems like a nice young woman," Orley commented as Lois stepped behind the counter with him. "Too bad they couldn't have stayed longer."

"I agree. Lisa did seem nice enough, but I believe she's a troubled young woman."

Orley tipped his head. "Oh? What brought you to that conclusion?"

"When I asked if she'd always lived in Sugarcreek, she said she used to live in Indiana and that she'd moved to Ohio after her parents died in an accident."

Orley's brows furrowed. "That's a shame. Did she give you any details on how the mishap occurred?"

"No, and before I could ask any more questions, Lisa announced that she had a *koppweh*, which was why she and Paul left our store so quickly." Lois pursed her lips. "The young woman couldn't even maintain eye contact with me when she spoke."

"We need to pray for her."

"Jah, and if Paul brings Lisa into our shop again, I'm going to see if I can get her to open up and share more about her past with me."

"Dear Caroline is at it again, huh?" Orley gave Lois a crooked grin.

She bobbed her head. "Only this kind of mentoring will be in person, not in my newspaper column."

***

Sugarcreek

"How's your koppweh?" Paul asked as they neared Lisa's grandparents' house.

She shrugged her shoulders. "A little better. It's not gone, but at least it's not pounding like it was back at the antique store."

"Glad to hear it. Guess you didn't find any of those musty-smelling books that caused the koppweh to be of much interest to you."

"No, but then I didn't get the chance to look at all of them before the headache came on."

"The next time we go looking for books, maybe we should check out the library or Christian bookstore here in Sugarcreek."

Next time? Is Paul suggesting that we should get together again? Lisa chanced a look at him but then turned her head back to focus on the road. "That'd be nice," she said quietly.

"How about next Saturday? Would you be free to go then?"

"I—I think so, but I'll need to check with Grandma first to see if she will need my help with anything that day."

"Okay. I'll give you a call sometime early next week to see if you'll be free, and if you are, we can talk about what time would work best for both of us to go."

"All right. That sounds good." Lisa didn't want to admit it, not even to herself, but she looked forward to spending time with Paul again. He was easy to talk to and didn't ask her a bunch of questions she'd wasn't willing to answer.

Maybe I could develop a relationship with Paul, Lisa thought as she fiddled with her purse straps. *But only as a friend—nothing else. I definitely have no romantic interest in him, and I'm sure he has none in me either.*

Chapter 16

"What time did you say Paul is supposed to pick you up?" Marlene asked as she and Lisa did the breakfast dishes the following Saturday.

"Ten o'clock." Lisa glanced at the clock on the far wall. "It's only nine thirty, so we have plenty of time to finish the dishes before he arrives."

Marlene nodded. She was glad the young man had taken an interest in her granddaughter. Lisa needed more friends and a social life. And maybe in time, Paul and Lisa would begin courting, which in turn could lead to marriage. That would put Marlene's mind at ease concerning her granddaughter's future. Marlene hated to think of what Lisa's life would be like if she didn't have a husband and family of her own by the time her grandparents died.

I can't worry about it, she told herself. *I just need to pray that things will work out for Lisa according to God's will.* Marlene smiled as she sloshed the sponge over another dirty dish. *And I guess it wouldn't hurt if I invited Paul to join us for a few more meals, although it can't be today, since I have already made other plans for the noon meal.*

Lisa dried the last clean dish and had put it away in the cupboard when she heard Maggie barking by the back door.

"I bet your excitable hund is letting you know that Paul must be here," Grandma said.

"I wouldn't be surprised, although I didn't hear a horse and buggy enter the yard." Lisa opened the door and looked out. No sign of Paul or his horse and buggy.

"No one is there," she said to Grandma. "I think Maggie must have been barking because she needs to go outside."

"You're probably right. She's only been out once this morning."

"I'll go with her." Lisa opened the door wider, and when Maggie bounded out, she followed. She'd barely stepped off the porch when Paul rounded the corner of the house and they nearly collided.

"Wh–where did you come from?" Lisa asked breathlessly as he reached out and clasped her arms.

"I stopped over at the harness shop to talk to your grandpa and left my horse and carriage at the hitching rail there."

Before Lisa could respond, Maggie darted up to Paul and gave a few barks as she pawed at his pant leg.

Lisa clapped her hands. "Maggie, stop it!"

"It's okay." Paul leaned down and patted the dog's head a few times. "How ya doin', girl? Are you happy to see me?"

Woof! Woof! Woof! Maggie's tail swished back and forth in perfect rhythm.

Paul laughed. "I'm glad to see you too."

"I'll take her out to the pen, and then we can go," Lisa said.

"I don't mind taking her while you get whatever you need for the trip to town."

"Danki. I'll meet you by the harness shop."

"I can get Chester and my carriage, so why don't you wait on the porch for me?"

"Okay." Lisa gave Maggie a few pats before returning to the house. On her way across the yard Lisa slowed to watch Paul walk and coax the tail-wagging dog to her pen. *It was nice of him to give me a break from taking care of Maggie so I could go inside to get my things.* Lisa felt a little anxious about going with him again, but maybe spending a few hours with Paul would help relieve some of her tension.

"Is Maggie still outside?" Grandma asked as she squeezed some hand lotion into the palms of her hands and rubbed them together.

"Paul's here, and he's taking her out to the pen while I get my things."

"Well, for goodness' sakes, I didn't even hear his rig come in."

"He stopped by the harness shop to say hello to Grandpa, so he tied his horse to the rail over there." Lisa took her jacket and outer bonnet down from the wall peg where she'd hung them last night and then picked up her purse from one end of the counter. "Paul will be picking me up out front shortly."

"I see." Grandma smiled. "I hope you two have a nice ride to the bookstore and that you'll find some books to your liking. Oh, and you may want to consider going to lunch afterward. Wouldn't that be nice?"

"Maybe, but—"

"I would invite Paul to join us for lunch here when you get back, but your grandpa will be attending an auction today. And I have plans to spend the day with my friend Clara, which will include having lunch together."

"That's fine, Grandma. I hope you and Clara will enjoy your day. If Paul and I don't go out to lunch, I'll fix something for myself after he drops me off." Lisa gave her grandmother a hug and headed for the front door. She didn't have to wait long before Paul pulled up with his horse and buggy.

Lisa couldn't help but notice the way Paul's horse pawed at the ground as though he was eager to go. Paul spoke to Chester in a soothing tone, and the horse calmed right down. She waved at Grandpa when he stepped out of his harness shop, and then Lisa climbed into Paul's carriage. A short time later, they were heading toward town.

It was a lovely fall day—a bit crisp, but the sun had come out, and Lisa felt cozy, wearing her warm jacket. She looked forward to visiting the Gospel Shop Christian Bookstore, because she hadn't been there in quite a while.

When they entered the bookstore a short time later, Paul went to look at the study Bibles, while Lisa browsed the section where Christian fiction was sold. He'd only been looking at the Bibles for a few minutes when one of the store clerks stepped up to him.

"May I help you with something?" she asked.

He shook his head. "I'm just checking to see what you have available."

The clerk smiled. "Okay. I'll be at the register if you decide to make a purchase or have any questions."

Paul continued to peruse the different Bible versions, but undecided, he left that section of the store and moved over to where Lisa stood. "How's it going? Have you found anything to your liking?"

She shrugged her slim shoulders. "There are so many good ones to choose from; it's hard to decide."

"Do you normally buy books or check them out at the library?"

"I do both, and sometimes, if I can part with them, I donate books to the library."

Paul smiled. "That's great. I'm sure they appreciate it."

Lisa nodded.

"Are you lookin' for historical fiction or contemporary?"

"I read both, but I favor historical."

Paul pointed to a book with a covered wagon on the cover. "That one looks interesting."

"Jah, but I already have it. In fact, it's one that I'm keeping to read over and over again."

"That good, huh?"

She bobbed her head. "Would you like to borrow the book? It's filled with a lot of action and gives interesting insight as to what the pioneers dealt with during their trip along the Oregon Trail."

"Sounds like something I'd enjoy reading, all right."

"I'll get the book for you when we get back to my grandparents' home."

Paul hoped he had made a little headway, talking to her on a topic she liked. All he had to do later was to accept the loaned book and give it a good read. *Who knows, maybe I'll get into the story and enjoy it.*

When Lisa smiled at Paul, a deep dimple formed in her right cheek. Now this was the old Lisa he remembered seeing so many times when they were children. Paul hoped he would eventually see more of that joyful side of her in the weeks to come.

~

"Are you hungerich? Would you like to go out someplace to eat lunch?" Paul asked after they'd left the Christian bookstore with their packages.

Lisa hesitated, remembering her grandmother's suggestion that she and Paul should go out for a bite to eat. Of course, Lisa would never be so bold as to suggest going out to lunch with Paul, but since he'd brought it up, she decided to accept his invitation. "That would be nice. Where would you like to eat?"

"How about Dutch Valley Restaurant on Old Route 39? We can order off their menu or choose from the buffet."

"I'm fine with that." Lisa hoped that if anyone they knew saw them together, they wouldn't think she and Paul were on a date, because they certainly were not. They were just two newly acquainted people who'd decided to eat lunch together, and Lisa definitely planned to pay for her own meal.

~

When Lisa and Paul entered the restaurant a short time later, the delicious aroma of roasted chicken mingling with other food items greeted them. The place was busy, but then again, it was the Saturday lunch hour. She wondered if they would be seated at a table out in the middle of the restaurant, near a window, or in a booth. Lisa didn't have a real preference, because at the moment, her stomach felt empty and she couldn't wait to eat.

Her mouth watered, just thinking about the food available on the buffet. She hadn't realized how hungry she was until now.

They waited their turn to be seated and a few minutes later were taken to a booth not far from the all-you-can-eat barn-raising buffet. Soon a waitress came and asked if they wanted to order off the menu or serve themselves from the buffet.

"I'd like the buffet." Paul gestured to Lisa. "How about you?"

She looked up at the server. "I will have the same."

The dark-haired young waitress smiled. "Good choice. The buffet includes the salad bar, and for an extra ninety-nine cents, you can also get a cup of soup."

"I'll be fine without the soup," Lisa said.

Paul gave a nod. "Same here."

"Would either of you care for something other than water to drink?"

"Water's fine for me," Lisa said.

"Think I'll have a glass of iced tea. With a slice of lemon, please," Paul added.

"Feel free to go up to the buffet anytime. While you're doing that, I'll get your drinks, and they will be waiting for you when you've returned to the table."

After the waitress left, Paul suggested that they bow their heads for silent prayer before going to get their food.

Lisa closed her eyes and lowered her head. *Bless this food to the strengthening of our bodies, Lord. And please help me to think of some things to say during our meal so Paul doesn't think I'm bored with his company.*

She opened her eyes and waited for him to do the same. Apparently Paul had more that he needed to pray about than Lisa did, for his eyes were still shut.

After Paul finished praying, they left their seats and got in line at the salad bar. When it was her turn and she'd picked up a plate, Lisa filled it with lettuce, shredded carrots, and several other fresh vegetables. After adding poppy-seed dressing, she sprinkled some sunflower seeds on top and returned to their table to put the plate down. Paul was right behind her, and they both went back to the buffet to get chicken, ham, mashed potatoes, gravy, and cooked green beans. Normally Lisa didn't eat this much for lunch, and she hoped she'd be able to finish everything she had taken. No doubt she wouldn't be eating much for supper this evening.

She set the warm plate down on the table and slid inside the booth. Then Lisa began to work on her salad, enjoying the tasty flavors of the fresh vegetables. Paul started with his salad too, but he soon went in for the chicken. Lisa took her time eating and noticed that he ate through his food at a quick pace. *I wonder if he'll be going back up to the buffet for seconds. Maybe Paul would get his money's worth here today.*

They ate in silence for a while, and then Paul engaged Lisa in conversation about the book she had told him about. "Does the historical book you have at home mention what kind of food the pioneers ate along their journey?" he asked.

"Yes, it does," Lisa replied. She went on to list all the food items she had read about.

When she'd finished what she had to say on the topic, Paul looked over at her and smiled. "I think I wouldn't mind another piece of that chicken. It's mighty good."

"They've got plenty, so why not help yourself?"

"While I'm up there, can I get you anything?" Paul waited by the table.

Lisa shook her head. "Thanks for offering, but I'm fine with what I still have here to finish."

"Okay." He left his plate and headed off to get back in the buffet line.

Paul has a good appetite, but the amount of food he eats sure doesn't show on him, Lisa mused.

A different server came by and picked up Paul's empty plate, then moved on to another table.

Paul returned, holding a new plate with a couple of things on it. "I sure like their chicken, and the rolls are good, especially with some apple butter."

Lisa nodded as she picked through her salad, skipping most of the lettuce and going in for the other vegetables. She'd eaten what she wanted from her warm plate, leaving some of it behind as well.

As they neared the end of their meal, the waitress came and asked if either of them would like a slice of pie.

Lisa shook her head as she placed both hands on her stomach. "I'm too full to even think about dessert."

"I can't eat anything more either," Paul said. "Maybe some other time we can come in just to sample some pie." He looked at Lisa, as though waiting for an answer, but she made no comment.

Lisa flinched at the eerie sound of sirens out on the road. No doubt there had been an accident somewhere nearby. Her hand trembled as she grabbed for her water glass and took a drink. At the moment, all Lisa wanted to do was go home and take a nap. She'd had enough excitement for one day.

"What's wrong?" Paul asked, leaning forward with his elbows on the table. "Are you grank?"

"No, I. . ." She held her hands against her ears. "The sound of those sirens just makes me feel. . ." Her voice trailed off. Lisa didn't want to talk about this right now.

Paul gave her an understanding nod and picked up the check. "I'll pay the bill now, and we can be on our way."

"Oh. . .uh. . .that's all right. . .I can pay for my own meal." Lisa's voice quivered as she struggled to keep her scattered thoughts from taking over.

He shook his head. "Nope. I invited you out for lunch, and I'd planned on paying from the start." Paul looked straight into Lisa's eyes. "Are you okay with that?"

"Jah, all right."

Lisa carried her purse, followed him to the register up front, and waited until he'd paid for their meal. Thankfully she could no longer hear any sirens, so that helped her relax a bit. When they got back to her grandparents', she would get the book she'd promised to loan Paul and politely tell him that she was tired and needed to lie down for a while. Maybe after a nap she would feel better and could put aside the fear she'd felt hearing those sirens. Lisa had never told anyone before, but whenever she heard sirens she remembered that dreadful day when she'd lost her dear family members in the tragic accident that had changed her life forever.

Chapter 17

When Paul entered his uncle's barn, his senses immediately recognized the aroma of nose-tickling straw and sweet-smelling hay. He'd come here to groom his horse before starting work and almost wished he could stay here the rest of the day.

Paul glanced at the wooden ladder leading up to the loft, remembering how he'd enjoyed playing in his father's barn when he was a boy. The sounds of rustling hay, creaking boards, and animal noises had always held an appeal for him. He'd even liked listening from the loft when grain spilled into the horses' troughs and bales of hay thumped to the floor.

Paul stood still for several seconds, taking it all in and thinking about the fun he'd had as a young boy. He could almost hear his father's heavy boots thumping across the floor as he headed into his horse's stall for feeding and grooming.

Moving on, Paul gathered the items to groom his horse from the cabinet where he kept them outside of the stall. The barn could be a place to do some deep thinking about his future. What was the Lord's plan for his life? How would he know for sure? Paul's thoughts went to Lisa and how he'd been doing a lot of praying for her. *I hope that I'll see some change in her life. Lisa is a good person, and I want to see her happy again, the way I remember her when we were children.*

Paul carried a couple of brushes he'd chosen, made his way into

Chester's stall, and was greeted by an eager-sounding whinny. As he stood inside the cubicle with the currycomb in his hand, Paul's thoughts returned to Lisa. Throughout the final weeks of November, he had stopped at the Schrocks' to see Lisa at least once a week. Although they'd eaten their Thanksgiving meals with their own families, Paul had gone over to see Lisa that evening. He'd enjoyed a piece of pumpkin pie and worked on a puzzle with Lisa, while her grandparents dozed in their comfortable living-room chairs, with Maggie stretched out on the floor between them. Who could blame the nice couple? After a day of eating too much good food, Paul figured most people had probably been resting or sleeping it off that evening.

The more time that Paul spent with Lisa, the more he enjoyed her company. It had even been fun to discuss the historical book she had loaned him previously. Although they seemed to be getting along okay, Paul had not yet mentioned that he'd known Lisa when she was a girl. He didn't feel that it was the right time yet. Paul had to be sure he had gained her trust before he opened up a sensitive topic. His worst fear was that if Lisa felt betrayed by Paul's knowing her previously and not saying anything, then she might become distant again and revert to her timid turtle-like shell. Would she back away from their established friendship? Paul wasn't sure how he would even know when he should tell her the truth. It was one more thing to pray about.

Paul's folks had been disappointed that he hadn't come home for Thanksgiving, but he wasn't ready to visit and take the risk of running into Susan or the so-called best friend who had stolen his girl. At this point, his gut told him to stay put in Ohio, where his heart could continue to heal from the disappointment and hurt he'd left in Indiana.

During a phone call on Thanksgiving morning, Paul's mother told him that Susan and Ervin were officially engaged to be married. The ceremony would take place next year in early May. Paul felt certain that he wouldn't be invited to the wedding, which was fine with him, because he had no desire to watch Ervin and Susan become husband and wife. That would be like pouring vinegar on an open wound. Paul remembered all too well how he'd once soaked a piece of tissue in vinegar and put it up his nose to stop a nosebleed. It had worked well, but not without the misery of burning and stinging like fire while the blood coagulated.

Chester nickered and stomped a front hoof, driving Paul's distasteful memory aside.

"Okay, boy, I hear ya. Let's get this job done." Paul pulled the currycomb slowly through the longer hair running down his horse's neck. As he fought against tangles in Chester's mane, his thoughts returned to Lisa again. "I wonder how long I should wait to tell her...."

"You talkin' to yourself?"

Paul's face warmed as he whirled around at the sound of his uncle's voice. "No, I...uh...was just thinking out loud."

Uncle Abe chuckled as he stepped inside the stall. "No need to be embarrassed. I do that sometimes too." He put his hand on Paul's shoulder. "Breakfast is ready, and we need to eat soon so we can go bid a few jobs. Kevin will do some cleaning in the shop while we're gone, and my part-time worker will be off today."

"Okay. I'll put Chester's grooming supplies back where they belong, close up his stall, and be right in to eat."

"All right then. I'll let your aunt know that we'll see you at the table soon."

"I'll hurry so I don't hold things up." Paul glanced at Uncle Abe while brushing a little more with the currycomb.

The older man slowed his steps on the way out and spoke to his horse. "I'll be back to get you ready to go, Cinnamon, so for now, enjoy your breakfast."

When his uncle left the barn, Paul expelled a deep breath. *Sure am glad Uncle Abe didn't ask who I was thinking out loud about. He'd probably make a big deal out of it and begin teasing me, saying that Lisa must be my new girlfriend.*

Lisa had no more than stepped onto the schoolhouse porch when it began to snow. She stood watching the fluffy white snowflakes as they drifted to the ground and quickly covered the grass. For a few seconds she had a mental picture of herself as a young girl, standing next to a fat-looking snowman with a knitted scarf around its neck and a man's straw hat on its head. A young brown-haired boy stood beside Lisa, holding a carrot in his gloved hand.

That's really odd, Lisa thought. *From the time I came to live with Grandpa and Grandma Schrock, I don't remember ever building a snowman in their yard, much less with the help of a boy my mind doesn't recognize. Why did that thought come to mind? Who was the boy with the carrot?*

Lisa felt a feeling of heaviness in her limbs as she struggled to remember. *Could this have occurred before the accident that took my mamm, daed, and grosseldere from me?*

Lisa's pensive thoughts evaporated when a group of five school-children filed into the yard, talking, laughing, and pointing up at the now-swirling snow.

"Teacher, can we build a snowman during recess?" Simon Burkholder asked, joining Lisa on the porch.

"That all depends on if there's enough snow built up on the ground by then," she replied. "It could quit snowing before noon-time, you know."

With a single-minded expression, he gave his head a vigorous shake. "I'm pretty sure it'll still be snowin' out here."

Lisa gave his shoulder a pat. "We'll have to see how it goes, Simon."

"But if it keeps comin' down like it is now, can we build a snowman?"

She smiled at the determined set of the boy's jaw. "Yes, anyone who wants to join in can help build a snowman."

Simon turned toward the others who had come into the yard, cupped his hands around his mouth, and hollered, "Teacher Lisa said we can build a snowman during noon recess."

A chorus of cheers went up, and Lisa couldn't help but smile. Sometimes, like now, she wished she was still a child. *But then,* she reminded herself, *I'd have to live through the pain of losing my family all over again.*

~

Walnut Creek

"Now would ya look at that? Here it is only the first Monday of December, and there's *schnee* comin' down hard out there." Orley pointed out their antique shop's front window.

Lois joined him. "Well, for goodness' sakes. That white stuff sure came out of nowhere. The last two weeks of November were chilly, despite the sunshine we had, but there was no sign of snow until now."

"Well, like it or not, looks like a new weather front's come in, and I kinda hope it sticks around for a while." Orley looked at Lois with a wide grin. "I'm sure lookin' forward to ice-skating and sledding again."

She squeezed his arm. "I'm not one bit surprised. I know how much you enjoy frolicking in the snow."

"Jah." Orley gave his full beard a tug. "I wonder if Jeff Davis will want to join me when our hill at home has enough snow for sledding, like he did last year."

"Don't get your hopes up, Husband. With all the responsibilities at the inn he and Rhonda bought before their baby came, Jeff may be too busy to go traipsing and sliding through the slippery snow with you this winter."

Orley's mouth slackened. He reminded her of a little boy who'd been told he couldn't have a bowl of ice cream before going to bed.

"If Jeff isn't available, I'm sure you can find someone else who'd be willing to go sledding with you—one of our neighbor children perhaps."

Orley's eyes brightened, and he snapped his fingers a couple of times. "I know who I can ask."

Lois tipped her head slightly. "Who would that be?"

"Paul Herschberger. It would be an opportunity for me to spend some one-on-one time with him and talk about his *druwwel.*"

"What problem is that?"

"The one concerning his friend Lisa."

Her brows furrowed. "Is there some trouble between them?"

"Not exactly. Paul wants to help Lisa regain the part of her memory she lost from childhood, back when they knew each other."

Lois's eyes widened. "This is the first time I've heard anything about that. How long ago did Paul share this information with you?"

"Last week he came by the store while you were at the post office picking up letters that had been sent to your Dear Caroline column." Orley cleared his throat a few times. "Paul shared it in confidence with me, but he said it'd be okay if I told you about Lisa's lapse of memory. I didn't think to tell you about it until now."

"Is there anything more you can share with me about the situation?"

"Sure, I'll tell you everything I know."

Lois listened quietly as her husband repeated the things Paul had told him concerning the deaths of Lisa's parents and paternal grandparents, and how she'd come to live with her maternal grandparents in Sugarcreek. Of course, Lisa had already told Lois about her parents' deaths, but Lois didn't want to interrupt Orley or remind of him of what she already knew.

"It must have been very difficult for a young girl to deal with a tragedy like that," Lois said. "I can't begin to imagine how terrible she must have felt."

"You're right—it had to be quite traumatic." Orley moved his head slowly up and down. "Paul also said that Lisa is kind of an introvert with very few friends. He's been working at establishing a friendship with Lisa and wants to tell her that they used to know each other when they were children. But he is waiting for the right time, when he's gained her trust."

"I see." She paused and tapped her chin. "That day he brought Lisa into the shop and I asked what prompted her folks to move to Ohio, Lisa said her parents died and that her grandparents raised her. It wasn't more than a moment later that she developed a headache. Although Lisa said the cause was the musty odor in the shop, I believe otherwise."

"What are you thinking?" Orley's brows lowered.

"I believe from the way she reacted when talking briefly about her past that Lisa has never fully come to grips with it." Lois folded her hands in a prayer-like gesture. "We should definitely keep her and Paul on our prayer list."

"Amen to that."

Their conversation was interrupted when an English couple entered the store and asked if there were any antique tables for sale.

Orley moved away from the window and went to show them where the vintage furniture was located, and Lois walked up to the front register to wait in case the couple decided to purchase something.

She glanced at a plaque hanging on the left of the room that read: God hath said, "I will never leave thee, nor forsake thee." Hebrews 13:5.

Lois closed her eyes briefly. *Heavenly Father, my prayer is that Lisa will know, if she doesn't already, that even though her parents and one set of grandparents are gone, You will never forsake her.*

Sugarcreek

By noon, the ground in the schoolyard was covered with at least two inches of cold, white flakes, and it continued to snow. Excitement ran high when the schoolchildren finished their lunches and hurried to put on their coats, gloves, and boots before running outside. Lisa and Yvonne joined them to watch and supervise.

In no time at all, the children had made numerous footprints, snow angels here and there, and a few snowmen in the yard. Squeals of laughter could be heard as some of the boys chased after a group of girls, with snowballs flying this way and that. The girls gave it right back to the boys, however, and it didn't take long before everyone was drenched with the heavy, wet snow that continued to fall.

Lisa watched as Linda, one of her youngest students, struggled to get up after she'd slipped and fallen. Sharon, an older girl from Yvonne's class, went over to help the crying child get back on her feet.

Lisa smiled as she thought about a saying she'd heard her grandma repeat on several occasions: *"Kindness is like snow: it beautifies everything it falls upon."*

Being kind to others was the way every Christian should act. The ministers in their church district had preached on that topic many times.

Lisa always tried to be kind and patient with her students, even when they became unruly or defiant. Her grandparents had been good role models, and Lisa appreciated the kindness they showed to her, as well as others.

"It's time for the children to go back inside now," Yvonne said, interrupting Lisa's musings. "While they are hanging up their outer belongings to dry, I'll go down to the basement, light the propane stove, and make a big pot of hot chocolate."

"That will be nice. I'll oversee the scholars while you're gone, and once all the younger ones are seated at their desks, I'll send an older student down to help you bring up the hot chocolate and cups for everyone."

Yvonne nodded. "Thank you."

After her friend hung up her outer garments and headed down the steps to the basement, Lisa put her own coat, gloves, and boots away, and then she directed the students to do the same. She hoped the snow would hang around for a few days so that the children could enjoy playing in it again. Truthfully, Lisa looked forward to doing the same. And when she got home this afternoon, she would let her dog out to romp in the snow too. It would give Maggie some exercise that didn't involve chasing the poor cats.

No doubt, Lisa thought, *playing with Maggie in the snow will make me feel like a kid again. And when we come inside, I bet Grandma will fix something warm for me to drink and serve it with some of those peanut butter cookies that she'd begun making before I left for school this morning.*

Although Lisa enjoyed teaching, she had to admit that coming back to the shelter of her grandparents' home would be the best part of her day.

Chapter 18

"I can't believe it's snowing again." Lisa's grandmother peered out the kitchen window, slowly shaking her head. "I thought when it first began snowing three weeks ago that it would have all melted and we wouldn't see any more for a while."

"Unless the weather pattern changes, it appears that we may get a white Christmas this year," Grandpa commented as he picked up the coffeepot and poured himself a second cup of the steaming brew.

The room felt cozy with the warmth and crackle of the wood-burning stove they used for extra heat. Her grandfather would keep it going most of the time during the winter months, and Lisa appreciated the kind gesture. It was nice to come in from the cold and park oneself near the cozy stove to warm up. And it was a good little dryer for all their wet boots they would place by it on chilly days.

"I hope the cold, snowy weather won't keep people from coming out for the students' Christmas program this evening," Lisa spoke up as she carried her breakfast dishes to the sink. "The kinner have worked long and hard on their parts, and they'd be disappointed if we had to cancel or attendance was low."

"I don't think you'll have to worry about that," Grandpa said. "People don't usually stay home because of a little schnee, and the weather report I saw in the paper yesterday made no mention of any severe storms on the horizon."

Lisa released a small sigh of relief. "That is good news." *All I'll need to do before the program this evening is to go over the younger children's parts with them sometime today. Yvonne will do the same with the older students. Hopefully, everything will go smoothly.*

"What a beautiful picture that makes." Grandma pointed out the window. "Look—four cardinals just came to rest on one of the snow-covered trees in our yard."

Grandpa stepped over by them and looked out. "Those are such beautiful *veggel*. And speaking of birds, when I was outside earlier I saw a pair of ducks near the barn where I spilled some corn the other day."

"Really, that's not something you see every day." Grandma pursed her lips as though in thought.

"I know, but it's true. I enjoyed watching them eat every bit off the ground and felt disappointed when the pair flew away."

"If there was a small pond outside, I wonder if those ducks would come around regularly." Lisa stepped over to the window and looked out just as one of the male cardinals flew out of the tree and landed on a nearby feeder. "Those redbirds are sure pretty, *jah*?"

"Most definitely. I can't believe how many birds we have in the yard right now. When it started to snow a few weeks ago we put more feeders out, and now the bird feed is disappearing so quickly."

"That's how it goes," Lisa said. "One bird tells another, and pretty soon a whole flock swoops in, just like those ducks Grandpa saw."

"True, but I don't mind paying the price for birdseed because they're sure fun to watch." Grandpa sipped on his coffee and set it back down on the counter. "I wonder, Marlene, do you think if we had a place to put a water feature in the yard that we could attract some ducks?"

She flapped her hand. "I think you'd be better off just leaving more corn out for them. You could put it in some type of pan, but only this time a little closer to where we could all see them from the house."

Grandpa smiled. "I could give that a try. I've got plenty of corn, so I'll just need a pan to put it in rather than scatter the seed on the ground."

"I'm sure I can find you a good-sized metal container that would be right for the job," Grandma was quick to say. "Maybe we could set the pan near one of the trees within our view while looking out the kitchen window."

"A flower bed farther out in the yard might work." Lisa pointed toward the window.

"Okay, we can try it your way first, and if nothing happens, then we'll put the corn near one of the small trees."

Just then Maggie let out a robust yawn as she stretched and rose up on all fours. Grandpa reached out and gave the dog some attention. She gave a contented grunt and leaned into his fingers as they scratched her back. "You're a good dog, Maggie, and you can be fun to watch too—just as long as you're not chasin' any birds." He shook his head. "They don't like that, and neither do the cats."

Lisa couldn't argue with what her grandfather had said. She enjoyed watching the various kinds of birds that visited their yard, which was why she would scold her dog whenever she bothered them.

Grandma joined Grandpa at the table, where he sat reading the newspaper. "Why are you wearing such a big grin?" she asked, pointing to the newspaper. "Is something funny written in there?"

He gave a nod and snickered. "I'm reading the Dear Caroline column."

"Is that a fact? And what did Caroline say that you think is so humorous?"

"It's not what she said. It's the question one of her readers asked."

"What did she ask?"

"Oh, it wasn't a woman who wrote the letter. It was a man."

Lisa watched in amusement as Grandma's eyes widened and her brows lifted high on her forehead. "I just assumed most of the letters written to Caroline would be written by women. What did the man have to say that made you laugh?"

Grandpa looked back at the newspaper and read in a clear, booming voice: " 'Dear Caroline, my wife fixes tuna fish casserole every Friday night, even though she knows I don't like it. How can I get her to fix something else?—Powerless Husband.'" Grandpa leaned his head back and chuckled. "Can you imagine that?"

"What—that he doesn't care for tuna fish? Is that what you think is so funny?"

Pulled unexpectedly into their conversation, Lisa waited to hear what her grandpa would say. He quickly responded to Grandma's question.

"I laughed because I think it's *lecherich* that this poor man would have to write a letter to a woman he doesn't even know with such an *eefeldich* question."

"It's not ridiculous, Jerry, and I don't think it's a silly question." Grandma crossed her arms as her chin jutted out.

Holding her hands behind her back, Lisa clenched her fingers into the palms of her hands. *Oh, boy. . . I hope they don't get into a heated argument over this—especially since it's not even important.*

Grandma looked over at Lisa with a hopeful expression. "What do you think? Would you agree that the man asked Caroline a silly question?"

"Please don't pull me into this or ask me to take sides. Don't you think you and Grandpa should just agree to disagree?"

Lowering her arms, Grandma shrugged. "Maybe, but not till he's heard the rest of what I want to say."

Grandpa looked at her and crossed his arms in the same manner she had a few moments ago. "By all means, please give us the rest of your opinion."

Grandma pulled her shoulders back and kept her back very straight. "I can understand fully why the man wrote the letter. He was clearly frustrated because his fraa didn't seem to care that he didn't like tuna and wouldn't fix him something else to eat on Friday nights."

"Be that as it may, would you like to know what Caroline said in response to his letter?"

"Jah, sure."

Grandpa picked up the newspaper and held it close to his face.

" 'Dear Powerless Husband: If you have asked nicely, and your wife won't fix you something other than tuna casserole on Friday evenings, why don't you offer to make supper or even take her out to a restaurant to eat? That should take care of the problem.'" Grandpa put down the newspaper and looked at Grandma with a smug expression. "Now wasn't that a good answer?"

Her lips formed a smile as she turned her hands palms up.

Before either of them could say anything more on the subject, Lisa grabbed her outer garments, along with her lunch pail and purse, and moved toward the back door. "I need to go so I won't be late to the schoolhouse this morning. I'll see you both when I get home." She turned back toward them and smiled. "I hope you two will have a nice day." Before either of her grandparents could respond, Lisa slipped quietly out the door. Although Lisa felt sure that her grandparents weren't angry with each other, it bothered her to hear them quarrel—especially over something as silly as some dissatisfied man's letter to Dear Caroline. *But I suppose all married couples disagree sometimes,* she told herself. *I'm just glad Grandma and Grandpa don't do it all the time, like that man and wife who used to live in the house closest to us. It seemed like every time I was outside and they were in their yard I could hear them arguing about something or other.*

Lisa had a momentary flashback and remembered seeing her parents in the kitchen the morning of the accident. They stood by the kitchen sink with their arms around each other, and a few seconds after their driver pulled into the yard and honked his horn, Lisa's father pulled her mother into his arms and gave her a kiss. Lisa was too young to be embarrassed by it then, but at the moment her face felt like it was on fire. She stepped into the barn, closed the door, and leaned against the closest wall. It always upset her when she had any kind of a flashback like that, but what really bothered Lisa was the fact that her early memories never came back. She closed her eyes and sucked in a deep breath. *Why can't I remember anything before the day of the tragic accident? Is there some reason I've blocked it all out?* Lisa had thought about discussing the situation with one of her grandparents, but the idea of trying to talk about it was too upsetting. So for now at least, Lisa would keep her thoughts and concerns to herself.

⁓

Feeling the need for a short break, and with Uncle Abe's permission, Paul stood near the shop window and watched the snow that seemed to be coming down harder all the time. Hopefully it would slow down before tonight.

"Are you looking forward to seeing Danny do his part in the Christmas program at the schoolhouse this evening?" Paul asked his uncle, who was sanding a nearly finished piece of furniture for an English customer.

Uncle Abe bobbed his head. "I think my youngest boy's a bit naerfich about playing the part of Joseph, though."

"Ah, he has nothin' to be nervous about," Kevin hollered from across the room where he'd been sweeping up some sawdust. "I played the part of Mary's husband once when I was still attending school, and it was as easy as brushin' my teeth." Paul's lanky-looking cousin cocked his blond head to one side. "All I had to do was sit there starin' at the doll that represented the baby Jesus lying in a manger. It was the easiest part in the whole play." Kevin made a kind of snorting sound. "Wanna know what I think, Daed?"

"What's that?" Uncle Abe asked.

"My little bruder worries too much. He'll do fine tonight, and then afterward, I will go right up to him and say, 'See, I told ya so.'"

Uncle Abe stopped what he was doing and pointed at Kevin. "You'd best get back to work on that heap of sawdust and quit making plans to tease your brother."

The teenage boy did as he'd been told, and Paul moved away from the window to resume work on the table leg he had previously been sanding. He looked forward to going to the program tonight and liked the fact that the backdrop of this weather made it feel more like Christmas. It would be fun to watch the kids recite poems, sing songs, and act out the story of baby Jesus being placed in a manger. Paul was also eager to see Lisa in her element as a teacher. *And maybe,* he told himself, *if her grandparents don't mind, I'll ask if I can give her a ride home after the festivities. It'll give us a chance to talk, and if I feel the time is right, I may even surprise Lisa with the fact that I knew her when she was a young girl.*

"All right, boys and girls, we're going to run through everyone's part for the Christmas program one more time before we go outside for our afternoon recess." Yvonne looked over at Lisa. "Why don't you start with the younger ones, since that's how we'll be doing it this evening? While your children practice, I'll sit with my students and watch."

"That's good," Lisa said. "You can let us know if anyone is talking too fast or not loud enough to be heard from the back of the room."

"Yes, and you and your pupils can do the same for us when it's our turn to rehearse." Yvonne took a seat near the back of the room while Lisa got her students in position to say or sing their parts.

Things went along fairly well until Lisa corrected Nancy and Nathan Burkholder after they'd said each other's parts instead of their own. When Lisa asked them to start over, Nancy began to sob. She cried so hard that Lisa wasn't sure she could get her to stop.

"It's okay. It was just an error. We all make mistakes sometimes." Lisa gently patted the girl's back. "Why don't you and Nathan take your seats for now while the others practice their lines? I'll give you an opportunity to try again later."

With her head dipped down, Nancy sniffled all the way back to her desk. Although Nathan didn't cry, his cheeks turned red as he mumbled something under his breath about his sister wanting his part instead of hers. Then the boy shuffled back to his seat and sat down with his arms folded.

Lisa pressed her lips tightly together. She hoped things would go better at the program tonight and that all the children would be able to remember their lines and behave appropriately. Otherwise, there would be some embarrassed parents and other family members in the audience. Lisa wouldn't be nearly as upset if any of her students messed up as she would be if they gave in to tears or refused to take part in the program.

Two more students said their parts, and Yvonne asked them to speak a little louder. Lisa feared the young girls might cry like Nancy had, but they kept their chins up and spoke their lines loud and clear this time.

As Melanie Beachy stepped forward to take her turn at reciting a Christmas poem, a disturbing memory flashed unexpectedly into Lisa's head. She saw herself as a little girl, standing in front of a roomful of people—many of whom she didn't recognize. But there, near the back, sat her mother and father wearing eager expressions as they waited for her to speak.

"Lisa," her teacher coached, "please share your Christmas poem with us."

Lisa opened her mouth, but the only thing that came out was a pathetic-sounding little squeak. Then, with tears rolling down her hot cheeks, she made a dash for her seat, put her head on the desk, and sobbed.

"Teacher, did I do okay?"

Lisa's mind snapped back to the present. She felt a bit shaken from having remembered something from her past that she'd obviously forgotten, especially when it had involved seeing her parents. *At least I remembered something, even if it did make me feel sad. Could it be that after all these years, I'm starting to get my memory back?*

"Teacher, did I do okay?" Melanie repeated.

"Umm. . .would you mind saying your poem once more?"

Melanie scrunched up her face. "Did I mess up? Is that why I hafta say it again?"

"I'm sure you did fine, but I didn't hear all of the poem, so would you please say it one more time for me?"

"Okay." The young, blue-eyed girl recited the poem in a clear voice, without missing a single line.

"Thank you, Melanie. Your poem was well done."

The child looked up at Lisa and grinned before skipping back to her desk.

As the rest of her students said their lines and sang a song together, Lisa made sure to keep her focus on them and push all thoughts of her scattering past to the back of her mind. If any more memories from long ago found their way into her head, Lisa hoped it would be when she had no distractions and could take the time to sit, think, and let it all sink in.

Lisa really wanted to remember more from her past—just not today, and especially not tonight during the play. She wanted everything to go perfectly and for everyone in attendance to enjoy themselves.

Chapter 19

"This is sure good stew," Paul said as he sat at the supper table with his aunt, his uncle, and their two boys.

Aunt Emma smiled and passed Paul the basket of buttermilk biscuits. "I'm glad you like it. I figured with it being so cold outside, some hot, hearty stew would be a good way to warm our insides before we head to the schoolhouse for the program." She looked over at Danny, who sat beside her, and nudged his arm. "You've barely touched your supper. Aren't you hungry this evening?"

The boy shook his head. "I'm too naerfich to think about food. I was hopin' I'd come down with a bad cold or somethin' so I wouldn't have to go to the Christmas program and do my part."

She gave Danny's shoulder a few pats. "There's no reason to be nervous, Son. You'll do a fine job playing Joseph."

"But what if I mess up and do somethin' stupid?"

"I don't see how you could mess up just sitting in a chair," Kevin interjected. "Unless you fall off it or miss the chair completely when you go to sit down." He chuckled behind his hand.

"It's not funny, and stop teasing your bruder," Uncle Abe spoke up. "Danny needs our encouragement right now and should not be teased."

"Sorry," Kevin mumbled around a piece of biscuit he'd put into his mouth.

Danny sat staring at his bowl of stew.

The tension in the room faded as Uncle Abe and Aunt Emma changed the topic of conversation to fixing the worn-out lock on the back door.

Paul couldn't help feeling sorry for his young cousin. He remembered how it felt when he was a boy and his brothers, Harley, Glen, Mark, and Amos, used to tease him. Sometimes he would think of something to say back to them. Other times Paul would try to ignore their catty comments. That always worked better than talking back or trying to be one up on the pesky brothers. Paul had learned a long time ago that it was better to keep quiet about some things than make a fuss.

Danny remained quiet, but he finally ate some stew and nibbled on his biscuit. The snow fell outside and could be seen through the kitchen window while they all ate their satisfying meal.

Paul was eager for this evening and had looked forward to it all day. Just seeing Lisa tonight would make it worth going. He smiled and envisioned her accepting his invitation to ride home with him after the program. *I hope she says yes.*

Paul buttered one of his aunt's flaky biscuits then enjoyed every tasty, moist morsel as he ate it. Following that, he finished his stew and took a drink of water. Paul had made up his mind that if he had the chance to be alone with Lisa tonight, he would definitely tell her the truth. The secret he'd been keeping weighed heavily on his heart, and no matter how she reacted, it would feel good to finally get the words out and wait for what he hoped would be a positive reaction.

Walnut Creek

"That was one tasty *reeschde*." Orley patted his stomach a few times. "It was so good, I'm tempted to help myself to a few more pieces."

Lois pointed at him and shook her finger. "You've already had several pieces of roast beef, and if you're not careful you'll be gaining more weight."

His mouth slackened as he gave his belly another thump. "Are you saying I'm *fett*?"

"You're not fat yet, but with the hypothyroid situation, you could become fat if you don't watch your calorie intake."

"I don't have time for calorie countin'." His brows furrowed. "If I'm gonna count anything, I'd like it to be something like money, old marbles, vintage buttons, sheep in my sleep, or. . ."

She held up her hand. "Okay, I get what you're saying, Orley, but have you forgotten what the dokder said about the importance of making good food choices and not overeating?"

"I remember." *How could I forget when you remind me so often?*

"If you're still hungerich, why don't you have a few of these?" Lois gestured to the dish of cut-up veggies in the center of the table.

He wrinkled his nose. "No thanks. I already had some, and I'm full enough."

She shrugged in response.

Orley loved his wife dearly, but she worried too much about his health, and he felt frustrated when she pestered him about it. Didn't Lois understand that he was a grown man and could think for himself?

"What do you plan to do after we finish eating?" Orley asked, seeking a safer topic.

"I have some letters that were sent to the newspaper for my Dear Caroline column that need to be answered."

"Oh, I see. I'd kinda hoped we could make a batch of popcorn and work on a puzzle together."

Her lower lip pulled in. "I don't know, Orley. You know how it goes when we begin working on a puzzle. We get so involved and often sit there for hours."

"How about if we set a timer? That way you can work on the puzzle for as long as you like, and there will still be time for you to answer some of those Dear Caroline letters."

"Okay, but only for an hour or so."

He smiled and reached for a few carrot sticks—just to make his wife happy. Then Orley pushed back his chair, picked up as many empty dishes as he could carry, and made his way across the room. After placing them in the sink and running warm soapy water over them, he looked out the window. It had quit snowing, but beneath the white glow of the moon he saw that their yard was covered in at least two feet of fresh snow. It was strange how the moonlight shining down from the sky to the ground caused the snow to look as though it had taken on a bluish hue. Orley had heard once that during the winter months, moonlight often appeared stronger because of the snow's ability to reflect it.

Orley went to the utility room and opened the back door. He shivered when a blast of cold air hit him in the face with the fierceness of a blizzard wind.

"What are you doing, Orley? Is the back door open?" Lois called from the kitchen. "I can feel some cold air seeping in that wasn't here before."

Orley quickly shut the door and went back to the kitchen. "I opened the door so I could see what the weather is like. It's mighty cold and windy, which means the roads could be icy tonight."

"We have nothing to worry about because we're not going anywhere this evening."

Orley nodded. "But others will be out traveling for schoolhouse Christmas programs and other things taking place. Several of our customers who came into the store today mentioned that they have children or grandchildren involved in plays this evening. And not all of them were from Walnut Creek."

"Jah, the week before Christmas is usually a busy time for Amish schoolhouse programs. Which is why we should remember to pray for everyone's safety." Lois folded her hands, holding them close to her chest, as she often did when preparing to pray.

Orley stood near the kitchen door and bowed his head to join her in prayer. *Lord, please be with those who are traveling on this cold winter-like night, and guide them safely to their destinations.*

Lisa watched with satisfaction as Nathan and Nancy said their lines perfectly during their part in the Christmas program. *No mess-up this time,* she told herself. *I'm glad they both did so well and remembered the correct words for their parts.*

When each of the younger pupils had taken a turn, all the children from the class Lisa taught sang a song. Although they were immature compared to the older students, Lisa was pleased with how well these young voices sounded as they sang each verse from "Away in a Manger."

When the song ended, Lisa and her students took a seat to watch the older pupils perform.

Everyone from Yvonne's class did a good job, including Danny, playing the part of Joseph. Originally, he was supposed to stand beside the chair where Barbara Miller, who played Mary, sat looking down at the doll representing the baby Jesus in the manger. But when Danny had told Yvonne that he'd be too nervous to stand and might cave in, she'd agreed to let him sit in a chair next to Barbara. The boys playing shepherds and the girls who had angel parts also did well as they'd gathered around Mary, Joseph, and the baby to sing "Silent Night."

In Lisa's head she sang each of the meaningful verses with her sweet students. During a moment like this, all the hard work of cleaning, decorating, and practicing for the program was well worth it. She felt sure that the parents and other family members of the students who had come out tonight appreciated the effort their children, as well as the teachers, had put into this special performance.

Lisa fanned her face with the piece of paper she held in case she'd needed to coach any of her students with their lines. Despite the cold weather outside, with nearly one hundred people inside the schoolhouse, the room had become quite warm and stuffy.

Better too warm than too cold, she thought. *It wouldn't be good for the scholars to be shivering as they said their parts.*

After the last song had been sung and the program was officially over, refreshments were served in the basement. Most of the children had gifts for their teacher or other students in their class, so the excitement ran high during this special time.

Her pupils with their families sat at one of the rows of tables to eat and visit with others. One long table off to the side had been filled with an abundance of cookies and cakes. Each of the desserts had been furnished by many of the women who'd come for the program this evening. The table next to it had a couple of clear punch bowls filled with bright red sparkling juice and cups ready for thirsty guests. The room hummed with conversations going on about upcoming plans for the Christmas holiday. The smiles on the children's faces warmed Lisa's heart. *It was a lot of work in the beginning, but it was worth it in the end,* she decided.

Lisa finished drinking a glass of fruit punch and had tossed the paper cup into the trash can when she saw Paul heading her way. He carried a plate with him, as well as a cup of the punch.

"I see you found the goodies." Lisa gestured to his plate.

"Jah, and there's sure plenty to choose from."

"I agree."

"That was a great program," he said, stepping closer. "Your students did very well, and so did Yvonne's."

She smiled. "The way things went during practice earlier today, I wasn't too sure how it would go this evening."

"That's how it usually goes. I remember during one of the Christmas programs I was involved in when I was a boy. . ." Paul's voice trailed off as he sat down at the closest table.

"What were you going to say?" She sat beside him.

"It wasn't really important. I was just thinking about a time when I forgot my lines and my brothers razzed me about it all the way home." Paul nibbled on a jelly-filled cupcake. "Say, I was wondering if it would be all right if I take you home when you're ready to go."

Lisa answered with no hesitation. "I'd like that, Paul. I'll just need to let my grandparents know. I'm sure they won't mind, because it will give them the opportunity to leave now if they want to, without having to wait on me."

"Great. Just let me know whenever you're ready to go."

"I'll need to help Yvonne clean up, so it could be a while yet."

"No problem. I'll help with the cleanup too."

"That's kind of you. We'll appreciate the extra pair of hands."

Paul finished eating the food on his plate, drank all the punch in his cup, and put the paper products in the trash can.

By the time Paul and Lisa got into his carriage, it had started to snow quite heavily again. He'd turned on the buggy's lights and got back out to clean off the windshield with a scraper. Paul also let Lisa know that a folded blanket lay behind them if she wanted more warmth. Because of scraping off the snow, he now had a good layer of flakes on his coat.

"Look at you," Lisa commented. "It is really coming down hard."

"Jah, and Chester's hair is turning white too. It's becoming a winter wonderland out there." He brushed off most of the snow before closing the door and getting the horse moving.

Paul would need to guide Chester at a slower pace than normal as he watched out for any vehicles on the road. The last thing he needed was a collision between a car or truck and his horse and buggy.

It wasn't long before they were on their way to Lisa's grandparents' place. Paul got his horse going at a steady pace and kept his focus on the road ahead. At least they didn't have too far to travel, but as cold as it was, it would be nice to stop in to warm up before he headed home for the evening, so he hoped Lisa would invite him into her grandparents' house when they arrived.

It's nice being with Lisa, and I hope she enjoys being with me. I wonder if she'd be available to go somewhere with me tomorrow eve-ning. Paul kept a good hold on the reins as he continued to think about the young woman sitting beside him.

Her sweet voice broke into his thoughts. "This is sure some weather we've been having. Just when we think the snow might let up, it starts up again."

"Jah. From the looks of it, my guess is that we're heading into what will probably be a pretty bad winter."

"Oh, I hope not. If it should get too bad, school might be canceled for several days, like it was two years ago during the first week of January. But of course, you weren't here for that," Lisa added.

No, but I wish I had been. If I'd been living here instead of Indiana, I would have never gotten involved with Susan and ended up getting hurt when she dropped me for Ervin.

Paul gripped the reins tighter as a car went past, going faster than he thought it should have, considering the ice and snow on the road. Fortunately, the vehicle stayed in its own lane, and Chester did well too.

I wonder if I should tell Lisa what's on my mind now or wait until we get to her grandparents' house to make my confession.

Paul had made up his mind that it was now time to say something when he saw a car parked along the side of the road with its flashers on. Thinking the driver might be having some sort of problem, he guided Chester over and stopped the carriage. In the headlights of the car, he saw a dog lying by the side of the road. A feeling of dread coursed through Paul's body when he heard Lisa scream, "Oh, no, it's Maggie! I don't know what she was doing out on the road, but she must have been hit by that car!"

Chapter 20

The joy of the evening had been completely wiped out as Lisa got down from Paul's carriage with tears streaming down her face. Unmindful of the cold and icy snow, she dropped to her knees beside Maggie.

"Is she alive?" Paul asked.

"I—I don't know." Lisa, barely aware that Paul had gotten out too and stood beside her holding Chester's bridle, could hardly speak around the burning constriction in her throat. She feared that her dog was in fact dead but couldn't say the words out loud. The tears escaped as Lisa remained by Maggie's lifeless-looking body. The overwhelming scene blurred her vision, and she wiped her eyes with the end of the jacket sleeve, trying to get a better view. *My poor Maggie. She looks so helpless.* Lisa looked up at her friend, hoping for any support from him.

Paul leaned closer to Maggie, and after a few seconds passed, he looked at Lisa. "The dog's right front leg is bleeding pretty badly, and there's a big gash on her head. However, she appears to be breathing. We need to get her some help right away, though."

All Lisa could do was nod in response.

The car that appeared to have been involved in the incident was still there with its flashers running. The woman behind the wheel opened the door and got out.

"Are you all right?" Paul asked.

"I—I'm fine." The woman's widened eyes were turned on Maggie. "Do either of you know the owner of this dog?"

Paul's voice sounded so somber as he pointed at Lisa. "It's her dog."

The woman stepped closer. "I'm so sorry. I didn't mean to hit your dog. As I'm sure you realize, the roads are icy, and I lost control of the car. I didn't even see the dog until it was too late." She paused for a breath. "I guess it must have been walking on the shoulder of the road, and when my car slid that way. . ." Her voice faltered, and Lisa knew that the young English woman was close to tears.

"My cousin Brent is a vet, and his clinic isn't too far from here. I'll call his emergency number right now and see if he can meet us at the clinic."

Lisa nodded slowly. She appreciated the woman's offer, but something deep inside told her that Maggie's injuries might be too bad and nothing could be done to save her.

Just like my mother and father, she thought. *The doctors couldn't save them or my Grandpa and Grandma Miller. Why does everyone I love have to die? Doesn't God care about me at all?*

Paul got a blanket from his buggy and wrapped Maggie in it. She opened her eyes for a bit but made no effort to get up. No doubt she was not able to do so.

With every fiber of her being, Lisa wanted to help her dog. She glanced at the woman, now talking on her phone. *I sure hope she can reach her cousin and that he'll be available to take care of Maggie.*

When the woman, who'd introduced herself as Judy, got off her cell phone, she said her cousin had agreed to meet them at the clinic. "I'll drive you and your dog there." She touched Lisa's shoulder as she looked at her with eyebrows drawn together in obvious concern.

Lisa was relieved that Judy had reached the veterinarian and he'd be meeting them soon. She got into the back of Judy's car, and Paul placed Maggie, securely wrapped in the blanket, on the seat next to her.

Lisa slid closer and put Maggie's head in her lap. "Please don't die, girl," she murmured as more tears fell. "We're gonna get you some help real soon."

"I'll go to your grandparents' house and tell them what's happened," Paul said. "Then I will meet you at the vet's office."

All Lisa could do was manage a brief nod. Her thoughts were fully on Maggie, and she barely heard Paul ask Judy for directions to the clinic.

Lisa sat in the back seat of Judy's car, gently stroking Maggie's head. Although it had quit snowing, the roads were slick, and she worried that the vehicle might slide off the road again.

Maggie gave a pathetic whimper and made an attempt to lift her head.

"Stay still, girl. We're going to get the help that you need." Tears seeped out of Lisa's eyes and splashed onto her cheeks. "I'm so sorry, Maggie. I should have made sure the door latch on your pen was fastened securely. If you don't make it, I'll be at fault."

"We'll be there soon," Judy called over her shoulder. "My cousin's clinic is about a mile up ahead."

With the dog becoming more active, it was apparent that the shock had begun to wear off. Also, the wounds poor Maggie had would hurt and make her uncomfortable.

Lisa hoped they would get there in time. Maggie had begun panting, and Lisa felt the dog's saliva on her hands. She also detected something warm, which she assumed was blood from the wound on Maggie's head.

"Don't die, Maggie. Please don't die," Lisa repeated once more as she squeezed her eyes shut. *Dear Lord, please don't let my dog die. I love her so much.*

When Paul knocked on the Schrocks' front door, he was greeted by Lisa's grandmother, holding a battery-operated light in her hand. She smiled then looked past him. "Where's Lisa?"

"She's at the veterinarian clinic with her hund."

Marlene leaned against the doorjamb, as though needing it for support. "Has Maggie been hurt?"

"Jah, she was hit by a car." Paul paused when he heard Marlene's sharp intake of breath.

"Come inside where it's warm and tell us about it."

Paul brushed the snow off his jacket and stomped his feet on the doormat. When he entered the house, he appreciated the warmth it afforded.

"Jerry's in the living room. Let's go in there, and you can give us both the details. We've been concerned ever since we got home and discovered that Maggie was not in her pen."

Paul followed Marlene into the living room where a nice, cozy fire burned in the fireplace, sending plenty of warmth into the room.

Jerry got up from his chair and shook Paul's hand. "I wasn't eavesdropping, but I heard your conversation with my fraa from in here." His brows knitted together. "How badly has Maggie been hurt?"

"We won't know until the vet examines her."

When Marlene suggested that Paul remove his coat and take a seat, he did as she said. Then he cleared his throat and proceeded to give them the details of what all had occurred.

Marlene wiped a few tears from her eyes, and Jerry rubbed the bridge of his nose. "I don't understand how Maggie got out of her pen. I saw Lisa go out there to put the dog in when I was getting my horse and buggy ready to take us to the schoolhouse this evening."

"Maybe she was in a hurry and just thought she had the latch on the door secured," Marlene said. "With everything there was to do because of the program, Lisa mentioned during supper that she'd had a lot on her mind all day."

"I can only imagine." Paul glanced toward the door. "I'd better get going. I'm supposed to meet Lisa at the veterinarian clinic. I'll bring her home as soon as we find out how badly Maggie was hurt and we know what will need to be done for the dog." He looked at Jerry and gave a slow shake of his head. "I hate to say this, but things don't look good for Lisa's hund. Her breathing was shallow, and there was a lot of blood seeping from her wounds."

Marlene stood up from her chair and went to stand in front of Jerry. "I think you and I should go too, because if Maggie doesn't make it, Lisa is going to need all of us there to offer our support."

"You're right," he agreed. "I'll get our outer garments right now."

As Lisa waited in the reception area of the clinic, it was hard not to give in to negative thoughts and despair. Judy sat in the chair next to her and tried to make conversation, but it was all Lisa could do to respond. She looked up at the electric clock on the wall, watching its second hand move steadily over the numbers. Lisa closed her eyes, trying to refocus her thoughts. *My grandparents must know by now what has happened since Paul said he'd go by there to tell them. It would be nice if they decided to come to the clinic with Paul. I'd really like to have them here with me.*

The time dragged on while Lisa waited for information on Maggie's condition. Any noise from the back of the clinic made Lisa look in that direction. Patience was the key right now, but she struggled to hold herself together. Lisa wished she could barge into that examining room and be with Maggie right now. But the doctor had asked her to wait out here and said he would let her know the extent of Maggie's injuries as soon as possible.

Minutes later, a car pulled into the lot, and soon a woman came into the clinic. She removed her coat right away and headed to the room where the doctor had gone.

Judy cleared her throat. "That was one of the doctor's assistants. He must have called her and asked if she could help out."

While Lisa appreciated Judy waiting with her, she didn't want to talk right now. Apparently the young woman must have figured that out, because she picked up one of the magazines lying on a small table nearby and began thumbing through the pages.

Soon after they'd arrived, Lisa had told Judy that she didn't have to stay with her because Paul would be coming here after he'd stopped by her grandparents' house and told them what had happened. But Judy had insisted, saying she wouldn't feel right about leaving and wanted to find out for herself how the dog was doing.

In an effort to keep her mind occupied, Lisa focused on the different things she saw in the reception area. The floor had been covered with blue-gray tile, which went well with the gray walls and light blue chairs. Across the room, several pet supplies had been displayed, consisting of shampoos, leashes, collars, toys, vitamins, and both nail and hair clippers that were all for sale. Looking on the other side of the room, Lisa noticed several posters showing different breeds of dogs and cats had been tacked to the walls.

Lisa tipped her head when she heard muffled voices behind the closed door of the examining room, followed by what sounded like water pouring into a sink. She wished she could be in there with Maggie right now, but it was probably for the best that she'd been asked to remain here. If Maggie had whimpered when the vet examined her, it would have been like a stab to Lisa's heart. She hoped her poor dog would be given something for the pain.

Lisa's nose twitched at the distinct odor of disinfectant, but at least that was better than the smell of blood and wet fur that had filled her senses on the ride to the clinic.

When the front door opened and Paul, along with her grandparents, stepped in, Lisa felt relieved. Grandma came toward her with open arms, and Lisa quickly stood and rushed into them, struggling not to sob.

"How is Maggie?" Grandpa asked in a tone of deep concern. "Is she going to be okay?"

"I—I don't know yet. The doctor and his assistant are still in with her, and I haven't been told a thing." Lisa gestured to the closed door of the examining room.

Paul crossed over to Lisa. "You look *mied*. This has been a difficult thing for you to be faced with tonight."

All Lisa could manage was a nod. Admittedly, she was tired, but her throat was swollen, and it felt like she'd swallowed a wad of cotton. How could such a wonderful evening have turned out so badly?

Everyone found a seat, but they'd only been sitting a short time when the veterinarian came out of the examining room and walked over to Lisa.

"Your dog has some head injuries that will require stitches, plus her right front leg is severely damaged." He paused for a few seconds, and his voice deepened as he spoke his next words. "I'm sorry to have to tell you this, Lisa, but your dog's leg needs to come off."

The doctor's words rang in Lisa's ears like a clanging bell as she sat there, trembling, unable to form any words.

"But she will live, won't she?" The question came from Lisa's grandmother.

"The dog has a good chance of survival, but only if the leg is amputated."

"Will it be expensive?" Judy questioned.

"I can't quote you an exact price at the moment, but it will likely add up to several thousand dollars."

The young woman released a heavy sigh. "Since I'm the one who hit the dog, I feel obligated to pay for the operation, but I don't have that kind of money. All I'd be able to contribute would be a few hundred dollars."

"Is surgery the only option?" Grandpa asked.

"Yes," the doctor replied. "It's either that or put the dog down. She won't make it without proper treatment."

"No, that's not an option!" Lisa cried. "I'll find some way to pay for it." A fresh set of tears streamed down her hot face. *I'm to blame for Maggie's injuries since I was the one who had put her in the pen before we left for the schoolhouse's Christmas program.*

"Don't worry." Grandma gave Lisa a hug. "We'll help with the expenses." She looked at Grandpa. "Right, Jerry?"

"Jah," he said with a firm nod. "We will do whatever we can."

"Same here," Paul interjected. "Maggie's a good dog, and she's worth saving."

Although greatly distressed about her dog's situation, Lisa felt a little better knowing that if Maggie had the surgery, she would likely live. But she couldn't imagine how the poor dog could possibly manage to walk on three legs instead of four. Lisa bit down on her bottom lip until she tasted blood. *My poor Maggie will never be the same.*

Chapter 21

When Paul left the Schrocks' home at two thirty the next morning, he felt a sick feeling in the pit of his stomach. It had been hard enough to see poor Maggie's injuries and think about the pain she must be in, but observing Lisa's reaction to it had really gotten to him.

I wish there was something I could have said or done to make her feel better, Paul thought. The fear he'd seen on Lisa's face when she'd signed the papers giving the veterinarian permission to operate on Maggie had been so obvious—especially after the doctor had explained the risks that went with the surgery and talked about any complications that might arise.

Paul smiled as the buggy rolled along. At the clinic, he'd seen the full extent of the love Jerry and Marlene felt for their granddaughter. They'd spoken of the need to be with Lisa no matter what the outcome would be for her dog and had offered to help with the expense of Maggie's surgery. When Lisa's mother and father died, despite their own grief, this older couple had taken on the role of being her parents in such a heartfelt way.

Maggie's surgical procedure had taken nearly three hours, and Paul thought about how, in addition to fatigue setting in, everyone seemed to have been on edge as they'd struggled to make conversation. The clock on the wall in the waiting room had showed that it was 1:00 a.m. by the time Paul, Lisa, and her grandparents left the clinic, and then they had nearly another hour to get back to the Schrocks' house. Paul had stayed for a short time, and now he had another half hour until he arrived at his aunt and uncle's place. Fortunately because it was Saturday, Paul didn't have to work today, so he could go to bed as soon as he got home and get some much-needed sleep.

Paul took it easy with Chester on the icy roads, and after arriving home, he didn't waste any time putting his horse and buggy away.

Using his flashlight, he made his way to the house and unlocked the back door. Upon entering the dark kitchen, he found the battery-operated light on the counter and clicked it on so he could see the room better. Certain that everyone had gone to bed, Paul quietly removed his coat and boots and put them in the laundry room. He was about to head upstairs when he realized how thirsty he felt. Paul got a glass down from the cupboard and filled it with cool water from the sink. After downing the whole thing, he realized that he hadn't drunk anything since the fruit punch he'd had at the schoolhouse.

He set the glass in the sink and shut off the light. With only the light from his flashlight, Paul headed through the familiar dark spaces to the upstairs.

Once in his room and after getting ready for bed, his mind played through the events of the evening. What a nice time he'd had at the schoolhouse seeing Lisa with the children and observing how attentive she'd been with them. After the program Paul enjoyed getting to talk to her as he'd helped with the cleanup. On the ride to her grandparents' home, things had been going so well until they'd come upon the scene of the accident. Paul was glad he hadn't said anything to Lisa about having known her before. For now, the topic of their childhood friendship was better left unsaid. She'd been upset enough about Maggie and didn't need anything else to feel anxious about. Paul would wait until her dog's injuries were healed and Lisa could cope with things better before he broached that sensitive subject.

Paul climbed into bed, stretched to get the kinks out, and

yawned. He was more tired then he'd realized. *I hope Lisa will be able to get some rest and doesn't lie awake worrying about Maggie.* Paul closed his eyes, whispered a prayer on her behalf, and within minutes gave way to much-needed sleep.

Lisa stared at the teapot sitting on the kitchen table. She'd had two cups of chamomile tea, but the mellow-tasting liquid hadn't made her feel relaxed or even sleepy. Her head was filled with thoughts of Maggie and everything the poor dog had been through and would have to face in the weeks ahead. Before performing the surgery, the vet had assured Lisa that her dog would adjust to having only three legs and, after a while, would be able to walk, run, and climb stairs again. It would take some time, but Maggie would learn to compensate for the missing limb.

Lisa felt some measure of comfort when Grandma stood behind her chair and began to massage her shoulders, neck, and upper back. "Maggie will be all right, Lisa." She spoke in a soothing tone. "Your hund is a determined one, and she will come through this just fine."

"I—I hope so." Lisa swallowed around the constriction in her throat. "Maggie will require a lot of care when she comes home, so I'll need to see if I can get someone to teach my class while I'm here providing for my dog's needs."

"That won't be necessary," Grandma said. "I'll be here all day, and I promise that I will take good care of Maggie."

"Really? You wouldn't mind?"

"Of course not. Maggie's a nice dog, and I know how important she is to you." Grandma continued to rub Lisa's tight muscles.

"Danki. I appreciate that." Tears welled in Lisa's eyes, and she swiped at them with the back of her hand. "I will want to be with her, though—at least for the first few days after she comes home. Maggie will be scared and uncertain about everything at first. She will need lots of love and reassurance."

"That's quite true, and we'll all do our part in helping her recover from the surgery, as we take one day at a time." Grandma ended her massage and stepped out from behind Lisa's chair. "Right now, however, I think the two of us should follow your grandpa's lead and head for *bett*."

Lisa nodded and pushed back her chair. She would go up to her room and get ready for bed, but with her thoughts still on Maggie, it was doubtful that she would get much sleep.

~

"We never heard you come in last night," Paul's aunt said as she handed him a plate of scrambled eggs. "Did you get home late?"

He let out an uncontrollable yawn and spoke in a groggy voice. "I didn't get back here till after two thirty this morning." Paul helped himself to some eggs and passed the plate on to Danny.

Uncle Abe's eyebrows shot up. "What were you doing out with Lisa at that hour? You took her home after the program, right?"

Paul nodded and cleared his throat a couple of times. "But we didn't get to her grandparents' house until way after midnight, because we were at the vet's with her *hund*."

Aunt Emma blinked rapidly. "What happened to Maggie?"

"She was hit by a car." Paul paused to pour some ketchup on his eggs and then filled the family in on the whole story.

Aunt Emma's fingers touched her parted lips, Uncle Abe jerked his head back slightly, and Paul's cousins looked at him with their eyes wide open.

"Is the hund gonna be okay?" Danny questioned.

"I believe so," Paul replied, "but losing a limb will be quite an adjustment for Maggie."

"I can only imagine." Aunt Emma heaved a heavy sigh. "Poor Lisa. I bet she was pretty *umgerennt* about the situation."

"You're right. She was very upset." Paul drank some grape juice and looked over at Uncle Abe after he set his glass down. "Unless you have some chores for me to do, I'd like to go over to the Schrocks' and see how Lisa is doing."

"My boys can handle any chores that need to be done. So feel free to go offer Lisa the support she obviously needs."

"Danki." Paul appreciated his uncle's understanding. Lisa had become a good friend, and he wanted to be there for her during this time of need.

⁓

As the sun streamed in through a small hole in her bedroom window shade, Lisa's eyelids fluttered and then opened. Looking at the battery-operated alarm clock on the small wooden table beside her bed, she saw that it was ten o'clock in the morning. Although she did not feel refreshed at all, at least she had been able to get a few hours of sleep.

Lisa forced herself to sit up and put her legs over the side of the bed. She wished what had occurred last night had only been a bad dream, but in reality Maggie was at the veterinarian clinic right now, recovering from her emergency surgery.

Lisa rubbed her eyes. *I wonder how my poor dog is doing after the rough ordeal she went through. I hope Maggie is comfortable and not in a lot of pain.*

Hoping the doctor or his assistant might have left a message for her, Lisa got up and hurried to get dressed. She figured her grandparents would probably be up and would already have eaten or at least started their breakfast. So the first place she planned to go was out to the phone shed.

Lifting the window shade, Lisa was glad to see blue skies and sunshine, with no sign of snow on the horizon, although the ground was still white. She hoped the clear skies meant their weather would be taking a turn for the better. If it warmed up and the snow melted, traveling would be easier on bare roads instead of ice and snow, like they'd been faced with last night.

Moving away from the window, Lisa left her room and hurried down the stairs. The door to her grandparents' room was closed, so she figured she must have been mistaken and that they were most likely still in bed.

In the entryway near the front door, Lisa took her outer garments from the clothes tree and put them on, then slipped into her boots. She'd no more than opened the door and stepped onto the porch when she saw Paul's horse and carriage coming up the driveway.

She drew in a deep breath and waited for him to join her on the porch.

"How are you this morning?" Paul asked when he came up the steps a few minutes later.

"I didn't get much sleep after you dropped us off last night, so I'm quite mied."

"It makes sense that you would be tired. I'm feeling that way myself."

"I'm sorry for keeping you up so long."

He shook his head and reached out to touch her arm. "I can do without sleep once in a while, especially when staying awake to help out an old friend."

She tipped her head slightly. "Old friend? I didn't know you saw me as old."

"Oh. . .um. . .it was just a figure of speech." Paul's cheeks reddened. "You definitely do not appear to be old."

Lisa lowered her gaze to the porch before looking up at him again.

"Have you heard anything from the vet this morning about how Maggie fared through the night?" Paul asked.

Lisa was glad for the change of subject. The strange, almost conflicted, way he looked at her right now made her feel something she couldn't explain.

"I was on my way out to the phone shed when you arrived," she said. "I'm hoping there will be a message letting me know how Maggie is doing."

"Mind if I go with you, so we can listen to the message together?" Paul stuffed both hands into his jacket pockets.

"That'd be fine." Lisa managed a smile, even though tears

pricked the back of her eyes. She hoped she could keep them from slipping out and dribbling onto her cheeks.

Paul led the way, and Lisa shuffled along through the snow, following in his footprints, which were much larger than hers. When they arrived at the shed, he opened the door and held it so she could go in.

Lisa stepped into the small wooden building and shivered. It felt colder in here than it had outside. She took a seat on the wooden stool, and Paul stood off to one side. The light on the answering machine blinked in rapid succession, letting Lisa know there was at least one message. She clicked the button and listened intently to the message, which to her relief was from the veterinarian.

"Hello, this is Dr. Hughes with a message for Lisa. I wanted you to know that your dog is resting comfortably, thanks to the pain and relaxation medication we've given her. She's also been given an anti-inflammatory to help with swelling. Maggie will be able to leave the clinic once she is able to stand, walk a few steps, eat something, and eliminate on her own. It's not unusual for a pet to remain in the recovery ward longer than a day, especially after major surgery. Please feel free to call my office with any questions you may have. We will let you know when it's time to pick up your dog."

Lisa felt a tightness in her chest as she held her hands tightly together. "I hate that Maggie's going through this, and I wish I could be with her right now."

Paul placed one hand on her shoulder and gave it a gentle squeeze. "She'll be okay, Lisa. You'll see."

"I hope so. I don't know what I'd do if Maggie didn't make it." Lisa's eyes burned with unshed tears, and she squeezed them shut in an effort to keep them from spilling over. "Danki for being my friend, Paul. I appreciate your support and all that you've done."

He patted her shoulder. "I only wish I could do more."

Lisa rose from the stool. "Let's go inside, and I'll fix you a cup of coffee or some hot chocolate. Although it's past our normal breakfast time, I'd also be happy to fix some eggs, toast, or whatever you like."

Paul shook his head. "That's okay. My aunt made the family some breakfast this morning. I would be glad for a cup of hot chocolate, though."

"Okay then, hot chocolate it shall be."

They left the phone shed, and Lisa pulled her jacket up closer to her neck to keep out the chill. Despite the cold, Lisa felt a warm bond with Paul through this experience with her dog.

Lisa's spirits lifted just a bit as she and Paul headed for the house. Until now, she'd never had a friend who seemed to care so much about her.

Chapter 22

Lisa's pulse quickened as she waited with Grandma for their driver to pick them up Tuesday afternoon. After spending four days at the veterinarian's clinic, recovering from her surgery, Maggie was finally ready to be brought home. Lisa hoped what they had come up with for the dog's sleeping arrangement and having foods to camouflage her pain pills would be just right for their patient.

Lisa had taught at the schoolhouse yesterday, and again today, which had helped to keep her mind occupied with something other than Maggie. But now that school was over for the day and they were preparing to pick the dog up, she could only think of one thing. Lisa was eager to bring Maggie home, but the thought of seeing her poor animal with one leg missing, not to mention the incision, swelling, and bruising, made Lisa's stomach feel queasy. The usual time frame for most pets that had an amputation was to remain at the vet's for one to two days. On the second day, however, Lisa had been informed that Maggie had managed to dislodge her drain tube, and some bleeding had occurred. The doctor thought it best to keep the dog and monitor her for a few more days.

Grandma paused from reading the newspaper and nudged Lisa's arm. "Please try to relax. I can see by your furrowed brows that you're apprehensive about picking up your hund."

"You're right," Lisa admitted, "and I am trying to get my mind-set in the right place before we head to the clinic. It's a good feeling to know that Maggie is alive, but at the same time it's hard to accept that her life with us will be different from now on."

"Not that different," Grandma said. "Remember what the doctor told us before we left the clinic on the night of Maggie's surgery?"

"He said a lot of things. What are you referring to?"

"The veterinarian stated that animals do better after amputation surgery than humans. In time you will see that Maggie can do many things she did before the accident, and she will become stronger. He also reminded you to keep a positive attitude and said if you do that, your pet will reflect positivity right back at you."

Lisa pushed a strand of wayward hair back under her head covering. "I'll do my best to stay positive and keep a cheerful attitude when I am talking to Maggie."

Her grandmother went back to reading, and they sat there together in the quiet of the living room. It was difficult not to be overwhelmed by all of this. Lisa wished she could be as confident as Grandma in her way of thinking. She tried to refocus by looking out the window and watching the birds as they flew to and from the feeders, keeping a steady stream of movement going. She especially enjoyed seeing the male cardinals with their pronounced red coloring. Outside, the corn sat in a metal pan for the ducks, but so far only the small wild birds had eaten any. Lisa figured Grandpa's sighting of the ducks had only been by happenstance.

She glanced at the battery-operated clock on the far wall. *Our driver should be arriving anytime now.* Lisa folded her arms as she thought about how things had gone in class today. The children had done well taking turns reading aloud from age-appropriate stories Lisa had chosen for them. During lunch break, she'd graded the spelling tests the children had also taken that morning. Many of them had good scores. It was obvious that her students had practiced at home, no doubt with some coaching from their parents or older siblings.

When a horn tooted outside, Lisa and her grandmother both got up from the couch and went to put on their outer garments.

Lisa also picked up an old towel and a sheet to put under Maggie on the ride home. She resolved to give herself a pep talk on the way to the clinic, so that when she saw Maggie for the first time since her surgery, she wouldn't give in to tears but would instead respond in a positive way.

When their driver, Herb, pulled into the parking lot of the clinic, Lisa's heart began to pound. *What if Maggie acts different toward me now? What if I can't deal with seeing her incision and the area where her right front leg used to be?*

"I'll wait here in the van," Herb said. "But if you need my help carrying the dog out to the vehicle, come get me."

Perspiration beaded on Lisa's forehead. Until now, she hadn't even thought about how they would get Maggie out to the van. Would she need to be carried, or could she walk by herself? But even if the dog was able to walk on her own, she would need some help getting up into Herb's vehicle. It was just one more thing to stress about, and Lisa certainly didn't need that.

She opened the back door of the passenger van and stepped down, thankful for her boots, because there was still some snow on the ground. Grandma had been sitting up front in the passenger's seat, and she got out as well.

When they entered the clinic, the faint odor of antiseptic made Lisa's stomach churn. It reminded her of the other evening, as they'd waited during Maggie's surgery.

Lisa stepped up to the receptionist's desk and told the young woman her name and that she was here to pick up her dog.

"Please take a seat." The woman smiled. "Your name will be called as soon as your dog is ready to leave."

Lisa hesitated a moment. "Oh, uh. . .what about my bill? Will you be sending it to me in the mail, or would you prefer that I take care of it right now?"

"If you're able to pay today, that would be appreciated."

Lisa reached into her purse and retrieved her checkbook. When the receptionist gave her the bill, Lisa wrote out a check. She was thankful for the substantial amount of money Grandpa and Grandma had given her and for Paul's help as well. Lisa felt blessed by their generosity and the moral support each of them had given her because of all she'd gone through with Maggie so far.

After Lisa received a receipt, she walked over to where Grandma sat and took a seat beside her.

Grandma smiled. "It'll be nice to have your dog back, and in a little while we'll be home getting her all settled in."

Using a light touch, Lisa drummed her fingers on the arm of the chair. *Will I be taken into an examining room to see Maggie, or will they bring her out here?* Lisa had never dealt with anything like this, and she felt quite confused and vulnerable.

Grandma took a magazine and began thumbing through it, but all Lisa could do was think negative thoughts as she picked at a hangnail on her thumb. *So much for trying to keep a positive attitude,* she thought.

Several minutes went by until Lisa was asked to go into one of the examining rooms. Grandma went with her, and Lisa was glad, because she desperately needed the moral support.

The doctor greeted them and then gestured to his assistant who stood by the table where Maggie lay.

Lisa heard a ringing in her ears, and every muscle in her body felt as if it had become frozen. Maggie whimpered, and the pathetic sight of her dear pet lying there with only three limbs nearly broke Lisa's heart.

"I am aware that the incision surgery site is a bit shocking," the doctor said. "It's not easy to see your dog looking so wounded and different, but try to remember that Maggie is happy to see you and wants to go home. So please look her in the eye, and don't focus your attention on the incision. Show that you're happy to see Maggie, because your positive attitude will set the tone for the dog's recovery."

"I—I will do my best." Lisa reached out with a trembling hand

and stroked the top of her dog's head, being careful to avoid the stitches.

Maggie whimpered again, and then she nuzzled Lisa's arm with her nose.

Maggie still loves me, and I'm sure she wants to go home as much as I want to take her there. I just hope I can do all the right things for her. Lisa swallowed around the lump in her throat. She had missed her dog so much and hated to see her suffer.

"My assistant has some instructions for you about Maggie's home care. We also have a sling available that you can put around the dog's belly, which will help her with mobility the first few days if needed. An e-collar may also be a good idea. It will prevent Maggie from licking or chewing at her surgical wound."

Lisa nodded, although her head felt like it was spinning with all the dos and don'ts she would be faced with while caring for Maggie.

The doctor's assistant gave Lisa a clear plastic bag, explaining that it had Maggie's pain medication inside, along with the instructions for her care.

"Please let us know if you have any questions or if any problems arise," the doctor said. "With the aid of the sling around Maggie's belly, my assistant will help you take Maggie to your vehicle now. Oh, and I would like to see your dog again by the first of next week, to make sure that everything is healing properly." He offered Lisa a reassuring smile. "I understand you must feel a bit overwhelmed right now, but once you get home and have established a routine, you will feel more relaxed and confident that everything is going to be all right for both you and Maggie."

Lisa looked at her grandmother and felt some encouragement when Grandma smiled at the doctor and said, "I will be helping my granddaughter with Maggie's care, and we'll both make sure that we follow the instructions you're sending home with us."

He nodded. "Good to hear, and please don't hesitate to call if any problems should arise or you have a question that isn't addressed in the list we're giving you. Now let's get Maggie ready to go home."

"Where are you going?" Lois asked when Orley entered the kitchen via the hallway entrance, wearing a heavy jacket, stocking cap, gloves, and boots.

"Thought I'd do a little sledding while there's still some *schnee* on our hill out back." He gave her a wide a grin.

"But it won't be long till supper. Besides, even if the snow melts soon, there will almost certainly be more as *winder* sets in."

"We might have a mild winter this year." Orley winked at Lois.

She gestured toward the window. "It's starting to get dark. What are you going to do—hold one of your powerful flashlights out in front of you as you sled down the hill?"

He shrugged. "That could work."

Lois rolled her eyes at him.

"Don't forget that my doctor said I should exercise to help keep my weight in check."

"Sliding down the hill doesn't take much energy."

"No, but trudging back up it sure does."

Lois lifted both hands in defeat. There was no way she could convince her determined husband not to get out his sled. "Okay, Orley, but supper will be on the table in one hour."

"I'll be back in the house by then, no problem." Orley kissed Lois's cheek, and with a whistle, he went out the back door.

Lois lifted her gaze to the ceiling. "For goodness' sakes, will that husband of mine ever grow up?"

She moved over to the refrigerator and took out a package of ground beef for making meatballs. "I guess I should count myself as fortunate to be married to a fun-loving man like Orley. If I had chosen someone else, I might not be so lucky. Some men, like that grouchy customer who came into our store this morning, would certainly be difficult to live with."

Lois got out an onion and the cutting board. "If all I have to complain about is a husband who likes to have a little fun, then shame on me," she scolded herself. "There are lots of people in our world right now facing bigger problems than mine."

Sugarcreek

Lisa knelt on the floor next to where Maggie lay on the comfy bed they had fixed for her. Under normal conditions, it would have been a nice sleeping arrangement. But Lisa wasn't sure her dog could be comfortable in any sleeping or resting arrangement or that lying on a cushioned doggy bed would help relieve the pain the poor animal must feel. Even the position the vet had said Maggie would need to lie in, with the amputation side toward the ceiling, looked uncomfortable.

Lisa had planned to mix Maggie's pain pill in a small amount of turkey-flavored baby food, as the instructions she'd been sent home with suggested. Some other suggestions to stimulate the dog's appetite had also been mentioned, such as offering her some smoked cheese like Gouda. Apparently the stronger smells were supposed to appeal, but so far, Maggie hadn't touched a bite, and she'd only lapped a little water from her elevated bowl. Lisa couldn't help but worry, because even if she had placed a pill in the food dish, Maggie probably would not have eaten it. The poor thing seemed so listless. Lisa felt sure her dog was depressed.

"How's it going in here?" Grandpa asked, stepping into the utility room.

Lisa shook her head. "Not well. I can't get her to eat, and if she doesn't eat, she won't get the medicine I want to put in her food."

"Is it time for her pill?"

Lisa nodded.

"Not to worry. I know of several tricks to get your pooch to take her medicine."

She tipped her head. "Such as?"

"One thing you can do is cut a marshmallow in two and wedge the pill in the middle of it. Then let your dog take a sniff of it, and offer it for her to eat." Grandpa jiggled his brows. "It's an inexpensive, low-calorie treat."

"I suppose it'd be worth a try," Lisa said.

"You could also spoon out a dollop of peanut butter, ball it up, and push a pill into the middle of it. Chunky peanut butter works best, because the peanut chunks disguise the pill inside." He paused and bent down to scratch Maggie behind her ears. "You could also try feeding her some thick, fruit-flavored yogurt with the pill mixed in."

Lisa's eyelashes fluttered. "Wow, Grandpa, how did you learn so much about giving a pill to a hund?"

"That's simple." He lowered himself to his knees. "I had plenty of pets when I was growing up and even in the early days of your grandma's and my marriage."

"Did any of your animals ever lose a limb?"

He shook his head. "But there were times when one of 'em got injured or sick and had to go to the vet's. So because they were my pet, I had the privilege of caring for them when they came home from the veterinary clinic."

Lisa's shoulders relaxed a little. She'd never thought of it as being a privilege to take care of Maggie, but now that she let the idea sink in, it made sense.

Lisa leaned closer to Maggie and gave her head a few gentle pats. "I'm going to the kitchen now, girl, but I'll be back soon with a special marshmallow treat for you."

The dog lifted her head just a bit and made a little grunting sound. *Hopefully she likes that idea,* Lisa thought.

Chapter 23

"Are you sure you can handle things with Maggie while I'm at the schoolhouse today?" Lisa asked her grandmother the following morning.

"Try not to worry. I'm sure we'll do fine." Grandma gestured to where Grandpa sat reading the newspaper at the kitchen table. "If a problem should arise and I'm not sure what to do, I'll go out to the harness shop and get your grandfather."

"Okay, good." Lisa felt better hearing that Grandma would seek Grandpa's help. She still couldn't get over how easily she had gotten Maggie to take her medication last night by taking Grandpa's advice and hiding the pill inside a marshmallow.

Last night Lisa had slept in the downstairs guest room, and with Grandpa's help she'd moved Maggie and her dog bed into that room as well. It was either that or Lisa would have slept on an air mattress in the utility room, because she wasn't about to leave her dog unattended overnight. She hadn't had the most restful sleep during the night. In fact, she'd woken up a few different times. And while Lisa was awake, her number one priority was to check on Maggie to see how things were. Each time she checked on the dog, Lisa had been pleased to find Maggie with her head down and eyes closed. She hoped that her faithful companion would get the sleep she needed to help with the healing process. Taking care of Maggie and doing all she could for the dog had given Lisa a taste of what it would be like to be a mother.

"Are you okay, girl?" Lisa called when she heard Maggie whimper from the utility room, where her doggy bed had been moved back this morning after they'd taken the dog outside to do her business. She tipped her head and listened, but there was no more noise. Lisa figured that the pain medication might have worn off. Or maybe the dog had bumped the tender area in her sleep. Lisa hoped things would go well during the time she'd be away from her dog. Truth was, she still felt apprehensive about leaving Maggie in order to teach school today, but tomorrow Lisa would be home all day, since it was Christmas, and she'd be celebrating the holiday with her grandparents. Paul would also be dropping by sometime on Christmas Day. Lisa had found a message from him this morning when she'd gone to the phone shed to let the veterinarian know how Maggie had fared through the night.

Lisa looked forward to seeing Paul again. This would be the first time she'd seen him since the day after Maggie's accident. He'd been busy working with his uncle, and she'd been busy teaching school. Lisa hadn't seen Paul at church either, because last Sunday had been an off Sunday when their district didn't hold services, so they'd both attended church with their families in other neighboring districts.

"Would you like me to pack your lunch box this morning?"

Grandma's question pulled Lisa's thoughts aside. "Oh, jah, it would be appreciated. And while you're doing that, I'll try to get Maggie to eat something."

"Good idea." Grandpa set his newspaper aside and stood. "I'm going to fix myself another cup of kaffi, but if you need my help coaxing your hund to eat, just give a holler."

"I will, Grandpa. Danki." Lisa left the kitchen and entered the utility room. She was glad to see that Maggie was awake and lapping water from her dish.

Lisa made sure to praise the dog when she drank, took a pill, or ate, hoping to encourage the positive behavior. It would be a tough road ahead for Maggie as she recovered from her surgery and the wound on her head. Lisa felt hopeful when occasionally Maggie's tail would wag in a slow manner after being praised or receiving attention. It made Lisa happy to see her dog trying to respond like she had before the accident.

Lisa placed the food dish in front of her dog. It contained Maggie's favorite kind of canned dog food with her pain pill mixed in.

Maggie sniffed the bowl, ate a few bites, and laid her head back down. Lisa figured the dog must have tasted the pill and didn't care for the bitterness of it.

"Oh, great." Lisa picked up the pill Maggie hadn't touched. Then she went back to the kitchen, got a marshmallow, cut a slice in the middle, and stuffed the pill inside. *I think Maggie has a sweet tooth for marshmallows, but then so do I.* She picked one out for herself and popped it into her mouth.

Returning to the utility room, Lisa squatted down beside her dog. "Here, Maggie. Would you like a tasty marshmallow?"

Maggie snatched the treat and chomped it right down.

Lisa smiled. "Good girl." *Guess if that's what it takes to get my hund to take her pill, then I'll just have to keep feeding her marshmallows.*

She stroked her dog's silky head. "Now you be a good dog for Grandma while I'm gone today. I'll miss you, girl, but I'll be back this afternoon, and tomorrow I'll be here all day."

Goshen, Indiana

"Your Christmas cookies are the best, Mavis." Daniel took a bite and sipped on his steaming cup of coffee.

"I hope you don't get carried away with what I've made and eat too many." Mavis shook a finger at her husband.

He flapped his hand. "It's all good. I'm enjoying these soft sugar cookies with the frosting, and they're sure tasty."

Frowning, she held up a paper. "I need to change topics. This is important."

He took another bite of his cookie. "What's up?"

"Would you look at this and tell me what's wrong with our son?" Mavis handed her husband the letter she'd received in the mail this morning.

"Is Paul sick, or has he been hurt in some way?" Deep wrinkles formed across Daniel's forehead.

"As far as I know our son is fine physically, but he is not coming home for Christmas and didn't even have the courtesy to call and tell us." She grimaced. "No, instead, he chose to convey the news via a letter."

Daniel's face relaxed, and he set the piece of paper on the table. "I don't see what the big deal is. Paul probably figured if he'd talked to you on the phone, you would have pestered him about staying in Ohio for the holiday."

Mavis placed both hands against her hips as she shook her head. "I would not have done that, although I may have asked for a better reason than he gave us in his letter."

"What reason would that be?"

"If you had read all of Paul's letter instead of tossing it on the table, you would know what I'm talking about."

Daniel picked up the paper and slipped on his reading glasses. His lips formed the words as he read Paul's letter. When he finished, he looked at Mavis. "Seems clear enough to me. Our son has an aldi, and he's staying in Sugarcreek so he can spend Christmas with her. I think it's fine that he has found someone new. It shows he's healing from the hurt of the previous young lady."

She released her hands from her hips and took a seat across from him at the table. "Paul never referred to Lisa as his girlfriend. He said she was a friend, plain and simple." Mavis paused. "I have to agree with you, though. It is good to see our son moving on, but I don't see any evidence of a relationship brewing."

He pulled his long fingers through the ends of his thick beard and made a grunting sound. "Come on, now. Who does our son usually talk about whenever he writes a letter or leaves a message on our voice mail?"

She moistened her lips with the tip of her tongue before speaking. "He has mentioned Lisa, of course. After all, they used to know each other when they were kinner. But he talks about other things too—like his job working for Abe, what the weather is like there, and—"

"He talks more about Lisa than he does the weather. And the fact that he wants to spend time with her during the holiday speaks volumes."

"It—it does?"

"Jah. Don't you remember how often I went over to your folks' place to see you when we were courting?"

"Well, yes, but Paul has never told us that he and Lisa are anything more than friends. I doubt that they are courting." Mavis rapped her knuckles on the tabletop. "If he is getting serious about her, and they should end up getting married someday, it would probably mean he'd stay in Sugarcreek. That is, unless he can talk her into moving here."

"I don't think that's likely. Remember, it was here where her parents and paternal grandparents lived. And you know the memory of the accident that took their lives might make it hard for Lisa to live here again." Daniel picked up his coffee cup and took a drink. "Also, in case you've forgotten, Paul left here to live with my bruder Abe and his fraa because his heart was broken when his best friend moved in on Paul's aldi. So in my opinion, our son's not likely to move back here again."

Mavis bit down on her lower lip. *Would it be wrong to hope, and maybe even pray, that Paul and Susan would get back together? That would definitely give our son cause to make Indiana his home again.*

"And while we are on the topic of Christmas," Daniel said, cutting into Mavis's thoughts. "We really can't complain, because we still have our sons Harley, Mark, Amos, and Glen living close by, and we'll be able to spend part of the holiday with each of them and their families."

"Believe me, I appreciate that. It would just be nice if all our sons could be with us for Christmas."

"Maybe next year Paul will come home."

Mavis looked right at Daniel and squinted until her eyelids were nearly shut. "He'd better not wait that long to come see us. I miss our son very much."

Sugarcreek

Excitement ran high in the schoolhouse as the children filed in the door, talking and laughing. Lisa heard several of her pupils say that they couldn't wait for tomorrow to get here so they could open their gifts and eat the delicious food their mothers would fix for Christmas dinner. Lisa wanted to share in their enthusiasm, but all she could think about was her dog and how Maggie would do today in the care of Grandma. She hoped things would go well and that Grandma could get Maggie to eat, drink, and take her pill when it was time for pain medication. Here it was, just the beginning of the school day, and instead of her focus being on teaching, Lisa's thoughts were on her desire for the day to end so she could go home and see Maggie.

If I can't concentrate on my job here and keep my attention on the students, then maybe I'm not cut out for teaching, Lisa told herself. *I do care about these children, though, so I must try to do better.*

She glanced at the clock on the far wall. The day would be over soon enough, and she had a job to do. Lisa turned her attention to the blackboard and the words written near the top: If We Use the Golden Rule at All Times, We Won't Need Any Other Rules.

She reflected on what the Golden Rule, found in Matthew 7:12, said: "Therefore all things whatsoever ye would that men should do to you, do ye even so to them: for this is the law and the prophets."

Although the schoolchildren in all eight grades memorized the Golden Rule in German and English, the most important thing was learning to practice it in their everyday lives. Lisa and Yvonne often stressed to the scholars the importance of using the Golden

Rule during playtime and all other situations here at school.

In addition to learning the Golden Rule, Amish children were taught in school to be cooperative; show respect to their teachers, as well as other students; and learn responsibility by helping to keep the classroom clean and orderly, which included keeping their own desk tidy. Another important thing the children needed to learn was obedience. It was the teacher's job to get her students to obey out of love and not merely because it was expected of them. Parental support made a huge difference in teaching the children the basic guidelines and values, because if children had been taught these things at home, they were more likely to comply in a positive way during school hours.

Once everyone had taken their seats, Yvonne read a verse from the Bible, and then it was time for the children to sing a hymn and recite the Lord's Prayer.

What a wonderful way to start each day, Lisa thought as she felt herself begin to relax. Hearing God's Word and singing along with the children had lifted her spirts, and she now felt ready to begin her day of teaching. Although some people who weren't Amish might not understand why an Amish education consisted of only eight grades, Lisa knew that Amish teaching provided a good foundation scholastically, as well as giving the children an emphasis on the value of hard work, community service, and preparation for eventually joining the Amish church.

~

Walnut Creek

As soon as Paul entered Memory Keepers Antique Store, Orley stepped out from behind the front counter and greeted him with a hearty handshake.

"Happy day before Christmas." The older man offered Paul a pleasant smile. "I haven't seen you in a while. How have you been?"

"I'm fine, but my friend Lisa nearly lost her hund last week,"

Paul replied. "I came here to see if I could find something she might like for Christmas. Lisa was pretty shook up when her dog, Maggie, got hit by a car, and she could use some cheering up."

Orley's brows furrowed. "I'm sorry to hear that. Is the dog going to be okay?"

"Her right front leg was injured pretty badly, so the vet had to amputate." Paul paused a few seconds. "But if there are no complications, the dog should be okay."

"When I was a boy, a friend of mine had a hund with only three legs," Orley said. "But the dog got along pretty well and was able to do most things that other dogs could do."

Paul pulled off his stocking cap and stuffed it in his jacket pocket. "I'll be seeing Lisa on Christmas Day, and I'm eager to see how Maggie is getting along."

Orley smiled. "So what kind of gift do you have in mind for Lisa?"

"I'm not sure. I'd thought about an old book, but the time I brought Lisa here she seemed to be sensitive to the musty odor of the books." Paul gave his left earlobe a tug. "So I'm kind of at a loss about what to buy for her."

"Let's go ask my fraa." Orley gestured to Lois, who stood across the room, rearranging some items on a table. "I'm sure she'll have some suggestions for what a young woman might like."

They made their way across the room, and when Orley explained to Lois that Paul had come in to find a gift for Lisa, she smiled and said, "That's very thoughtful of you, Paul, and I think I might know just the thing."

Chapter 24

Lois sat on the couch in their living room, looking at the cards she and Orley had received for Christmas this year. One stood out in particular. It was from her father and stepmother, Sarah, who lived in Kentucky. Lois had invited them to come to Walnut Creek for the holiday, but they'd declined, saying Lois's seventy-year-old father had a bad cold and didn't want to expose anyone.

Lois hoped that was actually the reason and that her dad wasn't using it as an excuse to get out of spending Christmas with her and Orley. It wasn't that he had a bad relationship with his son-in-law. It was his relationship with Lois that was strained and had been for a good many years.

Lois released a lingering sigh. The tension between her and Dad was mostly on his part, because she'd forgiven him a long time ago for being so controlling and insensitive to her needs.

Never mind about that, Lois told herself. *Orley and I had a nice dinner early today with his brother Ezra and Ezra's wife, Maryann.* Two of Orley's nephews had been there also, along with their families, and a good time was had by all. But truth was, Lois yearned to have that positive connection with her father and to have from him an unconditional love.

"Would you like a piece of pumpkin pie or something else to eat?" Lois asked Orley.

He set the book down that he'd been reading and smiled. "The pie sounds nice, and some fresh coffee would hit the spot too."

"I have to agree with you. That does sound good. So I will be back shortly." Lois got up and ambled into the kitchen. She got the pot of coffee started before pulling the pie and some whipped cream from the refrigerator. When Lois cut into the pie, its spicy aroma tickled her nose. Then she pulled a spoon from the drawer and dunked it into the heavy white cream she had whipped that morning. Each slice was adorned with a hefty scoop of the fluffy, sweet addition. Lois couldn't resist enjoying the remnant left on the spoon and smiled. She felt like a kid again, enjoying for a moment this fleeting pleasure.

When Lois returned to the living room with two slices of pie, she found her husband standing in front of the window, looking out. She set their plates down on the coffee table and went back for the coffee.

Returning to the living room, Lois was surprised to see that Orley still stood at the window. "What are you looking at, Husband?"

He turned to face her. "Just seeing how much the schnee has receded. With it being warmer today, quite a bit of snow has already melted." His shoulders slumped. "If we don't get more of the white stuff soon, it'll put an end to sledding for me."

"I'm sure we'll have plenty of schnee over the next couple of months, and you'll be able to do lots of sledding and horsing around in the snow." Lois gestured to the cups of steaming coffee and the mouthwatering pie she'd brought out. "Shall we eat it in here or sit at the dining-room table?"

"Here's fine with me, unless you're worried I might spill hot kaffi or drop crumbs from the pie crust on the floor."

"I'm sure you'll be careful, like always." Lois took a seat on the couch, and Orley sat next to her. She watched him take the fork and disperse all the whipped cream over the top of his dessert. Lois couldn't help smiling at her husband's happy expression as he ate the first bite of pie.

"Yummy. . .this is sure *gut karebsekuche.*" Orley smacked his lips. "Pumpkin pie is my favorite, especially at Christmas and Thanksgiving."

Lois smiled at her husband's exuberance. "I like it too."

Between bites of pie and sips from their cups, Lois and Orley talked about several things, including Paul Herschberger's visit to the store yesterday afternoon.

"I wonder if Paul's friend Lisa will like what he bought for her," Lois said.

"I don't see why she wouldn't." Orley wiped his mouth on the napkin Lois had provided. "What young woman wouldn't like a pretty teacup?"

<hr />

Sugarcreek

"That was a mighty good meal you ladies fixed for us. Danki." Grandpa's smile appeared to be directed at Grandma, but then he looked at Lisa. "The only problem is, I ate too much and now I'm too full for dessert."

"There's no hurry. We can have our pie once our stomachs have settled." Grandma pushed away from the dining-room table and picked up several dishes.

Lisa jumped up and helped her, and Grandpa carried some dishes out to the kitchen too. In no time at all the table was fully cleared and the kitchen sink was filled with hot soapy water.

Maggie sat whining at the back door, so Grandpa volunteered to dry the dishes while Grandma washed, allowing Lisa to take the dog outside.

Lisa put on a heavy jacket and a pair of boots, and she got Maggie ready by using the sling she'd gotten from the veterinarian clinic. This made it easier for the dog to go down the porch stairs.

They'd only been outside a few minutes when Paul's horse and carriage entered the yard. Lisa waved, and she watched as he pulled up to the hitching rail and got out.

Paul waved back. After he'd secured his horse, he reached inside the buggy and withdrew a small cardboard box. *"Hallicher Grischtdaag,"* he said as he approached Lisa.

"Merry Christmas to you as well." She was about to ask what he had in the box when he spoke again. "It's great to see Maggie. How's she doing?"

"As well as can be expected, I guess. She still has some pain, but I don't have to give her the medication as often as I did when she first came home."

Paul set the box on the top porch step and went over to pet Maggie. The dog responded by licking his hand.

"It's hard to see her with only three legs," Lisa observed, "but the vet said she will adjust to it."

"I believe she will too."

"Did you have a nice Christmas meal with your aunt and uncle and their family?" Lisa asked.

"I sure did, but we all ate too much."

She laughed. "That's what my grandpa said too, after we finished our meal. The three of us weren't ready for dessert right away, but Grandma will be serving some of her delicious pumpkin and apple pies soon. You will join us for some, I hope."

"Definitely. It'll give me that much more time to spend here with you."

The tender expression she saw on Paul's face caused Lisa to feel a fluttery feeling in her chest. *Does Paul see me as more than a casual friend? Do I want him to?*

She shook the thought aside by focusing on Maggie. "Are you ready to go in now, girl?"

Arf! Arf! The dog wagged her tail.

Lisa felt a sense of hope and calmness. Was it being in Paul's presence or the fact that Maggie seemed to be a little more like her old self? Of course, the dog still had a ways to go in her healing.

"Let's go inside now," Lisa said to Paul. "We can talk better in the warm house."

"Agreed." He looked down and gestured to Maggie. "Do you need help getting her back inside?"

"Thanks for offering, but I can manage. The sling helps a lot."

"Okay." Paul picked up the box, went up the steps, and opened the door. Then he stood off to one side while Lisa and Maggie entered. Once they got the dog situated in her doggy bed, Lisa led the way to the kitchen. When she and Paul entered the room, Lisa was surprised to see that the dishes were done and her grandparents were no longer in the room. She figured she'd either been outside longer than she thought or Grandma and Grandpa had figured out some way to do the dishes really fast.

"You can take off your jacket and stocking cap and hang them over there." Lisa motioned to the wall pegs near the kitchen door. After placing the box on one end of the kitchen counter, Paul used one of the wall pegs for his things, and Lisa used another to hang up her outer garments.

"Would you like to see the trick I use to get Maggie to take her pain pills?" she asked.

"Sure."

Lisa opened a cupboard door and removed a bag of marshmallows. Then she took one out and proceeded to cut a slice in the middle. Next, she opened the medicine bottle, took out a pill, and slipped it inside the slit she'd made on the marshmallow.

She smiled at Paul. "Follow me, and I'll show you how it's done."

"Would you like a yummy treat, Maggie?" Lisa held the marshmallow in front of Maggie's nose.

The dog wagged her tail and let out a couple of noisy barks.

Paul chuckled. "She seems pretty eager to eat the treat you brought her."

"Jah, she is." Lisa held out the marshmallow, and without any prompting, Maggie opened her mouth and snatched the sticky morsel.

"Well, what do ya know?" Paul shook his head in disbelief. "How'd you come up with that idea, Lisa?"

"My grandpa suggested it, and I'm glad it has worked so well." Lisa crinkled her nose. "I was afraid I might have to open Maggie's mouth and put the pill in at the back of her tongue in order to give her the medication."

"That wouldn't have been the most ideal situation, so I'm glad using a marshmallow worked out." He leaned closer to her and smiled. "I mean, who doesn't enjoy eating a sweet treat like that?"

"Exactly. So why don't we go back to the kitchen now? I'll fix us some hot chocolate with a marshmallow on the top."

Paul licked his lips. "That sounds great. And while we're drinking our beverages you can open the gift I brought you."

Lisa fidgeted and rubbed her hands on the front of her apron. "I wasn't expecting you to bring me a Christmas present, and I feel bad that I don't have anything for you. I've been so preoccupied with Maggie that I—"

"Don't worry about it, Lisa. I didn't expect a gift." Paul offered her a heart-melting smile. "Just being here with you is the only gift I need."

Lisa swallowed hard. She wasn't sure how to respond.

Paul reached into the box and pulled out a smaller box wrapped in green tissue paper and handed it to her. "I hope you like it."

When she tore off the paper and opened the box, Lisa was pleased to discover a delicate bone china cup with a gold rim. Dainty purple violets had been painted on the cup and matching saucer. "Danki, Paul. This teacup is so *schee*, it's almost too beautiful to drink from."

"Well, it's up to you," Paul responded. "You can either use it for drinking tea or sit it up on a shelf to look at and enjoy."

"I may do both."

"It's an old cup. Turn it over and see where it was made."

Lisa did as Paul suggested. The writing on the underside of the cup read Made in Germany.

"I bought it at Orley and Lois Troyer's antique store."

"It's a thoughtful gift, and I appreciate it very much."

Lisa's grandmother entered the room just then. "Hallicher Grischtdaag, Paul." She greeted him with a hug.

"Merry Christmas," he responded.

"I hope you're hungry, because I am going to set out some pies."

Paul gave a nod. "I believe I could manage to eat a piece."

"Would you like pumpkin or apple?"

"I like 'em both so either is fine with me."

Grandma looked at Lisa. "How about you?"

"I'll have the pumpkin, please."

Grandma got out the pumpkin pie and served Lisa and Paul each a piece. "Now, why don't you two young folks sit in here and visit while you eat your pie, and I'll take a piece for me and your grandpa to eat in the other room."

"Don't you want to join us?" Lisa questioned. "I'm sure you would enjoy talking with Paul."

"Of course, but your grandpa and I have a new puzzle started, so we'll keep working on that while you and Paul visit." She looked at Lisa and smiled. "I bet you'd like to talk to Paul about Maggie."

"Well, yes, but. . ."

"Very well then, I'll leave you two alone." Grandma scooped up two plates of pie and quickly left the room.

Paul took a bite of his piece of pie and followed it with a drink of hot chocolate. In the process, he ended up with a blob of melting marshmallow on his upper lip.

Lisa laughed and pointed.

His brows furrowed. "What's so funny?"

"You have marshmallow on your lip."

Paul chuckled and stuck out his tongue to swipe it off. "There, is that better?"

"Jah." Lisa giggled again. It felt nice to be here with Paul this evening, and it was good to find something to laugh about. Things had been too serious around here ever since Maggie's accident.

Marlene smiled when she heard Lisa and Paul's laughter coming from the kitchen. She was glad she had taken Dear Caroline's advice and played matchmaker with Paul and Lisa by asking him to build their kitchen cabinets.

I was even wiser when I invited him to join us for supper soon after that. He and Lisa seemed to be getting along well, and Marlene figured it was just a matter of time before the young couple would begin courting.

"What's that big grin on your face all about?" Jerry asked. "Did you find another puzzle piece when I wasn't looking?"

"No, I did not." She gestured toward the kitchen door.

He blinked a couple of times. "Huh? What about the kitchen?"

"Paul makes our granddaughter laugh," Marlene whispered. "Now isn't that a good thing?"

Jerry bobbed his head and ate some of his pie. "This is as good as always."

Marlene rolled her eyes. *Doesn't that man of mine think of anything but food? Is he completely unaware that Paul and Lisa are attracted to each other and could end up as a couple?* She took a drink from the cup of tea she'd brought in earlier. *I certainly hope that will be the case. I can't think of anyone better suited for Lisa.*

Chapter 25

The first day of January brought more snow, and by Friday of that week, a good twelve inches covered the ground. A lot of shoveling had been done at Uncle Abe's place, but with the snow continuing to fall it was hard to keep up.

Paul gritted his teeth as he tromped through the slippery snow toward the phone shed. A few minutes ago, he'd checked the outdoor thermometer hanging on the back porch wall. The gauge showed nineteen degrees.

Too cold for me. Paul shivered and tried to pick up speed. There was no doubt about it—winter was not Paul's favorite time of the year.

Wish I was in Florida with Grandma right now. He'd heard that his grandmother had traveled there to get out of the cold and wondered if she knew how lucky she was to be able to spend the winter months in a warm place.

Upon entering the phone shed, Paul saw the light blinking on the answering machine, so he took a seat on the wooden stool and clicked the button to retrieve all the messages.

The first one was from an English customer, checking to see how soon the kitchen cabinets they'd ordered would be coming in. Paul jotted the man's name and phone number down on the notepad by the phone and then waited to hear the next message. He was surprised to hear Orley Troyer's voice and even more astounded when Orley said that he had come across some old milk bottles in a box in the storage room that he'd forgotten was there. Orley also stated that he had bought the box at a flea market last fall and thought it was full of old magazines. He'd had no idea there were any milk bottles at the bottom of the box and was surprised to discover them that morning when he began rummaging through some things in the storage shed at his antique store and opened the box. Orley ended the message by saying that one of the bottles looked like the item Paul had described previously and had been searching for.

"I'll set the box aside for you," Orley said at the end of his message. "When you get the chance to drop by, you can take a look and see what you think."

Paul drummed his feet against the floor. He looked forward to going to Walnut Creek after work to check out those milk bottles. Even if none of them were the one he'd been looking for, it would be nice to talk to Orley and his wife again.

Since there were no other messages on the machine, Paul pulled off the page with the customer information for his uncle and stood. He was about to step out the door when the telephone rang. Since it was so cold inside the small building, Paul was tempted not to answer and to let the voice mail kick in, but he figured a few more minutes of enduring the frigid temperature wouldn't matter. He sat back down and picked up the receiver. "Hello."

"Hey, Paul, it's me, Harley."

"Hey right back to you." Paul gave a quiet chuckle. He couldn't believe his older brother recognized his voice when he'd only uttered a single word.

"I never expected you'd pick up. Thought for sure I'd have to leave a message."

"I came out to check for messages and was about to head back inside when the phone rang, so naturally I picked it up." Paul blew out his breath and watched as the warm puff of air drifted upward.

"I'm glad you did, because there's something I wanted to tell you."

"Oh, what's that? Everyone there is okay, I hope."

"Jah, all in our family are fine, but I figured I'd give you the news in case you haven't heard it already."

"News about what?" Paul leaned forward with his elbows resting on the counter where the phone sat.

"Susan and Ervin are making plans to get married sometime toward the end of May, but I don't know the exact date."

"Yeah, so I heard, and good for them. I hope they'll be happy in their marriage."

"Do you really mean that, or was that a *scheppmeilich* comment?"

Paul drew a stick figure of a horse on the empty page of the notebook. "I was not being sarcastic. I've moved on with my life, and I wish Ervin and Susan well."

"It's great to hear you talking in such an upbeat manner. I'm guessing it might have something to do with the fact that you have a new aldi. Am I right?"

Paul stiffened. "Who told you that?"

"Mom. She said that Lisa was the reason you chose not to come home for Christmas, and when she told Dad about it, he figured it out."

"Spending time with Lisa at Christmas was only part of the reason I stayed in Sugarcreek for the holiday. Oh, and you can let our mamm know that Lisa is not my girlfriend. We are just good friends." Paul drew in a deep breath, released it slowly, and closed his eyes. *But I wish it were more. If I could only be sure how Lisa feels about me, I'd ask her to go steady with me.*

Paul sucked in more frigid air. Even though he had promised himself that he wouldn't fall for another woman, somehow he had. There was something special about Lisa, like the way she cared for her students and even her dog. She seemed sincere and honest, and Paul felt certain that she would never hurt anyone intentionally.

"Umm. . .Harley, it's been nice talking to you, but I need to get out of this cold building and go back to the woodworking shop with a message for Uncle Abe."

"Oh, sure... Of course... I'll let you go. Take care, little bruder, and come see us soon."

"Maybe some time in early spring."

"Okay, you'd better, or I'll come to Ohio and get you. We all miss seeing your handsome face."

Paul let out a bark of laughter. "Yeah, right." He said goodbye and hung up the phone.

As Paul made his way back to the house, he thought about the news Harley had given him. A few months ago, hearing that Susan and his used-to-be good friend were planning their wedding felt like a stab to the heart. Now it didn't matter at all.

"Where's your brother today?" Lisa asked her student Karen Yoder when she entered the schoolyard after being dropped off by her father.

"After school yesterday, Gabe broke his arm in two places." The little girl blinked rapidly. "He was slidin' down the hill on an inner tube out behind our place and crashed right into a tree."

"I'm sorry to hear that," Lisa said earnestly. "Were you also sledding when it happened?"

Karen shook her head. "He went with our cousin Robert, and Mama said I couldn't go."

Before Lisa could form a response, her young student stomped the snow off her boots and went into the schoolhouse. Normally most of the children played outside until the bell rang, but with it being so cold outside, Lisa understood why Karen would want to get indoors quickly.

She shivered, watching from the porch as several more children came into the yard. Some stopped to make a few snowballs, but most made a beeline for the warmth of indoors.

Lisa was about to ring the bell when Yvonne came out and joined her on the porch. "I hope all this snow melts soon," she said. "Spring is still more than two months away, and I'm already longing for bright sunshine and warmer days."

"Same here. Winter is definitely not my favorite time of the year."

"There are some fun things to do in the winter, though, right?"

"Jah, like sledding on an inner tube and ending up with a broken arm." Lisa grimaced. "You'll never get me on one of those things."

"Sledding can be a lot of fun if one is careful."

"I suppose. Did Karen tell you about her brother's accident?"

Yvonne nodded. "Since he's in my class, I'll have to make a trip to his parents' house and take him some homework to do until he's able to come back to school."

"That makes sense. Otherwise Gabe will fall behind."

"How's Maggie doing these days?" Yvonne asked.

"She's getting around fairly well. Better than I expected. I guess the vet was right when he said that my dog would adjust to having only three legs."

"I'm glad she's doing better." Yvonne pointed to the bell in Lisa's hand. "I think it's about time to bring the rest of the children inside, don't you?"

"Yes, and it's time for a certain teacher to go indoors too. Brr... it's sure cold this morning." Lisa rang the bell and stepped aside as their students filed into the building. As the last two children—a boy and a girl—went in, a vivid picture popped into Lisa's head. She saw her six-year-old self, entering the schoolhouse she'd attended on a cold, snowy day. A young boy came in behind her and whispered in Lisa's ear, "I'm gonna marry you someday."

What a silly thought I just had, Lisa told herself as she stepped into the schoolhouse and closed the door. *Did it really happen, or was it only a figment of my imagination? And if it did actually occur, who was that boy?*

⁓

Walnut Creek

When Paul entered Memory Keepers that afternoon, he found Orley and Lois moving a small table from one side of the room to the other.

"Can I help you with that?" Paul hurried over to them.

"Danki for offering, but it's not heavy, and we can manage." Once the table was in place, Lois dusted it off while Orley came over and shook Paul's hand. "Good to see you. Did you get my message about the milk bottles?"

"I sure did." Paul glanced over at Lois and smiled when she waved; then he turned his attention to Orley again. "That's why I came by—to take a look at them."

"I wanted you to see the old bottles first, before I set them out to sell, so they're still in the storage room. Let's go there now and you can have a look-see." Orley motioned for Paul to follow him as he headed toward the back of the store.

When they entered the storage room, Orley turned on a couple of battery-operated lights and pointed to a shelf where six milk bottles had been placed.

After Paul stepped up and took a good look, he was pleased to see that one of the bottles looked almost exactly like the one his grandma used to own before he had carelessly broken it. He picked the ornate bottle up and studied it carefully. "This is it." He grinned at Orley. "It's very similar, if not identical, to the one I've been searching for. How much do you want for it?"

Orley quoted a reasonable price, and Paul said, "That sounds fair. Any chance you could gift wrap it for me?"

Orley bobbed his head. "I'm sure my fraa would be glad to accommodate that request."

"I'd sure appreciate it. My grandmother's birthday isn't till the end of April, and she won't be back from her winter vacation in Florida until close to that time." Paul fingered the raised bubbles on the bottle, feeling a sense of eagerness. "So I will wait until then to make a trip to Indiana and surprise Grandma with the old bottle for her birthday."

"I'm sure she'll be even happier to see you than she will be with the milk bottle."

"I hope so. It'll be nice to see her and the rest of my family."

"I bet they miss you."

"Jah, but they're well aware that I like it here and plan to stay."

"Sometimes change is good. A person can gain a new perspective when they start over in a new place."

"I agree with you on that." Paul left the storage room with the bottle and waited at the register to ask Orley's wife if she would be kind enough to gift wrap the milk bottle.

"No problem." Lois stepped behind the counter, pulled out some tissue paper, and began wrapping up the glass item with care. Then she showed Paul some samples of the different kinds of gift wrap available. "Which one would you like to use?"

Paul pointed. "I think she would like the one with the birds and flowers the best."

"You chose wisely." She smiled. "If there is anything else you'd like to look at, feel free to wander around the store. I'll have your gift wrapped by the time you come back to the register."

Paul thanked Lois and went to speak to Orley again. He found him standing near the front window, looking out. "Mind if I ask you a question?"

Orley gave him a wide smile. "I don't mind at all. Ask away."

"How long did it take you to know if Lois was the woman you wanted to date?"

There seemed to be a twinkle in the older man's eyes. "Not long at all. Course I waited awhile, till I was pretty sure she was interested in me too, before I asked."

Paul shifted his weight from one leg to the other. "I'm not sure what I'll do if she says no."

"Is Lisa Miller the 'she' you're referring to?"

Paul felt a rush of heat flood his face as he nodded. "Jah."

"I thought that might be the case." Orley moved closer and placed his hand on Paul's shoulder; then he gave it a couple of pats. "Look at it this way—the worst thing that can happen is she'll say no, and then you'll come to realize that she wasn't the right girl for you."

Paul wasn't sure he wanted to hear that, but Orley was right—he did need to find out where he stood with Lisa. He just hoped he would have the courage to do it soon.

"Oh, before I forget. . ." Orley thumped his forehead. "If you're not doing anything tomorrow afternoon, I'd like to invite you to join me on the hill out behind my home for some seriously fun sledding."

"That does sound interesting, but I don't have a *schlidde*."

"No problem. I have several old sleds in my barn, so if you don't have one, you're more than welcome to use one of those."

"That would be great." Paul hesitated a minute before asking a bold question. "Would you mind very much if I invited my friend Lisa to join me?"

"No problem. The more the merrier." Orley glanced over at Lois, who was still busy wrapping the gift for Paul, and she grinned in their direction. "If Lisa comes with you, I may even be able to talk my fraa into joining us. Normally she prefers to stay inside, but this time she might change her mind and come sledding."

"That would be nice. It will give Lisa someone to talk to in case she gets tired of sledding and decides to stand on the sidelines and watch."

Orley clasped Paul's shoulder. "All right, then, we'll look forward to seeing you tomorrow afternoon." He took a piece of paper and wrote down his home address, then handed it to Paul.

"What time would work best for you?"

"Oh, how about sometime between one and two?"

"Sounds good." Paul headed over to the register to pay for his purchase and wait for Lois to finish gift wrapping the milk bottle. As soon as he left, he planned to head over to see Lisa, and he sure hoped she would say yes.

Chapter 26

Sugarcreek

After Paul left Memory Keepers, he decided to stop by the Schrocks' place and see if Lisa would be interested in going sledding with him Saturday. He hoped she'd be able to, because it would be good for her to get away from the house for a while and have a little fun in the snow. Between teaching school and taking care of her dog, Lisa's life involved more work than play these days.

Paul urged Chester forward until the Schrocks' home came into view, and then he guided the horse up their driveway. Paul set the brake and got out of the buggy. A few minutes later, he had Chester secured at the hitching rail. After a short tromp through the snow, Paul stepped onto the sidewalk that had obviously been shoveled and sprinkled with ice melt sometime earlier today.

Stepping onto the front porch, he heard Maggie bark from inside the house. A few seconds later, Lisa opened the door with the dog by her side.

"Hello, Paul. It's good to see you. Would you like to come in?" She held the door open for him.

"Jah, sure." Paul stepped inside and bent down to pet Maggie. "How ya doin,' girl? Are you getting along better these days?"

The dog wagged her tail while licking Paul's hand.

He looked up at Lisa and smiled. "I think she likes me."

Lisa nodded. "I believe you're right. Maggie likes you a lot."

Do you like me too? Paul kept the thought to himself. It would be too bold to come right out and ask her that question. And it would be embarrassing if her grandfather or grandmother heard him ask that of Lisa. He gave the dog one final pat and stood to his full height.

"May I take your jacket?" Lisa asked. "We can sit in the living room and talk until it's time for me to help my grandma fix supper."

"You're welcome to stay for supper, Paul," Marlene hollered from the kitchen.

Lisa's cheeks colored. "I guess she was listening."

Paul chuckled. "I'd love to stay for supper, but I need to get home. I promised Aunt Emma that I'd pick up a few things for her at the store, and I haven't done that yet." Paul took a step closer to Lisa. "The reason I stopped by is to invite you to go sledding with me tomorrow afternoon. I was at the antique store in Walnut Creek today, and Orley invited me to try out the hill behind his house. He said I could borrow one of his sleds and mentioned that you'd be welcome to come too."

Lisa twirled the ties on her head covering around her index finger. "That sounds like fun, but I should probably be here to take care of Maggie."

Marlene stepped into the hallway. "Your hund's doing fine, and I'll be here to take her outside whenever she needs to go there." She gave Lisa's shoulder a tap. "After a long week of teaching school, you deserve to get out for a while and have some fun."

Come on Lisa. . .please join me tomorrow. Paul stood quietly at her side.

Lisa hesitated but finally nodded. "All right, Paul. What time should I be ready?"

"I'll pick you up around one o'clock. How's that sound? Or would you rather go a little later?"

"I can be ready by one."

"Great. I'll see you tomorrow then." Paul said goodbye to Lisa and her grandma, gave Maggie's head a few pats, and went out the door. When he got to the hitching rail and released his horse, he paused for a moment and stroked Chester's silky neck. "She said yes, boy. Maybe tomorrow, while we're traveling to or from Walnut Creek, I'll get up the nerve to tell Lisa how much I've come to care for her. I sure hope she feels the same about me."

The next day, dressed in a heavy jacket, scarf, gloves, and boots, Lisa stood waiting at the living-room window for Paul to pick her up. She looked forward to spending time with him again but felt bad about leaving Maggie for her grandmother to care for. Grandma had assured her, however, that she didn't mind and reminded Lisa that with the exception of going outside with the dog when needed, there really wasn't much else to do. Maggie was off her pain medication and didn't have to be coaxed to eat or drink anymore. The dog's stitches had come out, and she'd been getting around with little effort, while adjusting to her disability. Grandma had also commented that Lisa worried too much.

Lisa reflected on how well she and her dog had bonded when Maggie first came to live with them. She smiled, thinking about how one night a few days after she'd made the decision to keep the dog, she had discovered Maggie upstairs in her bedroom, curled up at the foot of the bed. Another time the dog had found a roll of her grandfather's quarters and managed to tear it open. Grandpa was none too happy when he'd discovered money all over the floor, but Maggie's winning personality won him over, and soon all was forgiven.

Lisa's attention reverted back to the present when she heard a horse's whinny. She shielded her eyes from the glare the sun had cast on the snow in their yard and was pleased to see Paul's horse and carriage enter the yard.

Lisa waited until she heard Paul's boots clomping up the porch steps before she went to open the door. Maggie hobbled into the hall's front entrance and stood beside Lisa.

"No, girl, you can't come with us," Lisa said when the dog whined and pushed her head against Lisa's leg.

"Maybe next year," Paul interjected. "She'll be completely healed and raring to go way before then."

Next year. Lisa smiled. *That must mean Paul is planning to stay and make his home in Ohio.* Lisa hoped that he would, and for the first time ever, she allowed herself to imagine what it would be like if she and Paul got married.

Now where did that thought come from? Lisa wondered. *I've never wanted to get married or establish a close relationship with a man. Besides, I don't know if Paul feels anything toward me but friendship.*

"Ready to go now?" Paul asked.

She nodded. "I'll just go into the kitchen and tell my grandparents goodbye."

"Mind if I go with you?"

"Course not. I'm sure Grandma and Grandpa would like to say hello."

Lisa clapped her hands and called Maggie to follow. The dog went obediently behind her, and when they entered the kitchen, Maggie bedded down on the throw rug near the sink.

Lisa's grandparents sat at the kitchen table finishing the last of their lunch. They both looked at Paul and smiled, and Grandpa got up and shook Paul's hand.

"As always, it's nice to see you," he said.

"It's good to see you folks as well." Paul glanced at the table, then looked at Lisa. "Did I get here too soon? Were you able to get some lunch?"

"Jah, I ate around noon."

"If you'd come by sooner we could have all eaten together," Grandma said in her usual cheery tone.

"That's okay. I ate at home." Paul's cheeks reddened a bit. "What I meant to say is, I ate at my aunt and uncle's home. I sure don't own it."

"Do you think you'll ever settle down and buy a place of your own here in Sugarcreek?" Grandma asked.

The color in Paul's cheeks darkened, and he lifted his shoulders in a brief shrug. "Maybe. . . I hope so. I've priced a few places, but I'm just waiting to see how things go."

Sensing that he seemed uncomfortable with this conversation, Lisa suggested that they get going.

"Jah, we probably should," he agreed. "It'll take us a while to get to Walnut Creek, and I don't want to keep Orley waiting."

"Is it necessary to go all the way over there?" Grandpa questioned. "Aren't there some places around here where you can sled?"

"I'm sure there are, but since Orley invited us to try out his hill and I already said yes, I don't want to go back on my word."

"That makes sense." Grandma gave Paul a wide smile. "I hope you and Lisa will have an enjoyable time."

Lisa and Paul said their goodbyes and hurried toward the front door. Lisa was glad that Maggie had fallen asleep or she'd have probably tried to sneak outside with them.

Paul steadied Lisa by putting his arm gently around her waist as they made their way through the slippery snow to his carriage. Although she couldn't feel the warmth of his hand through her heavy jacket, she felt a sense of pleasure at his touch, and knowing that he cared enough to keep her from slipping and falling in the snow made her feelings for him even stronger. Whether he felt anything more than friendship toward her or not, he certainly was a good friend, and she felt thankful for the comfortable relationship they'd developed.

⁓

"Would you like another cup of kaffi before you head out to the harness shop?" Marlene asked her husband.

He shook his head. "I'd better not. Too much caffeine makes me jittery, and I've already had two cups of coffee with lunch, not to mention the one I drank during breakfast." He smiled at her from across the table. "But danki for asking."

She nodded and fingered the napkin next to her plate. "What do you think about Lisa and Paul?"

Jerry shrugged. "What about them?"

"Their relationship, Husband. Where do you think it's going?"

His shoulders lifted again. "I have no idea. Guess time will tell."

Marlene tapped her fingers on the tabletop. "I believe they have gotten really close, and I wouldn't be one bit surprised if Paul asks Lisa to go steady with him." She looked at Jerry and blinked several times. "I think they're in love, and I'm wondering why Paul hasn't asked her already."

"Maybe he has, and our granddaughter has chosen not to say anything to us about it."

"That's lecherich. I see no reason why Lisa would not have mentioned it."

"It's not really ridiculous. She might like to keep her private life private." Jerry pushed away from the table and stood. "Would you like my help with the dishes before I go out to the shop?"

Marlene shook her head. "There are only a few, and I'll take care of them."

"Okay. I'll be back in the house in a few hours." He came over, bent down, and kissed her cheek. "Enjoy the quiet, and try not to concern yourself over Lisa and Paul. If they've decided to go steady or proclaimed their love for each other, I'm sure we'll hear about it when Lisa is ready to share the news."

"I hope so. She often keeps things to herself."

"Yes, most of the time. The fact is, all we can do is commit it to God." Jerry slipped on his jacket and knitted cap; then he went out the back door.

Marlene bowed her head in prayer. *Dear Lord, help me remember not to meddle in this or press Lisa about her relationship with Paul. If it's Your will for their friendship to go deeper, then it will happen in Your time.*

~

Walnut Creek

"Thanks for the loan of these great sleds," Paul said as he, Orley, and Lisa stood at the top of the Troyers' snow-covered hill.

Orley grinned like a child with a new toy. "No problem. I'm glad you could join me today."

Lois hadn't come out with them because she'd been busy writing some letters. She had, however, extended an invitation for Paul and Lisa to join her and Orley for some hot chocolate and cookies when they either got too cold and needed to warm up or had experienced all the sledding they could stand.

"Would you like to go first, Lisa?" Orley asked.

She shook her head. "Think I'll watch from up here while you two go down, and if nobody falls off their schlidde, I'll get on mine and meet you at the bottom of the hill."

Paul gave Lisa's arm a little poke. "Oh, so you're waiting to see if one of us gets hurt or ends up facedown with a mouthful of schnee?"

She laughed and poked him right back. "Exactly."

"Okay, well, here I go." Paul lay on his belly, grabbed hold of the wooden steering apparatus, and pushed off with one foot.

Lisa watched as he sailed down the hill, hollering at the top of his lungs, "Fun! Fun! Fun!" When his sled came to a stop, he got off, looked up toward them, and waved.

"You want to go next or shall I?" Orley questioned.

"I'll wait till you're at the bottom of the hill." Lisa hadn't been sledding since the first winter after she'd come to live with her grandparents. Although she didn't want to admit it, the thought of speeding rapidly down the snowy slope sent shivers of apprehension up her spine.

"Okay, here I go." Orley paused and gave her a silly-looking grin. "During my youth I was given the nickname 'Big O' because I was a good baseball player. Then when I became known by more and more people as Big O, it became almost like my second name." He gestured to his sled. "So stand back and watch Big O make his way down this snowy hill."

Instead of lying on his stomach the way Paul had done, Orley sat on the sled and took hold of each side of the rope that was connected to the steering apparatus. With a noisy huff, he pushed off with both feet and was soon on his way down the hill.

Lisa was impressed when he made it to the bottom with no problem. For a man in his fifties, Orley had a lot of spunk. She figured Paul would probably be the same way when he reached middle age. Lisa hoped she would still know him by then.

It was her turn now, and with Paul and Orley standing down there watching, she felt a determination to set her fears aside and make it safely to the bottom of the hill. She wasn't sure, however, whether to sit on the sled in the manner Orley had done or lie down on her stomach like Paul. Either way, if Lisa wasn't careful, she could end up crashing into something or simply losing her bearings and falling off the sled into a mountain of snow.

Finally, deciding to go facedown, Lisa positioned herself on the sled. She gritted her teeth. *It would be a lot easier to do this if those two men weren't down there, watching me and waiting.*

At the count of ten, Lisa pushed off. About halfway down, she gained momentum, and although the ride felt exhilarating, she lost control. The next thing Lisa knew, her sled hit a bump, and she bounced off, causing her to land facedown in the snow. She coughed and sputtered as a clump of frigid snow traveled up her nose. Lisa was thoroughly embarrassed, and her face felt like it had been frozen in place. She wasn't even sure if, when she opened her mouth, she'd be able to speak.

"Are you okay, Lisa?" Paul reached out his hand to help her up.

"I—I think so." Once on her feet, she brushed at the snow clinging to her face, scarf, and jacket.

"Maybe you should go inside and warm up for a while," Orley suggested. "You're pretty wet and shivering badly."

Lisa nodded and started walking toward the house, pulling the sled behind her. Although she enjoyed spending time with Paul, getting cold and wet with a face full of snow wasn't her idea of having fun.

Chapter 27

Lois heard a knock on the back door and went to see who it was. She had been engrossed in writing a couple of letters and getting them ready to send. Lois had always been a person who enjoyed crossing things off her to-do list. And for now she'd managed to check off everything and could toss that paper away.

When Lois opened the door, she was surprised to see Lisa on the porch, shivering and quite wet.

"Is—is it okay if I come in for a while?" Lisa's teeth chattered as she spoke.

"Of course. You need to get warm and dried off." Lois led the way to the laundry room where her gas-powered wringer washing machine sat. "You can take off your *schtiffel* and leave them here, and I'll set your jackets, scarf, and gloves near the fireplace."

"Danki." Lisa took off her boots and placed them near the washing machine before removing her other outer garments and handing them to Lois.

"How'd you get so wet?" Lois asked as she led the way to the living room, where the warmth from the fireplace greeted them. "I hope those eager fellows didn't start a snowball fight."

"No, no, they'd didn't." Lisa stood in front of the glowing fire, rubbing her cold, reddened hands together. "On my first and only attempt at sledding down the hill, I hit a bump and fell off the sled." Lisa grimaced. "I landed face first and ended up with snow up my *naas*."

Lois gave an understanding nod as she hung Lisa's jacket, gloves, and scarf on a wooden rack she had set up near the fireplace. "I've had that happen before too. Sledding used to be fun when I was a girl, but not so much anymore." She gave a quick shake of her head. "Of course, my fun-loving husband doesn't mind getting cold and wet. He will go out to sled or ice-skate on our neighbor's frozen pond whenever he gets the chance."

Lisa laughed. "I think Paul might be like that too. He seemed pretty excited about coming here to go sledding."

Lois's nose wrinkled. "If I had gone out sledding like Orley wanted me to, it probably would have been me who'd fallen off the sled and would be standing here, soaking wet. I've never cared much for activities in cold, snowy weather." She noticed that Lisa had quit rubbing her hands together. Lois bent down and checked the wood in the fireplace. *I wonder if Lisa would like a hot beverage to warm her up more. She'd probably appreciate being able to sit and relax after her unpleasant sledding experience.*

"Let's sit here in the living room where it's nice and toasty." Lois gestured to one of the chairs. "Feel free to take whichever seat you would like. While you're getting comfortable, I'll get us some hot chocolate."

"That's sounds good. Is there anything I can do to help?"

"There's not much involved in making it, so just relax and enjoy the warmth from the fireplace."

"All right. Danki for your kindness."

Lois smiled and hurried from the room.

While in the kitchen readying the hot chocolates, she peeked through the frosted window and saw the men walking back up the hill, pulling their wooden sleds. *If it weren't for my husband's long beard, I'd have a harder time distinguishing who is who out there.* Lois stepped over to the pantry to retrieve a bag of marshmallows. *My Orley is like a big kid at times. I can't help wondering if he'll ever start acting his age.* The water heated on the stove, and she began measuring and filling the mugs with her fragrant homemade chocolate powder.

When Lois returned to the living room with two mugs full of hot chocolate, she found Lisa on the couch with her head leaning against the back cushion and her eyes closed. Thinking she might have fallen asleep, Lois set the mugs on the coffee table and took a seat in one of the recliners. At the moment, the room seemed so quiet and peaceful.

A few seconds passed, and then Lisa opened her eyes.

"Sorry if I woke you," Lois apologized.

"It's all right. I really wasn't sleeping—just feeling fully relaxed."

"That's good. Everyone needs to take some time to relax." Lois got up and handed Lisa one of the mugs, taking the other one for herself. "Be careful not to burn your mouth. I'm afraid the hot chocolate might be a little too warm. There are some marshmallows right here too."

"Marshmallows are always so good in hot chocolate," Lisa said, "but did you know that they can be used to disguise a pain pill?"

"I'm not sure what you mean."

"When my dog first came home after losing one of her front legs, she wouldn't cooperate and take her pills."

Lois sipped on her beverage and listened attentively as Lisa explained how she'd used marshmallows to hide her dog's pain medication and was pleased when it worked.

"I'm glad it worked out okay and she cooperated."

Lisa sat quietly, drinking her hot chocolate, and Lois wasn't sure what else to talk about, since she didn't really know the young woman that well. *I could ask her if she and Paul are going steady.* Lois reached for some marshmallows to add to her hot chocolate. *She's a little timid, and that might seem like too bold of a question, so maybe it would be best if I ask more questions about her dog.* "How's your hund doing now?" Lois questioned.

"Much better, but she's not quite back to being her old self yet. The first week after her surgery was pretty rough."

Lois listened again as Lisa shared a few more things about Maggie's recovery and how terrible she'd felt seeing the poor dog in pain.

"I was so worried about her those first few nights that I set up a doggy bed for her on the floor in the downstairs guest room where I had decided to sleep. That way I could check on her frequently." Lisa looked away, then back at Lois. "At first I blamed myself for Maggie's injuries, since I was the one who'd put her away in her pen that evening."

"Do you know how she got out?"

"I suppose that Maggie could have played with the latch enough times to have gotten it open, but I'm not really sure." Lisa sighed. "I was so worried those first few nights, it was hard to sleep."

"You must care for your dog very much."

"Jah, Maggie is very special to me. She's a good companion and is ever so smart."

"I'd like to meet her sometime. Maybe this spring when the weather is nicer, you could bring her by here or our antique store. Or another thought would be for Orley and me to stop by your grandparents' place sometime when we are in Sugarcreek. Your grandfather owns the harness shop there, right?"

"Jah, and it would be nice if you could meet Maggie. She's a friendly hund, and I'm sure she'd warm right up to you." Lisa blew on her hot chocolate and took a sip. "This is really good. Is it a ready-made mix, or did you make it from scratch?"

"It's my own—well, my mother's, actually. I found it in her recipe book several years after she died."

"How old were you when she passed away?"

"I was still a young girl—just eight years old."

"Did your daed remarry?"

"Jah, he married a widow lady from our community in Mifflin County, Pennsylvania a year after Mama died, but that marriage only lasted a few years. Selma got cancer and didn't survive. It was hard to deal with because my siblings and I had grown fond of her." Lois swallowed hard in an attempt to push the lump in her throat down. Even after all these years, she still felt sad talking about her first stepmother's death.

"Did he find a third wife or stay single after that?"

"He chose a single lady who had never been married, but that wasn't till I was grown and had moved here. My daed is still married to Sarah, but they live in Kentucky and I don't see them very often."

Lisa took another drink from her mug, then set it back down on the coffee table. "Life is unfair, and there are so many uncertainties."

Lois drank some of her hot chocolate before speaking, which gave her a few seconds to think about how she should respond. "What you said is true, Lisa, but it's how we choose to deal with the unexpected happenings that occur. Some of them are tragic, to be sure, but we need to pray and have the faith to believe that the Lord will see us through."

Lisa pressed her elbows into her sides. "I try, but sometimes it's so hard. Ever since I lost my parents and paternal grandparents, I've feared that the worst will happen."

"In Second Timothy 1:7 we read, 'For God hath not given us the spirit of fear; but of power, and of love, and of a sound mind,'" Lois quoted. "Whenever I feel overwhelmed by fear, I try to remember that scripture."

"It is a good verse," Lisa said. "I'll try to focus on that whenever I'm full of doubts and fears."

⌒

When the men came inside an hour later, Lois removed Lisa's dried things, putting her jacket and scarf, along with her gloves, on the wall peg by the front door. Then she returned to hang the men's jackets, gloves, and stocking caps by the fire.

Lisa couldn't help but notice how red Orley's and Paul's noses were. Was it just from the cold, or had they both fallen off their sleds into the frigid snow? Before she had a chance to ask, Lois asked the men if they would like some hot chocolate.

"You bet we would." Orley looked at Paul. "Right?"

Paul bobbed his head. "Drinking something warm might help the inside of my body to feel warmer, and the cozy blaze in your fireplace will no doubt take away the chill my body feels. It sure has gotten really cold out there."

"I think it may have something to do with the fact that you and Orley both got so wet," Lois commented.

"That's true," Orley admitted. "Paul and I did fall off our sleds a few times. But don't worry, we never got hurt."

Lois gave a small laugh. "I figured as much." She turned toward the kitchen. "I'll be back soon with your beverages and some kichlin."

Lisa stood up. "I'll help you with that." She followed Lois into the other room. "What would you like me to do?"

"Would you mind going back to the living room to get our mugs? I'd like to have some more hot chocolate, wouldn't you?"

"Jah, I would."

"I'll slice some gingerbread while you're gone, and I'll get out some chocolate chip cookies I made this morning."

"Both sound yummy." Lisa left the kitchen and was almost to the door of the living room when she heard Orley mention her name. "How are things going between you and your aldi?"

Lisa tipped her head and waited for Paul's response.

"Lisa isn't officially my girlfriend, but I'm hoping she will be soon. When I take her home, I'm planning to ask if she'll go steady with me."

Paul had spoken quietly, but Lisa heard every word he'd said. She leaned against the wall, holding her hands against her chest as she pulled in a few deep breaths. *Paul wants me to be his girlfriend. When he asks me to go steady with him, what should I say? Should I give Paul my answer right away or say that I need to think about it?*

Sugarcreek

Paul's thoughts had been so scattered he'd barely been able to think of anything to talk to Lisa about on the drive back to Sugarcreek. But here they were, pulling into her grandparents' yard, and he still hadn't told Lisa how he felt about her or mentioned going steady.

She'd been quiet too, staring straight ahead most of the way and picking at the material on her gloves. *Is she still embarrassed about falling off her sled? Could she be upset because we didn't have much time to be alone with each other today?* Paul clamped his teeth together so hard his jaw ached. *When Lisa quit sledding and went into the Troyers' house, maybe I should have put away the sled I borrowed from Orley and gone in with her, or maybe we should have headed back to Sugarcreek.*

Neither Lisa nor Paul made an effort to get out of the buggy. They both sat staring out the front window at the backside of his horse.

What are you waiting for? he asked himself. *You can't put this off any longer.*

"Would you like to come inside for a while?" Lisa asked.

"Umm. . .jah, but there's something I'd like to say to you first."

She turned her head in his direction. "What is it, Paul?"

He moistened his parched lips with the tip of his tongue before clearing his throat. "As I'm sure you must realize, I enjoy spending time with you."

"I like being with you too."

"I'm glad, and, umm. . .well, the thing is. . ." Paul paused and took in some air. "I've come to care for you, Lisa. In fact I haven't cared about anyone the way I do you since my girlfriend back home and I broke up." He waited a few seconds to see if Lisa would say anything, but when she just sat there looking at him, he continued. "So I was wondering if you would go steady with me." There, it was out, and Paul felt a little better, but now he had to wait for her answer, and he didn't know what he would say if she said no.

"I have feelings for you too." Lisa's voice was barely above a whisper. "And jah, I would like to go steady."

Releasing the breath he'd been holding while waiting for her answer, Paul reached across the seat and took hold of Lisa's hand. He would rather have kissed her but didn't want to move too fast. Paul felt it best to take it slow and easy with Lisa, just as he'd done so far.

"Why don't you come inside, and we can tell my grandparents what we've decided," Lisa suggested.

"*Jah*, that'd be great. I hope they will approve."

"I don't think you have to worry about that. Grandma and Grandpa have said many times that they think you are a fine young man."

"Okay then, just let me get Chester secured at the rail."

Paul got out of the buggy, and as he went around to his horse, he reminded himself that he still hadn't told Lisa that they used to know each other. But he'd convinced himself that it could wait awhile longer. Maybe in another month or two, when their relationship had grown stronger, he would drum up the courage to tell her. For now, Paul would simply enjoy their courtship, and someday, if everything went well between them, he might even propose marriage.

Chapter 28

"Winter. . .winter. . .winter. . . Will spring ever get here? It seems like all we've had these first few weeks of February is ice and snow," Marlene complained to Jerry as they sat in the kitchen having a cup of coffee together before he headed out to his shop. "I can't believe our weather was so bad last week that school had to be canceled for two days. Although Lisa enjoyed being at home and spending time with Maggie, I think she missed teaching school on those days."

"It was pretty severe weather," her husband agreed, "but at least we have no blizzard-like conditions this week."

"Jah. Since today is Valentine's Day, and Lisa and Yvonne planned something special for their students, everyone would have been disappointed if there was no school today."

"What do they have planned?"

"In addition to a few of the parents bringing in hot lunches, Lisa took cherry-vanilla cupcakes to share with the children. As a special touch, she put a heart-shaped candy on the top of each one." Marlene paused to drink the rest of her coffee and set the cup down. "Before Lisa left for the schoolhouse this morning, she mentioned that Yvonne would be bringing two kinds of cookies."

Jerry chuckled. "Guess the kids will go home on a sugar high today. I bet their parents will love that."

She poked his arm. "Since it's Valentine's Day, I'm sure the children's parents will know what to expect."

"No doubt about that." Jerry started to get up, but then he sat back down. "Did I tell you what I heard about our bishop's son Eric the other day?"

"No, I don't believe you did."

"Es is ihm aartlich schlecht gange."

"In what way did things go badly for him?" Marlene questioned.

"After school yesterday, he went sledding with some of his friends. The boy wasn't gone very long before he came running into the house hollering like crazy, and with his mouth open and tongue sticking out."

Her eyes widened. "Oh, dear, what happened?"

"Well, the bishop said that Eric's *zung* had come in contact with the cold sled, and when it froze there, he just jerked his head back and pulled his tongue right off the sled."

"Oh, dear, I can't imagine how badly that must have hurt. It will probably take a while for the boy's injury to heal up."

Jerry bobbed his head. "I did some stupid things when I was a boy, but never anything like that. Makes me wonder what the young fellow was thinking."

"Maybe one of his friends dared him to do it. Or perhaps when Eric slid down the hill, in the excitement, he opened his mouth to scream and his tongue came out of its own accord and got stuck."

"Jah, either of those things could have been the reason."

Marlene pushed the plate of lunch meat closer to her husband. "Would you like me to make you another sandwich before you head back to work?"

Jerry gave his belly a few thumps. "No thanks, I'm full enough. I will have a few more chips though, and then I need to head out."

Marlene waited until he'd helped himself to a handful of potato chips before she spoke again. "Have you noticed the change in our granddaughter since she and Paul began going steady? I'd have to say Lisa seems like a different person since Paul came into her life, and that makes me so happy." She pursed her lips. "I'm also glad Aaron Wengerd has finally given up his quest to win our granddaughter's hand."

Jerry nodded. "I agree. I don't think Aaron would have been the best choice for Lisa."

"I hope the weather stays as it is right now so Lisa and Paul don't have to change their plans to go out for supper this evening."

"According to the weather report I read in this morning's paper, it's not likely to get worse. But even if it should, I'm betting Paul will put on some snowshoes and make his way over here just to be with Lisa."

Marlene smiled as she pictured Lisa's boyfriend blazing a trail through the heavy snow from his aunt and uncle's place to here. Every time Marlene saw the big smiles on Paul's and Lisa's faces when they were together, it brought tears to her eyes. If anyone deserved to be happy, it was Lisa.

Maggie got up from the braided rug she'd been sleeping on and gave a few loud barks.

"I know, girl," Marlene said. "You want to go out. Guess I'd better put my jacket on so I can keep a close eye on you out there." Even though Lisa's dog was doing so well, Marlene always went out with her. She couldn't take the chance that Maggie might leave the yard and try to make it to the schoolhouse in search of Lisa—especially after what had happened the night of the schoolchildren's Christmas program.

Marlene started to rise from her chair, but Jerry told her to sit back down and relax. "Since I have to get bundled up against the cold anyway, I'll take the hund out and bring her back in before I head to the harness shop."

"Danki, Jerry. Oh, and by the way—our granddaughter was thoughtful enough to leave us both a cherry-vanilla cupcake to celebrate Valentine's Day." Marlene gestured to the plastic container on the kitchen counter.

"It was nice of her to share. I'll get one after I bring Maggie back in and take it out to the shop with me." He turned to the dog and slapped his knee. "Come on, Maggie, let's go out."

Marlene watched them head to the door. Although her dear husband had never been the romantic type, he was a kind, generous man, and she'd never regretted marrying him. She hoped if Lisa and Paul got married that Lisa would feel thankful she'd chosen the right mate. Marlene casually anchored a hand against one hip. *And if I have anything to say about it, that marriage will happen.*

⁓

Lisa smiled as she watched her students give out their Valentine cards to each other. She and Yvonne received several too. The scholars had been served a hot lunch at noon and spent some time playing in the snow, and after a few more lessons, the party had begun.

Once the cards had been passed out, Lisa and Yvonne set out the treats they'd brought, along with some fruit punch left over from lunch. The kids ate the cupcakes and cookies, talking and laughing the whole while. Lisa was pleased that nearly all of them had said thank you. It was only right that the children were being taught proper manners at home as well as at school.

"Do you have any special plans for this evening?" Yvonne asked, stepping up to Lisa.

"Jah. Paul is taking me out for supper."

Her friend smiled. "You two make a really nice couple. I'm happy you've found someone special, Lisa."

"You'll find the right someone when the time is right."

A rosy glow erupted on Yvonne's cheeks. "I—I think I may already have."

"Oh? Is it someone I know?"

Yvonne nodded. "Aaron Wengerd has come over to see me several times in the last few weeks. And he invited me to join his family for his sister's birthday supper tonight. So that's how I'll be spending my Valentine's Day evening."

"That's wonderful, Yvonne. I hope things work out for you and Aaron." Lisa didn't voice her thoughts, but she was glad Aaron had quit trying to see her socially and found someone else.

As far as Lisa was concerned, there was no one better suited to her than Paul Herschberger.

"Are you excited about your supper date with Paul this evening?" Grandma asked as Lisa stood in front of the hall mirror adjusting her white head covering.

"Jah. Today was a busy day at school, and I'm looking forward to spending the next few hours relaxing and enjoying a nice meal at the restaurant he's chosen." Lisa's brows drew together as she looked at Maggie when she came in with her unique walk and sat down at Lisa's feet. "I wish it was springtime and Paul and I were going on a picnic. Then we could take Maggie with us." She leaned over and stroked the dog's ears. "You miss me when I'm gone, don't you, girl?"

Maggie whined and turned her head so she could lick Lisa's hand.

"Once school is out in a few months, I'll be here more, and we can spend a lot of time together."

As if she'd understood what Lisa had said, Maggie barked three times.

Grandma laughed. "That hund is too schmaert for her own good. Sometimes I think she can read my mind and knows what I'm going to say before the words come out of my mouth."

Lisa laughed too. *If I'm this devoted to my dog, I wonder how I would be if I had children someday. I can't believe how my life seems to be changing, because I never thought I would even be thinking about getting married and having children.*

A horse whinnied outside, and Lisa let her thoughts drift away. No doubt Paul had arrived, and she was eager to go. Even so, Lisa didn't want to appear too anxious, so she waited until he knocked on the door to open it.

Paul had barely stepped inside when Maggie began barking again and wagging her tail.

He bent to pet her. "Are ya happy to see me, Maggie girl?"

Woof! Woof! Woof!

Paul gave the dog a little more affection, then stood to his full height and handed Lisa a bright red gift bag. "Happy Valentine's Day."

Her cheeks warmed. "You didn't have to give me anything. Going out to supper with you would be gift enough."

"I wanted to do something a little extra special. Go ahead and open it."

Lisa reached into the bag and pulled out a book.

"It's a historical novel I found at the Christian bookstore," Paul explained. "It's set during the California gold rush days, and I thought you might find it interesting."

She turned the book over and read a short blurb that told a little about the story. "This looks quite interesting. I'll be eager to begin reading it. Danki, Paul."

"You're welcome." He offered her a wide smile. "I'd hoped you would like it."

Lisa's grandmother stepped into the front entrance, and Lisa showed her the book. "See what Paul gave me?"

"It certainly does seem like an interesting book." Grandma greeted Paul with a hug. "I hope you two will have a lovely evening."

"Where's Grandpa?" Lisa asked. "I'm sure Paul would like to say hello, and I want to say goodbye to both of you before we go."

"He went down the hall to get a new puzzle from the closet." Grandma looked in that direction. "Oh, here he comes now."

Grandpa appeared a few seconds later, holding a box with a picture of a covered bridge on it. Lisa figured he and Grandma would start to work on it as soon as she and her date left.

"*Guder owed*, Paul." Holding on to the puzzle box with his left hand, Lisa's grandfather extended his right hand.

With an eager expression, Paul shook Grandpa's hand. "Good evening. How have you been?"

"Right as *regge*." Grandpa put a sly little smile on his face. "Or maybe it would be more reasonable to say, 'right as snow,' since we haven't seen any rain in a good long while."

"That's true, but March is only a month away, so maybe the schnee will melt soon, and we'll get some rain clouds."

"If I had to pick between the two," Grandma chimed in, "I'd choose rain over snow any day." She sniffed deeply. "I've always enjoyed the clean, damp smell after we've been blessed with a good hard rain."

"Same here," Lisa agreed. "But I'd rather have plenty of sunshine, especially on days during the school year when I walk or ride my bike to the schoolhouse."

The four of them chatted a few more minutes, and then Paul looked at Lisa and said, "I don't know about you, but I'm getting hungry, so are you ready to go?"

"Most definitely." Lisa slipped into her outer garments, hugged her grandparents while saying goodbye, and gave Maggie a few pats on the head. "You be good now, ya hear?"

The dog cocked her head to one side and wagged her tail.

Paul opened the door, and the two of them stepped out onto the porch.

Once Lisa was situated in the passenger's seat of Paul's buggy, Paul undid the horse and climbed in.

Although it was a chilly night, Lisa didn't mind. With the carriage robe in Paul's buggy draped over the lower half of her body, she felt pleasantly warm. Besides, they would soon be sitting inside a cozy restaurant and wouldn't have to deal with the cold at all.

～

As Paul and Lisa headed back to her grandparents' house that evening after a delicious meal at Dutch Valley Restaurant, once again he considered telling Lisa that he used to know her when he was a boy. Something held him back as he looked over at Lisa. *Maybe now isn't the best time. If she were to get upset hearing this news, it would ruin the nice evening we've had.*

When Paul looked out the front window and saw white flakes on Chester's back, he realized it had begun snowing again. Fortunately there was not a strong wind, so it didn't look like they'd be faced with another blizzard like the one they'd had last week. On those days Paul and Uncle Abe had been able to get some work done in his shop, but neither of them had ventured out onto the roads.

"I can't believe it's snowing again," Lisa said, breaking into Paul's thoughts. "I want spring to come so bad, I can almost taste it."

"I hear what you're saying. It's a lot easier to get around when the weather is nice."

"It'll be better for Maggie too. She's able to walk easier now in the house, but all the snow in the yard makes it harder for her when she's outside."

"Makes sense to me. Even on my two good legs it's hard to get around in the snow. If I'm not struggling in snow up to my knees, I am slipping and sliding around on the paths that have been cleared."

"This colder weather isn't good for doing the wash either," Lisa put in. "My grandma doesn't like to hang her laundry outside where it freezes on the line, so she usually hangs everything that's been washed in the basement on a couple of drying racks. Sometimes, when we need things dried faster, she will set the drying racks in the living room in front of the fireplace." Lisa snickered. "Of course, that can prove to be embarrassing if those racks are full of wet clothes and someone drops by unexpectedly. That happened two weeks ago when one of our neighbors came over."

Paul laughed. It was nice to see how easily Lisa engaged him in conversation these days. It was a pleasant change from the quiet, shy young woman he'd met when he first arrived in Ohio. Paul liked to think that he'd had a little influence on her in that regard, but whatever the reason, it was good to see the outgoing Lisa he remembered from childhood resurfacing.

Paul saw the Schrocks' place come into view, and soon he guided Chester up the driveway. He hated to see his pleasant evening with Lisa end, but it had gotten late, and with both of them having jobs to go to tomorrow, it was time for them to say good night.

After Paul had Chester at the hitching rail, he did something he'd wanted to do for a long time. Paul pulled Lisa gently into his arms and kissed her lips. Warmth spread throughout his chest when Lisa didn't resist but responded to his kiss by putting her hands on the back of his neck. The nearness of her made Paul feel possessive. He wanted to take Lisa as his wife. But it was too soon for a marriage proposal, so instead of saying the words on his heart, Paul kissed her again.

Chapter 29

Winter moved on, and by the middle of March, spring had sprung. Flowering bulbs had begun creeping through the soil, robins were nesting, many lawns had turned green because of the rain, and sleds had been traded in for bicycles.

"What a beautiful day we've had so far," Lois commented as she and Orley entered the town of Sugarcreek with their horse and buggy. "It's almost warm enough that we could have taken our open carriage on the road today."

"That'll happen soon enough." Orley glanced to the left as they passed a well-kept farmhouse. "It's always nice to see bright green leaves filling out the trees and people outside working in their yards."

"Jah," she agreed. "And I always love the earthy smell when gardens are turned over in preparation for planting."

"At least our garden is tilled and ready for seeds and prestarted plants."

Lois gave a brief nod. "I have some ideas of what seeds I would like to put in this year. Since we didn't have enough small cucumbers for pickling last year, I'd like to get more of those plants too. Also some dill weed would be nice."

He smacked his lips. "Your bread-and-butter pickles are sure tasty, especially during those hot, sticky months that lie ahead. Yep, they're good, alone or on a burger."

"I'm glad you like them so much. Another thing I like to do

after I make pickles is give them as gifts to friends and family." She shifted on the soft, cushioned buggy seat.

They conversed more about their garden, until Orley pointed up ahead and announced that the Schrocks' harness shop was coming into view.

"I hope Lisa is home from teaching at the schoolhouse by now," Lois said. "I'd sure like to see that hund of hers."

"Me too, but I'm also wanting to pay Jerry Schrock a visit at his harness shop. I'm hoping he can fix that old bridle I got the other day, which I'd like to sell in our store."

"Should we pull up to the rail by the harness shop first?" Lois questioned as they entered the Schrocks' property.

Orley shook his head. "There's no point in you sitting in the carriage waiting while I talk to Jerry. How about if we stop at the house first, and if Lisa is at home, you can visit with her while I take care of business in the harness shop. When I'm done, I'll come back and join you. How's that sound?"

Lois hesitated a few seconds as she mulled things over. "I guess that would be okay, but I would feel uncomfortable if Lisa isn't home yet, and I would need to explain my presence to her grandmother."

Orley had opened his mouth as if to comment when Lisa rode into the yard on her bike. She stopped near the house, got off, and came over to Orley and Lois's carriage. "Well, hello. Did you come by to meet Maggie?"

"Our mission is twofold." Orley held up one finger. "We came to see your hund." A second finger came up. "And I have a harness that I hope your grandfather can repair."

Lisa smiled. "Maggie's not in her pen, so I'm sure she's in the house with my grandma. Come on in, and I'll introduce you to both of them."

⁓

"Grandma, we have company," Lisa called when she entered the house with the Troyers.

A few moments later, her grandmother came out of the kitchen and joined them in the entryway.

Lisa made the introductions, explaining that Orley and Lois owned an antique store in Walnut Creek.

"It's nice to meet you." Grandma gestured to the living room. "Let's go in there, where we can sit and visit." She led the way, and they all took a seat. "My husband's working in his harness shop right now." She looked at Lisa. "If he doesn't have a customer at the moment, why don't you go get him?"

"That's all right. There's no need to bother him," Orley was quick to say. "I brought something with me for your husband to repair, so I'll be going out to the harness shop soon anyway."

"Oh, okay. In the meantime though, would either of you care for some coffee, tea, or something cold to drink? I also have a loaf of banana bread that I made this morning." Grandma smiled. "Lisa and I usually have a snack when she gets home from teaching school."

"A glass of cold *wasser* would be nice," Lois spoke up.

"Water would be fine for me too," Orley added as he scooched over on the couch closer to Lois.

"Would you like my help?" Lisa asked her grandmother.

Grandma shook her head. "No need for that. I'll put the beverage glasses on a tray and carry it in."

Soon after Grandma left the room, Lisa's dog came in with her new tripod way of walking. "This is Maggie," Lisa announced. "She's quite friendly, so if you like dogs, don't be afraid to pet her."

Orley didn't have to be asked twice. He patted his leg and called Maggie over to him. The dog came without any further coaxing and laid her head on Orley's knee.

Lisa snickered as Maggie made a little grunting sound as she soaked up the attention. "She's always been a big baby, but even more so since her operation."

"With everything this poor *hund's* been through, she deserves a lot of attention." Lois leaned closer to Orley and reached over to stroke Maggie's ear.

"She's doing quite well now and has adjusted to her disability better than I thought she would. She's still playful and sometimes gets into things like she did before the accident." Lisa's nose wrinkled. "The other day I entered the kitchen and caught her ripping up a roll of paper towels that had been left on one of the chairs when we emptied the grocery sacks."

Orley chuckled. "When I was a boy, I had a dog that used to stick his snout in the trash can. He liked to pull out used napkins and wrappers." Orley slapped his hand against his leg and laughed. "That hund looked so silly when I came into the kitchen one day and found him with a paper bag over his head. I had a horrible time getting him to hold still so I could take it off."

"Do you have any dogs now?" Lisa asked.

Orley shook his head. "With our busy schedule we don't have time to take care of a pet." He looked at his wife as she scratched behind Maggie's ears. "Isn't that right, Lois?"

"Jah."

Lisa glanced toward the kitchen door. "I wonder what's taking my grandma so long. I should probably go see if she needs my help." She stood and was almost to the door when Grandma stepped into the room, red faced and carrying a tray full of water glasses.

"Sorry for taking so long," she apologized. "I was cutting some pieces of banana bread, and the next thing I knew, the whole loaf slipped off the counter and ended up on the floor in pieces." She set the tray on the coffee table. "It took me a while to clean up the mess, and I'm sorry that I don't have anything else to serve you all now."

"It's okay," Lois spoke up. "We don't need anything to go with our water."

"My fraa is right." Orley picked up one of the glasses and drank the water right down; then he rose to his feet. "Think I'll walk on out to the harness shop now." He smiled at Lisa's grandmother. "It was nice meeting you, as well as Lisa's hund. Oh, and danki for the water."

"You're welcome. Feel free to drop by anytime when you're in the area."

"We certainly will." Orley said goodbye and headed out the door. A few seconds later he popped back in. "I almost forgot, Lois—I'll come back here to get you when I'm through with my business at the harness shop."

She gave him a thumbs-up.

Lisa couldn't help but smile. It was nice to see how well this sweet Amish couple interacted with each other. Of course, her grandparents were the same way, and Lisa couldn't help but envy them. The nagging fear she'd felt for so many years had lessened some, but sometimes the thought of being alone when they died sent shivers of apprehension up her spine.

She looked down at her dog, now lying at her feet. Even the thought of how close she came to losing Maggie caused Lisa to feel tense.

Do not fear, Lisa told herself. *Remember to pray and trust God for all your needs.*

Paul gripped the reins tightly as he headed toward the Schrocks' place with Chester pulling his buggy at a good clip. He'd been invited to their house for supper this evening, and this was the night he planned to tell Lisa that he'd known her when they were children. In fact, Paul felt it was almost imperative, because he'd put it off longer than he had planned. Lisa seemed to be doing better now and had become more open to him, so Paul felt confident that she would accept the information he had to share. He hoped it might even bring them closer and could possibly jog Lisa's memory.

"I'll know soon enough," Paul said aloud. "Because I plan to talk to her after supper when we have a chance to be alone."

He let go of the reins with one hand and stroked his chin. *Or would it be better if I bring the topic up while her grandparents are in the room? At least that way, if Lisa should become upset, Jerry and Marlene would be there to help calm her down.*

Paul fought the urge not to tell her at all. *Would it really be so bad if she never found out?* He gave the side of his head a good thump. *No, it wouldn't be good to keep this secret from her forever. I'll tell her this evening, no matter what the consequences.*

"This sure is a good meal," Paul commented as he sat around the kitchen table with Lisa and her grandparents.

"I can't take any credit for it." Grandma gestured to Lisa. "My granddaughter made the pizza as well as the salad."

"You're a good cook." Paul smiled at Lisa, and her cheeks warmed.

"Danki." Lisa kept her gaze on her plate. She felt better when she changed the topic of conversation to something else.

"Orley and Lois Troyer came by this afternoon." Lisa directed her comment to Paul. "They wanted to meet Maggie and my grandparents."

"That's great. I bet they were surprised to see how well the dog is doing."

Lisa nodded.

"After Orley went out to the harness shop to speak with Lisa's grandpa, Maggie decided to put on a little show for Lois," Grandma said.

Paul reached for another slice of pizza and put it on his plate. "What did the dog do?"

"She disappeared for a while, and when she came back to the living room, Maggie had one of my husband's dirty *schtrimp* in her mouth, and she shook it like a rag doll." Grandma's brows lowered and then pinched together. "I tried to get the sock from her, but the stubborn *hund* did her tripod hop all around the room, and then she disappeared down the hall. Lois thought it was humorous, but Lisa and I were embarrassed."

Lisa nodded in agreement. "After the Troyers went home, Maggie came out of hiding and dropped the *schtrump* at Grandma's feet."

Paul chuckled. "Guess that's a good sign that the dog's feeling like her old self again."

"Jah, one never knows what that hund's gonna do next." Grandpa looked over at Grandma and winked. "Isn't that right, Marlene?"

"For sure. Maggie keeps life interesting around here."

When they'd finished their meal, Lisa helped her grandmother clear the table and do the dishes, while Grandpa and Paul retired to the living room to visit. It had been decided that they would have their dessert in about an hour, after their pizza had time to settle in their stomachs.

Maggie lay on the rug not far from where Lisa stood drying the dishes. Every once in a while the dog would make a grunting sound as she changed to a different position.

After all the dishes were dried and put away, Lisa hung the damp towel on a rack to dry. "Should we take kaffi in to the men now, or wait till we're ready to serve the cake you made?"

"Let's wait on the coffee for a while," Grandma replied.

"Okay. Guess I'll go see what Grandpa and Paul are up to now."

Lisa left the kitchen and was almost to the living room when she heard Paul mention her name. Although it wasn't right to eavesdrop, she didn't want to barge into the room and interrupt the men's conversation. She stood quietly near the door, planning to wait there until Paul stopped talking before entering the room.

"I need your advice on something, Jerry," Paul said. "It concerns Lisa."

"What about my granddaughter?"

Lisa's ears perked up, and she inched her way a bit closer to the door, being careful not to be seen.

Paul cleared his throat. "The thing is. . . Well, I used to know Lisa when she was a girl."

"Oh? You mean here or back when she lived in Indiana?"

"It was in Indiana. Our families lived in the same church district, and Lisa and I attended the same school." There was a pause, and then Paul continued. "I used to tease her back then, saying that I was going to marry her someday."

"Is Lisa aware of this, Paul?"

"No, not yet. I was planning to tell her tonight."

"Why'd you wait so long? Did you want it to be a surprise?"

"Not really. I. . .uh. . .was afraid of how she might react, since she doesn't remember much of her past before the accident. I also know it's difficult for her to talk about certain things, but I figure she has the right to know that the two of us used to be friends."

Lisa blinked rapidly as her mind tried to process what she'd just heard. She had no knowledge of having known Paul until he moved to Sugarcreek. She shook her head in denial. *No, what he said couldn't be true. Surely I would have remembered if I'd known Paul before.*

She flexed her fingers as she stood there trying to decide what to do. Finally, when Lisa could stand it no longer, she dashed into the room and stood directly in front of Paul's chair. "If it's true that we knew each other when we were kinner, then you should have told me right away." Lisa pointed a shaky finger at him. "I don't appreciate you keeping the truth from me, which means you can't be trusted. I—I never want to see you again." Lisa turned and fled the room.

Chapter 30

After climbing the stairs and pausing for a quick prayer, Marlene knocked on Lisa's bedroom door. When there was no response, she turned the knob and peeked in through the crack so she could see into the room. "Lisa, are you awake?" When her granddaughter gave no reply, Marlene opened the door wider and stood silently as she viewed Lisa lying on top of the quilted covering on her bed. With the room illuminated only by the small battery-operated light on the table beside the bed, Marlene saw that her granddaughter's gaze appeared to be focused on the ceiling. *I hope Lisa will listen to me and that she'll rethink her rash statement to Paul. The way that poor young man explained the situation to Jerry and me downstairs just now, I'm certain that he did not want to hurt her.*

Marlene stepped inside, shut the door, and went over to the bed, where she took a seat at the end near Lisa's bare feet. "I understand that you're upset right now, but you were rude to Paul, and I think you overreacted to what you heard him say to your grossdaadi."

Lisa sat up and folded her arms. "He lied to me, Grandma. Paul pretended to be my friend, all the while keeping a secret that he should have told me when we first met and he realized who I was." Her voice quivered, and she released a heavy, lingering sigh.

She is really upset, and I'm not sure if I can reason with her. Marlene shook her head. "He didn't lie. Paul was afraid to tell you for fear of your reaction. He's still downstairs in the living room, talking to your grandpa." She placed her hand on Lisa's leg. "Don't you think you should go talk to him about this—give him a chance to explain why he chose not to mention until now that he used to know you?"

"No, I don't want to talk to him." Lisa sat with rounded shoulders and a downcast expression. "I thought he was sincere and honest, but I know now that Paul can't be trusted."

Marlene felt bad hearing the pain in her granddaughter's voice, but for the moment, nothing she could say would convince Lisa that her anger toward Paul was unjustified.

I suppose I'll have to tell Paul that I've tried to reason with her, but she's just too upset at this point to want to listen to anything he has to say. She gave her granddaughter's leg a few pats, stood up, and quietly left the room.

Downstairs, Marlene still felt heaviness in the air from Lisa's response to Paul before she ran from the room. Marlene found Jerry and Paul sitting in chairs next to each other, engaged in a solemn conversation about Lisa.

Marlene dreaded letting Paul know that Lisa was done with him. It was obvious that the young man wanted to talk to her, but at this point, Marlene couldn't make Lisa do what she thought was the right thing. *My granddaughter can be timid, but I'm also seeing a streak of stubbornness too. She needs to listen to what Paul has to say and forgive.*

As she approached the men, Paul stopped talking and looked at her. "Is Lisa all right? Is she willing to let me explain and apologize to her?"

Marlene shook her head. "She's quite upset. Hopefully in a few days she'll be ready to talk, but unfortunately, not at this time. Lisa needs the chance to sort things out. Perhaps as she does, she will remember more of her past and be willing to talk about it."

Paul swiped a hand across his forehead. "I'm afraid I've messed things up real bad between me and Lisa. I should have either told her right away or said nothing at all."

"I don't see it that way," Jerry said with a slow shake of his head.

"If you'd kept silent about having known Lisa when you were children, and she had remembered it on her own, she'd have probably been even more upset, wondering why you didn't speak up."

"Maybe so." Paul lowered his gaze. "I'm afraid I've ruined my friendship with her."

"Please give Lisa some time. I'm sure she'll come around." Marlene hoped her words sounded reassuring. Truth was, she was not certain that her granddaughter would keep a relationship going with Paul now that she knew the truth. Above all, Marlene hoped that Lisa would not pull back into her protective shell again.

~

As Paul guided Chester in the direction of his aunt and uncle's home, he continued to berate himself for bringing up the topic to Jerry about having known Lisa when she was a girl. He let go of the reins with one hand and reached up to rub the back of his neck where a painful knot had formed. *It might have gone better if she'd heard it directly from me rather than hearing it secondhand,* he thought with regret. *She probably thinks I can't be trusted now.*

"Shoulda, coulda, woulda," Paul muttered. "Guess I'm not so good at fixing things after all, no matter how hard I might try." His jaw clenched. "Maybe Lisa doesn't want to be fixed. She may not wish to remember the past and prefers to live a guarded life, trying to keep a protective hedge around herself for the rest of her days."

He continued to replay the whole mess in his head, and all it seemed to do was add pain. Speaking with Marlene after she'd come downstairs with the bad news that Lisa didn't want to talk to him had only added to his frustration.

Paul figured when he arrived home that he would have to tell his aunt and uncle that his relationship with Lisa appeared to be over. He would have to retell the whole painful story again. "Good job!" he shouted into the night sky. "I've sure made a mess of things."

Chester's ears perked up, and Paul realized that his loud voice had frightened the poor horse. "Sorry, boy, I'm upset, but it's nothing for you to worry about."

As he approached his aunt and uncle's home, a realization came to him. *What I need to do more than anything else right now is to pray for Lisa and ask God to show me how I can restore my relationship with her. I'm also going to drop by Memory Keepers soon and have a talk with Orley. Maybe he can help me figure a way out of the mess I created. At the very least, I'm sure Orley will be understanding and sympathetic.*

~

Walnut Creek

Upon hearing the wind howling outside the bedroom window, Orley woke up and discovered that Lois was not on her side of the bed. *Could she be up late working on more letters to those who write to her Dear Caroline column?* He frowned. *I wish sometimes that Lois would give up that newspaper column. It takes up too much of her time, and I think she would do better if she stuck to mentoring folks one-on-one like I do when troubled people come into our store.*

Orley pulled himself to a sitting position, got out of bed, and put on his robe and slippers. Grabbing a battery-operated light, he padded down the hall toward the kitchen. Upon entering the dark room, however, he saw no sign of his wife. *That's strange. I wonder where Lois could be.* He paused and looked out the window. Even though it was dark outside, he could hear the wind pushing at the trees and, under the moonlight, see the branches being swished about. Orley hoped that things like their roofing would hold firm until morning.

As Orley made his way through the rest of the house and saw that each room he'd entered was dark, he began to worry. *Where could my fraa be? Surely she wouldn't have gone outside.*

Continuing on his trek, Orley went back down the hall. This time he stopped in the living room. With the light held in front of him, it didn't take long for Orley to spot Lois sitting on the sofa with her head bowed close to her chest. *Has she fallen asleep in that position or could Lois be in prayer?* He hated to disturb her, but the hour was late, and she really should be in bed.

—

When Lois had something on her mind to pray about, she didn't argue with God. It was like the Lord had prompted her to pray right now, and she figured it was good to follow her heart. The wind howled outside, and the homemade chime by the front door clanged loudly. When she'd first taken a seat here, the moon had cast a gentle glow through the windows and into the room, but now it was dark.

Lois had been sitting in the dark living room, devoid of light, with her head bowed for nearly an hour when she heard footsteps. She opened her eyes and saw Orley enter the room with a battery-operated light in one hand.

"I thought you'd gone to bed," she said when her husband approached.

"I did, but I was expecting you to join me, and I fell asleep soon after my head hit the pillow. So when I woke up and discovered you were not on your side of the bed, I became concerned."

"Sorry if I caused you to worry, but there was no need for concern."

Orley took a seat on the sofa beside her. "Did you fall asleep in here? Is that why your head was bent forward?"

"No." Lois shook her head. "I knew if I came to bed when you did, I wouldn't be able to sleep, so I came in here instead."

"How come? Has my snoring been too loud lately? Is that why you couldn't stay in the room with me? Or were you worried that I might fall out of bed again and wake you up like I've done several times in the past?"

"No, it was neither of those things."

He tipped his head. "What, then?"

"I don't know why, but I've been thinking about Paul's friend Lisa all evening and felt led to sit here in the quietness of night and pray for her."

"I see. Is there anything specific you believe she needs prayer for?"

"Not really. I just have this feeling that that she's dealing with something unsettling right now and needs the Lord's intervention." Lois placed one hand against her chest.

Orley reached over, took hold of Lois's hand, and bowed his head. "If that's the case, then I'll join you in prayer."

"Danki, dear husband," Lois said in a near whisper. "I appreciate your willingness to pray with me." She leaned her head close to his and prayed a heartfelt silent prayer: *Heavenly Father: Please be with Lisa tonight, and if there is something troubling the young woman, I ask that You give her a sense of peace. May Your will be revealed to Lisa in the days ahead, and may she seek Your approval in all that she says and does. Please give my husband and me an understanding heart and wisdom to know what to do and say if either Lisa or Paul reaches out to us again.*

~

Sugarcreek

Lisa lay on her bed, eyes closed and tears streaming down her hot cheeks. She hadn't even gone downstairs to say good night to her grandparents or to see how Maggie was doing or if the dog needed anything. *She's probably fine. Grandpa will take her outside before going to bed,* she told herself. *And Grandma will make sure a bowl of water is near the place where my dog sleeps at night.*

It had been at least an hour since Paul left for home. Lisa had heard his horse and buggy leave the yard and felt relieved. *I'm sure he's upset with me, but no more than I am with him. I still can't believe how he deceived me.*

Lisa's head ached as she tried to force herself to remember having known Paul when they were children, but nothing came to mind. It frustrated her to be unable to regain her memory, and it frightened her too. What if she never regained any memory about her life prior to her parents' deaths?

She pulled in a deep breath. If Lisa was being totally honest with herself, she would have to admit that part of her did not want to remember the past. In fact, just thinking about it caused her to feel terrified that something bad would happen if she opened herself up to remember the details of the life she used to know before the tragic accident.

Maybe I'm losing my mind, she told herself. *A normal person should not be thinking such things.*

Although Lisa had never spoken the words out loud, she felt guilty and unworthy for being the only survivor the day her parents and paternal grandparents died. After all, what right did she have to be alive when their lives had been snuffed out that fateful day? Lisa had battled with this issue many times, trying to make sense of it all. It seemed when she became upset about something it tended to bring these feelings she didn't understand right back to the surface. And since she'd felt betrayed and angered by Paul this evening, all the old emotions came back again. But the one obvious thing she had to think about was that the Lord had allowed her to survive for a reason. Even so, Lisa hadn't figured out what it was.

I still can't believe I let Paul gain my trust. Why would he wait so long to confess that he already knew who I was? She squeezed her eyes shut. *All I want to do is stay here in my room and not see anyone right now—least of all Paul.*

Lisa pulled her fingers tightly into the palms of her hands until she felt the pain of her nails dig into her flesh. *I wish I had never met Paul. It would have been better for me and him if he'd remained in Indiana instead of moving here.*

Lisa wondered what other secrets Paul had been hiding from her. Had he known she'd moved here after her parents died and then come to Sugarcreek to try to jog her memory? Lisa realized she wouldn't know the answers to her questions unless she asked Paul. But could she question him about it? Did she have the nerve?

Chapter 31

Lisa sat at the kitchen table, massaging her forehead. The morning light warmed the room, but its intense glow made her feel the need to squint her eyes.

Oh, dear. . .I hope I'm not working on a migraine, she thought. A bad headache that could end up making her stomach sick would not be a good thing since Lisa had a full day ahead with her students. She'd slept poorly last night and had awakened with her head throbbing. Lisa had no idea how she could make it through a day of teaching school, but she felt that she had no other choice. She had a to-do list in her purse to go through today, not to mention starting new books with her young scholars. Lisa had stored those new books away in the back room and was the only one who knew exactly where she'd put them. It was too late to see about getting a substitute, and it wouldn't be fair to ask Yvonne to teach all eight grades today. So with a determination she didn't feel, Lisa made up her mind that she would power through no matter how bad she felt. The pulsating pain made her realize it would probably increase if she rode her bike this morning, but on the other hand, it took more work to get the horse and buggy ready to go.

"Are you okay, Lisa?" Grandma's wrinkled brows and anxious tone of voice revealed her obvious concern.

Lisa cringed. *Does it look that obvious that I'm not feeling well?* "I woke up with a koppweh," she replied.

"Have you taken anything for the headache?" Grandpa asked.

She shook her head. "I'd hoped it would go away on its own."

Grandma rose from the table and opened the cupboard door where she kept all her medications and natural remedies. She returned with a bottle of aspirin and handed it to Lisa. "Here you go. Take two of these, and it should help."

"Danki." Lisa opened the lid, took out two pills, and swallowed them with the grape juice in her glass. She couldn't help thinking about last night when she and Paul had their falling-out. *I really don't want to discuss yesterday right now, especially feeling like I do, so I hope Grandpa and Grandma don't bring the topic up.* Lisa squirmed under her grandmother's scrutiny. She suspected there might be some questions about Paul forthcoming.

Grandma opened her mouth as if to say something, but to Lisa's relief, Grandpa spoke first, asking Grandma a question.

"Is there any more kaffi, or should I make another pot?"

She gave him a quizzical look. "There's still plenty of coffee, Husband, so feel free to help yourself."

"Oh, okay."

Lisa figured Grandpa would jump right up and pour himself another cup, but he remained in his seat and started another conversation—this time in regard to the work frolic that would be held at a neighbor's place in a few weeks to put a new roof on their home.

Lisa listened as her grandfather went on and on about the details of the upcoming event. Since she'd just taken the pill for pain, the homemade sticky buns in front of her called out, so Lisa helped herself to a small one from the platter. It didn't take long to nibble through the tasty sweet roll. Grandma's recipe was really good, so Lisa picked out a second bun and put it on her plate. She was tempted to have more but decided to stop at two.

"I'm glad you're able to eat, even with your head not feeling well." Grandpa smiled and reached over to pat Lisa's arm.

"It's hard to pass up Grandma's delicious sticky buns."

He bobbed his head. "I have to agree."

Lisa had to wonder if Grandpa might be deliberately trying to keep Grandma from bringing up the topic of Paul and what had transpired last night. If that was the case, she felt grateful, because the last thing she wanted to talk about this morning was the betrayal she still felt. It would be a struggle for Lisa until the pain relief fully kicked in. She hoped once she'd arrived at school that her head would feel better—it would be a good start to her day at least. Lisa figured that Yvonne would want to chat about this past weekend, and no doubt the subject of her and Paul could come up. Lisa hoped it wouldn't, though, because she didn't want to have to skirt around the topic or have to explain what had taken place.

Lisa looked at the clock on the far wall and drank the rest of her juice. It was time to put her dishes in the sink and head off to school.

—⁓—

"You look mied this morning, Paul. Did you not get enough sleep last night?" Aunt Emma asked.

"I am tired," he admitted before reaching for his cup of coffee. "Things didn't go well last night at the Schrocks' place, and I had a hard time falling asleep when I got home."

"Anything you'd like to talk about?" Uncle Abe questioned from across the breakfast table.

When Paul's cousins looked over at him with curious expressions, he realized that he should have kept quiet. *What was I thinking, blurting that out? If I'd wanted to open up about what occurred last night, I should have waited until I could speak to my uncle and aunt alone.* No way would he deliberately say anything about his personal problems in front of Kevin or Danny. They were both talkers and could end up blabbing whatever he said all over town.

"It's nothing I can talk about right now," Paul responded to his uncle's question. "I'm sure it'll work itself out in time." He fiddled with the fork beside his plate of poached eggs. *At least I hope it will work out. Truth be told, I'm not sure Lisa will ever speak to me again.*

Paul's uncle gave him a quizzical look. It seemed to him that his uncle might not be buying into his last comment. For the moment, the room had fallen silent, and Paul couldn't help but squirm in his chair. He felt relieved when the conversation at the table turned to other things and no one questioned him further.

"What's our first order of business going to be today?" Paul asked his uncle as he resumed eating his morning meal. "Will we be working in the shop all day or someplace else?" He grabbed a piece of toast and took a bite.

"Some things need to be done in the shop this morning, but I also have a few jobs I'll need to bid outside of Sugarcreek this afternoon." Uncle Abe sprinkled quite a bit of salt on his eggs, apparently unmindful of his wife's raised eyebrows.

Paul was surprised that his health-conscious aunt didn't come right out and say something, as she often did when her husband overused the saltshaker. *A little salt goes a long way,* Aunt Emma would often say with a shake of her finger. Today, however, she'd chosen to remain quiet.

Paul's nephews continued to eat like the growing boys they were. He couldn't help noticing how fast they could put away their mom's tasty home cooking, yet they were both skinny as rails.

Paul looked at his aunt. "I have an errand I need to run in Walnut Creek when I get off work today, so don't hold supper on my account. I may stop for a bite to eat on the way home."

She nodded. "No problem. If you change your mind and come home without having had supper, I can always heat something up for you."

Paul smiled. "Danki."

"I'm worried about our granddaughter," Marlene said as she and Jerry drank a final cup of coffee before he headed out to the harness shop.

"She'll be fine. I'm sure the aspirin you gave her will take away her koppweh," he responded.

"I'm not talking about her headache. I was referring to Lisa's emotional state." Marlene drew in a quick breath and released it with a huff. "I wanted to talk to her about it this morning, but you kept changing the subject."

"Remember last night, when you told Paul that he needed to give Lisa some time?"

"Jah."

"Well, your good advice was meant for us too. What Lisa needs now is the opportunity to think things through and reach her own conclusions rather than being told what she should do or how she ought to feel."

Marlene pursed her lips. "You're right, but I'm worried that she will use what she heard Paul say to you as an excuse to revert to her introverted ways. Her denial to face or even talk about the past is not a good thing, Jerry. She'll never fully recover from the trauma of losing her family until she faces her fears head-on." Marlene paused to finish her coffee and then rushed on. "We will not be around forever to shield and protect our granddaughter. Sooner or later she will have to deal with her future and accept the good and bad that goes with life. I believe it's our job to prepare her for that. Don't you agree?"

Jerry nodded with a sober expression. "But we can't force Lisa to come to grips with her past or find the courage to trust Paul or anyone else who has hurt her. Our granddaughter needs a spiritual awakening that will strengthen her faith, which can only come from God."

"So what are we supposed to do—just sit back and do nothing?"

He shook his head. "We can pray and be ready to listen when Lisa is ready to talk."

Marlene hated to admit it, but her husband was right. No matter how difficult it might be, she would take a step back and allow the Lord to work in Lisa's life.

Walnut Creek

At the end of his workday, Paul headed for Memory Keepers, where he hoped to speak with Orley. From what he'd been able to tell, the kindly Amish man was full of wisdom, and Paul certainly needed some sound advice concerning Lisa.

Upon entering the antique store, Paul spotted Orley down on his knees on one side of the room, emptying a box of vintage signs that advertised some products from the 1940s. Curious to get a better look, he crossed the room and knelt beside Orley.

"Well, hello there." Orley grinned at Paul. "It's good to see you again."

"Same here." Paul gestured to the box of signs. "Those look quite interesting. I especially like that one with a picture of an old soda pop bottle on it."

Orley nodded. "It's one of my favorites too. Now I just need to find the best place to hang these old signs where they'll get the most attention."

"How about there?" Paul pointed to a mostly bare wall near the front of the store.

"Jah, danki for the suggestion." Orley clambered to his feet. "What brings you into the store today? Are you lookin' for another vintage milk bottle?"

Paul stood too. "No, I. . .uh. . .need your opinion on something."

"Oh?" Orley tipped his head. "What can I help you with?"

Paul was quick to tell Orley what had transpired the night before and how Lisa had responded when she'd come into her grandparents' living room after hearing what he'd said to her grandfather. "She was really upset with me, and I don't know what to do to make things right between us."

"Did you try to explain your reasons for not telling her sooner that you used to know each other?"

"She wouldn't let me explain. Just ran out of the room after saying she never wanted to see me again." Paul clenched his teeth. "I realize now that I waited too long. I should have told Lisa right away that I knew her when we were children."

Orley placed his hand on Paul's shoulder and gave it a reassuring squeeze. "I'm sorry, Paul. Perhaps you should try talking to her again."

"How long should I wait to do that?"

"Well, that all depends."

"On what?"

"On how much time you think she needs."

Paul gave his earlobe a tug. "I'm not sure. I could wait a few days or maybe a week, but then what should I do if Lisa still won't listen to me? I'll be leaving for Indiana in a few weeks, and I'd sure like to get things resolved with Lisa before I go."

Orley's brows lifted. "You're moving back to your home state?"

"No, no, it's nothing like that. I'll be going there for my grandma's birthday celebration, and that's when I plan to give her the old milk bottle I bought from you."

"Oh, I see. Well, it might be good if you could resolve things with Lisa before you go, then."

Paul gave a nod. "Any idea what I should say, other than I'm truly sorry?"

"I have a suggestion," Lois spoke up from across the room.

Paul hadn't even noticed her until now. He waited until she approached them before asking for her suggestion.

"I didn't mean to eavesdrop." Lois looked at Paul. "But I was on the floor behind the front counter looking for something I had dropped this morning, and I couldn't help hearing what you said to Orley." She paused a moment, glanced at her husband, and then looked back at Paul. "Last night before going to bed, I felt a strong need to pray for Lisa, which I told Orley about. So we both prayed for her, even though we had no idea what the extent of her need was. Now I realize why God laid that upon my heart, and I see that we should have been praying for you as well, Paul."

"It's not too late," he said. "I could use your prayers and your advice to help me figure out what I should say when I see Lisa again and how long I should wait to make that happen." Paul pinched the bridge of his nose. "Do I wait a few weeks, till I get back from seeing my family in Indiana, or do I try to talk with Lisa before I go?"

"It's your decision, of course," Lois replied, "but I think it might help if you write Lisa a note of apology soon, and then say that you would like to talk to her in a few weeks, after you have returned from Indiana. That would give Lisa more time to think things over, and it would also give me the opportunity to speak with her."

"You'd be willing to do that?"

"Definitely."

Paul tilted his head from side to side as he weighed his choices. Giving Lisa more time might be the best thing, and writing her a letter rather than talking to her directly was a good idea too. He just hoped that when the time came for them to meet face-to-face, she would be willing to talk to him, and they could work things out.

Chapter 32

Sugarcreek

A sky filled with pretty shades of pink and orange greeted Lisa when she went to the kitchen window and lifted the shade. She watched for several seconds and squinted against the bright ball of orange rising up on the horizon. Lisa hoped that the weather wouldn't turn bad and thought of the old sailors' rhyme that said, "Pink sky in the morning, sailors take warning." But that was superstitious, and a beautiful sunrise should not be taken as a warning.

Lisa opened the window a crack, listening as the silence gave way to the sound of chirping birds swooping from tree to tree in search of food from the carefully placed feeders.

She felt thankful that today was Saturday and she didn't have to get up early to teach school. Yet here she was, up at the crack of dawn. Well, at least it was by her own choice and not because she had to fulfill a duty.

The past week had been difficult, as she'd struggled not to think about Paul's admittance to having known her when she was a girl. She didn't understand why he couldn't have been honest with her in the first place. Lisa was glad he had not tried to talk to her since then. She wasn't ready to discuss it with Paul, or anyone else for that matter. So far her grandparents hadn't pressured her about this either. She appreciated them allowing her to do what she wanted about the situation. Fortunately, Lisa's coworker hadn't brought up the topic of Paul lately either. Yvonne seemed to be absorbed in her blossoming relationship with Aaron.

Maybe my prayers have helped, Lisa concluded. *I did ask to be left alone to ponder things for myself.*

Pushing her thoughts to the back of her mind, Lisa glanced at the clock, surprised that Maggie hadn't heard her and come into the kitchen, begging to go outside. Apparently even her dog had decided to sleep in this morning. Maybe Lisa, Grandma, Grandpa, and even Maggie all had a touch of spring fever.

At least I got out of bed of my own accord and not because I'd set a blaring alarm to wake me up, Lisa mused. *But I'm glad I woke up when I did so I could fix a nice breakfast for my grandparents.*

Lisa's grandmother had been so kind the last few days, staying away from the topic of Paul and fixing Lisa's favorite meals. Grandpa had been pleasant and upbeat too, also refraining from saying anything about Lisa's relationship with Paul. It was the least she could do to let her grandparents sleep in this morning and have breakfast waiting when they got up.

She moved away from the window and took a loaf of raisin bread from the refrigerator. Grandma liked to store her homemade bread there to keep it fresh longer. *I wouldn't mind some french toast. It appeals to my urge to have something a little sweet this morning.*

She got out a carton of eggs and cracked two large ones into a deep-dish ceramic pan. To the egg mixture she added some milk, honey, and a bit of salt, then mixed the ingredients thoroughly. Next Lisa heated butter in a skillet on the stove. When it was ready, she dipped the bread slices into the honey mixture and fried both sides over medium heat until golden brown. When the slices were done, she placed them in an ovenproof baking pan and repeated the process with two more pieces of bread. Once six slices had been cooked, Lisa placed them in the oven to keep warm until it was time to eat breakfast.

She'd finished the last piece of bread and had put the pan in the oven when Maggie ambled into the room using her new gait. She paused in front of Lisa, lifted her snout, and gave a few barks.

"Smells pretty good, doesn't it, girl?" Lisa leaned over and rubbed the dog's ears. "I bet you'd like a taste, huh?"

Arf! Arf!

Lisa snickered and moved over to the sink to wash her hands. "Okay, but first, let's take a walk outside." Although the dog was housebroken, Lisa didn't want to risk Maggie getting too excited and piddling on the kitchen floor. Before readying her dog, she made sure the oven was on low so the french toast would stay warm.

Following that, Lisa got out the dog's purple harness, and a few minutes later they were in the backyard. Maggie loved being outside, and today she pulled on the lead to roam around the shrubs. Lisa thought it was neat to see the animal acting more like she did before the accident.

The sun was fully up, and birds were chirping everywhere. Lisa didn't know how the little creatures could always sound so cheerful. It seemed as though they didn't have a care in the world, despite the dangers all around. Predators such as cats and larger birds could be a threat, but the cardinals, sparrows, and other songbirds warbled on as they continued their hunt for food or rested on tree branches from above.

Woof! Woof!

Lisa turned to look at Maggie. "All done with your business and ready to go back inside?"

The dog let out a few more noisy barks.

Lisa put a finger against her lips. "Shh. . . Keep that up and you'll wake Grandma and Grandpa." She guided Maggie up the porch steps and into the house.

In the utility room, Lisa poured dog food into Maggie's dish and gave her a bowl of fresh water. From there, she returned to the kitchen, where to her surprise, she found Grandpa sitting at the table.

"Somethin' smells mighty good in here." He grinned at her. "Did you fix your special honey-raisin-bread french toast for breakfast?"

"You guessed correctly." She pointed to the oven. "I've been keeping it warm for you and Grandma. Is she up yet?"

"Jah. She's puttin' her hair in a bun and should be here shortly."
Grandpa glanced at the clock on the far wall. "We both slept later
than usual today. Guess we should have had our alarm set. I'd likely
still be asleep if I hadn't heard your hund barking from outside."

"Sorry she woke you."

"No, it's okay. There's plenty I have to get done today, so I needed
to get up and at 'em."

Lisa began to set the table with plates and silverware. "It's okay,
Grandpa. You and Grandma deserve to sleep in once in a while.
That's why I got up early to fix breakfast."

Grandma entered the kitchen just then, smiling from ear to ear.
"What's that delicious aroma in here? I could smell it all the way to
the bedroom."

"Lisa made breakfast for us, Marlene." Grandpa gestured to the
oven door. "And she deliberately let us sleep in."

"Well, for goodness' sakes." Grandma opened the oven and
peeked in. "Yum, yum. You're spoiling us this morning, Lisa."

"You deserve to be spoiled once in a while."

Grandma flapped her hand. "I don't know about that, but it sure
is nice to be treated to breakfast."

"Please take a seat and I'll put the french toast on the table."
Lisa grabbed two pot holders and moved toward the stove.

⁓

"Oh, my. . .this looks so delicious." Marlene's stomach growled in
anticipation when Lisa set the platter of french toast on the table.

"And I'm sure it'll taste as good as it looks," Jerry added, smack-
ing his lips.

Lisa set a jar of honey on the table, along with some apple butter and a bottle of amber-colored pure maple syrup. "Would either
of you like a glass of *millich* with your meal, or would you prefer
kaffi instead?"

"Milk sounds good for a change," Marlene said. "I'll wait till the
end of the meal to drink my coffee."

When Lisa looked at her grandpa, he nodded and said, "I'll have what your grossmammi is having. And I wouldn't mind some grape jelly to put on mine."

"I'll grab the jelly and set it by your plate." Lisa did that first then got out three glasses and set them on the table, along with a bottle of milk. After she'd taken her seat, they all bowed their heads.

Heavenly Father, Marlene prayed, *thank You for the wonderful breakfast our granddaughter so graciously prepared. Please bless, guide, and direct her life in the days ahead. And bless Paul too,* she added before opening her eyes.

As they ate, Lisa brought up the topic of the garden she planned to help Marlene plant after breakfast.

"I'll appreciate your help as much as I do you making this tasty meal." Marlene poked her fork into a piece of french toast and swirled it around in the amber-colored honey oozing off the edges.

"You're a good cook," Jerry interjected. "You'll make some lucky man a fine wife someday."

Lisa's cheeks colored, but she said nothing as she reached for her glass of milk.

Jerry liked grape jelly and had put a good amount on his first piece. Following that, he'd poured on the maple syrup. "Now this is the way to have tasty french toast."

Marlene wrinkled her nose. "I'm not sure how you can have so much sweetness on top of yours. It would make my teeth tingle with all of that sugar added."

"Nonsense. It tastes good, and this is how I've liked my french toast, and even pancakes, since I was a little boy."

Marlene rolled her eyes in disgust. "I doubt that even Maggie would eat a piece of french toast with all that sweet stuff on it."

"Bet she would." Jerry looked at Lisa. "Would ya mind if I gave the dog a taste of my french toast?"

Lisa shrugged. "I guess a small piece wouldn't hurt."

Jerry cut a piece from one of his, called Maggie over to the table, and fed it to her. "Here, girl, see if you like this."

The dog gave a quick sniff then consumed the morsel and appeared to be waiting for piece number two.

With a smug expression, Jerry announced, "See, I was sure Maggie would like it."

Marlene couldn't hold back her laughter, and neither could Lisa. The dog seemed eager to have another piece, but Jerry refrained from giving her one. He finally told Maggie to go lie down, and she obeyed his command. They chatted a little longer while they ate and enjoyed their breakfast together.

They were getting close to being done when Jerry snapped his fingers and pushed back his chair. "Forgetful me—I almost forgot about the mail I brought in yesterday after I quit working for the day." He made his way across the room and lifted a stack of envelopes from the rolltop desk. "There's a letter from your cousin Sara." He handed it to Marlene. "Oh, and here's one for you too, Lisa." He laid the envelope next to her plate.

Marlene couldn't help but notice that the crimson color in her granddaughter's cheeks was deepening as she stared at the letter.

"Who's it from?" Marlene questioned. "Did my cousin send you a letter too?"

Lisa slowly shook her head. "It—it's from Paul. His name is on the return address." She made no effort to open the envelope.

"Aren't you going to see what he has to say?" Marlene's curiosity was about to get the best of her.

"I—I guess so." A muscle in Lisa's jaw quivered as she tore open the envelope.

Marlene watched with mounting curiosity as Lisa read the letter silently. She fought the urge to ask, "What'd he say?" but pressed her lips together and kept silent.

Several seconds went by, and then Lisa set the letter aside and shifted in her chair. "Paul wrote to let me know that he'll be leaving for Indiana soon, where he'll attend his grandma's birthday celebration." She paused and swallowed a couple of times. "He didn't say how long he'd be gone, but he wants to talk to me after he returns to Ohio."

"Will you be willing to listen to him?" Marlene dared to ask.

Lisa lowered her gaze and gave a brief shrug. "I don't know yet. I'll need to think about it."

Marlene was on the verge of saying something more but stopped herself when Jerry cleared his throat and gave a quick shake of his head. She knew her husband well enough to realize that he thought it was best if Marlene didn't say anything more, so she honored his request. Marlene would, however, be praying that by the time Paul returned from Indiana, Lisa would listen to what he had to say and be willing to forgive.

"Would you like another helping of baked oatmeal?" Aunt Emma asked, moving the dish closer to Paul.

He thumped his belly. "No thanks. It was sure tasty, but I've had plenty. If I eat any more, I may not be able to get any work done today."

Uncle Abe chuckled. "Now that would be the day. I've never known a young man who could work as hard as you do, even on a full stomach."

"What about me, Daed?" Danny puffed out his chest. "I can eat a lot and still work hard, right?"

Uncle Abe smiled. "Jah, Son, you're a hard worker too." He looked across the table at Kevin. "You and your brother are both able to get a lot of work done."

The teenage boy shrugged and said, "On that note, can I be excused so I can get out to the barn and finish my chores?"

Uncle Abe nodded. "Of course, but please clear your dishes first."

Kevin picked up his plate and silverware and carried them to the kitchen sink. His younger brother did the same.

"While you boys are out there, would one of you run to the phone shed and check for messages?" Aunt Emma asked.

"Sure, Mom, I'll do it," Danny replied. "If you want, I'll check for messages first, before I start my chores."

Aunt Emma looked at her husband, and he nodded. "Danki, Danny," she said. "If there are any messages, please be sure to write them down and bring the piece of paper from the notepad into the house before you head out to the barn."

Danny gave her a thumbs-up and strolled out the door.

Paul smiled. His cousins were good kids and respectful to their parents. He hoped if he ever had children that he could raise them to be that way. *Of course, I'd have to get married first,* Paul thought. *And unless Lisa changes her mind about me, she and I will never be husband and wife.*

Paul thought about the letter he'd sent to Lisa three days ago and wondered if she'd received it by now. He leaned both elbows on the table and massaged his forehead. *If so, will she be willing to listen to me when I get back from Indiana?*

Chapter 33

Goshen

After paying for his ride and saying goodbye to his driver, Bob, Paul stepped out of the van and went around to remove his canvas satchel and the box with his grandmother's gift inside. Paul turned then and looked up at the house. It was hard to believe he'd been gone from here for eight months, because for the most part, everything looked the same. His parents' three-story white farmhouse still stood tall and stately, with pots of colorful flowers scattered around the porch and a neatly mowed lawn.

Paul's gaze went to the two hickory rockers situated between a two-seater wooden glider. Flashing back to the past, Paul thought about all the times he and Susan had sat upon that glider, holding hands and talking about their future after enjoying one of his mother's delicious meals.

Paul's fingers clenched around the handles of the satchel he held in one hand, while he gripped the thin piece of rope tied around the box in the other. He'd tried to fight those feelings that he'd felt sure had gone away. But being back home seemed to bring out his painful memories. *Susan and I would most likely be married by now, and maybe even starting a family, if Ervin hadn't stolen my girl. And now I've found someone I love even more, but it doesn't look like that relationship is going to work out either. Lisa has closed herself off from me, hiding behind a past that she's tried so hard to forget, and she may never open herself up emotionally to me again.* He gripped his satchel tighter. *What am I doing? I started with thinking of Susan, and now I've bounced to Lisa.*

Paul's thoughts were halted when the front door swung open, and with open arms, his mother dashed out to greet him. "Oh, Paul, it's so good to see you. It's been too long since you've been home, and we've all missed you so much."

"I've missed you too," Paul answered honestly. *I just haven't missed the unpleasant memory of Susan breaking up with me for the man I'd thought was my best friend.*

Paul resituated his belongings so he was able to slip one arm around his mother's slender waist as they entered the house. Her petite frame made it hard to believe that she'd ever given birth to five hefty boys.

"Where's Dad? Is he working today?" Paul asked.

She nodded. "He's had more orders than usual for rustic furniture, so he's been working sometimes six days a week at his store to try to keep up." She peered at him over the top of her glasses. "He really misses your help in the shop."

No pressure, please. I really don't want to come back here and work again. Paul's brows furrowed. "Hasn't Dad found a replacement for me? I thought he hired a man from Shipshewana."

"He did, but after a few months things didn't work out."

Feeling a little guilty, Paul figured he should follow up carefully on the topic.

"Really? I had no idea. How come Dad never said anything to me about it?"

"Guess he didn't want you to worry or feel guilty for leaving." Mom moved toward the kitchen. "If you haven't had lunch yet, would you like me to fix you a roast beef sandwich?"

"No thanks. My driver and I stopped at a place about an hour from here and had a bite to eat." Paul set the box with Grandma's gift it in on the counter. "If you don't mind me setting this here for now, the box is a gift for Grandma."

"No problem, it should be fine there." His mother smiled.

"Think I'll go upstairs to my old room and hang my clothes up so they don't get too wrinkled. I wanna look presentable for Grandma's birthday party tomorrow evening. It's being held here, right?"

"Jah, but if you have some shirts or trousers that are wrinkled, I'd be happy to iron them for you."

"I think they'll be fine once they're hung up, but I'll let you know if they're not."

"Okay. While you're doing that, I'll fix something cold for us to drink. Would a glass of apple juice appeal to you?"

"Jah, sure. Thanks, Mom." Paul hurried up the stairs to his room.

When Paul walked into his old bedroom, everything looked basically the way he'd left it. He noticed that the window was open, letting in a nice soft breeze. After he'd hung his clothes in the closet and put some other things in one of the dresser drawers, he headed back down the stairs.

When Paul entered the kitchen, he spotted two glasses of apple juice on the table. Looking at his mom, he picked one up and took a drink. "Ah, that sure hits the spot."

Paul's mother gestured to a chair and suggested that he take a seat. "It's been a while since we've talked, and I was hoping we could get caught up."

Paul could hardly say no to his mother's request, but he hoped she wouldn't ask about Lisa or start pressuring him to move back to Indiana and help with his dad's business. Paul pulled out a chair and sat down.

"Would you like some banana bread?"

"No thanks. I'm fine with the juice. Besides, I wouldn't want to spoil my appetite for supper later."

"Okay. Let me know if you change your mind." She took a seat across from him. "How is your daed's brother and his family these days?"

"Everyone's doin' okay. Uncle Abe's business is going real well, and we're keepin' plenty busy."

"That's good to hear." She sipped some of her juice and leaned forward, looking straight into his eyes. "How are things with Lisa? Are you two still going steady?"

I had a feeling she'd want to know about Lisa. Now that I've messed up my relationship with her, it's kind of embarrassing to talk about.

Paul moistened his lips with the tip of his tongue. "Well, uh. . . I'm not sure."

"What do you mean?"

Paul gave a brief explanation, ending it by saying that he would know more after he returned to Ohio and had spoken to Lisa. "That's if she's willing to talk to me," he added.

"I'm sure you're hoping things will work out, but have you ever thought that maybe Lisa isn't the right girl for you?"

Mom, you've never met Lisa as an adult—only when she was a child. Paul's stomach muscles knotted, and he felt sure that if he didn't leave the room, he was likely to say something his mother wouldn't like. He pushed back his chair and stood. "Is it all right if I borrow your horse and buggy, Mom?"

Her forehead creased. "Right now?"

"Jah."

"How come?"

"Thought I'd take a little ride into Shipshe and say hi to Dad. While I'm in town, I should buy a birthday card to go with Grandma's gift. But don't worry, I'll be back in time for supper," he quickly added.

She sat quietly for several seconds and finally nodded. "Sure, Son, you're welcome to use my horse, Holly, but before you go, I think you ought to know that—"

"Great! Danki, Mom. I'll see you in a few hours." Without bothering to finish his juice, Paul grabbed his straw hat and raced out the back door. He hadn't wanted to be rude, but he wasn't up to a lengthy conversation about Lisa with his mother right now.

On the way to the barn, Paul passed the chicken coop. The weathered wood framing and chicken wire created a safe yard enclosure for his mother's collection of ten fluffy hens and one noisy rooster. A few weeds poked up through the dirt around a dusting of wood shavings that had been scattered on the ground.

Paul glanced into the coop where the board rose on a slant and led to a raised area and the coop door. Bits of straw spilled over onto the exit platform—probably knocked out by the chickens from their nesting boxes. Cleaning the coop used to be Paul's job. He figured the responsibility fell on his mother now, since none of his brothers lived at home anymore. For the few eggs his parents would need, Paul wondered why Mom bothered with chickens at all. It would be a lot easier to buy them at the store or from some neighboring farm. *Maybe she likes having the freshest of eggs.* He reached under the brim of his hat and scratched his head. *Who knows—Mom might actually enjoy raising chickens.*

Paul moved on until he came to the tall double doors of his father's barn. When he opened them, he saw rough wooden walls with hooks made to hold various kinds of tack and equipment like shovels, rope, pitchforks, and brooms. Paul spotted Holly's harness and lifted it off the hook where her gear rested. The old barn was a welcome sight with its sweet-smelling hay. In the past, this place had often been his little getaway from life's problems—a quiet spot to think things through for a better perspective.

As he headed toward the horses' stalls, Paul glanced up, and his gaze came to rest on the wooden ladder leading to the loft overhead. He remembered fondly how he and his brothers had played up there during their boyhood. Since Harley was the oldest, he'd often played tricks on Paul, Mark, Amos, and Glen. Paul remembered one time when he and Amos had taken a nap in the loft and had been spooked by Harley, who'd dragged a large fake spider across their noses, awakening them both. Amos had screamed like he'd been stuck with a pin, but Paul had gotten mad and threatened to tell their dad. He hadn't done so, however, because he didn't want to be labeled a tattletale. Instead, Paul had gotten even with his older brother by hiding his good shoes one Sunday morning when it was almost time to depart for church. Harley had gotten a stern lecture from Mom about the need to keep better track of his things, and

Dad had been none too happy because they'd almost been late for worship service that day while everyone waited for Harley to locate his shoes. It had been a dirty trick to pull, and Paul had apologized to his brother later on, but he'd learned a good lesson that morning when Preacher John delivered a message on doing to others as we would want them to do to us.

The huffing of a horse's breath brought Paul's musings to a halt. He stepped into Holly's stall and was greeted by the mare's gentle whinny as she leaned her chestnut head against his shoulder. "Ready to take me to Shipshe?" Paul reached for the horse's bridle. "If you get me there in good time, I'll have a treat for ya when we get back."

Holly pawed a couple of times with her right front hoof and bobbed her head as though she understood.

Paul chuckled. "Okay, girl, I'm glad you comprehended what I said."

~

Shipshewana, Indiana

Paul decided to make a quick stop at Esh's to get a birthday card for his grandmother before going to Dad's shop to say hello. He'd only been inside the store a few minutes and had just begun looking at the cards when someone tapped his shoulder. Paul whirled around, surprised to see Susan Lambright. *You have got to be kidding! Out of all the people to see here on my first day back.*

"It's nice to see you, Paul." Susan's velvety eyelashes accentuated her dark irises as she offered him a dimpled smile. "You've been gone a long time. Are you here visiting your family, or have you decided to move back home?"

He moistened his dry lips with the tip of his tongue. "I. . .uh . . .just got here today. Came to help celebrate my grandmother's birthday, which will be at our place tomorrow evening."

"Jah, since my mamm and yours are friends, I heard about the celebration. Just didn't realize you would be here for it."

Why not? I guess you really didn't get to know me that well when we were dating. "Yep, and I brought her a special gift. It's a fancy old milk bottle almost identical to one she used to own before I carelessly broke it."

"I'm sure she'll be happy to have you at the party."

"I'm glad I can be here." Feeling a bit uneasy standing so close to his old girlfriend, Paul swallowed a couple of times. "How are things with you? I guess you've been real busy getting a lot of last-minute things done for your upcoming wedding."

"There won't be a wedding," she murmured with a slow shake of her head. "Ervin and I broke up a few weeks ago, so we won't be getting married next month after all."

Paul stared at her in disbelief and blinked several times. "Seriously?"

"Of course I'm serious. I have no reason to make up such a thing. Your mamm knows about the breakup. I'm surprised she didn't tell you."

Paul shook his head. He was hesitant to ask the next question but decided to go for it anyway, because he felt he had the right to know. "What went wrong? I thought you two were head over heels in love? Isn't that what you said when you broke up with me? Didn't you even say that you believed God had brought you and Ervin together?"

Susan's gaze dropped to the floor, and her voice lowered to a near whisper. "I—I did think that until he. . ." She stopped talking and folded her arms.

"Until what?" Paul prompted.

She lifted her face toward his. "Until Ervin found someone he liked better."

Paul's mouth nearly fell open. "Are you kidding?"

She gave a solemn shake of her head. "He used to go with Ava Miller when we were all running around together, remember?"

"Sure, I remember, but then her folks moved to Oklahoma and Ervin and Ava lost touch with each other."

"Jah, but now she's back, and all it took was one look at her, and Ervin practically fell into her arms." Tears welled in Susan's eyes. "I was never his first choice, but I'd convinced myself that I was. I think Ervin only wanted me because I was your girlfriend and he wanted what was yours. He always did try to be one up on you—even when we were kinner."

Paul stood almost frozen, trying to take all of this in. He'd been hurt terribly when Susan dropped him for Ervin, and now here he was, feeling sorry for her because she'd had her heart broken by his so-called friend. Some people might have gloated over the fact that the person who had hurt them was now facing the same kind of rejection and pain. Truth was, Paul felt sorry for Susan. She'd been taken in by Ervin's charms, only to be left with a broken heart.

Paul stepped aside when an elderly woman came up to the rack of greeting cards. Getting a card for his grandma could wait. All Paul could think about at the moment was offering Susan some needed support. He motioned for her to move over to the next aisle with him and said, "Should we go somewhere for a cup of coffee so we can talk about this more?"

Susan tipped her head back for a moment and briefly closed her eyes. "Jah, Paul, I would like that very much."

Chapter 34

Walnut Creek

Lois stepped up to Orley and nudged his arm. "Ever since Paul came by and told us about his situation with Lisa, I've had her on my mind. So I was wondering what you would think about going to Sugarcreek to pay Lisa a visit after we close the store this afternoon."

Orley stopped cleaning the front window and turned to face her. "That's a nice idea, but what reason would we offer for being there? Lisa would probably be upset if she knew Paul had told us what transpired when she overheard him telling her grandpa that he used to know her."

"You're right; we certainly can't blurt that out." Lois tapped her chin. "What if we make plans to eat supper at one of the restaurants in Sugarcreek, and we invite Lisa to join us?"

Orley gave his beard a tug, like he often did when he was thinking. "That could work, I suppose, but what if she has other plans for supper?"

"This is a weekday, and she's no doubt teaching school, so it's doubtful she'd be eating out." Lois poked her tongue against the inside of her cheek. "Of course, it would be rude to invite Lisa to join us for supper and not include her grandparents."

Orley's head moved slowly up and down. "Do you think she would open up and talk to us if her grandparents were there?"

"I don't know. It could be a problem—maybe even awkward in a way, I suppose." Lois placed her hand on his arm. "What do you think we should do?"

He sprayed more window cleaner and began to scrub the glass again. "I think we should go over to see Lisa and invite her and the grandparents to go out to supper with us. But it would not be a good idea to bring up the subject of Paul at a restaurant, so if they agree to go out with us, we'll wait till we take them home to bring up the topic of Paul."

Lois smiled. "Good idea, Orley. How thankful I am that I married such a schmaert man."

He chuckled and stepped back from his work. "How does this window look now? Have I got all the smudges and fingerprints wiped off?"

Moving forward and looking intently at Orley's hard work, Lois gave a nod. "You've done a good job. I don't think you could get that window any cleaner than it is." She patted his shoulder. "You're not only smart but a handy husband."

Shipshewana

"Are you hungerich? Would you like something besides kaffi?" Paul asked after he and Susan had taken seats at a small table inside the Corn Crib Café.

She shook her head. "I'm fine with the coffee we ordered. But if you're hungry, feel free to order whatever you like. Their sweet potato waffle fries are always good, and it'll be my treat." Susan offered Paul a smile that used to make him feel weak in the knees. Now Paul wasn't sure what he felt. Compassion for sure, because Susan had been hurt by Ervin, but he didn't think he felt anything other than that. He hoped not, at least, because Paul was in love with Lisa. Not that Susan wasn't a pretty young lady and a nice person at that. He figured in time she'd find someone new and would start fresh.

Paul had some reservations about the day he'd be speaking to Lisa after he returned to Sugarcreek. He fiddled with the menu their waitress had left on the table. *What if Lisa never forgives me and won't listen to what I have to say when I go back to Sugarcreek? Will there be any point in staying there if she rejects me?*

Paul glanced down at the menu but not because he was hungry. He just needed something else to focus on. *If Lisa and I don't get back together, I may as well return to Indiana and work for my daed. Mom made it pretty clear that he needs my help.*

"A dollar for your thoughts." Susan's shoe bumped the toe of Paul's boot under the table.

"Oh, sorry. I was just thinking about something is all."

"From the way you were frowning, they must have been some pretty heavy thoughts."

Paul gave no response. Instead he picked up the cup of hot coffee their waitress had just brought them, blew on it, and took a careful sip.

"Your mamm mentioned that you've been dating a girl from Sugarcreek." Susan looked at Paul, and her lips parted slightly. "Is it true?"

Boy, my mom and her mom sure must do a lot of talking to one another. I wonder just how much Susan knows about my private life. Paul drank some more coffee and swallowed hard, wondering how much he should tell her. Throwing caution to the wind, Paul blurted, "Her name is Lisa Miller. I knew her when she was a young girl. That was before you and your family moved here."

"I see." Susan fiddled with the napkin beside her cup. "So I assume at some point she moved to Sugarcreek with her family?"

"No, it was only Lisa who moved there." *Apparently Susan doesn't know everything.*

The next thing Paul knew, he'd told her the whole story of how Lisa had been the only survivor of the horrible accident that had killed her parents, paternal grandparents, and their driver.

After Susan offered some sympathetic comments, Paul continued by telling her that he hadn't realized who Lisa was when he'd first moved to Sugarcreek. "Then one day it dawned on me."

"Did she recognize you?"

Paul shook his head. "Apparently, the tragedy of the accident caused Lisa to forget most of her childhood before the deaths of her relatives. So until recently, she had no idea that she'd known me before." Paul finished the story by telling Susan how Lisa had overheard him telling her grandfather the truth.

"I bet she was surprised."

"Jah, but more than that, she was angry at me for keeping the truth from her all this time." Paul lowered his gaze. "I really messed things up between me and Lisa, and I'm not sure how to make them right, or if it's even possible." He looked away, wishing that the perfect answer would fall right into his lap, one that could fix all of this for good.

Paul continued to mull things over. *I miss Lisa so much, but I'm worried that we won't ever be together as a couple again.*

"We humans sure know how to make a mess of things, don't we?" Susan pointed to herself. "I know that better than anyone."

Paul sat quietly for a while. He was about to say something when Susan spoke again.

"I'm really sorry for hurting you, Paul. If I hadn't been swayed by Ervin's charms, you and I would probably be married by now."

He nodded slowly.

"But then, that would mean you wouldn't have reconnected with Lisa." Susan's words were spoken in a soothing tone. "I can see how much you love her. Your face seems to light up when you say her name."

As much as Paul wanted to deny it, he couldn't. Sitting here with Susan and telling her all of this had made him keenly aware of just how much he longed to be with the little girl, now a grown-up, he'd once promised to marry.

"I realize there's no chance of you and me getting back together," Susan said quietly, "but would you like a piece of advice?"

"Jah, sure. It couldn't hurt."

Susan leaned a little closer to Paul's side of the table and placed her hand on his. "If you care deeply for Lisa, then the day after your grandma's party, you should head straight back to Sugarcreek, Ohio, and declare your love for that girl. And if you really love her, Paul, don't take no for an answer."

Sugarcreek

Lisa was about to take Maggie outside when she heard a horse and buggy come into the yard. When she opened the door, she was surprised to see that the rig belonged to Lois and Orley Troyer.

Holding on to her dog's harness, Lisa stepped into the yard and waved. She figured the friendly couple had probably come by again to see how Maggie was doing.

By the time Maggie had finished her business, Orley had secured his horse, and he and Lois were headed Lisa's way. When they approached, Orley shook Lisa's hand and Lois gave her a hug.

"It's nice to see you." Lois pointed at Maggie. "It appears that your dog has made a lot of progress since we were last here."

Lisa nodded. "Maggie has adjusted quite well, and her disability doesn't hold her back from doing most of the things she used to do before the amputation."

"It's amazing how well an animal will adjust to something like that," Orley said. "We humans don't always deal well with physical challenges." He thumped his stomach and grimaced. "Take me, for example. I take medicine for my hypothyroid condition, yet I still have to watch what I eat in order to keep from gaining too much weight. I'll admit that I get frustrated sometimes."

Lisa, having never dealt with a thyroid issue or a problem with her weight, couldn't relate to Orley's situation. However, in Lisa's mind, her partial loss of memory was a disability, and it frustrated her to no end.

"Speaking of eating," Lois said, "My husband and I were wondering if you and your grandparents would like to go out for supper with us to one of the restaurants here in Sugarcreek."

"Maybe Dutch Valley," Orley put in. "A person can get filled up on their soup and tasty salad bar alone."

"That's kind of you, but I believe my grandma may have already started our supper."

"Indeed I have, and the Troyers are invited to stay and eat supper here with us this evening," Grandma called through the open screen door. She stepped out and gestured for them to join her on the porch.

"That's a gracious offer, but we wouldn't want to impose," Lois said after she and Orley had greeted Lisa's grandma properly.

"It's no imposition whatsoever. I have scalloped potatoes with ham in the oven, and there's more than enough to go around." Marlene smiled at Lois. "Please say you'll join us. It would be nice to have extra time to visit, and it will be much easier to talk in our dining room than at a noisy restaurant."

Lois looked at Orley, and when he gave a nod, she said, "Danki, Marlene. We would love to join you for supper."

"That was some delicious meal. Danki for inviting us to eat here with you." Orley patted his stomach before pushing away from the table. "Everything was so good, it was hard not to overeat."

"Jah," Lois agreed, "we appreciate the tasty food as well as your warm hospitality."

"It was our pleasure," Lisa's grandma replied.

Lisa's grandfather bobbed his head and grinned at Orley. "One of these days I may drop by your antique store. It would be fun to see some of the vintage items you have available."

"Feel free to come by anytime you like. We're open five days a week."

"Which five days?"

"Normally it's Tuesday through Saturday, but sometimes we'll close the store on a Saturday to go hunting for old things at yard sales, swap meets, or auctions."

Jerry got up from the table. "How'd ya like to join me in the living room for a game of checkers?" His question was directed at Orley.

"Sounds good to me, but I have to warn you, I haven't played checkers in a long while, so I may not be a competitive player."

Jerry winked at him. "No problem there. As I'm winnin' the game, I'll teach you my strategy."

Orley chuckled. "Game on."

~

"Have you heard anything from Paul lately?" Lois asked as she and Lisa did the dishes and Marlene put things away.

Lisa shook her head. "I assume he's in Indiana, where he was going to celebrate his grandmother's birthday." She grabbed another dish to dry.

"Jah, that was my understanding too. He came by Memory Keepers before he left and told us he'd be leaving."

Lisa stared straight ahead.

Lois cleared her throat. "Umm...I hope I'm not speaking out of turn here, but there is something I'd like to discuss with you, Lisa. In fact, it's been on my mind for several days."

"Oh, what's that?" Lisa barely glanced Lois's way.

Does she know what I'm about to say? Is that why Lisa won't look at me? Since Marlene had stepped out of the kitchen to use the restroom, Lois decided to plunge ahead, as it might be her only chance to speak with Lisa alone. "Paul mentioned that the two of you had a falling-out."

"I guess it could be called that. I suppose he told you that I walked in on him telling my grandpa that he used to know me when we were kinner."

Lois nodded. "He also said you refused to discuss it with him and said you never wanted to see him again."

"It's true." Lisa picked up some silverware to dry. "Paul sent me a letter before he left for Indiana, asking if I would be willing to talk with him when he returns."

"Are you willing, Lisa?"

"I—I don't know. Paul kept something very important from me—something that may have helped my memory return—and I'm not sure I can trust him now."

"Don't you think he deserves a chance to explain himself?"

"I suppose."

"If he apologizes, would you be willing to forgive?"

"I should, but it's hard for me to trust." Lisa's chin trembled. "I'm afraid of getting hurt—afraid of being alone—and fearful that I might never get my memory fully back."

Lois dried her hands on a towel and went across the room to get her purse, which she'd hung on a wall peg soon after she and Orley had arrived. She removed a writing tablet—one she often used when responding to letters she'd received in her Dear Caroline column—and brought it, along with a pen, over to the table. "I'm going to write down some Bible verses that came to me last night. Would you sit with me while I share them?"

"Jah." Lisa set her drying towel aside and took a seat in the chair beside Lois.

Lois wrote down three passages of scripture on the topic of fear and handed the paper to Lisa. "There have been times during the course of my life when I've felt fearful, and one or more of these Bible verses helped me get through whatever trial I had to face. I hope the same will be true for you, Lisa."

Lisa's chin dipped slightly as she studied the list. "I'll look these up tonight before going to bed."

Lois clasped Lisa's hand. "Please give me a call if you have any questions or would like to talk about this more. In the meantime, I'll be praying for both you and Paul."

Chapter 35

Lisa sat on the living-room floor with her back against the front of the couch, staring at the glowing embers in the fireplace. She was alone and had time to think and do some reading in pure quietness. Lisa wanted to take advantage of this time to reflect on some things. Grandpa and Grandma had gone to their closest neighbor's house for an evening of games and snacks. They'd invited Lisa, but she'd declined, saying she had some things she wanted to get done.

Lisa's day at school with the children had been busier than usual, and she'd been tired when she got home. Now she sat with her sleeping furry companion by her side. Maggie brought a soothing comfort and a sense of protection for Lisa, especially at times like now, when she was the only adult in the house.

Last night, after the Troyers went home, Lisa had spent some time reading the Bible passages Lois had written down for her. But she hadn't yet read the little self-help booklet Lois had given her right before the Troyers climbed into their buggy and left for home. Lois had shown Lisa such kindness, and her husband was supportive too. in the words he'd spoken before they'd left.

Orley and Lois are truly a special couple. I'm glad God brought them into my life. Lisa smiled. *The Lord knows each of us very well. He also knows what needs to happen for each of us at the proper time.*

The house was quiet, except for Maggie's snores from where she lay beside Lisa, so this was a good time to get some more reading done. Before settling down, she had grabbed a few cookies and some lemonade from the kitchen to enjoy while doing her reading.

I can't wait to try the chocolate chip cookies, since Grandma added pecans to them. Lisa took a bite of her first one and enjoyed its flavor. "This is sure tasty. Grandma knows how much I like pecans, so this was a nice surprise." Lisa ate the rest of it and sipped on some lemonade before wiping her hands on a napkin from the wooden tray she'd placed on the other side of her.

She opened the book to a page Lois had marked with a strip of paper. The words "Why me? Why wasn't I taken too?" seemed to jump off the page, and Lisa drew in a sharp intake of breath. *That's me. Whoever wrote this book must have been writing about me.*

Lisa rubbed her forehead as a sense of reality set in. She had never met the author before and didn't recognize the woman's name, so there was no way she could know Lisa or have any knowledge of her situation. Apparently others out there had lost family members and suffered with survivor's guilt. Those people may have been dealing with a similar type of problem as Lisa, and they needed help to deal with their fears and insecurities.

Tears sprang to Lisa's eyes, and soon after, they ran down her hot cheeks. Lisa knew this much—she had never fully come to grips with her parents' and grandparents' deaths and had always wondered, but never voiced out loud, why her life had been spared.

"I wasn't more important than the others in that van," Lisa murmured, barely able to get out the words. "Did God save me for some special reason?"

Lisa read on. "Love hurts, but we cannot avoid pain. Retreating into ourselves is not the solution." She paused to stroke Maggie's silky head before continuing to read.

"Fear doesn't stop death; it stops life. And worrying doesn't take away tomorrow's troubles; it takes away today's peace. Although we cannot understand why God does what He does, we can find comfort in knowing that He responds to us with love, comfort, and peace. Our heavenly Father is everywhere, and He knows everything about us. When we go through deep waters and feel that we are all alone, that's when it's time to remember that He will never leave us or forsake us. So if you're hurting from the loss of a loved one, or someone you know has let you down, your faith in God can be restored by trusting in Him."

Lisa closed her eyes and bowed her head. *Dear Lord,* she silently prayed, *please remind me daily that I am not to blame for the deaths of my family members, and I shouldn't feel guilty because I survived the accident. Help me to take one day at a time, trusting You and without fearing the unknown.*

~

Goshen

"It's so good to see you again, Paul. Danki for being here to help me and the rest of my dear family celebrate my seventy-fifth birthday." Paul's grandmother's blue eyes sparkled through the clear lenses of her glasses, and she gave him a hug.

"I wouldn't have missed it for the world," he responded, gently patting the slender woman's back.

She guided him off to one side of the living room, where no one else sat at the moment. "Your mamm said you have an aldi in Sugarcreek. Would you like to tell me about her?"

Paul looked away. *I had a feeling if Grandma found out about Lisa that she'd want to know all about it.* Belong within close proximity of the others made it harder not to be heard by someone other than his grandmother. All Paul could do was try to keep his voice down and hope that his grandma could hear him okay. As Paul searched for the right words, he felt the heat of embarrassment creep up the back of his neck and spread to his face. "Well, I. . .uh. . ."

"Has this girlfriend of yours filled an empty void in your life?"

"Jah or at least she did before I messed things up between us. But I'm hoping when I see Lisa again that she'll forgive me for being so stupid and saying something important to the wrong person rather than telling her."

Grandma gave his arm a tender squeeze. "I'll be praying for that."

"Come on, everyone. Let's gather around," Paul's dad called through his cupped hands. "Let us pause for silent prayer, and then we'll let my dear mother-in-law go through the haystack line first and help herself."

Paul felt relieved to hear his father's announcement, letting everyone know that supper was ready. That concluded the conversation between Grandma and himself about his situation with Lisa. Now he could enjoy the rest of the birthday celebration with his family.

Paul, along with the rest of the family, bowed his head. He prayed for his grandma, that she would remain healthy and live to serve God a good many more years. He thanked the Lord for his aunt, Mary Sue, who had taken Grandma into her home after Grandpa passed away five years ago. Paul also said a prayer on Lisa's behalf, asking God to pave the way before he spoke to her again. Even with his resolve to think positive thoughts, feelings of doubt had crept in off and on during the day as the time drew nearer to seeing her. Paul couldn't help fretting over this matter, which he felt sure was because things had not been resolved yet between him and Lisa. The last thing Paul wanted was to mess up and say or do the wrong thing when he saw her again.

~

After the meal, when everyone had gathered around to sing, Mavis smiled as she watched Paul play his guitar, while his four brothers accompanied him with their harmonicas. They all seemed to be having a wonderful time, and it felt good to see the whole family having fun as they spent precious time together again.

Mavis wondered if Paul would take his guitar with him to Ohio this time. When he'd left it in his room after leaving Indiana, it had given her a sense of hope that her son didn't plan to stay in Sugarcreek permanently. Now, however, with him having fallen in love with Lisa Miller, it looked doubtful that he would ever move back home on a permanent basis.

Mavis slid her tongue across her teeth and mulled things over. *Unless, of course, Paul returns to Ohio in a few days, and Lisa still won't talk to him. Maybe then our son will consider coming back to Indiana for good.*

—————

After playing and singing until his vocal chords felt strained and his fingers ached from chording and strumming the guitar, Paul set his instrument aside and went to the kitchen to get his grandmother's present. He found the box on the desk his mother used when she paid bills and wrote letters.

When Paul returned to the dining room, he handed the guest of honor the box. "Here you go, Grandma. Happy birthday!"

She smiled up at him and blinked several times. "You didn't have to get me anything, Paul."

"Yes, I did. And you'll know why when you see what it is."

"Oh, now you have me feeling quite curious." Grandma tore open the box and gave a little gasp when she pulled out the old, unusual-looking bottle. "Well, for goodness' sakes—this looks almost exactly like my old milk bottle. The one you broke and said you would replace someday."

Paul smiled. "Jah, Grandma, I've looked and looked for a bottle like that and finally found this one at an antique store in Walnut Creek, Ohio. The Amish man and his wife are the nicest couple, and Orley kept me informed whenever he got new milk bottles into the store."

Tears appeared in Grandma's eyes as she held the bottle close to her chest. "Danki, Paul. Although this is not the exact same milk bottle your grossdaadi gave me many years ago, it's very similar, and I will most certainly put it with my other vintage bottles."

Paul leaned down and gave her a kiss on the cheek. "I'm glad you like it."

"Jah, very much." Her voice choked up. "I'm sure if your grandpa was still alive that he would say it's a great bottle too—definitely worthy of being in my collection."

Paul felt good about bringing Grandma this special gift. Not only had it brought a smile to the dear woman's lips but it had released the feelings of guilt he'd carried around for having broken the one that Grandpa had given her.

Grandma opened a few other gifts then, which included a pretty vase with fresh flowers, a devotional book, a basket of yarn, a book with colored pictures of the birds that were native to their area, and a new daily journal.

Paul wondered how many pages and how many journals his grandmother had already filled up by now. His mother had told him once that her mother had been journaling since she was a teenager right out of school. Paul figured there must be plenty of stories in those journals—maybe enough to write several books if someone had a mind to.

It sure won't be me, Paul told himself. *I've never been good with words when it comes to letter writing. I'd sure never be able to write an entire book. Maybe someday, after my grandmother is gone, my mamm will try to get Grandma's journals published.*

"Should we have some cake and ice cream now that the gifts have been opened?" Paul's mother rose from her seat. "And when we're done with dessert, Amos has something special he wants to do for the kinner who are here this evening."

Paul glanced at his brother, wondering what he planned to do, but Amos's placid expression gave no indication as to what it could be. Of course, even when they were kids, Amos had always been able to get that composed expression on his face, giving no indication of what he was thinking or planning. It used to drive Paul batty, but now he was merely curious.

Harley's wife, Katie, along with Glen's wife, Sharon, went out to the kitchen with Mom, and everyone else gathered around the dining-room table again. A short time later, a delicious-looking chocolate cake with white icing, along with cartons of vanilla, chocolate, and strawberry ice cream, had been placed on the table, in addition to bowls, spoons, and forks. It had been a long time since Paul had eaten this much in one sitting, but he enjoyed every morsel of cake and each lick off his spoon of the cold strawberry ice cream he'd chosen.

After everyone finished their dessert, Amos set a chair in the middle of the living room and called his children, along with all of his nieces and nephews, to take a seat on the floor in front of him. Obviously curious about what Amos planned to do, all the adults found seats and sat looking at him too.

Paul couldn't help wondering what was in the cloth satchel Amos had now placed on his lap.

"You all ready?" Amos gave a wide grin as he looked at the children. When they nodded, he stood the cloth bag upright, reached inside with both hands, and pulled out two furry-looking critters. One resembled a sheepdog, and the other looked like a black-and-white long-haired cat. When Amos stuck his hand inside the critters' heads, Paul realized they were puppets. He bit back a chuckle. He'd never seen his brother play with puppets before—not even when they were children. He figured this must be something new Amos had decided to try in order to keep his five active children entertained.

"These are my new pets," Amos announced. He then gestured with his head toward the cat. "This is Patches, and my other friend here is Beau. They're not friends with each other by nature, but they've learned to get along, just like we humans should do."

The room got very quiet, and Paul noticed the wide-eyed expression on several of the children's faces when Amos made the cat say *meow* and the dog go *woof, woof!* Following that, Paul's brother launched into a full routine with the puppets, which included a silly song called "I Can Do Anything Better Than You Can." The most amazing part of the act was the fact that Amos had spoken and sung in both the cat's and dog's voices without moving his lips. This reminded Paul of the time Lisa had mentioned that a man and his wife had visited the schoolhouse, and the woman had used a puppet to entertain the children with ventriloquism.

When did my brother learn to be a ventriloquist, and how long has he been doing it? Paul asked himself. *Boy, a lot sure has happened in the time I've been gone. Think I should have kept in better touch with my family through phone calls and letters.* He gave his earlobe a tug. *If I stay in Sugarcreek, which I hope will be the case, then I must reach out to my family here in Indiana more often.*

Chapter 36

Saturday morning, when Paul came into the kitchen with his guitar and satchel, he found his mother at the sink, filling the teakettle with water. As he approached, she turned and smiled. "Guder mariye, Son."

"Morning, Mom."

"What would you like for breakfast—maybe some eggs? I can make them poached, fried, soft boiled, or scrambled—whatever you like. Oh, and I have a slab of bacon to go with the eggs." She placed the teakettle on the stove and turned on the propane burner.

"Thanks anyway, Mom, but I don't have time for a big breakfast." He glanced at the clock. "My driver will be here shortly."

"What?" Her mouth opened slightly. "You've only been here a few days. Why are you leaving so soon?"

"I told you last night, after everyone left. Weren't you listening?"

"Jah. You said you were eager to get back to Ohio so you could speak to Lisa, but I didn't think you'd be leaving today."

Paul felt bad hearing the disappointment in his mother's voice, but he distinctly remembered telling her last night that he'd talked to his driver, who'd been staying in LaGrange with some friends, and that he planned to leave this morning. He figured Mom either had been too tired to retain what he'd said or had hoped he would change his mind.

"Morning, Paul," Dad said as he strolled into the room. "Are you packed up and ready to go?"

Mom looked at Dad and frowned. "You knew our son was leaving today?"

Dad bobbed his head. "He told us last night—right here in this kitchen, as a matter of fact. Don't you remember, Mavis?"

"I heard him say he'd be leaving soon. I just didn't think it would be today." Mom's brows pulled inward. "We haven't seen Paul for a good many months, and I was hoping for a longer visit with him."

"I promise to stay in touch better than I have, and I will try to make my next visit here with you both last a little longer," Paul said. "I really feel the need to go home now so I can talk to Lisa."

"It seems strange to hear you call Ohio your home."

I'm sure, Mom, that you'd rather have me living in Indiana and not too far from your house either. If things don't work out between me and Lisa, you may get your wish. I'll probably end up coming right back here and begin working for Dad again, since he could use another person in the shop. Paul contemplated the best response to give his mother, but a horn tooted from outside. He peered out the window. "My driver's here."

"Why don't you invite him in to join us for breakfast?" Mom suggested.

Paul shook his head. "We need to get on the road before traffic gets bad." He gestured to the bowl of fruit in the center of the table. "Would you mind, Mom, if I take some fruit for the road?"

"Of course not, but I wish you could take the time to eat a bigger breakfast."

"I'll be fine, Mom." Paul gave her a hug, and his dad stepped forward and embraced Paul too.

"I hope things work out and you're able to find someone to work in your shop soon," Paul said. "I feel bad that I can't stay and help, but—"

Dad held up one hand. "Don't you worry about me. I've put an ad in the local newspaper as well as *The Budget*, so I feel confident that the right person will see that ad and respond to the request soon." Looking directly at Paul, Dad squeezed Paul's shoulders. "After all, I can't expect you to stay here just to help me when you've established a new life in Sugarcreek. None of your brothers have shown an interest in woodworking—especially the rustic kind. And I don't expect any of them to give up the jobs they like in order to help me either."

"Thanks, Dad. It means a lot to hear you say that." Paul heaved a sigh of relief. He was ever so thankful for his father's encouraging words.

When Paul's driver honked the horn a second time, Paul grabbed two apples and stuffed them in his pockets. Then he picked up his guitar and satchel, said goodbye to his parents, and went out the door. *Just think,* he told himself, *if everything goes well, before this day is out I'll be talking to Lisa.* The muscles in his jaw tightened as he put his stuff in the back of Bob's van. *At least I hope she'll be willing to hear me out. If she's not interested in what I have to say, I don't know what I'll do. Guess I could always get down on my knees and beg, but that might not be the best idea.*

⁓

Linsey, Ohio

It was about 320 miles from Goshen, Indiana, to Sugarcreek, Ohio, and they were at the halfway point in Linsey. Since they'd left Goshen a few minutes after six that morning, and it took about five hours, plus some extra time for any necessary stops, to get there, Paul figured they should arrive in Sugarcreek around noon.

He leaned his head against the headrest and tried to tune out the country and western CD his driver was playing. Paul didn't mind this type of music, but not with the volume way up. He wondered if Bob just liked it that way, or maybe he needed the loud music in order to keep himself from falling asleep at the wheel.

If Paul wasn't a member of the Amish church and was still going through his Rumspringa, he'd have a car of his own and wouldn't have to listen to any music if he didn't want to. Although Paul wouldn't trade being Amish for living a more modern, English life, he did miss a few things about owning a car. He'd thought for a while, when he had first put his vehicle up for sale before taking classes to join the church, that he'd really miss it, but he hadn't missed it as much as he'd expected. Normally, Paul was content to call upon a driver whenever it was needed and he couldn't travel with his trusted horse and buggy. But at the moment, he felt like a horse chomping at the bit to go.

"Did ya hear that loud boom?" Bob shouted against the blaring music, as the van slowed down as though of its own accord and then veered to the right.

Feeling a jolt when his driver accelerated slightly, Paul grabbed his armrest to steady himself.

"I think one of my back tires blew." A vein on the side of Bob's neck bulged as he let up on the gas pedal, turned on his emergency lights, and pulled the van off the highway and onto the shoulder of the road where it was safe. They both got out of the van and went around to check on the damage to the tire. Sure enough, it had blown, and now they had to put on the spare and hope it got them to the nearest place where Bob could buy a new tire. At this rate they'd never make it to Sugarcreek by noon, but at least the van was okay and neither Paul nor his driver had been injured.

"Whew!" Sweat beaded on Bob's forehead. "I'm glad there were no other vehicles close to my van when that happened. We could have ended up in an accident."

"That's for sure," Paul agreed. "God was watching over us."

Bob didn't respond, but then he rarely did whenever Paul brought up the topic of divine intervention or prayer. Bob had never professed to be a Christian and rarely spoke of religion, but he never seemed to mind whenever Paul brought God or the Bible into their conversation. Hopefully someday Bob would find a personal relationship with Jesus Christ.

"Well, we made it." Bob parked his van in front of Paul's aunt and uncle's home; then he looked over at Paul and grinned. "You glad to be back?"

Paul nodded quickly. The trip had taken longer than expected, but at least they'd made it safely back to Sugarcreek in time for him to see Lisa.

Paul paid Bob and told him goodbye; then he went around to get his guitar and satchel from the back. With a wave in his driver's direction, Paul headed for the house. He would say hello to whoever was at home this afternoon, wash up, and put on a clean shirt. Then he'd get on his bike, since it would be faster than getting the horse and buggy out, and head for the Schrocks' place.

Paul had no more than stepped onto the porch when his youngest cousin, bellowing like a wounded calf, ran around the side of the house, nearly bumping into Paul.

"What's going on, Danny?" Paul questioned. "What are you hollering about?"

The boy pointed to a blue Frisbee up on the roof.

Paul groaned. "For goodness' sakes, that's nothing to shout about. Just go get a ladder; then climb up there and get it down."

Beads of sweat appeared above the boy's upper lip as he pressed his arms tightly against his sides. "No way! I'm scared of heights, and I ain't goin' up there."

Paul was on the verge of telling his cousin that if he didn't have the courage to climb a ladder, then the Frisbee would have to stay where it was until a strong gust of wind blew it down. He changed his mind, however, when Danny moved closer and clasped his arm. "Would ya go up there and get it for me. . .please? I'll take care of feedin', waterin', and groomin' your horse every day next week if you get the Frisbee down for me."

Paul was aware that everyone had a fear of something, and apparently climbing a tall ladder was one of his cousin's greatest fears. "Okay, Danny, if you bring the ladder out of the barn, I'll go up and get your toy."

"Danki, Paul." Danny offered him a grateful-looking smile before he turned and hurried toward the barn.

⁓

"Where are you headed, Lisa?" Grandma asked when Lisa put on her black sweater and dark outer bonnet.

"I'm going to bike over to Paul's aunt and uncle's house and see if they've heard from him and know when he plans to return to Ohio."

"Can't you just call and leave them a message? I'm sure someone would get back to you later today."

"Grandma, I've been patient for days waiting to hear something from Paul, and I've reached my limit." Lisa shook her head. "I'd rather talk to one of his relatives in person than leave a phone message that might not get answered until Monday."

Grandma nodded. "I understand."

"So if you don't need me for anything, I'm going to get my bike and head over to the Herschbergers' now."

"That's fine, Lisa. We're having spaghetti and meatballs this evening. It will be an easy meal, since the sauce we canned months ago is setting there on the counter, and the frozen meatballs are thawing. Everything is set to go, even our canned green beans. The only other work that'll need to be done is warming the french bread in the oven and cutting up some fresh veggies to have with our meal. I won't need any help until it's time to start supper, which is still a few hours away."

"Okay, that sounds good. Thanks, Grandma. I'll make sure to be back in plenty of time to help with our evening meal."

⁓

I really hope when I get together with Paul that things will go all right. Lisa's stomach knotted as she gripped her handlebars and pedaled down the road in the direction of the Herschbergers' place. It would be great if Paul was there already, but there was a chance that he'd decided to stay in Goshen a few more days.

Or maybe Paul will stay there for good, since I'm almost sure he believes that things are over between him and me. Lisa clenched her teeth so hard her jaw ached. *I really messed up where Paul is concerned. I should have given him a chance to explain himself. At least in Paul's letter he said he wanted to talk to me. Grandma said this morning that I should take it as a good sign.*

Lisa glanced at a barking dog on the other side of a white picket fence and thought of her own pet she'd left at home. *I bet Maggie would miss Paul if we broke up for good and he moved away, but not nearly as much as I would.* Tears stung the back of her eyes, and she blinked, hoping to keep them from seeping out. *I can't start thinking negative thoughts or worrying about the what-ifs,* Lisa reminded herself. *I just need to have faith and remain calm.*

The closer Lisa got to his uncle and aunt's place, the more she hoped Paul was there. Her heart beat like a drum with the workout of pedaling as fast as she could manage. *I hope I don't break out in a sweat. That wouldn't be an impressive way to greet Paul or any of his family who might be at home.*

A short time later, Lisa drove her bike into the Herschbergers' yard. She stopped along one side of the driveway. Lisa was surprised to see Paul's cousin Danny standing off to one side of a ladder that was leaning against the house, and even more surprised to see Paul up on the roof holding a Frisbee. If Paul saw her, he gave no indication as he flipped the Frisbee into the air.

Lisa hopped off her bike and set the kickstand. While standing there, she couldn't take her eyes off Paul. Lisa watched as the object drifted to the ground, but she barely noticed when Danny picked it up. Her gaze was on Paul again, as he maneuvered himself toward the edge of the roof.

Lisa held her breath, and her body stiffened as he put first one foot, and then the other, on the top rung of the ladder. It appeared that Paul was about to step on the rung below it when a black crow swept down from nowhere, nearly hitting the top of Paul's head.

Paul leaned to the right, and then to the left, as the crow made another pass at him. Lisa wanted to call out to him, but fearful that he might lose his balance, she just stood there, continuing to hold her breath.

Suddenly, as though in slow motion, Paul lost his grip and tumbled downward.

Lisa and Danny screamed at the same time, as Paul's body hit the ground with a sickening thud. He lay there, unmoving, and Lisa rushed forward, shouting, "Paul! Paul!" She closed her eyes briefly. *Oh, please, Lord, let him live.*

Chapter 37

Lisa's heart thumped in her chest as she dropped to the ground on her knees beside Paul. Blood oozed from a gash on his head, and his left leg lay at an odd angle. She felt overwhelmed. Lisa didn't have a strong stomach when it came to seeing a good amount of blood, in addition to a leg not in its usual position. It was a lot to take in, but soon Lisa managed to open her eyes again and look at him. Paul was breathing, but his eyes remained closed, and he was unresponsive when she called his name.

Tears welled in Lisa's eyes as she laid a hand on Paul's swollen wrist. It felt pretty warm, and she noticed some discoloration–a good indication of a possible bruise. Lisa had no idea how badly Paul had been hurt. She just knew they needed to get some help, and soon.

Lisa looked up at Danny, who stood a few feet away with eyes wide and body shaking like a leaf being blown about the yard on a windy day. *I'll need Danny's help. I'm staying with Paul until the paramedics get here.*

"Danny, go in the house and get your mom or dad. Someone needs to go out to the phone shed and call for help. I don't want to leave your cousin here alone."

Danny stepped closer and looked at Paul for a moment; then he turned toward Lisa with a wrinkled forehead. "Is—is he dead?" The boy's voice quivered as he stared at his cousin.

"He's still breathing." Lisa gave her head a vigorous shake. "Go, Danny! Go get your parents right now!"

Within minutes of Danny's departure, the boy's mom and dad rushed out of the house. Emma held a towel, which she wrapped around Paul's head, and Abe instructed her to stay with Paul while he went to the phone shed to call 911. "And if Paul wakes up while I'm gone," he called over his shoulder, "don't let him move. I'm sure his leg is broken, and he may have a concussion or some internal injuries we don't know about."

"I won't leave his side," she called to Abe, and then knelt on the opposite side of Paul. "I hope we won't have to wait long for the ambulance to arrive."

With a trembling lip, Emma looked at Lisa. "It's hard to see him lying there so helpless, and it's frustrating not knowing how to treat his injuries as we wait here for help to arrive." Her eyes filled with tears.

As Lisa continued to wait with Paul's aunt, she explained how the accident had happened, giving an account of everything she'd witnessed from the ground below.

"He should have left the Frisbee on the roof." Emma's brows wrinkled. "But that's how Paul is—he's always been one to help out whenever he thinks there's a need." Her voice faltered. "When Danny came into the house with the news that his cousin had fallen, he followed me into the kitchen as I quickly grabbed a towel to bring out with me." Emma looked toward the house while speaking. "Danny admitted that he'd been the one who asked Paul to go up on the roof, and now he blames himself for what happened. He's sitting on the couch right now, in tears."

"People often have a tendency to blame themselves when something goes wrong." Lisa hoped her words gave Emma some comfort. Truth was, they were spoken as much for Lisa as for Paul's aunt. In addition to feeling guilty and unworthy because she'd been the only person who'd survived the accident that had taken her family, Lisa had often blamed herself for other events, even while teaching school, that logically were not her fault. It had been easy to blame herself and be miserable instead of enjoying her life the way she should. Lisa hoped those times of feeling guilty were behind her now and she could move forward with the Lord's help to a more positive attitude.

Lisa looked at Paul's pale face and grimaced. In this case, he could have said no to his cousin's request, but Paul chose to do what he felt was right. Truthfully, Paul probably would have gone up to get the Frisbee even if he hadn't been asked.

She breathed a sigh of relief when Abe showed up and said the call had been made and that help was on the way. Even so, the look of worry on Abe's and Emma's faces was unmistakable, and Lisa couldn't help feeling the same way. *My worrying won't help Paul's situation or me wishing I could've helped prevent the accident. The only thing left to do now is pray.*

Dover, Ohio

Lisa sat in the hospital waiting room between Paul's aunt and uncle. Kevin had been hiking with some friends when the accident happened, and Danny had remained at home to let his brother know when he got home. Paul's parents had been notified, and Lisa felt sure that once they received the message, one or both of them would come to the hospital. Lisa had also let her grandparents know about Paul's accident and explained in her message that she would be going to the hospital with Paul's aunt and uncle when their driver arrived but would try to keep them informed when she knew more. That had been three hours ago, and they still hadn't gotten word of Paul's condition.

Lisa glanced at the clock on the far wall. It seemed to be taking forever for them to hear the results of tests being done that would determine how badly Paul had been hurt. She felt helpless sitting here waiting, but she had spent this time praying and focusing on verses of scripture she'd committed to memory. Second Timothy 1:7 stuck out in her mind: "For God hath not given us the spirit of fear; but of power, and of love, and of a sound mind." How thankful Lisa was for the reminder found in God's Word that she should not be fearful.

Lisa thought about Lois and Orley and wondered if she should let them know that Paul was in the hospital. Since she didn't have anything specific to tell them about his condition, however, she decided it would be best to wait until she, Abe, and Emma learned something.

"I can hardly stand this waiting." Emma got up and began pacing.

Abe looked at his wife and shook his head. "Walking back and forth is not going to do you or Paul one bit of good, Emma. If you must walk about, why don't you go down the hall and get a cup of kaffi?"

She stopped pacing and turned to face him. "I don't need any coffee, and I'm feeling too anxious to sit still any longer." She sighed. "I just wish we would hear something."

"I want that too, but we won't hear anything one minute sooner with you walkin' the floor." Abe motioned to the chair she had left empty. "Please sit down and try to relax."

"I don't see how I'm supposed to do that." Emma sniffed deeply.

"Prayer," Lisa spoke up. "I've discovered lately that praying helps me relax and stop worrying."

Emma came back over and took her seat. "You're right, Lisa. I should be praying for my nephew, not fretting over something that is out of my control." She bowed her head and closed her eyes. Abe did the same, along with Lisa.

A few minutes later, Lisa heard footsteps approach. She opened her eyes and saw a middle-aged man dressed in hospital scrubs standing near their row of chairs. "Are you Paul's relatives?" he asked, looking at Abe, then Emma.

They both nodded.

"We've finished examining Paul and have done several necessary tests, and. . ." He paused and reached under his glasses to rub the bridge of his nose. "I am happy to report that Paul's injuries are much less than they could have been from a fall like he took. Besides a slight concussion, his left leg is broken, and he sprained his right wrist. The leg break is pretty bad, so we'll need to do surgery and put a few pins in it, but he should be able to go home in a few days."

Lisa slumped against her chair and reached over to clasp Emma's hand. *Thank You, Lord, for keeping Your hand on Paul. His accident could have been so much worse.*

Since Paul's surgery wouldn't be until the next day and he was sleeping due to the pain medicine he'd been given, Lisa, along with his aunt and uncle, decided it would be all right for them to go home. Abe said he would leave a message at the nurse's desk for Paul's parents, letting them know the details and that they should plan on staying at his and Emma's house for as long they wanted during Paul's convalescence.

It was difficult for Lisa to leave the hospital without talking to Paul, but what she had to say could wait until tomorrow, or even longer if necessary. The most important thing was that after a time of healing, Paul would be okay.

Sugarcreek

Lisa waited until Paul came home from the hospital to go to his aunt and uncle's house, hoping to talk with him about their situation. She wanted to make sure that he felt well enough to discuss things with her and was glad she had written Paul a note and left it on the nightstand in his hospital room, letting him know that she'd been there and would be over to see him soon after he got home.

With Paul's parents still there and his aunt Emma no doubt in the house, it might be difficult to speak with Paul alone. Even so, Lisa was determined that today would be the day she told Paul how she felt about him. She only hoped that, after all that had transpired between them, he felt the same way about her.

After parking her bike near the barn, Lisa hurried across the yard and up the steps to the front porch. She was about to knock on the door when it opened and a slender, brown-haired Amish woman stepped out.

"Are you Lisa?" the woman asked.

Lisa bobbed her head.

"I'm Mavis, Paul's mamm. I knew you when you were a little girl living in Goshen with your family, but you may not remember me."

"You're right, I don't, but there's a lot about my childhood I haven't been able to remember yet." Lisa gave Mavis a brief hug. "I'm glad you could be here, and I'm sure you must be thanking God that your son's injuries weren't life threatening."

Paul's mother gave a nod as she pressed a palm against her chest. "The moment I found out about my son's accident, I began to pray, and I couldn't stop doing so as we traveled in our driver's vehicle from Goshen to the hospital in Dover." She gave Lisa's arm a gentle pat. "I'm going out for a short walk, but why don't you go inside now and talk to Paul? I'm sure he'll be happy to see you."

"Okay." Lisa rubbed her sweaty hands down the front of her apron. She hoped she'd be able to talk to Paul alone, even if it were just for a few minutes. She needed to ask his forgiveness and let him know how she truly felt.

When Lisa entered the living room, she was surprised to see that Paul was the only one in the room. He lay stretched out on the couch, with his broken leg encased in a cast and propped up on a pillow.

He turned his head and smiled as Lisa approached. "I'm glad you're here, because there are some things I need to say to you."

"Jah, I've been wanting to talk to you too." She glanced around. "Where is everyone? Are we alone?"

"We are for the moment. Aunt Emma's out back hanging laundry. My daed and Uncle Abe headed out to the woodworking shop a while ago, and my mamm went for a walk."

"I know. I met her on the front porch before I came into the house."

"I hope you can stay awhile. I'd like you to get to know my folks."

"That would be nice."

Paul pointed to a folding chair that had been placed near the couch. "Please take a seat."

Lisa did as he suggested. She was about to say something, but he spoke first.

"I'm really sorry for keeping the truth from you for so long about us knowing each other when we were kinner. I should have been up front with you about it as soon as I realized who you were." He reached out his arm. "Will you forgive me, Lisa?"

She clasped his hand. "Jah, and will you forgive me for running out of the room the evening I heard you telling my grandpa the truth? I should have stayed and listened to your explanation."

"It's okay. It's in the past now, and we need to move forward."

"I agree. That's what I decided to do after Lois Troyer had a heart-to-heart talk with me. Would you like to hear about it?"

Paul nodded. "Most definitely."

Uncertain of how much time she and Paul would have to be alone, Lisa made short order of telling him about her conversation with Lois. "The things she said, along with the verses of scripture she mentioned, have helped me so much, Paul. I wish I had opened up to Lois sooner and talked about my feelings."

"You know what they say—it's never too late—and maybe it was the perfect time for you to hear what Lois had to say."

"You're probably right. I may not have been open to hearing what she said if it had happened earlier."

"There's something else I need to tell you." Paul stroked Lisa's fingers as he continued to hold her hand.

"What is it?'

"Before Susan dropped me for the man I thought was my best friend, I believed I was in love with her. But I've realized since then that I've never loved another woman the way I love you."

Lisa's pulse raced as she gazed deeply into his eyes. "I love you too. Very much, in fact."

Paul brought Lisa's hand up to his lips, and he grazed her knuckles with feathery kisses. "When I've healed from my injuries and the time is right, would you consider becoming my wife?"

Lisa couldn't keep the tears that had filled her eyes from falling over as she whispered, "Jah, I would be honored to marry you, Paul."

Lisa leaned closer to Paul, and he caressed her cheek with the back of his thumb. "I'm gonna hold you to that promise."

"Oh, I hope so," she murmured.

Epilogue

With a feeling of contentment, Paul sat beside his new bride at their corner table during the meal following the church service where they'd become man and wife a short time ago. The wedding had taken place at the nearby home of Grandpa and Grandma's Amish friend, and the noon meal was hosted right here at her grandparents' place.

Maggie was in her outside pen, letting out barks and watching the people coming in for the event. Paul couldn't help but smile every time he heard another yip, yap, or woof.

Looking out at all the other tables that had been set up for guests in this thoroughly cleaned barn, Paul's heart overflowed with happiness beyond belief. He could hardly comprehend that the girl he'd chosen back when he was a boy had actually become his partner for life.

Paul felt thankful that his entire family, including dear Grandma, could be here to help him and Lisa celebrate their special day. Lisa's grandparents were there too of course, smiling and laughing as they conversed with other guests. Although Paul had not gone fishing with Jerry yet, due to their busy work schedules, he looked forward to doing so sometime in the near future.

Paul smiled and nodded at Orley and Lois, who sat at one of the nearby tables along with several other visiting friends. Paul felt blessed to have met the nice Amish couple, and he appreciated the guidance he and Lisa had both received from the Troyers. Lois and Orley cared about people, and it showed.

Paul leaned close to Lisa and whispered, "Aren't you glad the Troyers could be here for our special day?"

Lisa nodded. "I hope by the time we're their age that we'll also have been able to mentor many people the way they do."

"If we're open to God's will and His leading, I'm sure there will be plenty of opportunities for us to help others. And who knows," Paul said with a grin, "we could end up with a whole houseful of kinner who will need our guidance."

"That could be, but only God knows what plans He has for our future." Lisa smiled and squeezed his hand under the table. "I am ever so thankful that we have put our lives in God's hands."

Lisa's Honey-Raisin-Bread French Toast

2 large eggs, well beaten
¼ cup milk
¼ cup honey

¼ teaspoon salt
6 to 8 slices raisin bread
Butter

Set oven to warm. Combine eggs, milk, honey, and salt with whisk or eggbeater. Dip bread slices into egg mixture. Melt butter in skillet over medium heat. Fry bread on both sides until golden brown. Place first finished slices in ovenproof dish and put in warm oven. Repeat with remainder of bread, two slices at a time. Keep french toast in oven until ready to serve.

Grandma's Chicken-N-Stuffing Casserole

STUFFING:

6 cups bread crumbs, browned
¼ cup diced celery
1 tablespoon chopped onion
1 tablespoon parsley flakes

2 eggs
¼ cup butter
Salt and pepper to taste

Mix all ingredients in a bowl and add enough hot water to moisten. Place in greased 9x13-inch baking pan.

CHICKEN:

¼ cup butter
4 tablespoons flour
1 cup chicken broth
1 can cream of chicken soup

15 ounces milk
1 whole chicken, cooked and cut up
Salt and pepper to taste

In a kettle, melt butter. Stir in flour to make paste. Add broth, soup, and milk. Cook until thick gravy forms. Add cooked chicken pieces and season with salt and pepper. Pour over stuffing. Bake at 350 degrees for 40 to 45 minutes until bubbly.

Discussion Questions

1. Lisa faced a terrible tragedy at the age of seven, when her parents, paternal grandparents, and their driver were killed. Lisa was the only survivor of the accident, and the emotional trauma left Lisa with a partial memory loss. Why do you think Lisa blocked out her childhood memories from before the accident?

2. Due to the accident and having been sent to live with her maternal grandparents, whom she didn't know very well at that time, Lisa became an introvert and feared the unknown. It was difficult for her to form a bond with anyone, anxious that something might happen to them. Do you think that was a normal reaction? Have you, or someone you know, ever been in a similar situation when you've gone through a tragedy? If so, how did you cope?

3. Lisa's maternal grandparents did all they could to help Lisa and give her a loving, stable upbringing, and she'd become quite attached to them. How wonderful it is when a relative steps forward to care for an orphaned child. Have you ever raised a child who was not your own? Did it strengthen the bond between you?

4. Lisa became an Amish schoolteacher, which filled a void in her life. She had no plans to get married and hoped she'd be able to teach for many years. Do you believe Lisa succeeded at filling that void in her life through teaching? Why do you think she would want to do that?

5. When Paul met Lisa during his first few days in Ohio, he had a feeling he'd known her before. He didn't know why, but he was drawn to Lisa and wanted to get to know her better. Have you ever felt that way after meeting someone for the first time?

6. Lois and Orley Troyer were open to God's leading whenever someone they felt needed mentoring came into their antique store. Have you ever known anyone like this Amish couple? Were you helped in some way by them, or have you ever been the one doing the mentoring?

7. Once Paul realized that he used to know Lisa when they were children, did he do the correct thing by not telling her right away? Did Lisa have a legitimate reason to be upset with Paul? Do you think she responded correctly, or would there have been a better way for her to deal with it?

8. Paul, a carpenter, had always enjoyed fixing things. Aware that Lisa dealt with some emotional things, he hoped that he could fix her problems by being her friend. Can friendship alone help someone who is dealing with something from their past that is affecting their current behavior? What are some ways we can help someone cope with a past trauma that still affects them?

9. Did Paul's mother expect too much by wanting him to live in Indiana, where he'd grown up? Do you think grown children should be allowed the freedom to move away from their parents without having pressure put on them or being made to feel guilty? Is there ever a time when parents should expect their adult child to live close to them?

10. How did Paul's broken relationship with a young woman from Indiana affect his relationship with Lisa? When Susan hurt Paul, he promised himself not to fall in love again. Was it too soon after the breakup with Susan for Paul to begin dating Lisa?

11. Taking in a stray dog, Maggie, was one of the first things Lisa did that helped her deal with her insecurities. Caring for Maggie gave Lisa a sense of purpose. How did Lisa handle it

when Maggie lost a leg? Did it make her a stronger person, or did Lisa's fear of losing someone she loved escalate?

12. What helped Lisa the most in dealing with her fears and anxiety? How do you deal with these emotions when faced with a frightening ordeal?

13. How can we help ourselves or someone we know who struggles with worry, fear, or anxiety? Do you have some favorite verses from the Bible about these topics?

14. Who were your favorite characters in this book? What stood out about the characters that made them special to you?

15. Did you learn anything new about the Amish way of life by reading this book?

16. Have you ever been to Amish country in Ohio? If so, what were some of your favorite places to visit there?

17. Did you learn anything specific from reading this story that helped to strengthen your faith in God? Were there any Bible verses that particularly spoke to you? In what way can you incorporate them into your life today?

About the Author

New York Times bestselling and award-winning author **WANDA E. BRUNSTETTER** is one of the founders of the Amish fiction genre. She has written more than one hundred books translated in four languages. With over twelve million copies sold, Wanda's stories consistently earn spots on the nation's most prestigious best-seller lists and have received numerous awards.

Wanda's ancestors were part of the Anabaptist faith, and her novels are based on personal research intended to accurately portray the Amish way of life. Her books are well read and trusted by many Amish, who credit her for giving readers a deeper understanding of the people and their customs.

When Wanda visits her Amish friends, she finds herself drawn to their peaceful lifestyle, sincerity, and close family ties. Wanda enjoys photography, ventriloquism, gardening, bird-watching, beachcombing, and spending time with her family. She and her husband, Richard, have been blessed with two grown children, six grandchildren, and two great-grandchildren.

To learn more about Wanda, visit her website at www.wandabrunstetter.com.

More Creektown Discoveries!

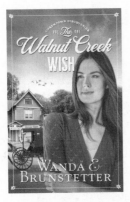

THE WALNUT CREEK WISH
(Available Now)

Welcome to Walnut Creek, Ohio, where Orley and Lois Troyer own an antique store they call "Memory Keepers." Though knowledgeable in antiques and their repair, their real talent is in mentoring folks who are hurting and don't even know it. Enter Jeff, a restaurateur, and Rhonda, a hotel manager, who recently moved to Amish country for the slow pace, but the change of scenery puts even more stress on their already strained marriage. Will an antique sled be the last straw to end their marriage, or will it lead to unexpected revelations and the fulfillment of dreams?

Paperback / 978-1-64352-741-3 / $16.99

THE APPLE CREEK ANNOUNCEMENT
(Coming August 2022)

A piano teacher and artist, Andrea Wagner has a fascination with painting the rural Amish landscapes around her home in Apple Creek, Ohio. She has made it to her thirties feeling like she has had a charmed life and finally has fallen in love with Brandon Prentice, a local veterinarian. But then she discovers she was adopted—and all she thought she knew about herself has crumbled. Andrea becomes so fixated on finding her birth mother that she pushes Brandon away, so she writes to the Dear Caroline column in the newspaper for romance advice. What will Andrea lose before she finds herself again?

Paperback / 978-1-63609-153-2 / $16.99

More from Wanda!

WANDA E. BRUNSTETTER'S AMISH FRIENDS 4 SEASONS COOKBOOK
(Coming May 2022)

Over 200 Recipes for Eating with the Seasons

A whole new collection of recipes from *New York Times* bestselling author of Amish fiction Wanda E. Brunstetter celebrates eating fresh within each season's bounty. Sprinkled with tips for growing and harvesting, the cookbook is divided by winter, spring, summer, and fall and has a bounty of recipes for various ways to use up seasonal fruits and vegetables. The well-organized book boasts contributions from Amish and Mennonites from across the United States. Encased in a lay-flat binding and presented in full color, it is a must-have cookbook for anyone who gardens, participates in a CSA, or enjoys farmers' markets.

Comb Bound / 978-1-63609-248-5 / $16.99